The Traitor's Blade

Book Cover by Bethany Gilbert

First edition 2026

ALSO BY

THE KINGDOMS OF ASSASSINS CHRONICLES

The Kingdoms of Assassins Anthology
The Glass Dagger
The Poisoned Crown
The Traitor's Blade

To My League of Ladies

Thank you for showing me that friendships like ours can exist at any age

I hope everyone else finds their rides or dies.

Rairene
Grecia

N
S
Trudel
Vicuria
Evrotia

CONTENTS

FOREWARNED

The Traitor's Blade is an adventure fantasy set in a dark fairytale adaptation world with teenage assassins. It includes elements regarding torture, war, combat, poisoning, blood, intense situations, death, and mental manipulation through poison that are shown on the page. Readers who may be sensitive to these elements, please be aware that you're entering into the dark fantasy world of the Kingdom of Assassins...

CHAPTER ONE

Drea

Three Months Before Drea's Accident

Drea smiled at Ana as they approached the palace's large, ornate double doors. Ana was dazzling in a pink ball gown with cap sleeves and beautiful gold embroidery in a sheer layer on top of the chiffon fabric. Her blond hair hung in waves down her back. Drea did a small twirl for Ana as they reached the doors and waited for them to open. This was their favorite ball of the year, the spring equinox when everything warmed up, the flowers were blooming, and for the first time in months, Drea didn't feel cold.

As the doors opened before her, Drea took a final breath and walked through.

They were at the top of the stairs for everyone to watch them descend.

It was a rite of passage none of them enjoyed.

Drea remembered the first time she was allowed to grace these stairs without her mother escorting her. She had almost lost control as the nerves fluttered sporadically throughout her entire body. Her hand had shaken so much she had to tighten her grip on the banister. It was the first time she had been so nervous since her training with her mother's instructors had begun. She had felt so foolish. But now she knew the dangers of the social pressures the staircase put on even the strongest.

Her fingers lightly grazed the golden banister as her other hand lifted the skirts of her dark purple dress just enough to avoid tripping.

She got to the bottom without once looking at her feet. When she got there, Henry waited for her. Anastasia, her elder sister, nudged her, smiling as she left to attend to one of her many suitors.

"As usual, I think half of the men in this room are in love with you," Henry said as he walked with her around the border of the dance floor.

"Only half?" Drea scoffed. "I must be losing my touch."

"Never," Henry whispered. He held his arm out to her, which she gladly accepted as they surveyed the dancers.

"I have to warn you, Mother is coming tonight."

Henry froze beneath her hand. He still despised her mother, not that she could blame him. If he knew everything her mother had done...hell, even she wouldn't be here. He would never talk to her again.

"I don't want to talk about your mother," Henry muttered as he swept her onto the dance floor.

"So you would rather gossip about everyone around us?" Drea laughed as she rested her hand on his shoulder and followed his lead in the waltz.

"Of course. Now, who do you think is going to falter first?"

"Let's look."

Henry spun them around effortlessly to get a lay of the land. She tightened her grip on his hand. Her magic danced within her, swelling and sparkling with each touch from Henry.

"Any guesses?" Drea asked a few seconds later. She gazed into his emerald eyes that seemed to glow in the candlelight.

"Any guesses?" Henry frowned. He kept his eyes on her, smiling as they transitioned into a new dance.

"About the dancers." Drea motioned lightly toward their surroundings.

"Not tonight, apparently," Henry said.

"What's wrong? One minute ago you were smiling and now you're not." Drea took a step closer to him, tilting her head farther to keep her eyes on his face.

"Everything's fine, Drizzie. I just got lost in my thoughts." Henry kept his eyes on her, smiling gently at her.

"Care to share? They must be highly entertaining if they kept you from determining Ana is dancing with some courtier who can't figure out which foot is his left foot."

"Quite entertaining, though not as entertaining as that," Henry replied as he spun them to watch Ana storm off the dance floor, her partner jumping out of the dance to follow her. But she had already found another to make up for his skills.

Both of their shoulders shook with barely restrained laughter. Ana was not subtle about her preference in dance partners.

"So, what are they?" Drea prodded. She was going to have to rip those thoughts out of him.

"Hmmmm?"

"Your thoughts," she teased, shaking his hand to get his attention. "You're distracted tonight."

"Yes, well..." Henry's cheeks turned a shade lighter than his red hair. "I was wondering—"

The large double doors felt extra loud as they were opened, and Lady Tremaine, Duchess of House Aumont and Ambassador for Trudel, was announced to the room. As usual, her mother was a stunning vision in her dark blue gown. The skirts swirled around her as she made her grand entrance. If anyone ever wondered where Ana got her flair for the dramatic, they needn't look far. Lady Tremaine walked among the whispers. Drea knew there would be some. This was the first ball her mother had attended in almost a year. Everyone blamed her for Ella being in another kingdom. But Drea saw the small smirk at the corner of her mother's lips. She loved this. She loved knowing

Ella was at home in Aumont, training, and not on the other side of the great ocean.

Out of the corner of her eye, Drea saw Queen Charisse stand and take the king's arm to join him on the dance floor. Being on the floor meant they didn't have to talk to her mother. Lady Tremaine's glimmer of a smile almost broke into a full grin.

Drea turned away and faced Henry, her breath catching as she locked eyes with him.

"What were you going to say before my mother walked in?"

"Come with me," Henry whispered. He pulled them off the dance floor, smiling as his hand gripped hers.

Drea hastened behind him, her magic dancing wildly as his hand continued to hold hers. The chill air of the night sky kissed her burning cheeks as they went outside to the large balcony over the gardens. Stars twinkled in the sky as the full moon shone brightly.

Drea spun around in her gown as she stared at the night sky. She stopped at the edge to lean forward on the stone wall. "I love this time of night. Isn't it just so beautiful?"

"It really is..." Henry mumbled.

She angled her body towards him, needing to see him in the moonlight. "What did you want to talk about?"

"I..." Henry rubbed his head.

It was the most normal movement, yet Drea was enthralled with everything he did.

He grinned at her as he kept his eyes locked on hers. "You know, I haven't the slightest idea anymore."

Drea moved until the hem of her skirt brushed over his boots. She leaned towards him and delicately moved one of his red curls out of his face.

"Henry, I—"

Drea bit her lip. Her magic swirled within her, waltzing to the beat of her heart. She longed to tell him all her secrets. To be fully, truly, herself with him.

Not this version she portrayed for all the court to see. But if keeping those secrets meant getting to share this moment with him, getting to...touch him...hold his hand...

"Drizzie," Henry said. He leaned in towards her, his hand resting at the base of her head as she tilted it.

Drea closed her eyes.

"Drizella, there you are."

Henry jumped backward.

If Drea thought her cheeks were already warm, they were ablaze now as her mother walked onto the balcony.

"Mother, do you need me?" Drea asked as she took a step closer to Henry.

Her mother looked at them in silence, a single eyebrow raised as they shifted.

"I'll see you inside, Lady Drizella." Henry walked away, his hands fisted beside him.

"Mother, did you have to—"

"Yes." Her mother walked over to stand in the exact spot Henry had vacated. "I have indulged in the dalliances you and your sister entertain. But I will not allow this one. This is dangerous, Drizella. I forbid it."

"You forbid it?" Drea scoffed. "I would never tell him anything, Mother. I would never betray our queen. I'm not so easily manipulated through love like Anastasia that I would divulge what we've done. Test me, like you did her, if you so choose. I will not fail." Drea stood tall against her mother.

"I cannot have Luca seduce you, as he did your sister. You're too clever. I'm trusting you to obey me without threat of punishment, but out of respect for our queen, and your love for me."

Her mother turned on her heel and left.

Drea looked at the stars she found so beautiful and found them judging her.

Present Day

Drea walked through the halls as briskly as her leg would allow. Assassins and students clamored around her, cleaning and repairing the damage. She felt their eyes on her, waiting for her to lead. But leading was the last thing on her mind.

She had sworn an oath to Queen Laila.

Now, Anastasia was returning home, and Princess Lena was coming with her. The novices worked on not only pulling themselves together, but the fortress as well. Everyone knew they didn't serve the crown of Rairene now; however, very few had been upset by the news. Another reason for concern. If they were so easily swayed...Drea shook the thought away. Those were problems for another day, because Anastasia was being escorted home by the king's champion, Lord Andrew, Henry's father. Henry might be with him. Her magic skittered around, gleeful at glimpsing him.

Tressa walked beside her. Her magic dissipated, stilling as Ella's former protégé fell into step with her. Tressa wore a maid's uniform to match some of the other novices in their facade. Though trained by Ella, she quickly fell in with Anastasia and Lucifer, and since Ella's betrayal, she'd become insufferable.

Tressa twisted her hands as they walked, a nervous habit that Ella had been unable to train her out of.

"Tressa, contain yourself. This is not the time or place to do something with your rage," Drea scolded as Tressa removed her hand from her pocket, leaving the dagger in its place.

"Are you sure we can't ask for Lucifer's body?" Tressa asked for the tenth time. Her hands switched to fidgeting with the tail end of her braided blond hair that fell to the bottom of her back.

Drea's magic relaxed when she saw there were no poisoned spikes sticking out of Tressa's braids.

Drea stopped walking down the hall, sticking her cane out to halt Tressa.

"I'm positive. It's bad enough everyone knows Lucifer worked here. I will not cast any further suspicion on us. That is the last time you will ask me," Drea commanded, channeling every ounce of her mother's tone. Gods, she hated being in charge.

Tressa muttered unintelligibly under her breath as the large double wooden doors parted before them. Two guards ascended the stairs, carrying Anastasia on a stretcher. Drea withheld her eye roll as they carted her sister inside. Ella hadn't injured her much; this was all for show.

"Thank you for bringing my sister home safely, Lord Andrew." Drea curtsied.

He looked just like Henry, with dark red hair and discerning green eyes. Drea glanced sideways at Tressa, who stared at him.

"Tressa, curtsy to his lordship," Drea whispered. "I hope you'll forgive my maid; she's not the brightest," Drea said. She straightened her back as she felt Tressa's glare.

"Not to worry, Lady Drizella." Lord Andrew studied the area as Princess Lena ushered herself past him.

"Princess Lena." Drea curtsied lower.

Princess Lena was a vision of lace and satin in a black dress that swirled around her. Her blonde hair was twisted into a high bun with a small tiara on top.

"Drizella, my love." Princess Lena wrapped Drea in her arms, hugging her close.

Drea shuddered internally.

"I'm going to get Anastasia all settled." Princess Lena left quickly.

Drea turned to find Lord Andrew following Princess Lena cascade up the stairs. His calculating eyes rarely missed anything.

"Apologies for your loss, Drizella." Lord Andrew paused as grief filled his eyes.

"My condolences for yours," Drea whispered.

"We had just gotten Ella back. Henry didn't show it well, but he was so happy."

"Knowing Henry, he'll find a way through this. All of you will." Drea walked him down the steps to his carriage, trying not to lean heavily on her cane. She clutched the cane tightly, holding back a scream. They were always just tall enough to make her journey on them uncomfortable.

"We have people out searching. Hopefully, we'll be able to catch her killer quickly," Lord Andrew assured her.

Drea kept her mouth closed to resist the urge to say more. The need to tell him that Ella was alive, to remove the grief from his eyes, was almost too much.

"We've missed seeing you at the palace, especially during the winter ball." Lord Andrew said.

"I've missed it as well, but I'm better off here." Drea moved her cane to make her point.

"I think you'd find that Henry, and the rest of the court, would disagree," Lord Andrew commented before stepping back into his carriage as the guards returned.

Drea didn't move until the carriage could no longer be seen. She twisted her cane around in her hands, ignoring the flash of pain that shot up her back. Her magic instantly cooled it, soothing the anger in her leg. Drea found Tressa standing at the top of the stairs, watching her.

By the time she reached the front doors, Lena was outside, ordering Tressa to do something. She was a woman on a mission. Princess Lena radiated righteousness and vengeance as she gazed around Aumont. Drea had to smile at the reason behind her wrath. Ella had no idea how much she had irked the princess, how important it was to Lena to become the Queen of Rairene...and Ella had simply walked into a ballroom and destroyed twenty years of scheming. If ever there was a time she wished she could have been at a ball, it would have been for that moment.

"I want her head on a spike." Anastasia charged into the meeting Drea and Lena were having with Queen Laila. Anastasia hadn't been back a full day and already she was on the warpath.

"Hello to you as well." Drea said, pinching the bridge of her nose.

Princess Lena sat across from her in the same black dress. Who brought mourning clothes on a diplomatic mission? Queen Laila gazed down on all of them through the enchanted mirror, her eyebrows raised at the intrusion.

Drea didn't care how familiar Anastasia was with Lena; you did not interrupt the queen.

"Send me to find Ella, Your Majesty," Anastasia begged. She pounded her fists on the table.

"Why do you think she's alive, Anastasia?" Drea whispered. Henry had been very convincing to everyone, from what Drea had heard.

Yes, Anastasia, how are you so certain? Queen Laila wore black as well, with a shawl wrapped around her shoulders.

Drea wore her mourning clothes, though her body was poised for her mother to burst through the doors at any moment, demanding answers or threatening punishment for their failures. How long would it take for her body to process what her mind had already accepted?

"Because I know Luca. He doesn't have it in him to kill someone he loves—"

"We are talking about the same Luca, right? The one who was banished by the emperor of Holodal for killing his brother?" Drea chided. It was a well-kept secret that almost no one in Aumont knew about.

"I know in my bones she's alive."

"Luca used an arrow laced with one of Snow White's most poisonous enchantments. An enchantment, I'll remind you, that was intended for David. While he may not have intended to hit Ella, he did."

"She survived. I know it as well as I know the beat of my heart and my skill with a blade. Why are you so adamant she's dead?"

"I don't want us to waste valuable time chasing a ghost when there are more important things to do," Drea growled. She leaned back and took a breath. Her magic had begun to dance within, and she had to remain calm.

"Let me go find her," Anastasia pleaded.

Drea had never heard her sister beg so much in all her life. Even when their mother had informed them they were leaving Trudel and moving to Rairene, Anastasia hadn't begged.

No. Queen Laila commanded.

Anastasia turned red, her fingers flexing.

You are needed here. You and Drea both have roles. Both of you must present a united front of grief. Lena, have our men find this Luca. I want answers about why he failed to kill Prince David that night. Queen Laila ordered.

Anastasia bowed her head, her hands clenched at her sides. "As you commanded." She took her seat beside Lena, blatantly ignoring Drea.

Fine, Drea didn't need or want her sister by her side. Though her heart ached at the rejection.

Drea paused outside her mother's bedroom.

Before anyone could notice, and before she changed her mind, Drea turned the handle and walked in. She needed some answers her mother could no longer provide. Drea lit a torch in her mother's oppressively dark room. All of her mother's secrets were in here, and she was the only one who knew about them. Not even Anastasia had been privy to this one, and Drea would never share it with her or Lena.

She looked at the small closet with no idea of where to start. She needed to figure out why her mother hadn't killed Ella when she'd been given a direct order by Queen Laila. Why had she lied to her queen and best friend?

Drea picked up her mother's quill and gently pulled on her magic.

She stilled as she stepped into the icy pond of her mother's feelings. She was writing a letter to the queen. Drea couldn't focus on the contents of the letter as the memory had become too degraded, but she did focus on how the memory made her feel. Her mother was tense. Her shoulders were tight, and there was a line of it going down her spine. Drea set the quill down and stepped out of her mother's memory. She longed to reach out and shake her, to make her see the queen was just using her to succeed where she had previously failed. Though close as girls, Drea always saw her mother's relationship with the queen as one-sided.

There had to be something that would help her. Drea peered around and found something she hoped held the key to both her mother and Ella; the whip her mother used.

Drea gripped it, the smooth leather cool beneath her fingers. She barely whispered her enchantment when hatred and joy poured into her. Drea lived through it all, as the whip that had touched Ella's back so many times stayed in her grip. She was frozen, unable to let go as the pain Ella had felt coursed through Drea's body, only to be rivaled by the unbridled hatred her mother held. The lashing of each whip strike hit Drea over and over on her back, legs, and arms. After what felt like a lifetime, Drea's hand was able to unwrap itself from the whip, letting it thump to the floor. Gods, how had Ella survived this?

Drea slumped onto the chair before her, more confused than ever about her mother. She paused, her fingers twitching as she stared at a portrait she had thought destroyed. Yet, there it was. The only portrait that held all of them together as a family. Ella was in her father's arms, head tucked under his, her piercing blue eyes staring back. Drea's mother stood beside him, while she and Ana stood in front, arms wrapped around each other.

Drea held it gently, tightening her hold as her mother's emotions spilled out. Drea hadn't pulled on her magic, and yet all the love her mother felt radiated out. She focused on those feelings, pulling them into her. Then she saw the last imprint, her mother holding it, her fingers gently brushing over Ella's dad, Lord Elliot. He was the only person her mother paid any attention to. All the love and heartache she felt were directed solely at him. Drea staggered backward, the portrait floating to the ground.

Her mother had truly loved Lord Elliot with everything she was. Drea didn't even think her mother was capable of that much love, yet there was all the proof she needed that her mother did, in fact, have a heart.

CHAPTER TWO

Drea

The sun had risen a few minutes ago, casting a silver light through the wispy fog as it rolled over the hedges. Drea's leg didn't ache as much, so she took the opportunity to stretch the muscles, followed by a deep massage that had her muscles relaxing. Today was going to be a good day.

Her magic cooed within, its gentle pull embracing her with warmth and peace as it slowly danced. Drea closed her eyes as it danced through her body, singing soft songs filled with sun, books, and the warmth of a body...Drea stopped the thought from forming.

It would only hurt, and today was a good day.

She grabbed her cane and rested it in the crook of her arm as she left her room. The hallway was always quiet this early in the morning. The novices were expected to be up and ready for breakfast at seven, but that was over an hour away.

Drea walked freely through the quiet. But she wasn't the only early riser now. Princess Lena was also an early riser, ready to conquer the day, ready to rule over the house until a crown rested on her head.

Drea rolled her shoulders as she gazed at the numerous stairs before her.

She took a moment before resting her hand on the banister and taking her first step down the stairs. And then another.

Today was a good day.

Drea continued walking down them, taking each step one at a time without the aid of her cane. Her shoulders relaxed after she got halfway down, her fingers resting gently on the wooden handrail.

Today was a—

Her leg cramped. Drea tried to hold onto the banister, but the muscle twisted viciously, sending shocks up her muscles and into her spine.

Drea tumbled down the final five steps, her cane bouncing across the wooden floor. It echoed in the foyer, disrupting the peace. Drea kept her mouth shut, refusing to let out a single whimper. She gritted her teeth as her muscles violently spasmed.

Footsteps quickly approached from above.

No, Drea thought, not right now. She didn't want anyone to see her lying on the floor, face down, trying to roll over and stretch out the pain.

"Dre..." Anastasia's voice washed over her.

Drea closed her eyes as her upper lip quivered.

"Let me help you." Anastasia's voice was below a whisper. Her hands were strong and gentle as she gripped Drea's arms and rolled her over.

Drea nodded slowly as she rubbed her head. Drea lifted her gaze to her sister, surprised to find Ana already dressed in a mourning gown, ready for the day. Drea sat, wincing as her leg continued to spasm. Ana pulled Drea's leg straight and reached under Drea's skirt to massage the muscles.

Ana locked eyes with Drea as her fingers dug in. "You know you're not supposed to push it on the stairs."

"I know," Drea mumbled. Drea pushed her hair out of her face before rubbing the tears away.

"Then why—"

"It was a good day," Drea whispered. "It was a good day." A tear constricted her throat.

Ana rubbed the tear on Drea's cheek. Ana's green eyes, the one thing they shared, were full of sorrow. "I wish you had killed him that night." Ana's eyes hardened.

"Should have and could have were two very different things that night. Should I have killed him? Yes. Could I have killed him? No," Drea said as her muscles relaxed under Ana's ministrations. Ana was the only one who could get her muscles to relax, not that she had let anyone else ever get close enough to try. Drea closed her eyes as the pain ebbed, and she could flex her leg again.

"We'll get him one day."

Drea nodded as Ana removed her hand and went to grab Drea's cane.

"There you are." Princess Lena walked down the hall, stopping as she took in the scene before her. "Is everything okay?"

Drea wavered under her gaze. To show weakness of any kind to Lena...was to show weakness of character and an inability to do her job.

"We're fine. I accidentally tripped Drea. Clumsy me. I'm going to call a maid for some coffee, would you like some?" Anastasia answered faster than Drea could respond.

Drea looked at her big sister as she slowly got to her feet, waiting for her muscles to cramp and ruin Ana's lie. The muscle quivered as it held, the shaking hidden by her skirts.

Princess Lena pursed her lips as she crossed her arms. "Please have some brought for me as well." She turned around and walked to her mother's office.

Ana handed Drea her cane, gently touching her shoulder before walking after Princess Lena. Drea followed in her sister's shadow, ensuring she didn't fall on the way.

Today was supposed to be a good day.

"Princess Lena, I was wondering what we're going to do to bring back some of our people who are out in the field?" Drea asked as she sat down, gripping her cane between her knees. Today could still be a good day. She could get Calla and Raven home.

Princess Lena took her spot in their mother's winged back chair behind the large wooden desk. "Nothing. Their mission continues."

"Nothing?" Drea did her best to hide her skepticism.

"Nothing. Their information is still needed for our mother's plan to succeed." Princess Lena examined her nails.

"What about Snow White and Belle?"

"Are their missions not vital?" Princess Lena locked her gaze on Drea, her light blue eyes flashing.

"Their mission is in crisis. Belle risked her life to reach out to me and let me know Snow White is compromised—"

"If she's compromised, that's her fault, and we will not intercede to save her life," Princess Lena dismissed.

Drea didn't push. She wasn't sure how she would tell Calla she was on her own, but she would. Calla deserved to know and plan accordingly.

"Have we heard anything from...what's her name again, Anastasia?" Princess Lena leaned forward, steepling her fingers together and resting her chin against them.

"Tressa, and not yet. She's only been at the palace for a day. She will need some time to get in and go unnoticed. Everyone is on high alert," Anastasia responded, sitting straighter in her chair.

"She has one more day."

"What's Tressa doing?" Drea sat. What was Ana planning?

"She's gathering information for us. Confirming a hunch," Anastasia replied, averting her eyes.

Drea looked at her sister for a few more seconds before turning away. Princess Lena continued with their plan for getting Rairene to declare war on Trudel. It was a trap Drea hoped King Matthias would be smart to avoid.

A piece of paper skittered across her bedroom floor the next morning.

Drea picked it up and read it four times.

Queen Laila demanded an audience with her, Anastasia, and Lena.

Tressa had news.

What the news was...Drea was about to find out. Drea applied deep pressure as she slowly rubbed her thumbs on her thigh in circular motions. The scar on her leg was rough under her fingers as she continued to massage it. As soon as the twitching stopped, Drea grabbed her cane and walked to the war room.

What had been her mother's office had officially been converted yesterday into a strategy room for all of them. The large desk had been replaced with a dining room table to give all of them a spot, while the mirror was moved to give Queen Laila a better view of them.

The room hummed with pent-up energy as she walked in and sat beside Ana. Ana was practically jumping out of her chair as Tressa joined them, taking a seat directly opposite the queen to present her news. Princess Lena relaxed in her chair, a small knife twirling in her fingers.

What's your report? Queen Laila asked.

"I figured out where Ella would have gone," Tressa reported. Drea would have expected her to be bouncing on her toes. Instead, she remained calm, the subservient spy, ready to please.

Where? Queen Laila stepped closer to the mirror.

"There's a stronghold up north that Ella and David used to go to."

Where and how did you get this information, Tressa? I didn't authorize any—

"I authorized it," Princess Lena smirked. She sat across from Drea, still garbed in black. Her hair was the picture of perfection as it fell around her face. "I wanted someone who was motivated to find Ella and David, and she did."

"Ella died; you're only going to locate David, who understandably went into hiding. It's almost as though there were too many attempts on his life," Drea said. Now that she had been filled in, she could without a doubt confirm there had been too many 'attempts' on his life.

"You're so adamant, Drea, yet there's no body," Anastasia challenged. "I say we send someone out to scout this stronghold and report back."

"I can do it." Tressa volunteered.

So that's why she was restraining herself. She wanted first dibs on Ella's flesh. Drea opened her mouth to protest, but closed it. Tressa shouldn't be allowed to go. She'd already lied about the stronghold. Drea knew which one they used to go to as children, and it was definitely not to the north.

I agree with Anastasia. Since Tressa learned of their potential location, we should reward her for confirming her hunch.

The matter was settled. Drea bit her lip. Tressa was going rogue, and she had no way of safely warning anyone. It would be odd for her to go anywhere near the palace right now, and though she could communicate through an enchanted mirror, she wouldn't know who else might hear.

"Mother, we have one more topic we wish to discuss," Princess Lena began. "We have been unsuccessful in locating Luca. However, I have a plan."

I'm listening. Queen Laila's voice was tinged with just enough disapproval to tread carefully.

"We want to have Drea release an image of Luca to the king. Tell them who killed Ella and have them flush him—"

"Ella won't be able to resist coming to the aid of her first true love," Anastasia chimed in, smiling from ear to ear.

Drea kept her sigh to herself. Ana was never very good at manipulating others. Ella would never be so foolish. She would be enraged, but not foolish. Not when she had a mission to complete, and if there was anything Ella did well, it was to put the mission first.

"Just how and when are you going to do this?" Drea questioned.

"I'm so glad you asked, sister." Anastasia glowed. "You see, the perfect person to deliver this information to is already coming here to visit you. To pay condolences for your loss. It'll be the best moment for you."

"Who?"

"Henry, of course."

CHAPTER THREE

ELLA

Circles darkened David's eyes as he sat on the couch in Oakwell Hold. It sagged beneath him as he fiddled with a worn blanket, his eyes trained on the frayed edges. They had been at an impasse for a few hours, neither one willing to talk.

"Why weren't we enough?" David asked.

"Why wasn't *I* enough?" Ella responded. It had weighed on her ever since she had come back to court all those weeks ago. Ever since she had told Henry and experienced his reaction to the life she had chosen, she had thought about how this conversation would go. "You were always enough. I always loved you for who you were and all you would become. I still—" she stopped, not daring to utter the word in the present tense. Ella sat and placed her feet on the cold wooden floor before looking at him. "Why wasn't I enough?"

"You were—"

"I wasn't David," Ella challenged him. "I would never be enough if I wasn't some silent, simpering lady of the court who did as she was told and could never do anything but appear pretty."

"That isn't true. There's so much you could have accomplished—"

"I wanted to be me. Me. Ella, the girl who fought pretend villains with her friends, protecting the kingdom we love." Ella sat tall, her hands fisted in her lap. The shadows had begun to play with her vision again, but she would not yield to the hallucinations.

"You became someone all of Rairene would like to see hanged."

"I didn't kill her," Ella whispered, keeping her eyes locked on David. "You know that. Why are we having this conversation if all you want to do is chastise me rather than listen to my side of the story?"

"I don't...I don't know how to trust you. I'm so mad, Ella. I'm mad at you. I'm mad at Henry. I'm just mad, and it's taking all I have to contain my magic and not lose control of it while allowing myself to feel some of my emotions." David threw his arms out. As if to make a point, his raw blue power flickered around his hands, then up his wrists.

Ella pressed her hands together and watched David pull his power back into himself. The circles under his eyes seemed to deepen with the effort.

"David...I don't know what to say that will help you trust me. Trust is earned, and I will endeavor to restore the trust you once had in me."

"You could have come back...you could have...but you became..."

"I know." Ella stood and walked past him.

She paused when he rubbed his eyes.

"I know you hate me. But until you can try to see past the villain you have made me out to be, for even a few minutes, I cannot, will not, tear open my wounds for you." Ella paused, taking a beat to keep her own emotions in check. Ella left, walking blindly toward her room as the shadows clouded her vision.

She made it to her room without giving in to the fear of the four poisons rampaging through her. Not once did she cower at the presence of those shadows caused by Mire. Gods, she couldn't wait for her body to finally be rid of them.

This was going to be harder than she thought. She would tell him everything...no matter how much it might hurt her.

She would do it.

Ella walked down an hour later to find David sitting on the couch, his knees tucked against his chest. He gazed outside, toward an unknown point out at sea.

"David—"

He jumped, the blanket tangling in his legs.

Ella leaped over the couch and stood in front of him. He blinked at her, his eyes dim.

"When's the last time you slept?" she whispered.

Ella rested a hand on his shoulder. David flinched away. She removed her fingers, doing her best to keep her face calm.

"I'm fine. I don't need it." David rubbed his eyes.

"David, you have to sleep—"

"Bad things happen when I sleep," he muttered.

"Bad things..." Ella thought of all the attempts on his life. Most had been while he slept...the late night assassination attempt, and then there was Sophie. Her latest protégé, who had been assigned to kill him. David had let her into his room. He had trusted her, given her a piece of himself, and she had tried to kill him.

"David." She waited for those beautiful eyes to turn to her. When they did, they held a level of revulsion she hadn't expected. Ella swallowed the well of sadness that rose within. "I could tell you that you're safe with me...or that I've already saved your life three times, but none of those facts will mean anything to you. You don't trust me. At least, you don't trust me as Cinderella. But Eleanor, the girl you grew up with, she's still here and you can put enough faith in her that she'll keep you safe while you sleep."

"I told you I'm fine." David rubbed his eyes.

"You're not. You need sleep. What can I do that would help you feel safe?"

"I, um..." David paused as he yawned. "I'm not sure."

"What if I did a perimeter check and then stood watch while you got some sleep?"

David nodded.

Ella got up and walked around the stronghold. By the time she got back, David had fallen asleep. Ella stayed awake for as long as she could. She didn't sleep while the shadows moved around them, or while the effects of Fenith turned her toes to ice . She stayed awake through it all, listening to the world around them. Eventually, she had to do something to stay awake so she searched Jaq's satchel. She found her daggers and a few bottles of potions, as well as a new pair of enchanted diamond earrings to communicate with.

However, the exhaustion crept in after a few hours and clung to the corners of her eyes, gripping until her eyelids acquiesced and sleep pulled her under.

Lucifer had her chained.

Her torture happened over and over, just as he had promised. He had strung her up, the chains biting into her wrists. No matter how much she begged, anything to get him to stop, he didn't. She screamed until her lungs burned and tears stained her face.

"Ella."

She slapped him as she woke up. Her breathing was rapid, her heart pounding as her eyes adjusted to the light streaming into the living room. As she blinked, Ella realized she had sunk into the couch beside David, who was currently holding his cheek.

"Are you okay?" Ella gazed at the red mark blooming on his face.

"I'll be fine." David stayed where he was, a few inches away from her, rubbing his jaw. "Are you okay?"

"It was just a nightmare or a hallucination, maybe both; I'm not sure right now."

"Did you want to talk about it?"

"Not particularly...it was my worst fear...my worst reality." Ella rubbed her hands over her wrists. "But thank you for asking." He wouldn't want to hear about it anyway, Ella told herself.

"Well, if you do, I'm here." David rubbed his eyes as he stretched.

"Did you sleep well?"

David shrugged. He turned away from her and stared off somewhere she longed to follow. She wished he would look at her with those beautiful brown eyes full of the kindness and friendship she had witnessed just five days ago, but now all she saw was a stone wall firmly separating them. How had everything changed so much in just five days?

"Can I examine your injury? I want to make sure it's not infected. The last time I saw it was at night, and we barely had time to make sure you lived," David said.

Ella nodded stiffly. David eased off the couch and left to get supplies, giving her a few precious moments to compose herself. It had only been a dream. Lucifer was dead. She had killed him. Ella got up slowly, waking her muscles as she stretched. She located an old, dusty shawl on a long forgotten chair and wrapped it around her shoulders as she loosened the ties on her tunic to allow David access. She let the fabric fall off her shoulder just enough to expose the cut from the arrowhead.

He wouldn't see anything else this way.

Not the scars decorating her back. Nothing.

It had never bothered Ella for Luca to see her scars, to see all she had endured, all that she had gone through. She hugged herself as she waited.

David walked back in and opened more drapes, letting the sunlight cascade over her. He stopped when he saw her in the sunlight, partially exposed to him. Ella felt her face flush as his eyes flew over her body before landing on her wound.

Ella gently pulled her long white hair to the side, draping it over her shoulder as she stared out the window and towards the waves crashing along the shore. Dark gray clouds had gathered on the horizon.

David's fingers were cool to the touch as he examined her wound. For a precious few seconds she had been happy on that dance floor, in his arms, gazing into his warm brown eyes. But everything else...Ella shook it away.

"It's healing well. There must not have been a lot of poison on that arrow," David muttered more to himself than to her as his fingers brushed over it once more before lifting her tunic. "Can I see the one on your side?"

Ella breathed in and nodded as she lifted the left side of her tunic and revealed the wound gifted to her by Lady Tremaine. Thankfully, the tunic was loose enough to keep the other scars hidden. She prayed to the gods he wouldn't study close enough to see some of the lighter scarring on her side. Ella clasped her hands together as they shook under his scrutiny.

"Do they hurt?"

"It's bearable; I've had worse," Ella replied absentmindedly.

"I can imagine."

Ella didn't bother responding as she walked towards the kitchen. She needed something to stop the shaking. Her body broke into a sweat as her head grew lighter. She hadn't felt so low in energy in a while. Their food supplies would need to be replenished soon, but there was still enough to last about a week before she would need to go into town, and by then they would be on the road again. Ella grabbed some cured meat and eggs, cooking them quickly as her body demanded food.

She turned to find David sitting at the table behind the kitchen, a box in his hands. After dividing the food, she approached him, watching everything he did. He watched her, too.

"Care for a match?" David asked, pushing the crownboard towards her. Crowns had always been his favorite game. Even at six, he had loved it. "Did you ever learn to like it?" he asked, smiling at her.

"A little." She shrugged. "I didn't enjoy the politics and warfare behind it so much then. Still don't, but I know it's why we were taught at such a young age."

"Groomed since day one to take the throne," David said.

"It's a good thing we never kept score," Ella said meekly.

"Five to three," he responded, his grin reaching his eyes. "I do love to win. I'm sure you've improved over the years."

"Uh-huh...sure." Ella sat across from him as he set up the board, and she ate, instantly feeling better.

Minutes passed in silence as they played and ate. David had improved a lot, but so had she. He missed some obvious moves, constantly protecting his queen.

"David, your queen is the strongest piece on the board; use her," Ella muttered.

"How did she do it?"

Ella looked up from the board. "How did the queen become the strongest piece? I don't know; it's the rules —"

"How did Lady Tremaine keep all of you in line? She had a house full of trained killers, and none of you stepped out?"

Ella kept her eyes locked on the board. "Some did...we quickly handled them. She paid all of us well, plus..." Ella trailed off. Ella bit the inside of her cheek. She didn't want to tell David that for nine years she had been manipulated. It was too embarrassing. "All of us thought we were serving the crown. There was some purpose to our work...we worked in the shadows so you didn't have to."

"You thought..." David paused, his hand gripping the counter, his knuckles white. "You thought my family was not only condoning but sanctioning those murders?"

"We had been given evidence to suggest they were traitors, abusers, or dangerous to the crown. We always did our own reconnaissance to verify the information, David. We...I...killed bad people. We never questioned it." Ella couldn't face him. She had been so blind. "I followed her every command, and I believed what she told me." Ella looked at her hands. "I wanted to make her happy and prove myself to her. Show her she had made the right choice in training me. And it was what I had always wanted…to serve the crown and protect those I love."

"But we never—"

"I know!" Ella paused. "I know. I never…" Ella hung her head. When she looked at David it was through tear stained eyes. "I'm still processing everything. I've only known for a few weeks, so I know it'll take you longer than a few days…but…I am trying to not let myself fall apart while telling you what I know. I understand you have questions, but making me feel naive for believing her…it isn't going to help me."

"I'll work on it." David shifted in his chair. "So, you never went against her wishes?"

"Once—"

"What happened?"

Ella gave him a pointed glare.

"Right—"

"Crowns." Ella moved her queen into position.

David stared at the board. His queen was out of position and wouldn't be able to help. He moved a pawn, delaying the inevitable.

"I don't tell you this lightly, David. It's embarrassing. But you need to know what we're up against. If we're going to do this, save your throne, defeat the queen of Trudel, and form an alliance with Holodal, you're going to need to know everything. You're going to have to learn how to use your queen."

"Are you the queen?"

"If you could protect me instead of putting me out there, but you knew you would lose without my help, what would you do?"

"Would you die?" David's eyes darkened.

"Dying is always a possibility, David, especially with what I do. Besides, wouldn't my dying make you—"

"Then I would protect you—"

"Wrong."

David opened his mouth.

"You will need to use all the resources at your disposal to keep your kingdom safe, and I am one of them. I have trained for this, David. I know you don't trust me yet, but hopefully by the time you realize you're going to need me, there's enough trust there to let me help." Ella moved her queen into position. "Crownmate."

CHAPTER FOUR

Calla

Calla had no memory of getting to her cell in the dungeon. No recollection of her beautiful gown being partially cut off to get to Lord Edouard's stab wound. None of it. All she could remember was Prince Adam stepping away from her, betrayal in his eyes. The guards had hit her over the head, and now she was in a moldy dungeon. Alone.

She had waited for the sun to rise to examine the bandage at her waist. It was wrapped tightly with a light tinge of pink where the blade had pierced her. She didn't dare remove any of the cloth for fear of infection. Calla gently pressed her fingers against it, wincing at the soreness and ripples of pain that spiraled out, clashing with her magic. She felt bumps under the wrappings, and Calla relaxed; at least they had stitched her up.

She counted the stones in her cell for the tenth time that morning. Of the one thousand four hundred and thirty-eight stones, four hundred were cracked.

"I am strong. I do not break. I am loved." Calla repeated those three sentences over and over, calming herself more each time she repeated those phrases. Sweat beaded on her forehead, and it had nothing to do with the weather. Her magic had become a constant roaring companion in her head, swirling throughout her body, kissing her skin. Calla was sure she glowed in the darkness. She hadn't been able to siphon her magic for days.

"I am strong." She pulled her magic back from her skin.

"I do not break." Calla summoned all of it to her core.

"I am loved." She balled it up and shoved it far down into her being. Calla let out a shuddering breath. She could do this. She had to do this because...Raven was going to die today. So she would do this. For Raven.

She would not show fear.

She would be in control of her emotions, in control of her magic. She would not cry over her lost friends, not yet, anyway. She hadn't been able to grieve for Ella or Jaq, and now... she would have to wait to grieve for Raven, alone. But those emotions would not be her undoing. She wouldn't allow it.

The noise outside her cell crescendoed.

Raven was dead. The crowd was cheering her death. Her best friend was gone. They had failed. Raven was gone.

Calla burst into tears, her magic rising to her fingers. "I am strong. I do not break. I am loved." She shoved it down. Made it smaller once more.

Calla curled in on herself, trying to find warmth. That was the hardest part — the cold. It seeped in through the stones, leeching her of all sense of comfort. If this was step one in their torture... Calla flicked the thought away. She would be okay. She had been prepped for this very situation by Raven and Ella. At least until she hadn't been able to withstand it anymore and had left. Thinking back, Calla realized she should have taken that training more seriously.

She closed her eyes, trying to get as much rest as she could. They would come for her any second, and she was determined to be well rested before they took her.

Calla did her best to work within the constraints of the shackles to press her hands to her head, digging into her hair with her nails, trying to massage the headache that had built up behind her eyes.

Her magic thrashed in its cage, cracking what she had thought were solid stone walls. She had to siphon it out of her before she lost what little control she held. But she had no vials to enchant or shields to strengthen. Calla wasn't even sure she could concentrate enough to effectively enchant anything. All she had was her gown and the stones beneath her. Two materials she had never attempted to enchant.

But she didn't care at that moment.

Calla pressed her hands against the cold stone and let her power flow into it. She focused her intention on the feel of a fire burning in the night, its flames giving you warmth, or the feel of an afternoon sun as it rose in the sky, and...the heat of Adam's hand as he held hers and how her whole body seemed to warm from the way he gazed at her.

There was no incantation for this enchantment, and she frankly didn't have the capacity for it. All she had were her intentions, which she twisted into a song for her magic as she channeled it through her fingers and into the two stones beneath them with a soft gentle hum.

She siphoned her magic until it felt almost manageable again and removed her hands from the floor. Calla held her hands over them, smiling when heat wafted off them.

She snapped her head up when footsteps echoed down the corridor to her.

They hadn't wasted any time in coming for her.

By the time the guards arrived, Calla was sitting on the stones so they wouldn't notice the heat, and her magic was once again contained. Three of them entered her cell. Two of them held her arms while the other unlocked her shackles from the ground. They adjusted the lock so that her hands were pressed together. She wasn't sure if she was offended or grateful they didn't deem it necessary to drug her before moving her. They did, however, blindfold her with a thick black cloth.

"Is that necessary? I did work in the palace."

None of them responded as they pulled on the lead of her chain, forcing her forward. She stumbled, but complied. After a few minutes of cautious walking on her part, two of the guards picked her up and carried her the rest of the way.

Once she was set down, it was onto a hard surface with straps that had her lying on her back. Calla took a breath and held in her shudder. This was probably the same place Raven had been taken to. She blinked against the candlelight as the cloth was removed.

Calla kept her mouth shut as a woman with gray hair and purple eyes circled her. She was strapped to a large wooden table, laying on her back. Calla didn't look at the woman. She stared at the ceiling, counting the wooden boards in her head. Her heart pounded, and she was sure the woman could hear its thunderous pulse. It was the first time Calla had been taken out of her cell since they had arrested her at the ball, and she did not know what to expect.

"My queen has yet to request any specific information from you. She mainly wants you to feel pain first. Pain is a desire I am more than happy to bestow on any unfortunate soul." The woman stopped next to Calla's head.

Calla still didn't look at her. Sweat beaded on her forehead as she counted the boards. She had had to start the count over multiple times. She could never get past thirty before something else happened that pulled her attention away from those old boards. Calla started the count again.

One, two, three, four, the woman walked over to a different table. Five, six, seven, Calla glanced over and saw the enchanter's mark on the back of the woman's neck.

One, two, three, it was light brown, common. Four, five, six, seven, she came back with a glass bottle in her hand; the contents hidden from the corner of Calla's eye. Eight, nine, ten, the woman let Calla see the glass bottle.

One, two, three.

One, two, three, Calla's heart was going to explode, she was sure of it. That glass bottle contained Leech, Raven's poison. How had they gotten Raven's poison? Only Raven's version of Leech was that dark a blue.

One, two, one, two, one, one, Calla saw the woman open the bottle. She kept her eyes locked on the ceiling. One...two...three... Calla would not ingest Raven's poison. She would not do it.

The woman grabbed Calla's nose and held it closed. Calla closed her eyes, trying to focus. She was not going to do it. She would rather die. Her body took the chance away. She opened her mouth, and the woman with purple eyes poured a few drops into Calla's mouth. Calla didn't move. She continued her count. She was going to figure out how many boards were on that ceiling.

"You know, I've never seen enchantments like these. It takes a special, twisted person to enchant this kind of poison. It's too bad I didn't get to truly speak with your friend to find out where she got them." The woman leaned towards Calla's ear and whispered, "she was too busy screaming to give me anything, anyway."

One, two, three, Calla didn't flinch as the woman walked away and put the poison in a locked drawer. Calla tried to continue counting, but eventually had to stop. Leech was doing its job in taking all of her body's heat. She shivered on the table. She was so certain she was cold enough that if she fell off the table, she would shatter into a million pieces.

Calla remained on the table, unable to move. Her muscles screamed at the ice, needing to move, to get the blood flowing again, but she couldn't. She couldn't move, and she couldn't stop getting colder. Even her magic had stopped moving, unable to respond to the burning freeze she was feeling. It had slowed to a glacial speed, and Calla didn't think she could access it if she tried. She could be thrown into a fire and it wouldn't make a difference. Her breath became shallow. How was she supposed to survive this? Did Raven's targets usually survive this? It was just a few drops. Calla thought frantically of the times Raven had used this particular poison. They had survived... right?

Calla's mind raced all the way back to Raven telling her about Leech. "The thing that makes it so deadly is your mind believes it's freezing cold. Once your mind thinks it's real, it's game over. Checkmate. But if they're smart enough, and few rarely are, they'll realize it's all in their mind, then the poison tends to not be as effective." Raven smiled at Calla, mischief in her eyes.

Calla stilled herself. She had to go to a place where she could forget the cold. She closed her eyes slowly, feeling each centimeter as the ice continued to crawl up her. When she felt the sun on her face, melting all the ice encasing her, Calla opened her eyes.

"It's about time you broke free."

Calla looked over at Raven as she sat, and saw her legs caged in ice while sitting in a field of grass. The rest had melted around her. Water dripped from her drenched hair and down her back.

"Where are we?" Calla surveyed the sloping hills covered in waist tall grass.

"I was hoping you could tell me." Raven lay down on the grass and gazed at the bright sky.

"I'm not sure." Why was she here? "It seems familiar, though."

"It's *your* mind palace, Belle." Raven shrugged.

"My mind palace... right... because..." Calla stopped. She couldn't say the words. She couldn't tell her friend she was dead. She would break, and that was not allowed. Clouds gathered above Calla as she stared at Raven.

"Nope. No, Calla, stop." Raven scrambled to her knees, dropping in front of Calla and holding her shoulders. "Don't get upset. You still have a way to go before Leech has run its course, and you need to stay here until it does.

So you don't get to be sad. You don't break. Remember? You don't break." Raven hugged Calla close.

Seven Years Ago

Calla was curled up in her room. Again. They were so mean to her. Why did they have to be mean? Just because she understood more than them didn't mean they had to do that to her. Hit her. Kick her. Call her names. Calla sniffled.

Someone opened her door. Calla shuffled farther into the darkness. If they were coming back to torment her some more, she would make sure they couldn't find her.

"Hello?" The girl's voice was strong and steady as she walked in. "Calla, are you in here? One of the little fairies said they saw you come in here."

"Raven?" Calla peaked her head out from under her bed.

Even at the age of eleven, Raven had more sass than most. She put her hand on her hip and observed down her new partner. They had both been told just a few weeks ago they would be working together.

"What are you doing under there?" Raven sat down beside her bed.

"I thought you were one of the other enchanters. They don't like me."

"Why?" Raven tilted her head.

"I don't know." Calla crawled out from under her bed.

"Of course you know why." Raven twirled a short strand of perfectly curly black hair around her finger.

"I'm better than them, and they don't like it," Calla mumbled, sitting across from Raven.

"So they beat you?" Raven arched a brow when she saw all the bruises marking Calla's legs. Calla pulled her skirts down more, though the damage was done. "How dark is your mark?"

"I don't know. I have an imprint covering it so no one will ever know. I don't even know."

"Well, it must be really dark. I don't think I've ever heard of someone pulling on their magic at the age of eight before," Raven mulled. "I have an imprint

as well. I think I used to know how dark it was, but then I was in an accident and forgot." Raven shrugged.

"Well, I don't like being special. I just want to learn how to be the best enchanter so I can protect everyone. I don't want anyone to get hurt."

Raven laughed. Calla's face flushed scarlet. "You know what I'm training to do, right?"

"Get rid of bad people?"

"Sort of. I'm training to kill people, Calla. That's who you're protecting."

"But I get to protect you, right? That's what Lady Tremaine said. I could protect you."

"Yes... that's correct. You get to protect me. Which means you have to be the best, Calla. I have big dreams, and that means I need an enchanter to have those dreams with me. Do you think you can do that? Be the best?"

"I will be the best. I promise." Calla nodded, new life growing in her honey-colored eyes.

"Good." Raven pulled Calla to her feet. "That means we do not break. Never. We never show them fear. We stand our ground. And-" Raven raised an eyebrow, waiting for Calla to finish her sentence.

"We do not break."

"We do not break." Raven reaffirmed as she wrapped her arm through Calla's and walked out the door back to where the other enchanters were training.

Calla blinked. Raven sat across from her, the sun's rays pulsing down on her long black hair. She hadn't cut it in months, apparently. Calla had never seen her with such long hair before. She liked it. It felt regal somehow to see Raven with hair that long. It was right. Raven opened her sapphire eyes and smiled. Gods, Calla missed those smiles. They had become so fleeting in the last few years. Ever since Jason and that poison she had made. Calla had dropped the poison when Raven and Ella had shown it to her. Ella had been quick enough to catch it. Both of them hid it, promising to never tell anyone. Calla hadn't needed her ability to read people to feel all of the hatred and anger pouring out of it. Whoever ingested that poison would die a hideous death, one she hoped she never had to witness.

"I miss you, Snowy," Calla whispered, staring at the clouds. They remained white and puffy.

"I miss you too, Belle." Raven scooted closer to Calla until their knees were touching. "Don't you think it's strange that bitch face Morgan doesn't know who I am? Or that *I* made those poisons? You would think Queen Lyanna would have told her, except she didn't."

"Why? And how did the queen know who you were?" Calla's head spun as Raven asked all of the questions she had been trying to sort out from the moment Morgan showed her Raven's poison.

"Maybe Queen Lyanna doesn't trust her as much as she would have you believe?"

Calla gasped in pain, falling backwards as ice crawled up her arms and legs. "What's happened, Raven? Why does it hurt so much?"

"You must be nearing the end. It always peaks before getting better." Raven grabbed Calla's hand, holding it against her chest. Tears, actual tears, fell down Raven's face. "I'm so sorry, Calla. I'm sorry you ended up here. It's almost over, I promise."

"I miss you. Why did you have to die?" Calla whispered.

"I know, my love. But remember, what don't we do?" Raven brushed a hand against Calla's cheek.

Calla blinked her eyes against the tears, watching Raven blur before her. Everything faded away. The grassy hills blurred in and out, so did the sun, until all that remained was Raven's perfectly beautiful face, that for the first time in years, was expressing genuine emotion.

"We do not break," Calla mumbled.

"We do not break." Raven leaned down and kissed her cheek.

Calla opened her eyes, gasping against the cold. It was worse now that she was aware of her body. But she survived. She could move her fingers just enough that she knew it was wearing off. Calla gazed at the ceiling and counted. One, two, three. She counted all the wooden boards in the ceiling, only stopping when the guards came in to bring her back to her cage. If Morgan had said anything, Calla hadn't heard it. She had zeroed in on the boards and blocked everything else out as her mind regained its clarity and Leech left her body, bringing back a semblance of warmth to her.

The guards chained her wrists tightly together before throwing her over one of their shoulders and walking down to the dungeon with her. They blindfolded her again, not that it mattered. She knew the route. She had mapped it when Raven had been taken. If the opportunity had arisen, Calla had made sure she would be ready to help get Raven out. But the chance had never come, and now she was stuck instead, and Raven was dead.

CHAPTER FIVE

Drea

Two Months Before Drea's Accident

Drea rode Dream hard through the forest. Her magic soared in the wind whipping through her hair. Drea closed her eyes for a moment, feeling the breeze as it raced around her. She wished she could let go of Dream and let the air gather her up to soar over the kingdom and view its beauty from above while free of the constraints of her responsibilities. She sighed away the exhaustion that pulled at her limbs. Last night had quickly faded into the early morning as she hunted her latest target. The reconnaissance of him had led her through the fifth, fourth, and third circles of Riset as he went from brothel houses to pubs to gambling dens. She learned he was cautious at the brothel houses and always requested women he already knew. Getting access to him at a pub would be harder, as he seemed to just stumble into whichever one piqued his interest at the moment. However, there weren't many gambling dens, and he seemed to prefer one over the others. That was where she would make her approach. She would lure him away from the tables, and once they were alone, she would get him to take her to his place where she would not only kill him but also search his home for the illegal enchanted potions he was selling in the lower circles.

Drea knew this job served no purpose for the queen of Trudel. In fact, she would probably benefit from the citizens of Riset being strung out on enchanted potions, but she also hated when potions were being exploited and had thus ordered the hit on the man who had fled Trudel and snuck into Rairene.

"Drizzie?"

Drea opened her eyes and smiled at him. "Finally caught me, I see."

"Maybe I let you get away. What's the fun if there's no chase?" Henry asked.

"That's got to be the reason. We can't have it known that the Prince's champion is so easily beaten," Drea said as she laughed.

They plodded along on their horses. The forest lay to their right, and the long stretch of beach sprawled out on their left. The beach they were on overlooked the great ocean that separated them from the other kingdoms of Trudel and Evrotia. It was a minimum two-week sail to either one. The ocean crashed thirty feet below them, spray drifting around them.

"Do you ever think about going back?" Henry asked.

Drea turned in her saddle to look at him as she tilted her head. Had she missed part of a conversation?

"Trudel. Have you ever wanted to go back?"

"Once," Drea replied. She kept Dream walking along the cliff edges. They were away from everyone out here. Henry had wanted to come to Aumont, but that couldn't be allowed. So she had offered the beach as an alternative. "When we first got here, I didn't understand the culture or why we had to come. I was so mad at the queen for sending Mom to be the ambassador. I got as far as sneaking onto a ship heading to Trudel"

"I don't remember that," Henry interjected.

"You wouldn't have. It was at night, and it was Lord Elliot who found me. He knew exactly where I would be. He gently chastised me for scaring everyone by running away, before picking me up and taking me home. I hadn't experienced that in Trudel whenever I ran away. I was always left alone while my mother went out with the queen, and she never noticed I was gone. It was

always a servant who found me for fear of being punished if I wasn't home. After that, I decided I would see what life was like here."

"What about now that things are different?" Henry prodded.

Everything was different now. Lord Elliot was dead. She was fighting a secret war. Her enemy was right next to her, and yet...she was happy.

"It would take a lot to get me to leave now. I'm happy here." Drea made sure she was looking at him when she spoke.

"Good," Henry said, gazing out at the ocean as he shifted in his saddle. "Is Anastasia excited for Princess Lena's arrival?"

"You know she is." Drea replied. Saying Anastasia was excited for Princess Lena's annual visit was an understatement. Every spring equinox, Princess Lena made the journey from Trudel to spend three months at the palace. It was part of the treaty that had been drafted eighteen years ago. Every year, Princess Lena would visit to ensure she and Prince David were on friendly terms with each other. Unfortunately, that couldn't be further from what was hoped for by both royal families. Prince David did all he could to be around her for just long enough that she couldn't be fully offended.

"You're not excited to welcome her?" Henry asked.

Drea watched him out of the corner of her eye and stuck her tongue out at him. "We should get back. I don't want Mother to notice I was gone."

"Does she usually notice when you're gone too long?" Henry responded.

No, she didn't. But Drea wasn't about to say that to Henry. He had already observed a lot, and she didn't need to confirm any more thoughts he already had about their family dynamic.

***

Drea read the missive from Princess Lena one more time. Anastasia was twirling around in her aggressively pink room as she gushed over the invite. The plush carpet beneath Drea's feet seemed to pull her down and root her to the spot instead of providing the grace Ana demonstrated.

"I don't understand your excitement, Ana. We were already going to the ball," Drea said as she tried to temper her sister. The three of them had grown

up together in Trudel, but Ana had always worshiped the ground Lena walked on.

"Yes, but she's inviting us to spend it with her, with the other royals—"

"We know them." Drea tried to reason with her, but it was no use. Ana was lost in the fantasy.

Drea set the note down and turned to leave. How Ana coped with that much pink and frills, Drea couldn't fathom. She opened the door and stepped out as Ella walked by, her protégé Tressa beside her.

"Drea," Ella said. Ella glanced to her side, noticing that her protégé was staring into Ana's room. "Tressa, it's rude to stare."

Tressa stared at her feet, her shoulders slumping. She mumbled something incoherent to Drea, which earned a small glance of pity from Ella.

Ella whispered something to her that had Tressa smiling before nodding and going to Ana's door. Drea stepped sideways and closed it when Ana beckoned Tressa in.

"Are you sure you want to encourage that? I ask as her sister," Drea commented.

Ella sighed. "No, but if I discourage it, she'll only turn away from me and listen only to Anastasia." Ella crossed her arms.

Drea nodded. "Princess Lena just invited us to spend the evening there with her."

"But aren't you already going?"

Drea grinned. "That's what I said." She began to walk to her room, leaving Ella in the hallway. "I wish you could be there with us."

"If they wanted me there, the queen and king would have invited me," Ella replied as she turned away from Drea.

Drea remained silent, knowing the queen and king had no idea Ella was in Rairene at all.

The last thing Drea did before meeting Ana and her mother downstairs for the carriage was grab her purple lace butterfly mask. It had been a while since a masquerade ball had been thrown at the palace, and they were going all out this year. She delicately placed it on her face, pulling the black strings back and binding them. Her brown hair fell in loose curls down her back, with wisps framing her face. Anastasia continued to adjust her outfit and mask, their mother beside her, reassuring her the entire time of her beauty and charm.

By the time they got to the palace, Drea leaped from the carriage. She briskly ascended the towering stairs leading to the entrance. The ball had started a while ago, and Drea's heart pounded with the thought. Her mother may relish being fashionably late, but it only brought an accelerated pulse and sweaty hands to Drea. Her magic spiked as she approached the doors.

Shhh, we'll be dancing soon. Drea soothed her magic.

She walked in through the doors, smiling at those who turned to see her. Squaring her shoulders, she moved gracefully around the edge of the room, listening to the chattering of court gossips. Princess Lena had yet to grace everyone with her presence, and Prince David was stewing beside his parents. He couldn't dance until the princess had arrived. Queen Charisse whispered something to him that brought a smile to his face. Drea turned away from them and headed towards a corner of the room to watch and listen.

"Since when have you ever been one to stand in the shadows during a ball?" Henry asked as he leaned against the wall beside her. He wore a decorative black mask that covered the space around his green eyes.

"Since I needed a dance partner," Drea replied, looking at him expectantly.

"Is that the best idea?" he asked. Henry moved a small curl off her mask and tucked it behind an ear. "I assumed after your mother..." Henry glanced away, "well, I thought we might pause the dancing?"

"I don't care about what my mother says. Besides, she'll be too busy preening for Princess Lena tonight to notice," Drea assured him. She waited for him to ask her.

Henry held out a hand, which she gladly accepted.

Her magic spun around, twirling effortlessly as they danced. Drea savored the feel of Henry's calloused palm pressed against hers, or how he guided her perfectly with the support of his arm under hers. The soft fabric of his jacket soothed her magic as she rested her hand on his shoulder. This was her favorite part of dancing with Henry. They knew the steps the other would take before they were taken and could move in perfect symmetry with each other without saying a word.

By the time the dance was done, Drea's cheeks were flushed, not that Henry could see, and her magic had spiraled down into a calm sway that relaxed her entire soul.

"Announcing Her Majesty, Princess Lena of Trudel," the court announcer proclaimed.

Henry groaned softly. "Duty calls. I need to be with David." Henry excused himself as they walked off the floor.

"Duty calls me as well," Drea whispered, spotting her mother and sister behind Princess Lena.

The two parted, with Henry going to the dais and Drea standing beside her mother.

"Where have you been?" Lady Tremaine asked through gritted teeth at a level only Drea could hear.

"I didn't think I would be needed to watch Princess Lena's maids get her dressed," Drea mumbled.

"Your absence was noticed."

"My apologies, Mother." Drea wanted to say more, but thought that saying she felt she wasn't important enough to warrant such attention would fall on deaf ears.

"Your Majesties. Thank you for allowing me to stay in your home, and thank you for this wonderful ball. I do enjoy a reason to dance with the prince," Princess Lena said as she curtsied low to King Matthias and Queen Charisse.

"We're always thrilled to have you visit us, Princess Lenaria," Queen Charisse said. Her voice was soft as it floated over to them. She nodded her head to Princess Lena, indicating she could get out of her curtsy. "I look forward to seeing you on the dance floor."

Once they were done, she waited to be dismissed by the slight nod of her mother's head. Drea slowly walked over to a table laden with meats, breads, cheeses, and her favorite, chocolate cakes in an assorted variety.

"You know, even with that mask on, I would recognize you anywhere."

Drea's heart stuttered as a deep voice whispered in Trudelian behind her. It couldn't be. She spun around to see a tall man with shoulder-length blond hair, pale skin, light blue eyes, and a charming smile she hadn't seen in almost ten years.

"Liam?"

"Hi, Little Butterfly." Liam grinned wider as he bowed. He held his hand out to her.

Drea grasped it without hesitation as he swept her into a fast-paced waltz.

"What are you doing here?" Drea asked in Trudelian. Her voice was rusty as she spoke in her native language.

"Not happy to see me?" Liam asked, pressing his hand and hers against his heart.

"I am..." It had been so long since she had seen him. In fact, she had been nine and tried to kiss him, if memory served her. "How have you been?" Drea shook off her embarrassment and focused on him. She wasn't used to tilting her head to look at him. Laughter danced in his eyes as they spun around the room. Her magic spun with them, giddy as they waltzed.

"Well, at least you're happy to see me," Liam said as he squeezed her hand as her cheeks flushed.

"How have you been?" Drea reiterated. She continued to speak Trudelian, finding the words flowing back to her.

"All that changed was that life was duller without you there," Liam said.

Drea glanced away from him as they continued to sway around the floor. She didn't notice the dances shifting and the evening passing them by.

"Will you accompany me outside?" Liam asked.

Drea nodded as Liam escorted her off the floor and outside into the cool air. The moon's absence brought the stars to life as Drea's eyes adjusted to the darkness. She rubbed her arms, smiling softly when Liam placed a cloak around her shoulders.

Drea removed her mask and turned to face him.

"There's my butterfly," Liam said. He stood beside her, leaning against the banister.

"What brought you out here with Lena?" Drea asked.

"I can't come see my friend?" Liam responded.

Drea cocked a hip and stared at him.

"I came on orders from the Queen. You know how it is for me there, the bastard son of the queen's consort."

Drea remembered how hard it was for Liam at Trudel. Queen Laila constantly used him as a pawn against his father for his father's betrayal of her. If he wanted to stay at court, he would have to prove himself worthy of remaining at court.

"At least here you'll hopefully get some reprieve. What does she have you doing?" Drea asked.

"I can't tell you that, Queen's secrets and all." He winked as he leaned closer to her. "I've been tasked with babysitting."

"Sounds incredibly entertaining."

"Well, if I continue to see you, then it will be," Liam spoke softly, his hand gently touching the same strand of hair Henry had moved earlier, and holding it behind her ear, as he stepped closer and kissed her temple.

"When might I see you again?" Drea mumbled through the haze that enveloped her and her magic as Liam remained close to her.

"Tomorrow? I'm sparring with the prince and his friend. You should come watch me beat them." Liam grinned.

"I would love to."

Present Day

Drea waited in the hallway across from Tressa's room. She still slept in the wing with the novices, something Drea was certain grated on the uppity assassin. How Ella had handled mentoring and training her, Drea couldn't imagine.

Drea shifted on her feet. Tressa should have come back from the basement armory in Aumont by now. She didn't need many supplies for this trip. Drea flexed her feet and walked over to Tressa's door as she removed a small black leather pouch from a hidden pocket within her skirts. Drea's lock picks hadn't been used in a while, but she liked to keep up with her skills, not that she would ever need to pick a lock again. Drea quickly grabbed her tension wrench, inserted it into Tressa's lock and used the pick to run it along the inside of the doorknob, feeling each pin release. She twisted the handle open and slipped in before anyone saw her.

Drea had expected something minimal with a vanity and wardrobe. No personal items or details. Since Tressa had grown up on the streets of Riset until the age of ten, Drea had thought she wouldn't have much in the way of belongings. However, the room was an explosion of random objects and trinkets. A pile of clothes sat on top of a chair in the far-left corner. The vanity had several knives scattered over it and the long spiked hairpiece Tressa wove into her braid. The four-poster bed was the only spot in the room that wasn't in pure chaos. The blankets were in perfect order; the pillows were fluffed.

Drea walked over to the bed and sat down as Tressa walked through her door.

"Get out," Tressa said. Her arms were full of several items, including a large pack. She walked across the hardwood floor to the vanity and set down a pile of clothes, weapons, and enchanted items.

"Remind me again, Tressa, what's the name of the stronghold in the north that Ella and David are supposedly hiding in?"

"I didn't say the name." Tressa grabbed Drea's cane from its resting spot on the bed and held it out to her.

Drea took it and looked down on Tressa. "And you're sure it's a spot to the north?" If Tressa were going to the north, Drea would not give her more cause to search elsewhere. Tressa's eyes widened just a little.

"I'm certain; is there a reason I should search somewhere else?" Tressa confidently asked, keeping her eyes locked on Drea's.

"Is it Summerswind Fort?" Drea listed the one stronghold in the north that Ella had despised as a child. It was run down, and when the wind blew in through the old stone hallways, it sounded like a haunted ghost was screeching through the rooms. Drea hoped they hadn't gone that way.

"No, the other one. There were a couple of portraits in the prince's room of the stronghold. Why keep them if they don't mean something to you?" Tressa shrugged as she turned away from Drea.

Drea straightened her spine at what Tressa had pulled off. "I see. Well, I'm glad you'll be the one to bring your former mentor home. If she is alive." Drea added.

"You still doubt Anastasia's claims?"

"I don't doubt Anastasia believes she's alive. But I wonder if it's because she wishes she could kill Ella herself. Keep that in mind when you go there. I would hate to think of what Anastasia would do to someone who kept her from exacting her revenge." Drea spoke softly. She walked towards the door, not setting her cane down on the wooden floor.

Drea left Tressa in silence, her mind a churning sea with storm clouds on the horizon. There were too many possibilities and nothing she could do, and now she had to face Henry.

Drea stopped at the edge of the stairs. Her cane hovered over the next step, waiting for her lower leg to hold her weight. She should go back to her room. Henry could deliver his condolences to Anastasia. She didn't need to see him. Didn't need to...her left hand crunched the portrait of Luca she had been commanded to deliver. She could just as easily order one of the novices to hand it to him. It didn't have to come from her. Drea took a step backward, bringing the cane with her. She shifted her weight to lean on the cane, transferring the portrait to a pocket. She had sworn a new oath to Queen Laila. She would do as she was told. Her magic skittered inside, sending her heart into spasms.

She was going to see Henry...for the first time in two years.

And it wouldn't be from behind a curtain or while hunched over a bleeding Ella, but in the light of day. She should have known the day would come when she would eventually have to face him, especially after the death of her mother.

Drea massaged her leg one more time. When she glanced down at the foyer, Henry stood at the bottom, his back to her as he spoke with a guard.

She was in one of those moments she had read in all of her romance novels. The beautiful girl standing at the top of the stairs, wearing a dazzling gown with perfectly curled hair. Then the man looks up and sees her, his mouth dropping open just slightly in awe as he witnesses her descent, as though his life were tied to hers.

Except Drea's dress was black and unflattering, and her curly brown hair was loosely pulled back to keep it out of her face. Her walk down the stairs would be anything but graceful as her cane echoed on each step, its resounding thud a reminder of why she could no longer see him.

Henry turned his attention to her, and she almost tripped at the sight.

Gods, he took her breath away. His wavy red hair curled around his square jaw. His green eyes were locked on her, watching her every move. His black mourning uniform was wrinkle-free, and the black cloak he wore shrouded him in a layer of soberness. He was...Henry...as perfect now as he had been since the last time she had danced with him at the palace. But now...she was no longer the same dance partner. Her fingers twitched with the need to cover the thick scar trailing from her left temple to just under her chin. The face she had once known how to read so well was emotionless as she reached the bottom of the stairs.

"Henry," Drea spoke softly as he helped her down the last step with the gentle support of his arm. Being allowed to say his name again was like rereading a book for the first time in years, relaxing yet exciting.

She moved towards the garden. Henry wrapped her free arm around his, an added layer of support as they walked in silence through Aumont. The stronghold was lit with candles, appearing like a normal home of nobility. Not like the house of horrors he had seen just days ago. She wondered what he was thinking about after all that had happened. He would of course realize every time he asked about Ella over the years, or mentioned missing her, Drea had been lying to him. He would never forgive her for all she had done.

"Drizzie, where are we going?" Henry asked.

Her magic flared at the nickname, warming her soul with joy. Drea pulled it back into its normal dancing position. Every time her cane touched the ground, she felt him wince beneath her fingers. So, he was still embarrassed by her deformity. Drea straightened her back and walked with confidence, dropping his arm. She didn't need him to want her anymore. She would tell him this one piece of information and be done.

"Do you trust me?" she asked, turning to watch him.

"No." He didn't look at her.

"I simply thought you would wish to pay your condolences to me in private." Drea continued walking, one step at a time, her cane touching down a little lighter with each step so as not to draw any more attention than was necessary. They walked down toward the section of the maze that was mostly abandoned by novices.

She sat down on one of the stone benches, her back stiff. She didn't want to do this.

"I have some information for you—"

"How could you do it?" Henry asked at the same time.

Drea paused, waiting to see if he would ask again. He didn't. Instead, he sat beside her, his hand resting on the stone bench just inches from hers. Her magic demanded she reach out and rest a finger against his. Just a finger to feel his skin again.

"You're so good at your job, Henry." She twisted to keep him in sight. His deep emerald eyes were inches away, and instead of finding the longing she had once seen within their depths, all she discovered was loathing. She gulped. "You're so good at protecting those you love. I know there's no way they could have disappeared without your help. You're too smart. I know you know everything...you have to know everything." Drea searched his eyes for confirmation. Any sign. There was none.

"Was that what you wished to tell me?"

"No...um...we have a portrait of Luca to hand over to you and the king. It's information we're providing to aid in the capture of Ella's killer."

"Luca?"

"He's the one who shot the arrow in the ballroom. We can't locate him, so we're giving you his portrait to use however you see fit." Drea withdrew the portrait of Luca from her pocket and handed it over to Henry.

"Is there anything else?" He took it, not once glancing at her.

"I know," Drea bit her lip and turned away, "I know you have a lot to protect...I guess both of us have become servants to our roles...doing all we can to protect the people we love...no matter the consequences." She could do it. She could tell him about Tressa. Henry would warn them. But Henry hadn't indicated anything to her...for all she knew, Ella was truly dead. She had seen nothing after they'd left Aumont. Even if he didn't know, there had to be a way to warn them. Somehow.

Drea opened her mouth. "Henry—"

"Lord Henry, your father scried me. He's wondering where you are and has ordered you to the palace." Princess Lena walked into the gazebo, her black skirts swirling around her. "I was wondering where you two had gotten, Drizella. It's not like you to wander off. I know how it tires you."

Henry stood and bowed. "Thank you for letting me know."

"I trust Drizella delivered our good news?" Princess Lena asked.

"She did. It's very helpful."

"If I were you, I would put it on every mirror. Just to make sure everyone knows what he's done. Betraying Ella and Prince David...I could hardly believe it."

"Me too," Henry muttered. His brow furrowed as he looked between them. His eyes darkened before he nodded and left.

CHAPTER SIX

Ella

Ella set her plate of food down when the mirror behind the black cloth glowed. It flashed three times. A special announcement from the palace. David ripped it off as the message began.

Ladies Anastasia and Drizella of House Aumont have provided valuable information that will aid in the arrest of the man responsible for the death of Lady Eleanor and the attempted assassination of Prince David. The killer of Lady Tremaine, Trudel's ambassador, remains unknown.

Ella couldn't move. *Couldn't think.*

Luca's face was in the mirror. His face was being sent out throughout the entire kingdom.

He would have nowhere to go now.

"They can't do that." Ella shook.

"Ella —"

She flinched away.

"I know it's bad they revealed his face. I know you care about him."

Ella rubbed her hands over her eyes, wiping away some tears. "Maybe one day long ago I cared. But when enough people let you down—"

"We didn't mean to let you down."

She took a moment for herself, centering the well of emotions in her heart. "I know." She wiped away more tears. She didn't know if they were for Luca or herself.

Ella paced around the room, her hands twisted together. Luca's face remained in the mirror. His green eyes seemed to lock and hold onto hers. It was the portrait she had painted when they had been courting. Her heart ached at having ever painted it. If she hadn't...they wouldn't have had a single image of him to use. He would have been safe.

Ella turned to David and saw the questions forming in his eyes.

"Ella—"

"I can't talk right now, David. I want to. I do. I want us to talk and find a way to put everything on the table. But right now..." Ella glanced at the mirror. "Do you even know what his image there means?" Ella stood."I need to breathe, and that means I can't be in this room right now." Ella brushed aside another tear.

She turned on her toes before he could say anything, relying on the trust she had in him to give her the space she needed. Ella walked out of the stronghold and charged down the stone path.

Sand squished beneath her toes, and she reveled in the coarse grains rubbing over her skin. Waves tickled her ankles, singing their song of joy to her, pulling her farther out into the ocean. Ella didn't stop until she was up to her knees and closed her eyes. The waves gently brushed against her, caressing her. She tilted her head back, gazing at the white clouds overhead.

Ella took in the calmness of the waves, it settled her mind and gave her the clarity and peace she needed. This time, Ella knew why tears trickled down her cheeks, and she let the emotions rock through her.

Everything she had done in the last few weeks had all been for David. She had given up so much for him. She had been...broken. She realized that now...nine years later. She had been broken. Her mom had died. Her father had died. The people she loved had loved their idea of her, not who she was. So she had left.

Ella slid out of the armor she had built up and let herself feel her emotions. Sank into them as she sank into the ocean and sat down, letting the water wash over her chest. She couldn't let her emotions cloud her judgment or guide her in making a rash decision. So she sat with them, tears on her face, eyes closed, as she let her emotions wash out with the waves.

A while later, Ella stood and headed back to the stronghold, spotting David sitting on the threshold, waiting for her. His hands held his head, his black hair falling gently over his face. His other hand held a stick, drawing lines in the sand. She wondered what he saw as she approached. Did he see the villainous assassin who killed his mom, or the girl he had grown up with rising from the history that weighed her down?

Ella shook her head and shifted her thoughts to the problem before them.

Luca was exposed.

Which meant they didn't have him. But they wanted to use him as bait to get her out of hiding. Well, they would be very surprised when she didn't. She knew better than to play that game. This would not keep her from going to Holodal. If they caught Luca, he would never betray her. He never had before.

***

Ella walked down the hallway of the stronghold she had once loved. She touched the rough stone walls, letting her fingers dance over their imperfections as she wandered down toward the kitchen later that evening.

"You don't understand, Henry, *I can't—*"

David stopped talking as Ella presumed he was cut off by Henry. She paused in front of the living room. David stood in the center of the room, talking to Henry through the large mirror that hung on the wall. Ella watched Henry, examining his tangled red hair and wrinkled uniform.

David, we don't know what she went through—

Because she won't tell us. She chose to go through it. Chose that life over us, over me... David paced around the room, running his hands through his hair.

You said she wants to explain—

She said she wanted to follow her heart and that we never thought about how she got to the point of leaving us.

Henry rubbed a hand over his face. *We never did, David. Maybe you should ask her.* Henry shifted his eyes to her.

She leaned against the doorframe, eyes focused on her nails. "If I told you that you couldn't be an enchanter anymore, while still being able to access your magic, what would you do?" Ella kept her eyes trained on her nails, clearing the sand from her cuticles as her heart raced.

"That's different. I can't help it, I was born with—"

"Neither can I." Ella cut David a look.

David opened his mouth.

"I cannot help the desire I feel to fight and defend any more than you can help the desire to heal and protect. They're the same, David, and just because you were born with your gift doesn't make it more important than mine. All I ask is we move forward without judgment and build a stronger friendship with no secrets between us."

Henry and David looked at each other.

"We'll work on it," David said with Henry quickly nodding.

"Henry, how are you doing?" Ella asked, desperate to shift the conversation.

If you two could quickly form an alliance with Holodal, that would be fantastic. The king is livid that I won't tell him where you are. Henry rubbed his face once again as though it would wash away the sleep in his eyes.

What about Luca? Did you have to—

I did. Drizzie...Drizella brought the information to me. What was I going to say, 'they're both alive, no need to put his face out to the kingdom'?

What do you mean? She knows I'm alive—

Drizella has to do as her queen commands, Ella. Queen Laila has designated her and Anastasia as interim ambassadors. You may as well write her off as an ally, Henry said, his eyes dimming.

But…she… Ella ran her hands through her hair. Drea knew she was alive. But she wasn't telling the queen. Nor was she telling Anastasia about the role she played in helping her…in helping Ella kill Lady Tremaine. *I wouldn't give up hope on her, Henry,* Ella commented before she started to leave the room.

Ella, Henry called. She turned to face him, pausing as he pinched the bridge of his nose. He hesitated, glancing between her and David.

What? Ella cocked a hip as she crossed her arms. Henry shifted in the mirror, visibly uncomfortable.

You should know Drizella also told me Luca was the archer the night of the ball. He's the one who shot you.

If Henry said more, she didn't hear it as blood rushed through her ears. Luca had been the archer. Henry wouldn't tell her that to hurt her, but to warn her. She knew that. Yet her heart could not accept what her mind had suspected. Luca had shot the arrow at David. It would have landed had she not gotten in the way.

Ella stumbled out of the room. She hadn't seen him at all during the ball, not that she had had time to find him. But he hadn't been there afterwards either. He hadn't shown up until she was running out of Aumont, barely functioning. He had known exactly where she was injured…had been ready to bandage it…Luca had shot her.

She leaned heavily against the cool stone wall, closing her eyes.

Henry's words ravaged her delicate lake of emotions. The ice she had built on her emotions cracked as the words 'Luca shot you' struck at it like an ice pick, over and over again. She ambled back to her room, her mind whirling as she processed the information and shifted the pieces on her board.

"Can I come in?" David leaned against her doorframe, hands behind his back.

"Depends on what you're holding in your hands." Ella crossed her legs, watching his cheeks flush. She tried to crack a smile but stopped when her lips quivered.

He stepped inside and handed her a cookie.

"Can I show you something?"

David raised his eyebrows as she reached into Jaq's satchel. She had finally finished going through it. If she were honest with herself, she needed the distraction. It worked. Ella stared at the last item he had hidden at the bottom.

Her shackle.

Just one of them. But somehow, Jaq had known she would need it.

"Are you able to control how much you read from an object?" Ella asked.

David nodded.

"So if I give you something, do you promise to just read the emotions? No memories?"

David nodded again, slower this time.

"I, uh...I only have one, and I don't know if you need the set, but I hope it's enough to show you." She could let him read it. It was just the emotions. Nothing else. He didn't need to see the punishments...or hear her crying when the monster in the dark stalked her. He wouldn't need to see any of that. Just her emotions. Just the strength and determination she had built. She would do this. She would mend the bridge between them.

"The set?" David questioned.

Ella withdrew her hand, the shackle gripped in her fingers. "They, uh..." Ella froze as she moved closer to him and pulled up the sleeve of her tunic to show him her wrists and the scars that had embedded themselves there.

David studied at her wrists. His magic flared out around his own as his hands moved to hover over her wrists. His magic continued to wrap around his fingers as he continued to stare, his body frozen, his brown eyes darkening the longer they stared.

Ella gently touched his hand and placed the shackle in it. She leaned away as his magic engulfed the chunk of metal.

David closed his eyes, his entire body shuddering as what the shackle gave him passed through his body.

A moment later, the shackle clattered to the floor, and David ran for the washroom.

The sound of him vomiting reached her ears.

Ella ran over, stopping at the door. "David, are you okay?"

David heaved again.

"I don't understand. Why are you sick?" She waited outside the washroom as he cleaned himself.

What had he read? Ella scrunched her lips together. He shouldn't have felt anything that bad...right? Had she forgotten something? Ella walked back to her bed and picked up one of the cookies. She had experienced pain, fear, and anger while wearing those shackles. But there was also strength and determination. Ella continued to eat more cookies while she waited for him.

"Are you sure you're okay?" Ella questioned through a mouthful of cookies.

"Am I okay? Are you okay? Do you realize...Ella..." David knelt before her, his hands on her knees as his magic continued to flare around his fingers.

"David?" Ella put a finger under his chin and lifted his head until she could look into his molten brown eyes. "I'm sorry, I shouldn't have had you—"

"Don't apologize. Not for feeling. Never for that." David gently touched one of her wrists, rubbing a thumb over the scars. "I just didn't expect...all of that pain and loneliness. Or the fear...the terror that coursed through you..."

"It was nothing—"

"It was everything. It consumed you, and I'm so sorry we didn't listen to you, see you, or open ourselves to the idea that you should be able to be yourself. " David stood and sat beside her, his hands clasped between his knees. He took slow breaths, his magic flaring less as he regained control.

"I...thank you..." Ella whispered.

"I already knew you were strong. I've never questioned that." David took one of her hands, turning it over in his. "Thank you for showing me."

Ella nodded as she watched her hand turn in his. "How did you not lose control? Your magic was flaring, yet you kept your control of it."

"It's one of the first things I learned at the academy. You can't truly test your power until you know how to maintain it while feeling powerful emotions. If you don't...well, it controls you."

Ella found herself in front of a ladder at the end of a long hallway. She climbed the ladder that had been forbidden to her as a child. Dust and the scent of long-forgotten items assaulted her nose. Large white linens covered boxes and trunks filled with unknown treasures. Ella laughed as she opened various boxes and uncovered vases, plates, and artwork.

"So, were our outrageous ideas correct? Is this room filled with swords and gold?" David called as he walked up the ladder.

"Afraid not." Ella stared at the portrait of Queen Charisse and her mother. They were so young, Ella realized. Both taken too soon. Queen Charisse's black hair cascaded in curls around her arms, while Ella's mom, Lyra, had hair just as white and wavy as hers. Both wore smiles that would melt a kingdom. It reminded her of Raven, her heart aching for her friend.

"We should hang it up," David said.

"It seems like they didn't want anyone to see it." Ella motioned to the other items in the room she had found. They were all portraits of them as children, as their two families grew up.

"They did, but pain does funny things to us. All of us respond to grief differently, and sometimes that means putting away what you love most."

"Sounds like a coward's response—"

"And not talking about the person at all is different..." David challenged.

Ella turned away. He was right, of course. Who was she to judge for hiding them away? She moved to another trunk, one that appeared older than the others and had been pushed into a corner. Gowns that hadn't seen sunlight in gods knew how long were nestled on top, along with an envelope displaying Ella's name. Her eyes widened as she lifted the envelope in shaky hands while staring at her mother's handwriting. Ella gazed between the envelope, the gowns...her mother's gowns, and found herself unable to move. Unable to let herself touch the fabric that had once been worn by her mom. Ella sat on the floor and stared.

"David...will you...will you read this, please?" She handed him the envelope, her eyes fixated on the truck.

"Are you sure?"

Ella nodded.

"My Little Snowstorm —"

Ella snapped her head. Queen Charisse called her that. She had always thought...Ella shook her head and turned away, letting David continue. As he spoke, his voice drifted away, and the sound of her mother's soft whisper of a voice washed over her.

My Little Snowstorm,

I'm sorry I've had to leave you. I know the years ahead will be hard, but I want you to know just how loved you are. I did not leave you willingly and believe me when I say the enchanters tried everything. They did all they could to ease my pain and keep this illness at bay for as long as they could. Some things just can't be healed. But the years I got with you were worth any illness. Ella, your father was the light of my life, but you were the love of my life, and I couldn't have asked for anything more than the time I got with the two of you.

I only wish I could have shown you my kingdom and the home I loved so much. I see you running around with Henry and David, and I wish I could share my memories of growing up in Trudel with you. There's nothing like waking up in the winter to a field covered in fresh snow and racing your horse across the hills. One day, I hope you get to meet my family. Even though I may be gone, I'm certainly not lost, not so long as you're alive. I've asked Charisse to pack my trunk with my most cherished memories of home so that when you're ready, you might learn a bit about me and my first home.

Love you endlessly,

Mom

David remained silent after he finished. She felt his presence behind her, waiting. But Ella couldn't think of anything to say. Her mother had loved her. She had wanted her to meet her family in Trudel. Ella ran her hands through her hair, braiding it back.

"I uh..." Ella stood.

"Are you okay?"

"I'm fine." She didn't believe herself for a second. Ella walked toward the hatch and climbed down.

"Where are you going?"

"Running," Ella replied. "I'm going running."

"But you hate running," David called as she walked to her room to change.

She was already too far away to let him know she loved the escape it gave her.

The wind rushed past her as she blocked out everything but the sound of waves crashing beside her and the feel of the fog kissing her cheeks. She ignored the pulling in her back and side as best as could. Ella got as far from

Oakwell as she was comfortable with before turning back. She sprinted the rest of the way, her lungs burning with effort, salty sweat blurring her eyes. As soon as she reached the gate leading to the stronghold, she collapsed on the beach, her chest heaving. She didn't want to see her wounds, but she had a feeling they were bleeding.

David stood over her, blocking the morning light.

"Want to train?" Ella asked.

"It won't be fair; you're injured." David swallowed his excuse.

"I just ran up and down a beach. I think I'm okay. But you're welcome to do the same run if you wish," Ella replied as she stood, hoping that whatever wound had cracked open wouldn't be visible.

"What did you have in mind? Basic drills?" David asked as he stretched.

"I've seen you train. Do you still do 'basic drills'?" Ella cocked her hip.

"I practice all forms of combat."

"Then that's what we'll do —"

"Ella —"

She jogged into the stronghold before he could say anything else and grabbed her daggers from the couch.

"David, let's fight. I'm not afraid of you, are you afraid of me?" Ella moved into a defensive position, her glass daggers ready. David froze, his eyes locked on the daggers. Ella flipped them and drove them into the sand.

"These were not the weapons that killed her." Ella eased toward him. "If you would prefer, we can practice hand-to-hand."

David nodded. Ella refocused herself and got into a strong base position. Her palms were up and open, her balance centered.

She waited for David to make the first move. It needed to be him.

"Come on, show me what you've got. I've been dying to see —" Ella baited him.

David moved.

Ella blocked him.

They sparred for several minutes, neither one of them getting the upper hand. Evenly matched, for one, Ella thought.

Ella threw a punch and David caught it with his hand. He held on as their eyes locked. Ella held her breath as her heart raced, and it wasn't because of the fight.

David still held her hand.

Ella shook herself and swept her leg out and knocked him down.

The sand did nothing to assist them, as their feet sank in with each step. Ella's thighs burned with the effort. They ended up next to the crashing waves, neither one realizing just how close they were until a wave licked Ella's toes and she lost her balance. David got through her guard and pinned her down, pressing her into the sand and holding her hands above her head.

Ella yielded as she locked eyes with David's, which were mere inches away.

She relaxed underneath him, his legs resting on either side of her.

He was so close if she lifted her head off the sand just a little bit, their lips would meet.

"Good job," she whispered.

David had yet to move. His eyes roved over her face. She wondered what he was searching for...and if he found it.

A wave brushed against them, breaking them out of their moment.

David stood, removing his hands from hers as he cleared his throat.

Ella got up before pushing him over as she walked away laughing. David scrambled after her, chasing Ella as she continued to laugh. He caught her farther down the shore, wrapping his arms around her waist. He picked her up and carried her back toward the water before promptly tossing her in.

Ella coughed as salty seawater crashed over her. David reached out a hand to help her up, both of them laughing as she leaned against him. Ella lightly ran her fingers up his chest.

David broke away, turning his back on her.

"David —"

"Don't. Please."

Ella turned to face the ocean, giving him space. She breathed with the waves, calming her rapid heart and the desire to touch him again. To see his uninhibited smile once more. She balled her fists. None of it mattered. He didn't care for her. Even before he knew who she was, he had always flinched away from her.

"I'm..." David stopped talking. It became such a long pause Ella turned around.

"David?" She frowned.

He didn't say a word as he walked around her, examined her back. Ella spun to face him.

"David?"

"Stop." David held her shoulders and moved to her back once more.

"David—"

"Who..." His hands touched her back.

It was then Ella realized her thin white tunic had become plastered to her skin.

"Ella..."

Ella pulled up the edges of her tunic to show him. She let him see her back in all its scarred glory. The whip scars on her back that were so old, so faint, they could barely be seen beneath the others, and David saw them all as his hands gently touched the history of her skin.

"Who did this to you?"

Ella faced him, hiding her back once more.

His hands remained on her shoulders. "*Who did that to you?*"

"It doesn't matter. I killed them," Ella whispered. She turned away from him, stopping when his hand gripped her arm.

He released her when she looked at him and kept his eyes locked on hers as he lifted his tunic.

"You showed me yours, I'm going to show you mine."

Ella stared at the red lightning marks that scarred him. They streaked from his hips to the center of his back. They were the marks of an enchanter losing control. The marks of David losing control. Only he could have caused those marks. Ella noted each line, five on each side, that ran until they collided in an explosion at the base of his spine.

He had been in pain and had tried to hold himself as he lost control.

"How—"

"I'm the one who found my mom."

He didn't have to say more.

Ella could picture it perfectly. Finding the queen dead, with an explosion of raw power around her, and he had almost...who wouldn't have lost control?

"David...I'm so sorry."

It was no wonder he hated her...hated Cinderella. He had suffered at Lady Tremaine's hands as well. Ella saw that. He could never move past viewing her as his mother's killer. She couldn't fault him. David locked eyes with her as he put his tunic back on.

"Let's go inside and get some food," Ella said.

David nodded as they walked toward the stronghold. At least now she knew he could never see beyond her as more than an assassin, and Ella would have to learn to live with that.

CHAPTER SEVEN

Raven

Raven stumbled backward in shock from Aleks, bumping into Rowan. What had Aleks just said to her? Surely she had heard him wrong, and it was because of the literal noose around her neck that she thought he had said something that made her gut churn.

Aleks had said...he had been sent to find *her*, the lost princess of Evrotia...and bring her to his kingdom. He had just...he had saved her so he could complete *his* mission?

Raven's heart pounded in her chest, her limbs numb. The sensation twisted up and around her arms and legs until Raven reached for something to keep her standing. These feelings had nothing to do with the rope still loose around her neck, or the adrenaline rushing through her from escaping the palace on horseback.

Aleks stood before her, his blue eyes locked on hers. His white hair windswept, one of his braids tangled in his quiver. The man who had just saved her life had only done so, not because he cared for her, but because she was his mission.

She had...sacrificed so much...was tortured...

"I went through that torture...*your torture*...it should have been you in that cell." Raven threw the words at him as she shoved Aleks to the ground.

They rolled together as she got in some well placed punches, the shackles hindering her wrists. Raven's magic thundered in her veins, commanding her to use it as she screamed at him. It rose violently, swirling near the surface of her skin. *Not yet*, she told it, pulling the power back from the brink of a delicious cliff she longed to explore.

"Let me finish what I was saying—"

"I will not trade one dungeon for another. I did not endure that pain...and loss...just to lose my freedom again." She tried to keep the upper hand on him, but even when she wasn't bound, exhausted, and in pain, he was her equal.

"I know," Aleks whispered. "I know." He flipped her underneath him, gripping her arms, her legs bound between his.

"Let. Me. Go." Raven commanded, ignoring the twisted pain on his face. She refused to blink despite the tear that broke free and rolled down the side of her face.

"I will, once you let me finish," Aleks said.

Raven stopped struggling against him. Aleks stood, offering her a hand. Rowan extended his as well, which she gladly accepted. She stood away from Aleks, watching him as he ran a hand through his hair. Rowan stood just behind her, his arms crossed, as he stared at Aleks.

"We're waiting," Rowan grumbled.

"I was sent to find you...well, I didn't know it was you," Aleks explained as he paced in front of them. "My mother had heard the rumors for years that somehow you had escaped and were being raised in Evrotia by a former staff member of King Stewarts. I spent my time searching for those map pieces the king had given to his trusted friends."

"Why didn't you ask your aunt for help with those map pieces?"

"My aunt wasn't supposed to know."

"You have a very...interesting family, Aleks. Why couldn't she know?"

"My mother loves her sister, but she wanted you found secretly. She didn't tell me why. But, I never thought...I don't know how my aunt found them in my room and then placed them in yours...I promise...I didn't know."

Aleks stared at her, his eyes pleading with her to understand.

"I...I never told my mother about you. She doesn't know about our relationship or who you are."

"How chivalrous of you," Raven muttered.

"I want to take you to King Stewart's advisors," Aleks blurted.

"What?" Raven cocked a hip as she did her best to cross her shackled arms.

"You're Princess Astrid, and I want to take you to the people who can help you take back your throne."

Raven looked at Rowan. She had not expected that answer. At worst, she had expected him to bring her to his mother; at best, she had hoped he would let her go. He appeared just as shocked as she felt.

"Why?" It was the only thing she could think to ask him at the moment. Though she wasn't sure if the 'why' was about going to her father's advisor's more than a general request to know why he had bothered with her at all.

"Because my aunt shouldn't be ruling over a land she got through a coup."

"Then unshackle me." Raven held out her wrists to him. Would he do it? Or was this all a ploy to get her to trust him long enough to blindly follow him into some trap?

Aleks stepped up to her and withdrew a lock pick, removing the shackles without hesitation. Raven pulled back her wrists before either of them could see how raw and shredded her skin was. She hid them behind her, not daring to touch her skin for fear of the pain it would evoke. All too quickly, their lifted weight brought on a wave of emotions. She was free. The shackles would no longer hold her.

Raven clutched her neck as the sensation of water strangling her ran over her skin. *It wasn't there.* Raven repeated it three more times as she shook herself free of the memories. Queen Lyanna, her *stepmother*, was an excellent torturer. Raven loathed admitting it, and had an even harder time digesting that her stepmother had done that to her. That day...had been the worst of her days as a prisoner. It was also the queen's favorite way to inflict pain. Raven shuddered. Never again. She would take being drugged by her own poisons any day. Queen Lyanna's assistant, Morgan, had enjoyed it as well. A match made by the gods. Raven had never figured out who Morgan was. Definitely one of Lyanna's mysterious enchanters. Raven had memorized her face from her perfectly placed silver hair, dark purple eyes, and down to her red lips, adding it to the ever growing list of people she would kill.

She turned away from those memories as the sky lightened to illuminate their campground. Rowan slept near her, his hand resting on the pommel of his sword as he lightly snored. The campfire had died long ago, a tendril of smoke curling from the ashes. Raven gently sat, rubbing her hands over her biceps, breathing in the cool mountain air.

Her wrists were still covered in dried blood, her skin raw from the shackles. She could leave. Right now. She could get up, take a horse and go...where? Ella was dead. Lady Tremaine was dead. She had no home. She could go find Calla and Mira and disappear into the woods. What she did know was she didn't want to go find her father's advisers, who, if Lord Cenric was correct, had abandoned her. She didn't want any of this.

Throughout her entire life, she had wondered who she was. If she had a family. If they had loved her, missed her, wanted her. Now...she didn't want this life. Didn't want to be some long lost princess who would come and save the kingdom from a cruel queen and bring peace to the land.

She didn't want that.

She wanted to live in a small cabin with her friends, her poisons, and a dog.

She wasn't meant to rule over anyone. She could barely take care of herself.

Raven looked from her hands and directly into Alek's ice blue eyes. He sat across from her on the forest floor, his cloak wrapped around him. Dark circles deepened under his eyes as he adjusted his sitting position and got settled. He still wore his mourning clothes for Ella, his white hair disheveled.

"Morning," Raven whispered

Aleks nodded his head. "How are you feeling?"

"I'm okay..."

"You went through some pretty bad withdrawals. Do you think the enchantments are completely out of your body?" Aleks asked.

Raven brought her knees to her chest. She had only survived those days of torture because of him. Aleks had kept her going.

"Don't worry about me. You don't have to keep pretending you care."

Aleks opened his mouth, stopping when Rowan shifted. He sat and looked between the two of them.

"What's the plan?" Rowan asked as he got up and stretched.

Raven flicked her eyes to Aleks, curious to see what his master plan was. It couldn't really be taking her to the king's advisers and starting a war. Could it?

"I didn't lie yesterday. My intention is to bring Raven to her father's advisers and get back her crown for her," Aleks replied.

"And if I don't want to meet the men who ignored my father's wishes in keeping me safe?" Raven sat up straighter.

"None of us were old enough during the coup to know what truly happened or why they didn't take you with them," Aleks replied.

"You didn't answer my question. What if I don't want to meet them?"

"Then leave," Aleks stood, his hands fisted. "But just know that everything we did, everything Rowan and his father risked, will have been for nothing, and you will regret it for the rest of your life."

"I didn't ask for this." Raven stood and walked until she was inches away from him. "I don't want to be a queen, Aleks. I never wanted...I'm not worthy of being a ruler." What Raven didn't voice out loud was she never wanted to rule in any capacity. She knew how to follow orders and to have others follow them. But ruling over a kingdom...she could never be worthy, not with all she had done. What Aleks was asking of her...it was too much.

"At least hear what they have to say," Aleks whispered.

"You don't know what you're asking me to do."

"Then explain it to me, help me understand why you won't even go to them."

"They abandoned me, Aleks. They left me. If they thought I was worth keeping alive, then they would have followed their orders and gotten me out. But they didn't. So what could I possibly have to hear from them other than how much of a disappointment I've become?" Raven blurted before she could process what she was saying. They had left her behind. All she heard about was how loyal they were, how they wanted her to be queen, and yet...they had left her.

Aleks's arms dropped to his sides. "You are anything but a disappointment, Raven. They would be privileged just to breathe the same air as you. Whatever their reasoning was then, could never apply to who you are now. If anything, go to them to show them the errors of their behavior."

Raven trembled as she let herself feel her heart break at all of the feelings she had repressed. She stared blankly ahead, only focusing on Aleks when he touched her. She locked blurry eyes with him.

"I'll try," she whispered.

Aleks nodded. He squeezed her shoulders. "I would never abandon you. I promise."

Raven needed a break. But Aleks was intent on getting to these advisers as quickly as possible, which meant fewer stops.

They had been riding nonstop for over a day through the forests at the base of the mountain range, heading east if she was tracking the sun's movements correctly. No one could follow their trail through here. Hell, for all she knew, they were lost and Aleks just wasn't saying anything.

"Are we ever going to give our horses a break, Prince Charming?" Raven grumbled. Her stomach did too. They hadn't eaten since the morning, and by the sun's position, it was well past noon.

"Are you ever going to stop calling me that?" Aleks questioned.

"It's too endearing to ever stop," she replied. Raven's horse drew even with his. "How long will it take to get there?"

"I'm not sure. The last report my informant gave had their position somewhere near the depths of the mountains bordering Trudel and Vicuria."

"You're not sure?" Raven's magic spiked at the unknown. Aleks was leading them on a blind hunt.

"There's a reason they've evaded capture for eleven years, Raven. They're very good at covering their tracks. We just need to get close enough and one of their sentries will intercept us."

"I say we stop for now, Aleks," Rowan said.

"Fine." Aleks dismounted and tied his horse to a nearby tree. "We'll camp here for the night."

"Finally." Raven got off, falling to her knees as her muscles gave out on her.

Both men leaped to her side.

"I'm fine," she grumbled as she shooed away their outstretched hands.

Raven took a breath and closed her eyes. Her magic fluttered through her body, trying to soothe aching muscles that had long since given up on supporting her. The hard earth did nothing to tempt staying on its surface for any longer than was necessary. Slowly, Raven got up on quaking legs before leaning heavily against her horse.

As she groomed her beautiful brown speckled mare, Raven took the moment to relax and let her muscles unwind. Once done, she pulled out her sleeping mat and sat down to stretch. Aleks got the rest of the camp ready, moving around her in silence. Rowan had disappeared, probably gathering firewood, if Raven had to guess.

"Come with me," Rowan said next to her.

Raven yelped as Rowan lifted her to her feet and pulled her along with him.

"Where are we going?" Raven asked as he led her farther away from the camp and deeper into the darkening woods. "Rowan."

"Here." Rowan stopped suddenly. "I was taking you here," he said as he motioned towards the stream of water in front of him.

A stream of fresh, flowing water.

"I smell that bad, huh?" Raven smiled as Rowan opened his mouth. She knew it was true, though. She hadn't bathed in...gods knew how long.

"It'll be cold, but—"

"Doesn't matter, I get to be clean." Raven walked to the edge of the stream. Her booted feet rooted her to the shore as she stared at the water flowing by.

Raven clenched her fists until her nails dug into her skin.

She could get in the stream.

She could do it.

She could finally wash everything away. All she had to do was get in...

Chains kept her captive on the table.

A coarse sack had been thrown over her head.

Water poured endlessly over her face.

"Raven?"

Raven heard Ella's voice whisper over her, only to be drowned out by the water rushing over her. It choked her as laughter echoed all around.

"Raven."

Rushing water diluted her hearing until all she heard was her heartbeat rapidly beating to be free and the rush of her magic rising to face the threat. Her heart hammered a tune she had come to know well during her time with Queen Lyanna.

"Raven, are you okay?" Rowan asked, his voice faint as the memory held her firmly within its grasp.

"I uh..." She continued to stare at the rushing water.

"I didn't think water would—"

"I um...Rowan..." She clutched her cloak, grinding the wool between her palms.

"Raven."

Strong, gentle hands lightly touched her shoulders. One of them moved to the center of her back and rubbed light circles over her.

Just as he had done every night she was in that dungeon.

"I can't get in." It was a whisper on the wind blowing through the trees.

"Then we'll try again another day," Aleks responded.

"I want to feel clean...to wash all of it away..." Raven choked out. She twisted her hands together before hugging herself tightly.

"May I help you?"

Raven turned her head to see Aleks.

He stood beside her, his eyes not once breaking from hers as she wavered. Her pulse quickened the closer she got, while her magic softly cooed at being close to Aleks. Her dried blood and sweat seemed to tighten on her skin, crawling up and over, until all she felt was the filth encasing her. Then she looked back at the water, and it rushed over her face again, drowning out anything but the sound of water running over rocks.

Raven nodded, barely noting the shift in Aleks's shoulders as they relaxed and he eased his stance.

"Let's start by sitting down." Aleks knelt down, waiting for her to follow him.

She did so slowly, sitting down and awaiting further instructions.

"Put your feet in the water."

Raven paused, examining her boots.

"No need to remove them. I'm sure they could use a good washing." Aleks spoke softly as he put his own boots in with hers. "We'll keep your uniform on."

Raven glanced down at herself. She had forgotten she had her uniform on. What had once been her royal guard uniform was now clothing coated in the trials of her torture. She hadn't taken the time to examine it, or the way it forever creased where the blood had pooled and dried.

"Where did Rowan go?"

"He went to grab fresh clothes for you."

"What's next?" Raven flicked her eyes to him.

"We sit in the water."

Aleks slid forward, with Raven following him. The stream was shallow, barely covering her legs as it flowed around her. Raven wrapped her arms tightly across her chest as she watched the dirt and blood wash into the clear water. Her heart pounded as she took rapid, shallow breaths.

"I can't go any further, Aleks," she said.

"That's okay. You've come far enough. I'll use my hands to wash you off if that's okay?" Aleks moved to his knees and cupped water in his hands before drizzling it down her back. He did this for several minutes, moving deliberately each time he poured the water down her.

Raven kept her eyes open, staring at the surrounding forest. She kneaded her magic back into her core. It was rough and sticky, refusing to be so constricted. But it was contained, so she left it where it was.

"Where is she hurt?" Rowan's voice pulled her out of the meditative state she had fallen into.

Rowan set the clothes down and stomped into the water to stand before her.

"Rowan —"

"Where are you hurt? You should have told us." His green eyes grew as he looked her over.

"Rowan, I'm not hurt," Raven reassured him. "This is all just..." Raven watched the dark red streaks paint the surrounding water. "I was hurt...but I'm not now. I promise."

"I'm sorry," Rowan whispered.

"Rowan, you didn't do anything —"

"You're my friend...my queen...and you had to..." Rowan stammered. "I brought you to her..." He stared at his feet.

Raven stood, her legs shook, either from the cold or the fear, she didn't know, but at that moment, she didn't care. "None of what happened to me was your fault. If you hadn't brought me to her, she would have killed you. I would rather have you standing before me now than grieve the loss of another friend."

"I still should have done something."

"You did. You helped Aleks get me out." Raven rested her hand on his shoulder and squeezed. "You didn't let me die."

Rowan nodded his head, his green eyes full of guilt. He rested a hand on her shoulder and squeezed before stepping back to let her finish. Raven kneaded her magic back slowly, finding it more difficult than before to keep it contained as it continued to rise.

She faced the stream again and repeated what she had done with Aleks to get into the stream.

Raven sat down before Aleks and fixed her gaze on the cedar trees bordering the stream, watching the birds fly through the early morning sun rays breaking through the canopy. Water continued to pour over her, numbing her body as it washed away the last remnants of her torture.

Aleks rested a hand on her shoulder as he crouched in front of her. "Do you want me to wash your hair?"

Raven's magic spiked at the thought of water pouring over her head. She lifted her hands to her head, attempting to run her fingers through greasy, knotted strands that fell to her shoulders, and failing when the tangles became too large.

Raven clenched her hands to stop the shaking and nodded stiffly.

"It would be faster if you lay down in the water. It's shallow enough that it won't cover your face."

Slowly, she eased back, wanting nothing more than for all of this to be over. Aleks pulled out a washing bar and, as soon as her head rested on the rocks, he began scrubbing her scalp. She stared at him as he worked quickly above her. His usually well-kept hair was messy, with even one of his braids fraying at the end. Though his biceps moved quickly while washing her hair, his hands remained gentle as he lifted her head and got to the underside of her hair.

Before she could turn her focus back to the forest, the birds, or anything but the water surrounding her, Aleks was lifting her up out of the stream by her arms and giving her a final once over.

"I'll go change back at the camp. Take your time getting out of these and into the ones Rowan brought. He also brought a brush for you," Aleks said as he handed her the pile of clothing.

Raven took it, watching as Aleks left without so much as a mild attempt at flirting. She set the clothes down on a dry log and began removing the uniform that had become her jail clothes. As much as they had washed off, it still hadn't been enough to remove the sweat stains or burn marks from the metal stick Queen Lyanna and Morgan had used on her body.

Raven didn't look at her body. Not yet, anyway. She would hold off on that discovery for a little while longer. Before the coldness of the water and crisp air could settle on her exposed skin, Raven pulled on what felt like the most luxurious, simple black tunic and black pants. The fabric wasn't even that soft, but it felt like velvet on her body as she rubbed warmth back into her muscles. Next were the wool socks that had never been worn, followed by a sturdy pair of thigh high lace-up black boots. The tunic had loose sleeves that gave her the freedom of movement she had been missing.

The last thing she tackled was her hair. Though it was clean, the tangles remained. Raven set about slowly moving the comb through her hair and working each knot out until her curly black strands were silky smooth once more. As Raven stood taller and stretched out muscles that no longer quaked, she turned inward, towards the bubbling mass of power in her core. She beckoned to it, whispering sweet encouragement as it slowly reached out a tendril to her.

Raven gripped the small dagger she had found hidden in her clothing and formed her intention. It had been so long since she had enchanted. No wonder her magic was a sticky mess. She pulled more to her, watching it writhe around her fingers before climbing up the blade.

"*Interficiam per os sicut filum*," Raven muttered under her breath, building her enchantment's power until the simple dagger vibrated in her hand. She felt the enchantment settle as her power flashed. The glow faded into the cool metal as Raven sheathed it and stuck it in her left boot.

CHAPTER EIGHT

Mira

The last time Mira had been on a boat, she had been fleeing her father's rage. Her sister, Maliah, had concocted the solution to ease their father's wrath. Mira would travel away from their sandy home island with its tall glittering palace, warm air, and perfectly sculpted beaches of Grecia and move to a strange kingdom named Rairene. Since Mira had failed to understand how a lady behaves under the governesses assigned by her father to tutor her, she would live at the academy for noble women to learn what it meant to be a proper noblewoman or she could never return home and see her six sisters again.

Mira chuckled to herself as she leaned against the ship's railing. If only her sister had known precisely what it was she was going to be trained on. She gazed out at the view before her. After traveling across the open sea for two weeks, she had finally reached Evrotia. The large harbor and capital city Aslar, sprawled out before her. Dozens of ships were docked, with men and women chaotically moving around them. The palace loomed over the city, its gray stones casting a shadow over everyone it watched. From a distance, Aslar appeared beautiful and full of life. But up close, Mira knew the homes would be barely considered livable as they piled on top of each other in a series of boroughs that would lead to the gates of the palace.

Not a single person who was part of the noble class lived outside the palace gates.

From what Mira understood, none of them would be allowed should such a request be made. Queen Lyanna liked to keep her most loyal subjects close and living a life of luxury in their cages. The ship neared its dock, and Mira went to her room to gather her belongings. Three massive trunks awaited her in one of the ship's nicer rooms. She couldn't have the queen see her arrival at the palace as anything less than opulent. Until she got there, Mira had to go undetected. She adjusted her simple green gown that bore no elaborate lace or detailing like she was accustomed to. She couldn't wear one of her fancy gowns, not yet, anyway. Next, she braided her long, wavy red hair into a fishtail down past her waist.

She finished her appearance by washing her face to ensure she appeared as common as possible to anyone who might look too closely at her. She didn't want any of the citizens who saw her to think she had anything worth stealing or that she could be taken advantage of. The boat docked and unloaded around her with her belongings. All of her trunks were left on the uneven wooden dock with a nod from the sailors before she was left alone.

Mira searched around until she found a man driving an empty carriage. She hailed him down and helped him lift her trunks. He carried her to an inn in a nicer part of Aslar, the part Queen Lyanna deemed acceptable for visitors. Though the lone enchanter hanging from a noose at the entrance to the city was an image she would not soon forget.

That could have been Raven or Calla...

Mira shook herself. It hadn't been them. They were still at the palace. They were safe...ish...she conceded. She would locate Lord Conrad in the city and then...well...Mira would become the last person she ever wanted to be.

Mira wandered around Aslar in the early morning, assessing which market would fill all of Lord Conrad's desires. Somewhere close to the palace, but far enough away that he could scamper into a little hole if needed. But he would also want to be around people who wouldn't care to look too closely at him, so as much as he would have preferred one of the nicer markets, Mira assessed he would choose one of the more unpleasant ones. Which meant all of the markets she had been through were wrong. It also meant her clothing was wrong. Thankful for being an early riser, Mira went back to her small, could-barely-be-called-a-livable-space of a room and changed.

Gone was the beautiful, modest, green gown, to be replaced with a frumpy beige dress that dropped to her ankles and did nothing to flatter her figure. Just as intended. She had a hard enough time making her face boring. Her hair went up into a plain bun at the nape of her neck, and any jewelry she owned was locked away. She strapped a dagger to her thigh that was accessible through a cut in her dress and put on a pair of leather slippers with just enough padding to keep the cobblestones from becoming too much of a nuisance.

By the time she got to the nearest market that met hers, and thus Lord Conrad's aloof desires, the people of Aslar were awake and beginning their day. Mira perused the luxurious wares of jewelry, clothing, and even some rugs, observing the buyers around her and noting anyone that matched Lord Conrad's tall, bulky frame, and, no matter how much he tried to hide it, he always walked around with an air of superiority.

As she waited, Mira couldn't help but notice the depression that seeped through the air. These people lived at a level of poverty she had never seen before, but the feeling was more than just sadness. There was a restrained anger and fear twisting their way through them. Despite that, there were very few guards, and the surrounding people moved with the caution of someone doing their best to go unnoticed.

"Don't often see your lot here," a woman said.

Mira turned to the owner of the stall. Mira took a moment to actually observe the woman's items. She sold beautifully crafted jewelry that could have been sold for so much more. Mira picked up a silver necklace with a single drop pearl on it.

"I beg your pardon," Mira whispered.

"You're from Grecia?" The woman's accent was heavy as she said Mira's homeland.

Mira nodded. "What gave me away?" She asked as she motioned toward her entire body.

The shopkeeper grinned. "Used to see yer lot all the time, but now..." She looked around the market before shrugging.

Mira hadn't kept up with the trade between Grecia and other kingdoms. She wondered why there had been a change.

"Anything else change?" she whispered.

"Something 'appened at the palace. I would avoid being sent there if you can."

"What happened?" Mira tried to mask her concern behind wide, curious eyes that wanted gossip.

"No one's sure out here. Few days ago the palace closed its gates. They 'aven't opened since."

"You mean no one has gone in or out since?"

The shopkeeper nodded.

"What about the staff? Surely..." Mira trailed off as the woman shook her head.

She had to find Lord Conrad, get information, and get into that palace. Immediately.

Mira purchased the pearl necklace, donning it so that it rested just above her breasts, before moving on to locate Calla's tormentor of a mentor.

Mira shuddered at having to speak with him. Though he may be a talented enchanter, she had always been repulsed by him. Her instinct proved her right when she found out that he enjoyed pushing Calla to her limits until a potential burnout was near. He would work her until she could barely lift a hand to enchant, and even then, he forced her. Though Calla didn't see it that way. Lord Conrad had conditioned her into believing he could barely do anything with her training because he didn't know her true potential and never would, thanks to the marking on her back.

Mira walked through the market in a haze of rage the longer she thought about coming face to face with him.

"I thought I sensed entitlement nearby."

Mira whipped around and stared at the towering lord. Though tall, Lord Conrad had never made Mira feel intimidated.

She'd faced worse after all.

"Lord Conrad, I've been searching for you," Mira spoke softly.

"So I assumed. Come quickly before you draw more attention to us."

Mira harrumphed after him, following him down alleys and twisting through some of the poorest conditions she had seen before arriving at the humblest home she had ever seen Lord Conrad occupy. The inside was as expected, filled to the brim with opulence and poor taste. Mira hid her scowl as she noted the room overflowing with items of perceived wealth like the gold framed mirror, lavish pillows, and rugs that overlapped on other rugs. The walls seemed to loom large over her, tilting inwards as though at any moment all of the adornments would come crashing down.

"What's happening at the palace with Raven and Calla? Have you heard anything?" She didn't waste time.

Lord Conrad huffed. "I warned her to stay away. Calla, that is. She visited me two weeks ago. I haven't seen her since."

"And you haven't bothered to attempt an entrance into the palace?" Mira challenged.

"The palace is on lockdown."

"Why? What happened? No one in the city could tell me."

He heaved a sigh so large he appeared to visibly age before Mira as he sat down and motioned for her to do the same.

"I'm going to tell you three things, and I need you to hear them before you go charging headfirst into danger." Lord Conrad waited for Mira to nod. "First, Ella is dead. Second, Raven is dead. Third, Calla is stuck in the palace, most likely about to lose control over her flimsy magic, and there is nothing I can do to get in."

Mira rolled through everything he said to her. She let it hit her square in the chest like a wave crashing on towering cliffs. She remained composed as she stood and moved toward Lord Conrad's door. She paused when his hand wrapped around her wrist.

Without looking back at him, Mira said, "you cannot stop me. I will not lose another friend...another sister...to this plot." Mira ripped free and strode away.

CHAPTER NINE

Drea

Two Months Before Drea's Accident

Drea walked over the uneven stone pathway down to the training fields. It had been easy to sneak out before the sun rose. Only the army was up this early after the masquerade ball. The fog had rolled in, and the grounds were covered in a light mist. As much as she wanted to take her time and enjoy the silence and peace that came with it, she knew Liam would notice if she were late.

She twisted her hands together, her magic itching to shed her dress for loose training clothes to join them. Maybe one day. One day the kingdom would change, and she, and maybe even Ella, would be able to fight alongside them freely. But not now.

She walked over to the fighting ring at the far end of the field. It had been left alone by all of the others as four young men practiced, the prince's uncle and instructor looking on. Drea stayed back, watching from a distance. She knew Liam noticed her, but didn't want to draw any attention to herself.

Prince David sparred with Liam, the match ending in a draw. Henry went up against Liam's guard next. Henry defeated the guard in a few moves. Liam helped up his guard and challenged Henry to a match.

The two of them sparred for several minutes before Henry came out the victor. Drea saw David turn away to hide a grin as the two walked over to the wooden fence. Their instructor gave Liam and his guard some pointers before David faced off against the guard. On and on it continued for the next hour. At some point, several knights had joined and sparred against their prince and champion. Drea watched all of it, her heart longing to test herself against them. It was one thing to know she was good and another to truly test all she had learned.

At the end, Liam walked over to her with sweat dripping down his back. The sun had fully crested the horizon, and the rest of the palace was up and getting the day started.

"Thank you for inviting me. You did well." Drea lied.

"I did okay, but I don't expect you to know the difference," Liam responded.

Drea held in her retort. Not even Liam knew what she truly did, and she couldn't let him in on the secret now.

"Maybe one day you can help me understand."

"Maybe," Liam mused. "Will you sit with me tonight during dinner? The king is hosting another boring dinner for us to attend, and I would be more excited about it if I knew I had something to look forward to."

"You would look forward to my company?" Drea asked, her cheeks flushing.

"I would look forward to anything that involves your company."

Present Day

Drea fiddled with the edge of her sleeve. The black satin fabric grew heavy on her shoulders in the mid-spring sun. Her foot ached from riding a horse into Riset, but she had been desperate to get a croissant and to shake the feeling of eyes watching her every move. To know she could move freely without judgment or sorrow seeping into the pores of her skin. Drea stared at the cafe, Bird and Mouse, and went inside.

It was a quaint cafe Ella frequented, and ever since she had met Ella there a few weeks ago, she had become a regular. The shop owner exuded the warmth of the sun shining on your face. It was an attitude Drea hoped to one day have. For now, she would have to survive off the limited interactions she could have with the shop owner.

"Good morning, Drizella, your usual, I presume?" he asked from behind the small glass counter. Several pastries decorated the display case, each one as tempting as the last.

"Yes, please."

"Right away, Miss Drizella," Albert said as he grabbed a croissant and brought it to the back to be warmed up.

Drea left her coins on the counter as she went outside and sat down at one of the two small round tables Albert provided. When she had first met Ella here, she hadn't understood the appeal. It was a small cafe off to the side of the main market square. Not many people ventured this way, and those who did were hurrying about their day. She understood now why Ella loved it. The delicious food and tea aside, the cafe offered a modicum of privacy while allowing her to still see and hear what was happening in the square.

"Can I join you?"

She hadn't heard him approach, but the moment Henry's voice raced over her skin, her magic sparkled in response inside her. It pleaded to be let out to dance with him. Drea pulled it in softly, shushing it with soft strokes of comfort. She made sure her magic was under control before she locked eyes with Henry. He wore his plain clothing of soft spun white tunic and black trousers with military boots. A cloak hung from his shoulders down to his calves.

"Of course." Drea motioned to the chair across from her.

"Should I bring another cup of tea, Miss Drizella?" Albert asked as he set down her scone and pot of tea.

Drea gazed at Henry, raising her eyebrows in question.

"Yes, please, I would love to have some," Henry responded, shifting in his chair. His red hair was tied back, and dark circles underlined his dim green eyes.

Once Albert left, Drea poured herself some tea and sipped it, watching the people of Riset move around them. "What brings you down here, Henry?"

"I needed to get out of the palace. I don't know how much longer I can bear Celeste's grief and the king's anger," Henry confessed. He pinched the bridge of his nose before rubbing his hands over his face. "Ella had talked about this cafe a couple of times, so I wanted to see what her obsession was."

"How is the princess?"

"She's confused. Ella just got back, and now she's gone. Truly gone. I don't know how to make her feel better. She's already lost so much. It'll take a while for her to recover. How are you doing?" Henry turned to face her, pouring his cup of tea.

"You should take her out of the palace as well. If you need a break, I'm sure she does. Maybe take her to a bookstore?" Drea suggested. Her heart ached for Celeste; she didn't deserve this pain.

"What about you? How are you and Anastasia?" Henry probed.

"You don't want to hear about how we're doing." Drea dismissed his query. She didn't want to tell Henry about Anastasia's need for revenge and how it fueled her. Or how Drea wanted to tell Henry she had been relieved at first, but now she wished her mother were alive if only to take Lena out of power.

Henry reached toward her before pulling his hand back. "I do. I want to make sure you're okay. I'll always be there —"

"I know," Drea whispered. "I'm okay...Ana's okay."

"That sounded confident," Henry joked.

Drea gave him a timid smile. "We're grieving too. It'll take time."

"Can I ask you another question?" Henry leaned toward her.

Drea's magic fluttered to life. She pulled it back, heart racing for him to lean just a little closer. Just close enough to his scent of metal and earthy magic to fill her senses. She nodded while she waited for the question.

"You said we sacrifice ourselves for those we love. What did you mean?" Henry tilted his head, watching her.

She paused and sat back in her chair.

"Um...just that you and I have given up a lot for the people we love. That's all." Drea couldn't meet his eyes.

"What did you give up?"

You. That was the answer she wanted to give. *Our friendship. Your love. Everything.* A tumble of answers fell through her heart. None of them possible to give a voice to. Not even now.

"What did you give up?" Henry pressed, his hand fisted on the table.

"I can't tell you," Drea whispered so softly she could barely hear it. "I can't tell you, Henry. But I hope you know it was more than I've ever been able to bear losing." Drea's heart cracked at the confession. Even with her mother dead, it would just make him upset. Besides, he had moved on, and there was no point in hurting both of them.

"That's not enough," Henry said through gritted teeth. "We...you and I..." Henry paused as he ground his teeth and pinched the bridge of his nose.

The green eyes she had fallen in love with so long ago now looked upon her with nothing but pain. For a moment she thought she had glimpsed them softening towards her before hardening once again.

Henry opened his mouth to say more, but Drea interrupted him. "Have you heard anything about the search for Luca?"

Henry pulled back. "No."

"I hope you find him before we do," Drea muttered.

"Is that a threat?" Henry remained slouched in his chair as Drea got up.

"No, it's a warning."

Drea continued her walk through Riset, walking wherever her feet carried her. The morning sun rose in the sky, warming her beneath her heavy clothes. She glanced up when the ground beneath her feet shifted from even cobblestones to bumpy rocks mixed with mud. She had wandered down to the lower-class border between the third and fourth circles.

The lower circles were alive with people. They created a current around her, moving easily through the streets to their destinations. The air smelled of baked bread, horses, and ocean air. Children chased each other, squealing as they ran away from mothers and elder siblings. Though all of the circles they had patchwork clothing and shoes that were barely held together, there was a happiness in the air that Drea hadn't felt in years. She wandered through all of them, her mind centering.

Drea stopped suddenly when something small crashed into her legs. Her cane kept her up as she looked down to find a little girl staring at her. The girl backed away with wide brown eyes and an open mouth.

"Liza," a woman yelled. A woman a few years older than Drea, with frazzled black hair and a flushed face, ran over as she wiped her hands on her apron. "My apologies"

"Everything's fine, truly," Drea reassured her.

"Liza, apologize to the lady." Her mom commanded.

Liza walked over slowly, her eyes locked on Drea's feet as she swayed beside her mom. "I'm sorry."

"You're forgiven," Drea said. "I promise no harm was done."

"This time. She's run too fast before," the woman tsked lightly.

Liza stared at her feet. "Would you like to come in for some tea?" Liza asked.

"Oh, um..." Drea bit her lip.

"Please join us. I've already got a kettle going."

Drea nodded and followed the two toward their home. It was small and nestled between two stores that appeared to be keeping the home standing. While the outside was discouraging, Drea could see where they had put in effort to keep it sustainable. A patchwork of stones and wooden boards dotted the exterior while being covered with some well-placed ivy and small potted plants. The inside was a similar scene, but filled with far more love. The kitchen sat to the left of the door along the front wall with barely enough counter space to cut a carrot. The fireplace had a small, dying fire on the far left wall with a kettle hanging over it. Two chairs slumped before the fire, with a small wooden table in the center of the room decorated with some flowers in a vase. The smell of breakfast still coated the air with scents of burnt toast and burnt porridge.

A small door led through to what Drea assumed was their lone bedroom, which she was certain all of them slept in. Liza's mom bustled around the fire when the kettle screamed, as Liza herself fetched some small cups and set them on the table.

"Um, Miss, would you mind grabbing the dried tea herbs? I have them up there." Liza's mom gestured toward a cabinet high above and well out of Liza's reach.

"She doesn't like me getting into the tea," Liza mumbled when Drea saw a forlorn face.

"It must be some delicious tea then." Drea chuckled as she walked over, leaving her cane resting against the table.

"It's a family secret reci—OW," Liza's mom howled.

Drea twisted to help, her leg spasming at the sudden movement. Drea fell towards the counter, gripping the edge to stay upright.

The door to the bedroom smashed open, and a scrawny, bushy-haired man stumbled out as he tied an apron around his waist. "What happened?" His light voice echoed around the room as he assessed everything. "Who are you?" he asked, his eyes landing on Drea.

"I burned my hand on the kettle again," Liza's mom said. "That's um...I never asked for your name."

"Drizzie," Drea responded without thinking. Black spots dotted her eyes as she did her best to keep Liza and her mom from seeing how weak she was. She turned back to them, pretending to reach for the herbs, while in reality she was giving herself the space she needed to let a tear fall down her face as the pain ebbed and flowed throughout her. She calmed her magic as it writhed, its dance unfolding the longer the pain went on. Drea breathed in, pulling her magic back in with each second until it was well contained and content to dance slowly again.

With her moment taken, Drea reached for the tea and delicately faced the room again. Liza's mom sat next to the table, her hand cradled before her, the kettle resting on a hotpot on the table. The cups had scattered across the floor. Liza's dad moved swiftly around the room, gathering up Liza and wiping away any hot water as he searched for something to help his wife with her pain.

"Are you sure you don't want me to get a healer?" he asked for what sounded like the tenth time.

"Yes," she whispered.

Drea hobbled over, wincing as her leg continued to voice its grievances. "May I?" Drea asked as she sat down next to her. "What's your name?"

"Danielle."

"Can I see, Danielle?" Drea asked, holding out her hand.

Danielle cautiously extended her arm toward Drea, her fingers curled in to protect the burn. Drea slowly extended them to fully expose the palm that was blotched with red marks and deeply burned. She needed a healer. But based on their living situation, Drea knew they could never afford one, at least a good one.

"Liza, would you grab me a cup of your cleanest and coldest water?" Drea asked quietly.

"I'll be back." Liza was gone, a question poised on Drea's lips.

"She has to go to the pub for cold water," Danielle said.

Drea nodded in understanding. "Danielle, this is a deep burn, and it appears it's not the first one."

Danielle nodded, staring at her hand with watery eyes.

"I would like to do something for you, but I can't promise it will work as well because I don't have time to purify everything. But I can tell you it will do its job; it just might take a day longer."

"What is it?" Danielle could barely speak, and Drea imagined the pain to be incredible. How she had even been able to get through the first burn and let it heal naturally was a mystery.

"I'm an enchanter. I can easily enchant a potion for you—"

"We could never repay—"

"You won't have to. I insist you let me do this for you, for the tea." Drea looked Danielle in the eye, making sure she understood the sincerity of the offer and the severity of what it would do to her hand if she refused. "Please let me help you."

"You don't even know us."

"That should never matter over something like this," Drea added.

"Danielle, listen to the enchanter who is being kind," her husband added.

Danielle nodded as Liza came back with a cup of water. Drea withdrew an empty vial from her satchel and poured some of the water in. Drea closed her eyes and searched inside herself to the core of power that gently swayed within her. She delicately pulled on her power, summoning a ribbon of power to her fingertips. As she pulled, Drea focused on health and the bonds of friendship that heal the body and soul. She thought of Henry. Drea envisioned his smile whenever he read something funny, or the way he laughed when they went horseback riding. Then she focused on how she felt during those moments and how her heart soared on the wind. Drea took those feelings of growth, happiness, and love and poured them into her enchantment.

"Statu sano corpore instauraretis," Drea whispered. She hadn't enchanted in front of people in years, and all three of them were staring. Drea focused on the vial in her hands, thinking only of Henry to drive her intention of healing and regeneration. *"statu sano corpore instauraretis,"* Drea repeated it over and over as her magic built around her hands. The energy swelled around her before it began twisting into the vial and turning the water into a thick, dark, shimmering blue. She cut off her magic, pulling the ribbon gently back inside her as the enchantment completed.

"I need some flour." Drea requested. All of them gazed at her with slightly open mouths. "Liza, some flour, please."

Liza blinked before going to the cabinets and bringing over a jar of flour. Drea put some in her palm and let a few drops of her enchantment drop onto the flour. She stoppered the vial and then mixed it into a paste that held a light blue hue. Drea gently smeared it onto Danielle's palm until her entire hand was coated. Relief instantly crossed Danielle's features as they smoothed out and the pain in her eyes disappeared.

"This is your potion without pure water?" Danielle gazed at her hand in awe. "I've had some enchantments before, but never like this."

"I'm very good," Drea muttered. "You should apply it the same way twice a day. You'll need just a few drops each time, and it should be better in a day or two."

"Thank you; how can we ever —"

"Some of that family tea is payment enough," Drea replied.

"Here, it just finished steeping. I'm Erik, by the way," he said as he handed over a cup of tea and sat down.

Her eyebrows rose as layer after layer of spices with mild floral notes hit her taste buds.

"I can see why you keep this out of Liza's reach. This is delicious." Drea took another sip. "You should sell this to the cafes. They would forever be at your heels for more. Of course, you would need to draft a contract with them stating they could not attempt to reproduce it themselves."

"I'll think about it," Danielle replied as she continued to work on her hand.

"So, how did you join the club?" Erik asked.

Drea took a sip of the tea as she thought about Erik's question. "What do you mean by club? Being an enchanter?"

"The amputee club," Erik said as he lifted his leg and pulled back the pant leg to reveal a wooden peg.

"Oh, I never would have guessed that about you," Drea said, shocked by what she saw. He had been moving around with such ease.

"I just figured I wasn't about to let something like that keep me from living my life."

Drea took another sip of the tea, wanting to make every drop last. "How did you lose it?"

"Horse accident. I used to work in the stables for a noble lord, but when this happened...well...you can see," Erik motioned around their home.

"I was...hurt by someone I cared about," Drea spoke softly, careful of her words around Liza.

"Well, I'm happy to see you haven't let it keep you from your life as well," Erik said. He got up and moved around the house easily as he put things back where they belonged.

Danielle watched after him with so much love Drea had to turn away. She finished her tea and gently massaged her leg under the table.

"Thank you so much for the tea, but I must be going." Drea got up and shook out her skirt. "I meant what I said about selling your tea. I've never had anything like it. It's its own type of magic." Drea winked.

Danielle got up and walked with her to the door, her hand no longer cradled against her chest.

"Thank you for everything, truly. I don't know what we would have done..." Danielle sucked in a shuddering breath. "Can I...could I possibly see you again to discuss how to sell my tea?"

"Of course. Do you know about The Bird and Mouse?"

Danielle nodded.

"I'll meet you there for breakfast in two days? Gives you time to think everything over and maybe some of the cafes you would want to sell to."

Danielle nodded again. Drea reached into her satchel when Danielle wasn't watching and pulled out her coin purse. She hugged Danielle quickly, dropping the coin bag into Danielle's skirt pocket and left before Danielle could notice.

CHAPTER TEN

Drea

Two Months Before Drea's Accident

"Why were you at the training field?" Henry asked Drea the next day. He stopped her while she was on her way home to get ready for the dinner Liam had invited her to attend with him.

"Was there something wrong with my being there?" Drea questioned. If he had stopped her over this...

"No, you've just never observed before."

"You never invited me, Henry, and Liam did."

"How do you know him, anyway?" Henry had kept his voice level until this moment. But when he tightened his hands into fists, turning his knuckles white, his voice went down an octave.

Drea laughed to lighten the mood. "I know him from Trudel. We used to play together as children before my mother brought us out here to marry the duke. Why does it matter to you?"

"He's paying you a lot of attention."

"That's because he doesn't know anyone else here," Drea chided. "I would say you're jealous."

Henry's cheeks flushed. "I'm not jealous. I'm concerned. I don't want him to swoop you off your feet and leave you behind when he returns to Trudel."

"Well, you can be reassured my feet are not easily swept," Drea replied. "Now, will it be a problem when I'm at dinner tonight with him?"

"No."

Though he was quick to answer, Drea could have sworn she heard an underlying grumble in his voice. She rolled her eyes and walked back with him to the palace. She would have to ride home quickly to get dressed in time.

"Drizzie, I..." Henry stopped talking, running a hand through his hair.

"Yes?" She turned to face him.

Henry shifted back and forth on his feet, eyes downcast. "Never mind."

Present Day

Drea unfolded the message again. *Lord Henry, the Prince's Champion, requests your presence at the palace midday today.* She had no choice. She had to go. To defy an order from a royal representative was akin to defying an order from the king.

Drea stared at the palace one last time before stepping through the doors for the first time in two years. It was as though she had never left. The carpet runners beneath her feet were still the same forest green with a golden detail trim. All suits of armor were perfectly polished. If it weren't for the muffled sniffles or hunched over servants, Drea would have thought nothing was wrong. Sadness seeped into her toes through the stone itself. She kept her heart walled as everyone darted around her. Did they see her as a member of the noble class who also grieved the loss of a mother and sister? Or a deformed interloper? She wasn't sure which one she preferred.

Drea was halfway to the gardens when Henry strode toward her, a flurry of advisers and assistants behind him. They converged on him, asking questions and demanding he answer. Her Henry...no...he wasn't hers. Not anymore.

Not ever. He had never been hers. Despite the way her magic danced in his presence, it could never happen.

Her mother had made sure of that.

Henry towered over all of them, standing firm against a sea of upset men.

"Enough. I will answer nothing else. Each of you knows where I stand; it will not change. My loyalties lie with Prince David, and Prince David alone." Henry dismissed all of them, crossing his arms and glaring.

He took a moment to straighten his uniform. Knowing him, he also shook off his annoyance.

"Drizzie..." Henry cleared his throat. "Lady Drizella, thank you for coming. I know it's a bit of a journey," Henry remarked.

He held out his arm to her, waiting for her to loop her hand over it. Her heart lurched at the warmth of his arm against hers.

"I didn't realize I had a choice." She ignored how he had corrected himself. She loved hearing him call her Drizzie. It was his nickname alone for her. "I know you're busy, so this must be important."

They walked out to the gardens as the sun gently touched her face.

"Yes." Henry glanced back. "I've been trying to shake myself free of them all morning."

They continued in silence. It wasn't lost on her how much this mirrored their last interaction. She did her best not to hold him back from a brisk pace, though she eventually let go of his arm and slowed down after a few minutes. The muscles in her leg hadn't spasmed yet, but she could feel it coming, felt the tightening under her skin the longer she stood on it.

"Henry, why was I summoned?" she asked. The sound of rocks crunching beneath her feet grated on her.

"I, uh...wanted to have an excuse, and I wanted to see you—" Henry paused when he realized how far behind she was. He bowed his head and walked back to her.

"Henry—"

"Plus, I wanted to ask you about Ella," Henry quickly finished, running a hand through his hair.

"I see…well, thank you for the excuse. Even as the interim ambassador, it's suspicious for me to be here. I'm certain Princess Lena will have a spy in here by now."

"Then why come at all?"

Drea looked at him, keenly aware of how close they were. Her magic spun in delight. Drea soothed it, pulling it into a slow waltz. She steadied herself, re-gripping her cane.

Her foot stumbled over a rock and her leg seized.

It ground her muscles together into a tight ball of burning pain.

Drea covered her mouth as she fell sideways, refusing to make a sound.

Henry caught her, his muscular arms pulling her tightly against his chest. He swept an arm under her legs and carried her to a marble bench, where he gently set her down. She bit her lip in protest at being put down.

"What can I do?" Henry whispered as he knelt before her. His green eyes darted rapidly between her leg and face.

Drea pressed her hands to her cheeks, trying to hide the tears that welled and gathered around her scar.

"I uh…I need to massage it."

"May I?" Henry waited for her nod before massaging her thigh through her skirt.

"It will work better, um…" Drea blushed, "if you don't have my skirts between your fingers and my leg."

Henry's face was as red as his hair as he slowly reached under her skirt and massaged her thigh. The coarse scar tightened under his touch, shocks of fire racing through her. Relief eventually came as the minutes ticked by and the muscles loosened. It had to happen right now, in front of him. Henry hadn't seen her in such a pathetic state…as if the cane and scar weren't enough of an embarrassment.

"Thank you, Henry, I can take over," Drea whispered. The pain was bearable now. She could bend over and not worry about the sensation of tearing her muscles apart.

"Does that happen often?" Henry sat beside her, his hands clasped between his knees.

"It depends on how much walking I've done and whether I massaged it in the morning. Some days it doesn't matter, but I've learned how to get through it."

"I wish..." Henry turned away. "Never mind." He gazed at the sky. "Was it so horrible for Ella here that she would rather subject herself to that training than be with us?"

"She wanted to protect the kingdom she loved. That's all there is to it. She didn't fit into the role of a lady. Why is it such a bad thing for women to train? To be knights?"

"Men are fighters. We're the ones who protect and defend those we care about...those we love. It's how the kingdom works—"

"It doesn't have to be, Henry. It can change. You could let women train to defend themselves. I don't understand why that's hard for everyone here to accept when you're so accepting of everything else."

"Because of this." Henry motioned at her leg as he stood and paced. "You should not have to suffer like this. You shouldn't have to be in constant pain for something a man could have..." Henry stopped and gathered him. He pinched the bridge of his nose and breathed. "If your being unable to fight meant that you wouldn't have experienced this injury...then I will always choose the option that ends with you not in pain."

"Henry, women are in pain every day. Just because you are honorable and noble doesn't mean there aren't men out there who beat and hurt the women in their lives. Women who have no one to turn to for help, or to show them how to defend themselves." Drea stood, standing almost as tall as Henry. Her eyes narrowed as she left her cane on the bench. Her magic spiraled in confusion before morphing into a tight tango. It was violent as Drea understood how frustrated Ella had been.

"That's the same thing. You willingly put yourself in danger by becoming who...whatever you are...and it ended everything between us...everything. At least that's what I'm assuming since you never told me." Henry ground out, not backing down from how close she stood before him.

Drea arched her brow in challenge.

He was right, of course.

He just didn't know why.

Could never know why.

It would destroy him. It had almost...Drea shook herself.

"This injury..." Drea swallowed. She would not think of that day. She had gotten adept at it. "It was not because of who I am. What happened to me..." Drea squeezed her eyes shut, fighting off the images that flashed before her. The shack. The ballroom. The dark blue eyes that belonged to him. The rope binding her wrists. She squeezed her eyes until the images vanished and then turned to Henry. "It would have happened no matter what." Drea blinked, refusing to go back to that place. Refusing to remember the torture by...No.

"Who I am...it kept me alive that day. Not being a helpless creature who has to wait to be found. If I had...I would be dead right now," Drea snapped.

She could vividly picture lying in that decrepit house in a pool of her blood, gasping for breath as she reeled in her magic.

Their magic sparked between them, and Drea wanted to unleash hers and let it dance with Henry's. It sang and begged to touch him, to feel him under her fingers once again. But she couldn't. She would explode if she touched him. Her magic was already convulsing around her fingers with barely any control left.

"What does that mean?" Henry questioned.

Drea took a step back.

"It means nothing would have changed that day. Everything between us still would have ended." She turned away from him as her pulse raced and her cheeks flushed.

The events of that day...and the weeks leading up to it would have happened no matter what. Henry was a casualty of her mother's scheming, and...he would think it was his fault. She couldn't give him that pain, as untrue as it was. So Henry couldn't know that that day cost her everything. She had chosen to fight, yes, but she hadn't realized just how fractured she was until confronted by him and all he represented to her. Drea tightened her magic back into a slow dance.

"Can you please tell me why you wanted me here?" she mumbled.

"I..." Henry looked around. "Are you okay to walk again?"

Drea nodded.

"There's very few people I trust, and you—"

Drea chuckled softly. "You trust me? After all you've learned—"

"You're the only one who knows the truth, and I need someone I can talk to." Henry shrugged. "Plus, Ella still trusts you."

"So you want an...alliance?"

"I need someone on my side. So I'm asking to build that trust back." Henry reached out and gripped her shoulder.

"I would like to rebuild that trust. I need to think about betraying my queen and sister, but to start rebuilding the trust, you should know that an assassin by the name of Rapunzel has been sent to find David and confirm if Ella is alive. She told everyone she was going north, but I'm certain it's a lie and that she's going south. She's been told to only confirm, but her impulse control isn't good and I think she'll attack them."

"Thank you," Henry replied.

"You're welcome. I'll give you an answer soon."

CHAPTER ELEVEN

Ella

Ella finished washing and put on clothes that made her wrinkle her nose as she looked between them and her filthier clothes before walking downstairs. David set down a mirror before going back to cooking.

"That was Henry telling me that someone named Rapunzel had been sent out to find us. Who is she?"

Ella slumped her shoulders. "She was my protégé—"

"I thought Sophie was your protégé?"

"She was. Rapunzel, Tressa, was before her. She became obsessed with Ana and Lucifer. She'll be upset if she finds us."

"You don't think she will?"

"She might. She's smart enough, but she's also rash and makes impulsive decisions. But we should be prepared to leave," Ella explained. "Until then, rematch?"

He had beaten her the last three times they'd played.

"Are you sure you can handle losing again?" He put the bowl down and turned to her.

"I handled it just fine when we trained earlier."

"You went easy on me. I may not like you fighting, but I can still see when someone is holding back," he remarked.

Ella flushed but didn't deny it. "You went easy on me as well when you held back on your punches."

David went back to his cooking. He kept his eyes trained on the food in front of him, the knife deftly chopping the carrots and onions.

"I don't know what to do," Ella murmured as she stared at the board.

"Move your pawn —"

"Not with Crowns. The queen." Ella frowned as David moved his pawn. "Tremaine has planned this with Queen Laila for years, and none of us knew. I need more information."

"Isn't that what this Huntsman is supposed to give us? Answers?"

"As long as we can find his contact in Holodal, if not..."

"Would anyone else know where to search?"

"Snow might...she would..." Ella paused. The image of Raven sobbing and collapsed on her bedroom floor after Jason had left her flashed before Ella's eyes. "That's a last resort. Though there might be some very motivated guards we can talk to first."

"Why would some guards be willing to help?"

"They work for Luca's father, some high-ranking nobleman in Holodal. They'll want to ensure his safety and might have some connections that can help us."

"Then it sounds like we have even more reason to go. It'll take us a couple of days on horseback to reach the border and another four to get to the capital." David furrowed his brow as he did the math.

Ella bit her lip. They needed to leave, and she needed to be healed.

"Would Vivifica help heal my wounds?" Ella muttered. She would take the risk. Just this once. "Could you sprinkle some on my injuries?"

David assessed her. "Only if you're certain. As I said, I'll never force an enchantment on you."

"I know, but we need to leave, and I need to be at my best."

"Give me one minute." David set aside his cooking and walked out, coming back with a glass bottle filled with a pure, enchanting solution. His hands began to softly glow as he spoke. *"Statsu sano corpore instauratetis."* His magic surrounded the bottle, the water turning into a thick, dark blue liquid the longer he enchanted it.

Ella pulled the top of her tunic to the side with shaking fingers.

"Ella, are you sure?" David asked. His hand held hers as he gently ran his thumb over the back of her hand.

Ella nodded, closing her eyes. David's gentle fingers spent shocks across her skin as he applied his potion to her arrow wound before moving to the one Lady Tremaine had gifted her. Ella flinched as he lifted her tunic.

"Did that hurt?" David mumbled.

Ella shook her head as her cheeks flushed. It had hurt a little bit, but she wasn't about to mention she had flinched at the sensation of his hands on her skin. Once he was done, he gently patted her shoulder and went back to cooking.

"Thank you." Ella spent the rest of the day cleaning their clothes while David prepped everything in the kitchen. Her clothes were the worst from being covered in her sweat and blood. She let her mind wander as she cleaned, hoping that by not thinking about the problems she needed to solve, her mind would begin to form a plan. Holodal felt like a long shot, yet it was their only shot. Even Queen Laila would think twice about coming after a kingdom aligned with Holodal. It was their mountain border that had always kept them apart. The mountainous terrain had steep slopes that would appear out of nowhere, with only rugged animal paths to guide them over. There was only one safe way through that promised no bandits or criminals, and it was the one path they could not take. It was heavily guarded on both sides, and everyone who went through the cavern had to be given permission. They would have to travel over the mountain without being seen or killed. It had been her main reason for David's healing potion. She would have to be at the top of her game to protect David.

Ella walked across the hall to David's bedroom the next morning and threw open the door.

"What did you put on me? Was it Solacium?" She had trusted him, and he had thrown it in her face with a significantly more potent potion.

"What's happened?" David sat in bed, his black hair sticking out at odd angles. "Ella?"

"What potion did you put on me? My wound is completely healed. If you had put Vivifica on me, it would still be healing. Henry's potion never—"

"I used Vivifica, El. You saw me enchant it. It's just the difference between my magic and Henry's."

"He seems just as powerful as you—"

"He is. Henry doesn't love—"

Ella laughed as her hands shook. "Henry doesn't love?" She couldn't help but think about the pain that had filled Drea's eyes when she saw Henry.

"Of course, he loves. Henry doesn't love the same way. Everyone displays their love differently. Henry shows his through protection and defending those he holds closest. That's why his enchantments for battle are so powerful. Whereas those with an affinity for healing show their love through complete sacrifice. That's why healing potions can be so powerful."

"I see. So you would rather die than say...see me dead?"

David didn't hesitate. "Always. I will always put you first."

Ella's heart stuttered. He had to be lying. He would do that for anyone. "That's...that's..." she paced around his room, a new fury burning through her. If everyone knew that all they had to do was threaten someone he cared for, then..."You can never tell anyone. The power that knowledge has..."

Ella left. She couldn't be in the room anymore. He didn't know what he was saying to her. He didn't love her. He couldn't. She walked aimlessly around the stronghold, muttering to herself about enchanters and princes. Ella stopped in the kitchen and took a breath. She splashed her face with some water and closed her eyes. She couldn't focus on this. They had to go and she had things to pack.

She walked to the attic and stared at her mother's trunk. She wanted to take all of it. Each piece was something her mother had left her. She held a shawl in her hands that was soft and delicate, made of the finest wool with enchanting horses embroidered along the edges. She had never seen it before, yet it had been loved over the years.

"Do you think we should leave soon?"

Ella jumped at David's voice.

"We should leave today. We've been here too long, and Henry is depending on us." Ella stood and gathered a few items. She'd come back for the rest one day, she promised herself. Ella walked downstairs and grabbed one of her saddlebags in the living room.

"Are you upset?"

"I'm fine, I—"

The horses' scream was the only warning they got when the back door opened.

Ella shoved David to the ground.

A dagger vibrated in the door, right above them.

"Get inside," Ella commanded as she withdrew a dagger and turned towards their assailant.

A woman with blond hair braided past her hips launched herself out of the shadows, entangling herself with Ella.

Tressa.

Only a year younger, her former protégé had never lived up to her potential. All she could hope for was that Tressa had been naïve enough to not share anything with Anastasia.

Tressa got close to Ella, pushing her close to the wall and forcing close combat. Their daggers interlocked as they fought, moving away from the door.

"What are you doing, Tressa? You know you can't beat me." Ella grunted as Tressa got in a lucky punch.

"I'm going to fix what you ruined," she hissed as Ella shoved her against the side of the stronghold.

"You aren't good enough. Yield." Ella pressed a dagger lightly against Tressa's neck. Her brown eyes were red, her hair was covered in dust from a long journey, and she desperately needed a bath.

"You took him from us...from me," Tressa growled.

"I know." Ella relaxed her hold slightly as she took in her former friend. "But he wasn't a good person. Tress...he didn't deserve—"

Tressa kicked her leg up and broke out of Ella's hold, shoving her back with enough force that Ella landed on the ground. Ella hit her head, blinking against the pain. She looked up in time to lift her dagger and block Tressa's blade from impaling her. The two of them twisted on the ground until Tressa disentangled herself and Ella leapt to her feet.

"I don't want to kill you, Tressa, but I will." Ella was resolute in her decision. She would do whatever it took to protect David.

Tressa laughed as they circled each other. "I'm surprised you haven't already. Has my mentor gone soft? Has a few days with the prince unmade who you always wanted to be?"

Tressa broke through Ella's defenses, punching her to the ground.

To Ella's horror, David ran out, sword drawn, and attacked.

She knew how to beat Tressa. She'd done so many times; hell, she'd been the one to train her. David, she knew, could easily handle Tressa. He just didn't know the one thing he needed to avoid.

Tressa's long golden hair was braided with spikes.

Poisoned spikes.

Ella watched Tressa's grin widen as David fought her. She dramatically thrust her dagger at him, a fake out Ella had seen her pull off many times.

An exploitation men always fell for.

Everything happened in a blur. There was no dramatic pause that let Ella watch in slow motion as she tried to scream at him to duck. There was nothing she could do. Gods knew what would happen if those spikes were poisoned today. All Ella could do was hope Tressa had slept in so much dirt that the poison had faded.

In one moment, David stood before her.

Next, he was on the ground.

David clutched his face as her spikes ripped open his cheek and the hand that had moved to catch her hair. David screamed.

She didn't wait to see if he would start convulsing from any potential poison. She hoped he didn't lose control. Ella launched herself at Tressa, no longer concerned about anyone's safety.

Ella rammed her hand up and into the roots of Tressa's hair, getting a firm grip as she plunged her dagger into Tressa's heart.

Tressa clutched Ella's arm, her mouth open in shock. Her eyes locked on Ella as both of them sank to the ground.

"What did you do?" David's voice was frantic as he crawled over, clutching his face, blood dripping between his fingers.

Ella ignored him.

She eased Tressa to the ground as she convulsed. Her warm brown eyes gazed into Ella's with a fear so profound Ella could hardly bear the weight of it.

"I asked you not to make me kill you," Ella whispered as she brushed Tressa's mangled hair out of her face.

Tressa gripped Ella's arm in a vice, blood pooling around her. "I don't want to die, El."

Tears streamed down Tressa's cheeks.

"I'm sorry." Ella didn't hide the tremble in her throat. She had killed her protege. Her friend. "I'm so sorry." Ella held Tressa close.

"Let me see her." David collapsed next to them, ignoring his injuries as he removed a clear vial of liquid from his trousers. "I can help," he mumbled. His fingers were slick with blood as he attempted to hold it.

"David, don't—"

"I can help her! I have to help her. See what you did to her. You can't...you can't just kill people. Let me help her. I can save her...please..." David's voice choked off as he frantically focused on the vial gripped between both hands.

Ella glanced down at Tressa and the blood beneath her. She could barely keep her eyes open as they stared at Ella. Although they had known each other for years, they had grown apart when Tressa found friendship with Anastasia and Lucifer.

"I always...admired—" Tressa began.

"I know. You were a beautiful fighter, Tressa," Ella whispered. She stroked her hair as Tressa took her last breath. Ella closed her eyes, letting the tears fall.

"I can save her," David snapped. He began his enchantment for healing, his hands flaring dimly. He viciously rubbed them on his trousers to remove the blood. "I can do it this time. I'll save her. I have to save her this time."

"David, stop." Ella reached over and grasped his arm.

He whipped his head around, his dark brown eyes filled with loathing and fear. Fear of not being enough. Fear of not being strong enough.

He screamed as he tried his enchantment again.

The vial shattered in his hands.

"No. I can do it. I can do this." He withdrew another vial, his magic flaring brightly, the vial shattering instantly.

"David." Ella set Tressa down and wiped away her tears before shaking him, trying to get his attention.

He was too far gone, lost in a memory.

"It's okay, David...she's already gone. There was nothing you could have done."

"I could have saved her. I should have—" David sat back on his feet, rubbing his eyes. He grimaced as the dirt fell from his hands onto his cheek.

"She's not your mom," Ella whispered. "You couldn't have saved her."

"She was right there, Ella. I should have been able to save her," he pleaded as he rocked back and forth, his hands pressed to his head.

Ella moved until she was in front of him. She gripped his wrists and rested her knees on his feet, holding him still. Ella gazed into his wondrous brown eyes and saw someone who still held the blame and burden of grief.

She gently cupped his face, careful to avoid the torn skin. She wiped away some of the dirt and locked eyes, letting him see the truth. "Not everyone can be saved. It will hurt, and you will always carry that wound with you. But you cannot let it continue to define you." Ella spoke softly, letting her words wash over him. They would not be easy to absorb, and he would hate her for them.

"You're not one to talk about being defined by the pain you carry."

"You're right. I carry a lot, and it has molded me in its fire. I took what was in my control and made it my own. You need to realize that even though you are one of the most powerful enchanters I have ever seen, not even you can save someone who has taken a dagger straight to the heart."

CHAPTER TWELVE

Raven

Raven sat down before the fire as they finished setting up for the night. They had continued eastward, staying within the depths of the forest. If Queen Lyanna had set anyone after them, they seemed to be doing a good job at evading them. Though if her stepmother...Raven paused as she absorbed that fact. If her stepmother was smart, she was sending a small elite group of trackers after Raven. The last thing she would want is for the entire kingdom to become aware of Raven's existence. Which meant everyone who had been forced into that courtyard to witness her execution were now liabilities. Raven's only reassurance that everyone there was alive was that the queen couldn't simply kill her entire staff. Right? Raven shook the thought away.

She rubbed her hands together before the fire. The sleeve of her tunic fell down her arm, revealing her tender wrists to her. Angry raw skin glared at her, with bruises where she had pulled too tightly against her chains.

Aleks walked out of the forest carrying a rabbit he had skinned and promptly strung it over the fire to cook.

"Can you tell me about our time in the palace as children?" Raven mumbled. She had been at war all day with herself about asking. It had been her greatest dream to know who she was...and now...she wasn't sure she wanted to hear it, but curiosity had won in the end.

"You really don't remember?" Rowan asked.

"You heard your father in the dungeon. The enchanter he took me to was really good."

"I think that enchantment is fading, though," Aleks commented.

Raven raised her eyebrows for him to continue.

"You had those nightmares in the palace. Whenever you spoke about them, they sounded just like the coup that happened. You even saw Rowan in one of them. I think the inking from that enchanter worked only so long as you weren't in a place that held memories for you." Aleks supplied. "I'll bet if we looked at that ink on your back it would be faded."

Raven pulled her hair off her back, twisting it on her head before turning her back to the fire. Aleks knelt, leaning around to examine it. His body brought her more warmth than any fire ever could as he got closer and ran his calloused fingers gently over her skin.

"Well?" Raven asked after a few heartbeats of silence.

"I can't tell," Aleks spoke slowly. "I think the edges are fading, but the color isn't. I wonder why he inked you at the base of your neck."

"It makes sense to me," Raven replied, "It's as close to my mind as you can get without it being exposed."

"I guess." Aleks sat back from her. He turned his attention back to the fire and rabbit, turning it.

"What story did you want to hear?" Rowan asked. He shifted on his bedroll to hand over a piece of bread and a flagon of water.

"When did I get Feather?"

Rowan grinned as Aleks laughed.

"Well, believe it or not, you were always the troublemaker in our group, and I don't know if I've ever seen King Stewart so mad before," Aleks said.

"What happened?" Raven leaned forward as she gnawed on the bread.

"We ended up crawling through the rafters of the stables somehow, and Aleks got it in his head that it would be fun to try to drop onto a horse from up above," Rowan explained.

"I'll bet he thought that was a good idea." Raven winked at Aleks.

"Well, before we could try, which we were going to do, with *you* positioned to drop," Rowan said, pointing a finger at Raven, "when we paused long enough we heard something whining."

Raven sat up straighter as she pictured the memory Rowan was sharing. It didn't feel like an actual memory as she envisioned what it must have been like for three children to be dangling over horses from the rafters.

"An angry voice came from a few stalls over, quickly followed by a yelp," Aleks added. "Before either Rowan or I could do anything, you had dropped to the ground, startling the horse, and ran over to the other stall." Aleks paused as he turned the rabbit again. "By the time we got to you, the stable hand was in tears, and you were holding a whimpering puppy the color of the darkest night to your chest. To this day, I don't know what you said to that stable hand, but he was terrified of you after."

"He was abusing the dogs, right?" Raven asked. Both of them nodded their heads. "I'm sure I threatened some kind of violence. Was my...father...mad?"

"He had expressly forbidden you from having a pet. He knew they were a lot of responsibility, and he didn't want it being passed to a servant who had other duties to attend to," Rowan said. "But the moment he saw you with Feather, he couldn't say no."

"Did I take care of her?" Raven asked.

"You didn't let anyone else care for her. She was your puppy, and no one else was going to feed or walk her," Rowan said, smiling.

"Thank you for caring for her after," Raven said.

"It was my privilege," Rowan whispered.

Raven remained still, listening as she counted seven different footsteps. Seven men, probably part of Queen Lyanna's army, if Raven had to guess, were circling their camp. Raven moved just enough of her arm to reach for the small dagger she had hidden in her pants. She dared the smallest movement of her head, turning towards the flames where she knew she would find Aleks. He always took the first shift.

He barely spared her a glance.

His legs were in an open defensive stance, his hands open and ready with his sword. Raven couldn't turn without alerting their attackers to see Rowan. They did a decent job of sneaking up on them until they started rustling the brush and stepping on dead leaves. The men finally revealed themselves and walked past her to approach Aleks. One of them even stepped right over her.

"Gentlemen, what —"

"Give us all of your belongings and horses, and we'll leave you alive," the leader demanded as he interrupted Aleks.

"Funny, I was going to give you a similar offer. Leave now, and I'll let you live."

Raven heard the smile in Aleks' voice.

Raven could see enough of the men to make out they wore old boots with patches covering the worn out holes. Their clothing wasn't much better. Those who were lucky enough boasted tattered fur cloaks, while some wore the resemblance of a cloak around their shoulders. Guards they were not. Raven had only heard minor rumblings about the Mountain Men in Evrotia during her time in the palace. The queen didn't care to deal with them, even when they raided the towns that struggled to support her. These men were a law unto themselves, and would not hesitate to kill any of them.

The men surrounding them chuckled.

"You need to count again. You're outnumbered. There's seven of us, and two of you. Three if you count the woman."

"I would definitely count the woman," Aleks remarked.

"Surrender," the leader ordered.

"No."

Raven heard Aleks pick up his sword as the men attacked.

She took that as her cue to jump into the fray, right as Rowan leapt up as well.

While Aleks tussled with the leader and one of his men, Raven and Rowan engaged the others. She took on three of them, pulling her sabers from the pack on her horse. Rowan fought the other two scrawny men. Her opponents weren't in better condition. They were sloppy in their technique and had probably never lifted a blade until they were forced to. One of them lunged at her, leaving himself open for a killing blow, a strike she took without hesitation.

He would have done the same to her.

The remaining two became wary as they took different positions and confronted her again. They looked at each other several times before attacking her. They were careless and sent random jabs to her waist and arms. Raven moved to dodge, stumbling over a log. Raven thrust her blades from her knees before they could get the upper hand, killing both of them.

Her fight done, Raven turned to see Rowan and Aleks had handled theirs as well. She moved so that her legs were stretched out in front of her as the cramps continued to pulse in her legs. She leaned over and reached for her toes, squeezing her eyes tightly against the pain.

"Are you hurt?" Rowan walked over as he sheathed his sword.

Aleks walked around the circumference of the camp, searching for any other attackers.

"I'll be okay," Raven reassured Rowan.

Aleks came over and put out a hand to her. His fingers sent shocks down her magic, causing it to flare and stick to her veins.

"We should go." Raven pulled her fingers away as soon as she stood, rubbing them together. She kneaded her magic back, pulling it in as much as she could.

"It's the dead of night, Raven —" Rowan said.

You want to sleep next to a bunch of dead men?" She asked.

"No, but what choice do we have? We can't guide the horses through the forest with no visibility." Aleks motioned to the pitch black sky.

"We'll have to light some torches and go on foot." Raven packed her sleeping roll and was eventually joined by Rowan and Aleks.

They got their horses saddled quickly and began walking towards whatever destination Aleks had in mind.

CHAPTER THIRTEEN

Calla

The guards dumped her on the ground, chaining her to the floor. Once their footsteps were gone, Calla curled up and let herself break, just a little bit. She hid her face in her hands, hoping to stifle any sobs that escaped. She could do this. She could remain strong until she found a way to break free. Calla wrapped her dress around her legs, trying to keep in some warmth as sleep slowly tried to drag her under.

Before sleep could claim her, the sound of footsteps reached her. They were quiet and careful, but nothing could hide in this dark hall. Her eyes had adjusted enough to see someone in a black floor length cloak step to the edge of her cell, their face hidden.

"Are you... are you okay?" Adam's voice echoed quietly.

"Adam." Calla turned more to see him. Her heart exploded at the sound of his voice, her magic coming to life, swirling throughout her.

"Are you okay?"

"I, uh... I don't know how to answer that." Calla tried to sit, but slowly fell back down to her side. She couldn't get her body to respond just yet. It had been a very potent batch of Leech, apparently.

"What did they do to you?" Adam crouched down. His brow furrowed; it deepened the longer she tried to get up.

"Poison. One made by an extremely talented enchanter," Calla whispered. Warmth from the stones slowly crept into her hands, her fingers finally bending. She continued to lie on her side, watching Adam. His chiseled jaw was covered in a light stubble that only enhanced his cheekbones. The scar he had gotten from his wolf attack across his face was healing nicely now. It would still be there, but it wouldn't ruin his chances of being more than just a consort anymore in Princess Arianna's court. But it was his dark green eyes with flecks of gold that had her wanting to reach her hands out to him, one last time.

"Poison? Which one? Maybe I can enchant an antidote for it."

"It's not one you've heard of—"

"Maybe I have." Adam sat down, tucking his cloak around him.

"Adam, there's no antidote for it. It just has to work its way through me."

"You seem to know a lot about this poison. If you're just a maid, how could you possibly know anything about it?" Adam asked as he crossed his arms.

Calla remained silent. She was too tired for this. She didn't want to lie to him anymore. She didn't want to lose him more than she already had. But she would never betray her sisters, even if it meant not answering his questions.

"I can't tell you."

"They're right, aren't they? Arianna... she was right." Adam leaned away from her. Even though they had bars between them, he still gave himself more distance from her.

Calla found the strength somehow; she made her muscles move. She crawled on hands and knees until she was at the bars. Calla leaned against them, wheezing as she looked at him. She pulled the tears back. He didn't look at her.

"Do I seem like an assassin to you?" Calla whispered. "Adam, please." Calla choked on some tears. "Have you ever thought I could kill anyone?"

Adam slowly turned toward her, his emerald eyes roving every inch of her. "Was it all a lie?"

"No. You have to believe me. I never lied to you."

"Then why did you automatically think I thought you were an assassin?" Adam snapped. He ran his hands through his hair.

"Because Princess Arianna said I had been sent to kill you. I can't even kill a rat, and they scare me." Calla tried to pull on the chains more, tried to get closer to him somehow. If he would only come over to her. "Adam... please...after everything..."

"That's why this hurts, Calla. If that's even your real name. How could I ever trust you again?"

"Because of what you feel in your heart...I feel it too." Calla felt her magic trying to soothe her, rising now that Leech was finally leaving her system.

"It was all a lie. Everything you said was so you could get closer to me," Adam growled.

Calla tried to calm herself. Her heart was beating too fast, her magic answering the breaking of her soul.

"Everything we shared...was a lie."

"It wasn't...I promise." Calla was too tired to hold the tear back. She pressed her hands to her eyes, white spots dancing in the darkness.

When she opened her eyes, Adam was just inches away from her, his white knuckled hands gripping the bars beside her head.

"I want to believe you, Calla. I really do...but Arianna has too much proof and you have none." Adam's hand lightly touched her cheek. Calla leaned into the feel of him. Her magic sang at his touch, rushing throughout her.

"Adam, I didn't lie about why I was your maid. I promise." More tears slipped through, only to run over his hand. "Talk to the head housekeeper if you want proof."

Calla closed her eyes and memorized the feel of his hand against hers. The warmth that seeped in from him. He was going to leave her. She could feel it; her magic quivered at the knowledge. He was the only friend she had left here. Raven was dead. Lord Conrad wasn't going to save her; she had resigned herself to that fact.

"I love you." Calla made sure to speak Evrotian. She couldn't tell him in Vicurian how she wanted to let him know all that she was. She wanted to show him she was an enchanter too. That she loved to bake, ride horses, and more than just a maid. Gods how she wanted to tell him everything. But she couldn't. He would tell the queen, she was certain.

CHAPTER FOURTEEN

Mira

Mira gracefully stood out of her perfect curtsy. Her fingers twitched with the need to adjust the minor imperfection in her gown. Instead, she clasped them in front of her as she gazed at Queen Lyanna and her throne.

The queen had foregone her mourning black already, opting to wear a gown the color of freshly dried blood with gold lace trimmings. All of her hair was piled on top of her head with a crown of obsidian spikes. So, this was the woman who had tortured and killed Raven and now held Calla captive.

Mira stood taller.

She might have cowered before her in years prior, but not anymore. Mira wore the armor of her hard learned lessons under her skin. It wrapped around her bones and lent her the strength she needed. She may not be an enchanter, but she found she didn't need to be one to be strong.

"Princess Miraya of Grecia, welcome to Evrotia." Queen Lyanna's girlish voice flitted over the air with boredom.

"Thank you, Your Majesty. It is a pleasure to finally visit your kingdom," Mira replied. She ignored the piercing headache that was growing because the edges of her tiara were pressing into her skull. How Queen Lyanna wore her own dominating crown was beyond Mira's comprehension.

Mira glanced to the queen's side and froze once she saw one of the royal guards had golden skin and dark red hair just like hers.

"Tell me, what brings you to my court?"

Mira pulled her attention back to the queen. "My father sent me. I am almost of age to truly have a role in court, and he desires for me to learn about other courts so I might better myself."

"Ah, yes...that." Queen Lyanna paused. "How is King Arthur? I haven't enjoyed his company for many years."

"He's well, thank you. Long may he reign," Mira quipped.

The court seemed to sway around her like kelp drifting in the sea. The all consuming silence rippled into a low, steady hum now that her surprise arrival was deemed boring. Queen Lyanna wouldn't be killing the princess of an ally. She wouldn't dare. And that was what Mira had counted on.

"Once you're settled, make sure you join us for dinner tonight. It's been so long since I've had someone decent to talk to," Queen Lyanna commanded.

"I wouldn't dream of missing it." Mira replied, taking that as her dismissal. She couldn't walk fast enough.

***

Mira shook herself in front of the mirror. It was dinnertime, and nausea rolled around in her stomach and throat refused to settle. No matter how many dresses she put on, or different styles of braiding her hair, the nausea and anxiety remained.

She settled on a light purple dress that flowed around her with airy fabric. The sleeves flowed down from her shoulders and split down the middle to kiss the ground. A white sash was tied around her waist and trailed down to the floor. Her hair was pulled back with multiple braids that she twisted around on her head.

Mira took a final breath and stared at the golden tiara in her hands.

The last time she had worn this tiara...

The image of her father's fist flew towards her.

Mira closed her eyes and placed the delicate tiara encrusted with pearls and crystals on her head.

She straightened her back and left, wandering down endless, twisting hallways. Everyone walked past her with efficient speed and downcast eyes. By the time she got to the smaller dining room, the servants were setting down the first course.

"Princess Miraya, I was beginning to worry," Queen Lyanna said as she walked in.

"My apologies, Your Majesty." Mira searched for her seat, stumbling when she saw who she was sitting beside.

"Princess Miraya," Prince Adam said as she took her seat next to him.

She faced forward. What was he doing here? "Prince Adam," Mira muttered.

"Ah yes, it completely slipped my mind earlier to mention our other guest." Queen Lyanna couldn't quite hide the childish glee in her voice. "You two are well acquainted with each other, right, Princess Miraya?"

"Yes, we've met before," Prince Adam replied.

Mira shot him a glare. Prince Adam shrugged his shoulders in apology.

"Well, I hope you two enjoy each other's company," Queen Lyanna said.

Mira glimpsed the smirk on the queen's face before turning back to her meal. As much as she wished she could ignore everyone around her and eat in silence, she had a mission to achieve. She would find Calla. No matter what.

"What brings you to Evrotia?" Mira asked.

"I'm engaged to Princess Ariana."

Mira did her best to not choke on her food.

Prince Adam turned away from her, and she was content to let him be. Instead, she shifted her focus to the guest on her left, a woman with silver hair and purple eyes. She wore a beautiful gown made of black silk with silver embellishments. Mira noticed she was paying attention to their conversation with the slight tilt of her head while she did everything she could to not look at Mira.

"What's your name?" Mira asked her.

"Lady Morgana, but you can call me Morgan," Morgan replied. Her voice was smokey like Raven's, but unlike Raven's, hers sounded like it came as a side effect to either too many potions or screaming. Mira wasn't sure which one she wanted it to be.

"In what capacity do you serve the queen?"

"In any capacity she wishes." Morgan turned to Mira.

If Mira hadn't felt a wave of unease wash over her, she would have found Morgan enchanting. Her purple eyes held Mira captive as she stared at them. Mira gave her a coy smile.

"Isn't that true for everyone here? I mean, what do you do specifically for her?" Mira asked. She leaned closer to her, letting her hand rest just close enough that she was touching Morgan's arm.

"I discover things for her. And when I'm not doing that, I like to entertain myself from the doldrums of court life," Morgan answered. She also leaned closer to Mira, whispering conspiratorially.

Mira wasn't going to push further on what she did for Queen Lyanna. She could already tell it was the most she was going to get out of Morgan.

"It must be so strange for you to be here compared to Grecia," Morgan said.

"Have you been?" Mira leaned back for a moment to take a bite of her food and to see how interested Morgan was.

"I've only ever read about it. Never been able to make the journey, unfortunately." Genuine longing to travel flashed in Morgan's expression before being replaced by a coy look. "Maybe one day you can show it to me."

"Maybe. It is a beautiful island. I've missed it terribly. My father has been sending me around to other kingdoms for a few years. The sand at our beaches is so white it could be snow, the water is so blue and clear you can see to the surface beneath it if it's shallow enough, and the sun warms you from the inside out." Mira rested against the back of her chair as she thought about home.

"Is all of that true, Prince Adam?" Morgan asked.

Mira tried to hide the frown as Adam was brought into the conversation. If Morgan's goal had been to turn her off, that had certainly accomplished it.

"Princess Miraya tells the truth. Grecia is truly a sight to behold," Adam commented. He turned back to his meal, doing his best to detach from the conversation.

Mira turned her back to him and faced Morgan directly.

"What about your home? Are you from here?"

"I'm from Trudel, the queen's homeland."

"I've heard it's a winter wonderland there, being covered in snow almost half the year." Mira's gaze lingered on Morgan's lips.

"It's true. The snow is beautiful, though after two months you tire of it."

"Did you come here when the queen did?"

"Yes. I was one of her ladies sent to support and ease her transition into this court. I found I enjoyed it here and have never been back home."

"Surely you visit your family?" Mira asked.

Morgan shook her head. "I don't have any. What about you? Don't you miss your family? You have six sisters, right?"

Mira laughed. "Yes, plus a younger brother. We are certainly a handful for our father."

"I've heard he doesn't take well to people who misbehave." Morgan turned to her wine and took a sip.

"He is a strict father. But to answer your question, yes, I miss them." Mira meant it. She missed the chaos of her elder sisters and her younger brother. All of them brought unique personalities to their family that made their governesses quit within months.

"Hopefully, you'll get to see them soon." Morgan gave Mira a gentle touch before turning back to her meal.

Mira ate the rest of her meal in silence, contemplating her interaction. It was odd. Morgan had given her almost as much information as she had divulged, yet somehow she felt as though Morgan had gotten more out of the conversation than her. Mira would have to play with her more. There was something about Morgan that instantly made her wary, but intrigued at the same time.

CHAPTER FIFTEEN

DREA

Drea winced as a novice flipped another over their back and onto the mattress before straddling them and pressing a practice dagger to their opponent's throat. Despite the upheaval, Gus had kept the lessons going, ensuring everyone would be ready for anything. Drea pulled on her dress, trying to find a comfortable position as her training clothes underneath bunched.

She waited patiently inside the room next to the door for the class to end. Several novices had noticed her and paused just long enough for their opponents to take advantage. Gus lectured each of them, his bulky frame towering over even the tallest of them. They were dismissed quickly, with Gus shaking his head as he walked over to her.

"A little warning next time would be appreciated, Miss Drizella," Gus said as he stopped before her. He wiped his brow, his brown hair still perfectly brushed back from his round face.

"Of course, I just didn't...they've never reacted that way before," Drea replied.

"You're the mistress of this house now; they see you differently," Gus explained.

Drea remained silent. She wouldn't be able to sneak around the house easily if everyone paid attention to her.

"What brings you down here?" Gus asked.

"I want you to help me fight again," Drea said before she could change her mind.

Gus's eyebrows shot up at her request. "Of course, we can try. I've always offered that to you. I can't make any promises about how successful we'll be, given how long it's been."

"I understand," Drea replied, nodding as she straightened her back.

"Might I ask why now?"

"I don't want to be helpless anymore," Drea muttered, more to herself than to Gus.

"The only people who held you back were your mother and yourself. The former I never understood, but the latter...well, it's hard to come back after that." Gus walked around the room, setting up the space for her. "I don't have anything for a few hours, so let's get started." Gus stretched his muscles as he walked onto the large mattress in the middle of the room. "I won't say anything to anyone unless you ask me to." Gus added.

Drea nodded her thanks as she removed her skirts and corset. They fell in a pile on the ground as she stepped out of them, wearing her old training clothes.

She had been surprised to find the black clothes still fit her perfectly. The pants hugged her in all the right spots, and her tunic still allowed for movement without being too loose. Her black boots were tied up to her knees, offering extra support. A dagger was strapped to her right thigh, an adjustment she would have to adapt to. As she walked onto the mattress, Drea tied her hair back into a ponytail, her long curls falling between her shoulder blades.

"What are we starting with?" Drea asked as she twirled the dagger.

"Stretching," Gus replied.

"Stretching?" Drea cocked a hip.

"Followed by strength training. Prepare yourself for a lot of squats, lunges, and more," Gus said, his voice filled with mirth.

"Evil man," Drea replied, a hint of a smile pulling at her lips as she followed his instructions.

"You already know how to be ruthless. But your leg is inhibiting you and will continue to do so until you strengthen it." Gus explained as he walked around her, correcting her stance.

Before the strength training began, Drea sat on the floor and massaged her leg one last time, digging in deep to break up the tendons and cartilage that had tightened. She closed her eyes, feeling the muscles beneath her hands as they relaxed.

"I want you to do a series of three exercises. I don't care how long it takes, so long as you finish them," Gus said as he helped her to her feet.

She got through five squats when the muscles twitched.

Drea completed the first set before the muscles spasmed.

She sat down before her leg gave out on her and waited a few minutes until the twitching beneath her hands stopped. Then she got up and finished her second round of squats.

Each time she felt a flicker in her leg, she waited until she couldn't stay on her feet any longer, and then she got back up until she finished every last exercise Gus threw at her.

Drea sat in her bedroom nook with a cup of tea in her hands and watched the late spring storm roll in off the coast. Any training today would have to be inside. She took a sip and closed her eyes.

Henry's question from the other night bounced around her mind. She wanted out of this life. But she couldn't leave Anastasia. She would never subject her sister to that betrayal. If Drea could have had it her way, she would have grabbed Anastasia the night of the ball just seven days ago and run away with her. But Ana never would have left. She loved their life and the power she got from controlling the turn of the court from the depths of the shadows. Most importantly, she was addicted to the sense of importance she got by having the ear of the queen.

Drea leaned her head back against the wall and let her mind rest, if only for a moment.

A soft knock drew her attention right before Anastasia walked in. She was quiet as she slid inside and eased the door closed. Ana wore her training clothes, the black fabric clung to her narrow waist. Her weapons, two twisted daggers, were sheathed at her hips. Her blond hair was pulled into a tight chignon.

"You're going to get soaked if you train outside today," Drea commented as Anastasia sat down across from her.

"A little rain never hurt anyone." She leaned back, her hands resting on top of her knees. "How's your leg today?"

"It's fine. I massaged it a few minutes ago." Drea replied. She didn't want to tell Ana it had cramped so hard from all of the training with Gus she had woken up screaming and had been unable to fall asleep since.

"I'm worried about you. You've been doing too much recently. Your leg rarely gives you this much trouble." Anastasia reached out and rested her hand on Drea's ankle, playfully shaking it.

"I'm fine, Ana. We have more to do now that Mother's gone."

"You'll let me know if you need me to do some of it. The queen wouldn't need to know," Anastasia reassured her.

Drea didn't respond. The queen may not be told, but Princess Lena would be. Anastasia would say something about it to make herself look better while painting Drea as the incompetent one. It wouldn't be done maliciously, but it would still happen.

"What updates do you have?" Drea asked.

"Luca hasn't been flushed out...yet. He can't go home. With his face everywhere now, it's only a matter of time." Anastasia took the mug of steaming tea from Drea and took a sip, scrunching her face before handing it back. "I always forget how much I dislike tea until I have some again."

Drea said nothing. Anastasia loved to talk, especially when it meant sharing information Drea hadn't known about. So she sat and waited for her sister to continue.

"Tressa scried me early this morning."

Drea noted her sister's smug face. She knew she had Drea's attention now.

"Oh? Did she do something useful?" Drea couldn't stop the dig from coming out.

"She found them. David went to a nearby village wearing only a cloak as a disguise. Of course, the villagers didn't recognize him. Why would they? But Tressa was able to follow him back to where they've holed themselves up."

"She saw Ella?" Drea pressed. It would be one thing to find the prince in hiding than another to find the assassin who was supposed to be dead.

"Not exactly. But there are two horses, so who else could it be? We know it's not Henry; you just saw him yesterday."

Drea hadn't told her sister where she had been yesterday, just that she had had an errand to run. She had, however, informed Lena about the summons. Drea said nothing in reply, knowing her sister expected information in return.

"What orders did you give Tressa? Is she waiting for backup?"

It was no secret between her and Anastasia that Tressa would be unable to take down both David and Ella. She would be outmatched. Something that had not been shared with the queen before she sent Tressa to find them.

"I told her to observe and we would send some of our best to help."

"Ana..."

"She'll listen to me. She hangs on every word I say." Anastasia dismissed Drea's comment.

Tressa would go after them. Drea knew it. Ana knew it. Tressa was blinded by her infatuation with Lucifer and would seek her revenge, one way or another.

"Tell me you've woken some of the men and sent them north to her," Drea muttered. She'd almost said, south, but was quick to remember Tressa's lie. If Tressa wanted to bury herself, Drea wasn't going to try to help.

"Of course." Anastasia shifted in her spot beside Drea. "So…what did Henry have to say? You must be happy to be seeing him again?" Her sister kept her eyes locked on the storm rolling in.

"He wanted to update me on their progress in searching for Luca and to see if we needed anything."

"Always the knight in shining armor," Anastasia commented. "What was his update?"

"They've had as little luck as we have. Wherever Luca is hiding, he's done well to remain hidden."

"How are you doing with seeing Henry?"

Drea turned to her sister to find only genuine concern painted on her face. Ana was now the only one alive who truly knew why things had ended. She had always supported their mother's decisions, but she had also held Drea late into the night when the pain had been too much for her heart to bear alone.

"It's been okay. My magic is…delighted, and I have to keep it tightly controlled. But otherwise…it's fine. He's formal around me, just as I am toward him."

"If it becomes too much, let me know."

"If the queen demands I interact with the palace more so that you and Lena may move about unseen, then it is a burden I'm happy to carry," Drea replied quickly. She grabbed Anastasia's hand and squeezed it. "I've gone through worse."

"I know. I just don't want you to leave me too. I adore Lena, but sometimes I need my little sister."

"I would never leave you, Ana, I promise." Drea continued to hold her sister's hand. "You might be my big sister, but I will always protect you."

With that reassurance, Anastasia hugged Drea and left her with more thoughts about what she should do next.

Drea listened at her door for several long minutes before she cautiously turned the doorknob and slipped out of her room. She left her cane resting against the wall and padded down the carpeted hallway. Everyone was asleep as she moved about Aumont in her nightgown. Her primary concern was getting down the stairs without Lena or Ana hearing.

Drea straightened her shoulders and gripped the railing before taking her first step.

And then the next.

Drea's leg shook by the time she had five stairs left. An improvement from her training. She would make it. She would reach the bottom without falling and without the assistance of her cane.

She could do it.

Drea held her body tight as a cramp twisted its way through her scarred leg. She gripped the railing with her left hand as her right hand covered her groan.

She would not fall.

With shaking fingers, she moved her free hand down to her leg and massaged the muscle as best she could, giving herself enough relief to make it down those last steps. While the hardest part was over, she still had to walk down the never-ending hallway to the kitchen and out through the kitchen gardens.

Drea gritted her teeth as she walked. Her eyes adjusted to the darkness as she focused on the door near the end of the hall. She moved more slowly than her heart demanded. Her ears strained for any sound other than her own. Drea reached the kitchen and eased the door open, thankful for its well-oiled hinges.

She sagged against the wall. Her leg kindly reminded her of its annoyance when the cramps swelled. This time she eased herself down onto the cool stone floor and took precious minutes to rub the muscles into submission. Drea glanced at the back door leading to her destination, a small garden filled with some fruit trees and a tapestry of herbs.

She shoved herself off the floor and stood determined. Her magic spun out of its dance as Drea stared at the damn door that was twenty paces away. She had already improved so much. She could get there without her cane. She had already come so far.

Drea straightened her spine and walked through the kitchen and outside. The cresting moon shone dimly over the garden, casting long shadows from the trees. She would be hidden here. She crossed her arms as a shiver passed through her in the cool night air.

Her nightgown had been necessary to wear on the off chance someone saw her. It was worth suffering the cold for the excuse.

"Here, take my cloak." Henry walked out of the shadows along the far wall, his black cloak already in his hands.

"Then you'll be cold." Drea protested as he gently settled the thick, warm cloak over her shoulder. She did her best not to breathe in his scent.

"I'll be fine. I warmed up on my ride here," Henry said. He stood in front of her, his arms relaxed at his sides. He wore a loose black tunic and dark trousers.

Her fingers twitched to run through his tousled red hair, her magic flitting through her entire body, pressing against her skin to touch him. *Shhhhh*, she pulled it back into a tight, slow foxtrot. Drea wrapped her arms around her waist, hidden in the depths of Henry's cloak and far away from him.

"Thank you for coming here," Drea said, starting the conversation as they moved farther into the garden.

"I have to admit I was surprised to receive your scry," Henry replied.

"I would have gone to the palace, but I have to be careful. Anastasia already asked me about being there." Drea commented.

"You know the whole time I was out here waiting, I couldn't help but remember that one time I had snuck out here," Henry said, smiling softly.

"I remember. Ana had just done something obnoxious and I...I needed to talk to you," Drea whispered. He had always been there for her. Even now...he was here...for her. She wilted inside as he once again showed her that she could never deserve his love. Not anymore.

"So, what did you need to discuss?" Henry leaned toward her, his green eyes open and curious...or, if she was being honest, she would say they were hopeful as he looked at her.

"I want to help you...but I need you to promise me that Ana won't be imprisoned or harmed."

"Drizzie, I can't..." Henry pulled back from her.

"Henry, please. You don't know what it was like growing up with our mother. Her sole focus was the queen's mission, and thus ours...since we were five..."

"Then why are you considering helping me?" Henry stood before her, arms crossed.

"I'm tired, and I want it to stop." She didn't add anything else. It would only lead to more questions she wasn't prepared to answer. Drea gazed at him, and her heart ached to wrap her arms around him. "Please, Henry, are you able to promise me anything?"

"I can promise I'll do my best to protect her. But if she does something that could hurt David, I can't guarantee the king won't want her punished for her crimes." Henry stepped closer to her and rested a hand on her shoulder. "It's the best I can do without actually going to the king."

"I understand." Drea kept her eyes locked on his. She pulled a small mirror from her nightgown and handed it to him. "Take this. I enchanted it so that only you and I can communicate through it. Should I have anything for you, I'll reach out using my mirror."

"Drizzie —"

She stepped away from him, her magic dancing a tango filled with desire. Henry stepped back as well, the mirror clutched in his hand. Drea pulled the cloak off and held it out to him, an arm's distance away, a thousand heartbeats away. He took it from her, wrapping it back around his shoulders.

"I'll be in touch," Henry whispered before turning away and climbing over the low stone wall.

CHAPTER SIXTEEN

Ella

"Let me see your hands," Ella commanded.

Tressa lay beside them, but she couldn't focus on that. Right now, Ella needed to see David's hands. Tressa loved using pretty flowers with deadly consequences.

"We have to clean your hands and face. Now." Ella grabbed David and shoved him inside. She did not just kill someone she had trained to lose David over his arrogance. She plunged his hands into the wash basin and scrambled to find a wash cloth. The sooner she got it out of his system, the better.

"Ella, what poison is it?" David asked. He vigorously cleaned his hands.

"I don't know. Some type of flower...I never paid enough attention," Ella confessed.

David's shoulders relaxed. "It's not enchanted?"

"No. But it's still toxic. It could cause a fever and vomiting."

"Well I've handled worse," David mumbled.

"Let me check something." Ella left before David could say anything, racing for her packs. She dug through them, searching for her healing kit. She grabbed a small jar and sprinted back.

"Dry your hands and face. I have something that will help." Ella opened the jar and wrinkled her face at the smell.

David grimaced. "What is that?"

"My friend created it. It'll help heal your wounds and prevent the poison from spreading."

"It's enchanted?"

"Yes, but she made it for enchanters. It doesn't infect your magic. I promise."

David nodded as he dried his hands and face. He sat down on the kitchen floor. Ella sat across from him and hesitated, stinky goop on her hands, as she locked eyes with him. The spikes had lightly grazed David's cheek. She started there, gently spreading Calla's concoction over the scrapes.

"Why was this made and why is it awful?"

"I have no idea about the smell, but it was actually created after someone we know got injured. My friend didn't want to feel helpless trying to save another enchanter...so, she found a way."

Ella moved on to David's hands. They were torn, but not deep. Hopefully, Calla's serum would work quickly.

Ella carried her saddlebags out to the horses and dropped them on the ground. Both horses were lying down, each with a broken leg. She walked over to them, examining them further. Drea's horse, Night, gazed at her in pain. Ella patted her, searching for more injuries, though the broken legs would be enough to hinder their journey. David came up behind her, his hands completely wrapped and gauze covering the strikes on his face.

"Change of plans," Ella ground out. "We need to find her horse and lighten our supplies. Can you scry Henry and inform about what happened?"

David nodded as she walked back inside and repacked their bags down to their bare essentials. Two sets of clothes, food, water, and weapons. She glanced around for anything else, grabbing Jaq's satchel. The last thing she did was braid her hair and put on her wig.

"Ready?" She looked at David. He had strapped his sword to his belt. Ella touched her own, resting her hand on her father's sword. Both of them clasped their cloaks together before shouldering their packs.

Tressa had to have come on a horse. They swept through the forest, looking for how she had journeyed there. There was no way she walked, Ella adamantly thought.

Ella stopped abruptly, David running into her at the sight of a beautiful, large black stallion that stood in the sun rays breaking through the trees, his hide glistening. How Tressa had gotten her hands on a steed like him...Ella shook her head and approached slowly.

The horse stared at them. His ears were slightly back as she got closer. He shuffled a hoof, warning Ella. She waited, stepping closer when he stopped moving. Ella put out her hand, waiting for him to smell it. As he did, she watched his ears relax and point directly at her before resting his nose in her hand. Ella motioned David over, putting his hand under the stallion's nose.

The stallion didn't back away. David and Ella walked to his left side, stroking him as they went. She strapped the saddlebags on as David untied his lead. Ella mounted, swinging her leg over and settling on top of him. She waited for his reaction. He stood still, calm, waiting. David came up behind her, adjusting his seat.

Slowly, Ella turned the horse, leading him deeper into the forest.

"What do we do now?" David asked.

"We stick to our plan."

"It'll take us longer with one horse."

"I know," Ella murmured.

Ella and David rode in silence for hours, listening for any sign that they had been followed. Ella had insisted on it. Who knew if Tressa had someone else with her? She doubted it, but given that Tressa had found her, she wasn't taking any chances. Only once they made camp for the night did Ella break the silence.

"I don't think we were followed. I think she was dumb enough to be working by herself."

"Dumb enough? She seemed pretty capable to me," David remarked, placing some pieces of wood in a small clearing.

"Well, she's never beaten me in a fight before, so why she thought she could do it while injured..." Ella shrugged. "I suspect her love for Lucifer is what motivated her to react irrationally."

"Her love for Lucifer?"

"She was infatuated with him. I have no idea why. He barely ever glanced at her, only kept her around because she would do whatever he told her to." Ella sat on her sleeping mat.

"What was it like there?" David sat across from her. Ella raised her eyebrows at him. "Henry was right. The two of us don't really know each other, and I would like for us to know each other. The real versions of ourselves."

"That's uh... that's a hard question to answer, David... didn't that shackle give you that answer?" Ella whispered.

"Well... I felt your emotions as you asked. I didn't dive deeper, and in our rush to flee, it was left behind. So... if you don't want to tell me about it, I understand." David searched the forest. "What about your best friend? Snow White? What's she like?" He leaned forward, watching Ella.

"Snow White....she's my rock. I miss her so much. She's not usually gone so long for an assignment, and the last time I saw her... she wasn't doing well.

But she's the strongest person I know, a strong enchanter too." Ella added, smiling as she thought about Raven.

"That would explain her poisons." David commented. "But who trained her? She couldn't have gone to the Enchanters Academy. They never would have taught her how to make poisons."

"She was trained by an enchanter at Aumont. All our enchanters were. They were all taught very specific things. Snow wanted to learn about poisons, so she was taught."

"Where did Tremaine find enchanters who were willing to help her?"

"I would imagine they were enchanters who didn't enjoy having the palace monitoring them." Ella remarked, thinking of Lord Conrad. He hated the palace for its rules about enchanting. He was from a wealthy family; he had left so that he wouldn't have to answer to the king."

"I see." David shifted. "Is there anything I can answer for you?"

Ella bit her lip. There was so much she wanted to ask, but wasn't sure if she wanted to know the true answer, or keep the ones she had been told the last ten years. "Why did you keep writing letters?"

David snapped his head to look at her. "Where—"

"I had to leave the letters at the stronghold, but Drea had given them to me a few weeks ago."

"I kept writing you letters hoping you would return one to me." He rubbed his head. "I know it sounds silly, and deep down I knew I would never hear from you, but I wanted to... I needed to keep that hope alive. It's all that kept me going, especially after Mom. I wanted you to know I still thought about you, still cared. I don't know...it sounds silly now—"

"It isn't." Ella interrupted. "I wish Drea had given them to me years ago... I know why she didn't... but still... I guess better late than never," she said, "at least she didn't burn them... and thank you for writing them."

"Have you read all of them?" David raised a brow.

"Not all of them. Just a few. You were mad at Lady Tremaine for sending me away to Evrotia and complaining about Princess Lena." Ella laughed.

She rubbed her left wrist absentmindedly. David lifted his hand and reached for her wrist. She let him touch her. Let him run his hand over the first scar she had ever gotten in that room.

"I wish…Gods, I wish we had done so much differently back then. I feel like we let you down," David whispered.

"Do you think…do you think we'll ever truly know everything we were lied to about?" Ella whispered. She locked eyes with him, waiting for his answer.

"I hope so. I think that to start unraveling those lies, we need to talk, and learn, and listen to each other." David smiled gently.

"Well, where should we start?" Ella leaned away from him, tucking her wrists between her knees.

"What makes you laugh? Is it still seeing me and Henry slide over a wet floor?" David asked.

Ella chuckled. "Apparently, yes." She watched the fire crackling before her. "Planning pranks with my friends makes me laugh. Racing on horseback still makes me laugh…" Ella paused, thinking about what else made her laugh and found the memories were not fun anymore. "That's it, I guess. What makes you laugh?"

"Celeste and Henry always make me laugh," David said, sobering quickly.

Celeste. Ella's heart ached for him at what this must be doing to Celeste. She reached out to him but stopped when he moved away.

"I need us to resolve this quickly, Ella. Not only is Rairene at stake, but so is my sister."

"I know. I would never let anything happen to her, David," Ella promised.

"I would rather die than see Celeste perish," David said, confirming Ella's worst fears. He would always put everyone else before himself. That was not something she could allow to happen.

They rode on horseback for two days, learning about each other and sometimes arguing with each other. "What's it like being an enchanter? I always wished I could have been one growing up." Ella asked. Her mind had once again wandered, and she found herself asking a question she had been longing to know the answer to.

He was so close, and it took all of her willpower to not lean back into him and feel the steady presence of him pressed against her. If they had been back in the garden all those days ago, she wouldn't have hesitated. She would have turned around, kissed him, and wrapped his arms around her. But she couldn't do that. Not anymore, because even though they were rebuilding their friendship, she still sensed that barrier from him.

David chuckled softly in her ear. "I remember. You were obsessed with the palace enchanters, always chasing after them, wanting to see them enchant something, usually jewelry." David paused. "It's hard to explain. I have this power that lives within me. It's connected to my soul and responds to all that I feel. It sings in my veins and purrs in happiness. It flares in anger and erupts when I'm in pain. I have to constantly monitor it and soothe it. The biggest part of our training is learning how to keep it from overpowering us and forcing us to lose control."

"You mentioned you learned how to let it flare without consuming you?" She had never heard Calla or Raven talk about any kind of training like that.

"Yes. Our magic is tied directly to our emotions. If we experience an abnormal amount of pain, grief, anger, even joy, our magic rises to meet that emotional threshold. It sees pain as a threat and that you need help, so it floods your body. You become overwhelmed because it surpasses the amount of magic you can contain, and the enchanter is forced to unleash it as raw power. It typically has devastating effects on the enchanter and anyone around them." David paused. "Most enchanters die if they don't regain control quickly, or if they don't know how to harness their power productively."

"They die?" Ella whispered. Why wouldn't Lady Tremaine have trained any of the enchanters on what to do? Raven was terrified of losing control.

David nodded. "The magic just pours out and refuses to be contained. Once the enchanter is depleted of all magic, it continues to pull on them until their life. I've only ever heard about the strongest enchanters being able to pull themselves back from burnout. It's why they train us to work with our power."

"That doesn't sound very enchanting." She'd never worried about Calla or Raven losing control, but now...she hoped her sisters were okay in Evrotia.

David sighed, adjusting so that he sat closer to her. "It's not. But I still wouldn't trade it away. It's like having a constant companion. You never feel as alone."

"You felt alone?"

"All the time. Especially after you were gone."

"David," Ella paused, biting her lip. "I'm sorry you felt alone."

"You were my best friend, Ella. I hope we can get back there."

"Me too." Ella whispered. "Can I ask you something else?" She turned to see him nod. "You mentioned that no enchanter would have trained Snow White on how to make poisons...why?"

David blew out a breath. "Because they're dangerous. Not just for the recipient, but for the enchanter. Our enchantments are fueled by our intentions and emotions. When I enchant the potion Vivifica, I'm fueling it with the intention of healing, love, and safety. It's tiring, but I actually felt more at peace afterwards because of the emotions I had to use. An enchanter who uses poisons, especially ones that kill, their intentions would have to be death, anger, manipulation, and sorrow. Those emotions being used like that would only grow within the enchanter until eventually they became twisted within them." David took a moment. "The last time I heard about an enchanter creating poisons it was because they went insane from making too many poisons. They don't have good endings, and it's why they're forbidden to be taught. Are you concerned about your friend?" David leaned closer to her.

"Yes." Ella could barely utter the word to the worry that had been building for months. "Ever since she...her heart was broken a while ago, and she's struggled to recover. It only got worse after she made the one poison; it was pure black, and our friend Belle saw it and almost dropped it from the pain she felt crawling out of it. She's an enchanter as well," Ella added when David scrunched his face. "Snow White became different, more driven, more reserved. I've barely seen her smile since."

"I bet if she turned her anger towards enchanting potions for healing, it would get better. Typically, those who know how to carry that much pain are our best healers, and doing something good should help counteract whatever that one poison was."

"I don't even think she knows what it will do. She simply poured everything into it. She collapsed in front of me afterwards."

"You were there?"

"I was always there for her. She's my friend, and a lot of the poisons she experimented on were beyond her mentor's skill, so she practiced in private with me to watch over her." Ella leaned back into David, absorbing his warmth. She hoped she could get word to Raven soon about David's idea. Maybe her sister would start to come back to her.

CHAPTER SEVENTEEN

Raven

Raven watched in horror as Queen Lyanna approached Calla, as she was held between two guards and shoved the gauntlet into her chest.

Her mouth was open, but no sound came out as Raven sprinted to her side, trying to catch Calla as she fell, her heart in Queen Lyanna's fist.

Raven woke to hands shaking her.

"Raven, wake up." Aleks's wide eyes shone through the dim firelight.

"What's happening?" Raven sat up quickly, blade in hand. Calla's face, twisted in pain and fear, was crystal clear in her mind's eye.

"You were screaming, and unless you want more mountain men to find us, I needed to wake you up." Aleks sat back from her, tilting his head. "Do you want to talk about it?"

"It was nothing." Raven ran her hands through her hair, closing her eyes as she took steadying breaths. Calla was safe. Aleks had said she'd gotten away. She had escaped. She wasn't being tortured. She would never have to live through that.

"It didn't sound like nothing," Aleks whispered. He scooted closer to her, his leg pressed against hers.

"Just one of my normal nightmares. I thought you were used to them."

"I never got used to seeing you in pain. Never will." Aleks surveyed their makeshift camp. "If you ever want to talk about them, or about...what happened while you were arrested...I'll always be there to listen."

"Thank you," Raven mumbled, ducking her head down. She couldn't look at him right now.

Raven stuffed everything down, pulling her emotions back just as tightly as she pulled on her magic. She pushed both of them down into small balls that could be ignored. Since she couldn't bake to focus her mind, Raven did the next best thing, she got up and fell into her old morning routine. She dusted off her exercises and brought life back to her body. The three of them had barely stopped moving for the last three days, and she was exhausted. It would be another four days at least before they reached a distance to her liking before they attempted contact with anyone.

Her least favorite part was that their path walked between the borders of Evrotia and Trudel, and she did not want to go anywhere near Aleks's home kingdom. She had heard many stories about the Tarntan Castle. Most of them described its towering walls of white stone as terrifying. Trudel was a kingdom that spent most of its time blanketed in snow. The castle was built high on the tallest mountain, jutting out of the very mountain itself, so they could watch over everyone. Its stone was said to be enchanted to always remain unbreakable and therefore always remain pure white, just like the hair of those who ruled over it. She hoped as they searched for King Stephan's advisers, she wouldn't see more than a fleck of its shadow.

Rowan got up shortly after she began exercising, joining her with his own warm-up. Both of them moved seamlessly while Aleks worked on packing up the camp.

It was the horses shuffling their hooves that pulled Raven from her thoughts.

She stood and moved around slowly, searching for attackers. She walked carefully to her horse, catching the attention of both Rowan and Aleks. They also shifted their positions, both of them pulling out small daggers from their boots.

She got to her dagger right as a man leaped from the trees.

Raven struck him quickly in the chest with her blade. He landed on top of her, the blade sliding in deeper as he died. Raven's magic surged as she struggled to get him off her. She squirmed out from him, kneading her magic back. It felt sticky as she continued to pull it in, folding it over and over. Raven stood and spun around, searching for more men.

She turned around as Aleks took down the other one.

"How many mountain men are there?" Raven asked. She knelt down and cleaned her blade on the man's tunic. Her magic tried to roll free of her grip. She pulled it back, straightening her spine.

"Too many. Most of them have families who lost their homes and ran to the mountains to survive," Rowan said as he walked around the perimeter of their camp.

"We should move on. I don't like that we keep coming across them." Aleks mounted his horse.

Raven and Rowan got on theirs quickly, riding off into the forest.

CHAPTER EIGHTEEN

Ella

Ella and David stared at the mountain. The forest had gradually gotten denser until the terrain had gotten too hard to navigate safely on the stallion's back. Fog coated the range, obscuring the peak.

"We can't," David commented as they dismounted and stared at the climb. "We can't leave him, Ella."

"What do you recommend then? It's not as if we can continue riding him? We're at the Holodalian border, a border that has kept both kingdoms at peace due to how hard a climb it is."

"I know, but we might need him."

"David, we will not get a stallion over this mountain. Luckily, he should be able to find his way home." Ella stoked the horse's nose, letting him snuffle her hair. "I love horses, David, you know that. Which means I don't suggest this lightly." Ella continued to pet him. "Let's get him unsaddled." Ella moved to the horse's side and removed the saddlebags, along with his saddle and reins. He looked at her. She knew he could see into her, see the dark twisting of her soul. He stayed beside them, grazing as they got ready.

"I don't think he's going to leave us," David said as they began their climb. He adjusted the weight on his back, groaning.

"I think you're right." Ella smiled as he followed them. "What do you know about these mountains?" Ella asked.

"Henry and I have studied them in war strategies for years; plus, we've always dreamed of crossing them. It'll take us three days on foot to cross. It's a wet forest and is always covered in fog and rain. It also means the forest ground will be muddy, and on a steep incline...well, we're about to get very dirty. But...it'll have to be enough until we get to Holodal. We'll use animal paths to cross. It might take us longer, but we can't be discovered."

"Let's get started," Ella said, taking the first steps up the steep mountain. She focused on putting one foot in front of the other. The incline forced her to stare straight ahead, ensuring she didn't tumble down. Ella removed her pendant to protect it and tucked it into her pocket for safekeeping.

Ella took out her water-skin and drank, relishing the cool water. The horse had followed them, as David had predicted. He moved slowly behind them as the incline worsened. Ella leaned forward to keep her balance.

"Do you think we should pause for a bit?" David asked, through a ragged breath. "Maybe eat? Catch our breath."

Ella looked at the sun, swaying on her feet. She glanced down, leaning backward to keep herself from falling down the path. She sat down heavily as she nodded. Ella lay on her back, blindly digging through her pack for some dried meat.

They found a spot a few hours later that would be safe to sleep on without falling downhill, both of them collapsing on the ground once they were done for the day. "I don't think I've been so exhausted in my life." Ella surveyed the thick canopy. They had mustered enough energy to make a small fire, just big enough to warm themselves. "Though, there was that one time Snow White, and I had to run laps around all of Aumont...that was exhausting."

"Every day for the first year of combat training, I could barely get out of bed. This feels like that."

"I don't remember that."

"I didn't tell you. I guess we've always kept secrets from each other."

"David—"

"Just tell me, how long did you make Henry lie to me?" David asked. He stared at the dark, starless sky.

"Just a few days. He had snuck into Aumont to speak with me and saw me training some novices a before the ball."

"I see...and neither one of you felt the need to tell me?"

"Henry wanted to...I wouldn't let him."

"Henry is his own man and could have told me without your permission."

"Would you have trusted me? Would you have still let me near you?" David twisted his lips, stirring the flames with a stick. "If you had known, you would have blocked me out, like you've been doing, and Lady Tremaine would have seen it and had you killed sooner."

"If you had told me the whole truth, everything, I would have gone along. We could have gone to my father and —"

"And done what? We only had my knowledge of what she had done. We still don't know the complete plan, David. We knew almost nothing, and her being the Ambassador to Trudel, your father could not move against her without starting a war. We would have been fools, and you would have died. I would have died. I know it all blew up anyway, but at least we're still alive. I wish I could have told you sooner I'm Cinderella, but given your hatred towards me, can you really blame me for keeping that secret?"

David grumbled unintelligibly as he stared at the fire.

"I hope one day you'll be able to see why we did things the way we did. I accept it can't be right now."

He turned away from her, pulling his bedroll out to sleep. Ella finished her meal and sat in silence, listening to the wood crack in the fire. The stallion had stayed with them and was laying down near them. She had never been more thankful to have a horse who could carry their packs as they climbed higher. She reached into her pocket and held the necklace in her hand, twisting it in the firelight. How much protection could it really offer her? Could it only protect her from direct threats by a person? Or could it do more? Ella put it back in her pocket, knowing she would probably never know the answer. Jaq was dead, and she didn't feel like asking David right then. He would come around eventually. He had to see that her lies had been for his protection, not just for her heart.

Ella and David traversed enemy territory and steep inclines that stole their breath away. By midday they had crested the first mountain and begun their trek back down to the gorge below. They would have to do this several more times before entering the unknown land of Holodal. Ella found herself thankful with every step that the stallion hadn't run off, saving her back and energy.

David kept them at a good pace, though sometimes he had to urge Ella along when all she wanted to do was lie down and potentially never get back up again. How anyone did this for fun was beyond her. She had always considered herself a nature person before this moment. She loved trees, and walking through forests, and going on long horseback rides. But this, hiking through dangerous terrain, barely able to find her breath, sweating so much she felt like she had swam through a lake. She would be happy if she never had to hike another day in her life.

Nighttime was the worst. Every single ache and pain she had ignored reared back in the night's stillness. They had set camp near the base of the mountain by a small stream, but it offered little in the way of quenching their thirst with its mud infested waters. David actually went as far as forbidding it.

On their third day, the trail got easier, and they found more animal paths they could follow.

"Any idea of when we'll be out of this range?" Ella huffed. She needed some conversation. Anything was better than this suffocating silence.

"What? Henry didn't share his master plan on how to navigate this with you?"

"David—"

"You mean he kept important information from you?"

"You're being an asshole right now." Ella stepped into the dark and muddy riverbed. It was their only way across, and she hoped it didn't get too deep. The last thing she needed was for her sweat soaked clothes to become mud covered sweat soaked clothes. Frogs and insects buzzed around them.

"I have a right to be upset, Ella."

"I'm not saying you don —" Ella paused. She could have sworn something brushed against her leg. She held still. Waiting. Nothing. There were just the quiet ribbits of the frogs and the chirping of birds around her. She moved on, trying to see through the muddy waters as best she could with each step. The last thing she needed was for some creature lurking in the river to decide she was its lunch.

"Now you get to feel what it's like to be left in the dark."

"*I was left in the dark* because there wasn't time to explain the plan to me, what with everyone descending on my home, and me killing Lady Tremaine, and saving you." Ella snapped.

David was a few steps ahead of her in the river, the stallion beside him.

"It still doesn't excuse —"

"Shh, be quiet." Ella snapped. She needed to listen. The air had shifted around her as a subtle quietness blanketed them.

"Oh, now you want me to be quiet. You're the one —"

"David, *please* —"

"No, there's nothing out here. We're completely alone. Just you and me on the border of Holodal trying to be friends again —"

"David, I need you to be quiet."

The forest had gone silent. The insects and frogs were gone. The birds had stopped chirping. Ella looked at her feet in the black water, and she knew something brushed against her calf this time.

"—which I don't know how we're supposed to do that if you keep your secrets —"

A wire flashed in the sunlight before her. Ella jumped towards David, tossing him backward before he could activate the tripwire in front of him. The idiot.

Ella fell in the opposite direction.

Black water rose over her, swallowing her as she hit the bottom of the riverbed, arms splayed out behind her. This time, a wire tightened around her wrist, restraining her to the floor. She pulled hard, trying to get to the surface.

Ella pulled and pulled on her wrist, each one stronger than the last. The riverbed was just deep enough that no matter what she did, she couldn't get her head above the water.

Blinding pain erupted in her vision as a foreign object pierced all the way from her back through her chest.

Ella let out a garbled scream, her lungs filling with water.

She pulled again. Somehow she pulled, but couldn't get free.

David had left her. He would probably be glad she was gone. He hated her after all.

Ella tried to pull again, but her vision darkened before fading to black.

Ella gasped for air as she was violently awoken by someone pounding on her chest. David's face was inches away from hers, his brown eyes wide.

"Hold on, Ella. I need to get us out of here." He picked her up and carried her over to the horse. He leaned her against the stallion's neck as he got on behind. Ella faded in and out of consciousness. All she could track were the jumps and jostles that jolted her back to her body.

She was hurt. It was bright and painful, but she couldn't figure out its origin, only that a throbbing mass of nerves wouldn't stop screaming at her. Luckily, the darkness took her again before the pain became too much. All she felt was the steady heat of someone behind her, holding her close. That presence whispered to her, and she did everything she could to stay and listen just a little bit longer.

Ella opened her eyes, and she was in her garden again. But her mother wasn't there. Ella had a feeling she would never see her mother here again. She smiled when she saw a figure walking towards her.

"Raven."

Raven didn't say a word as she walked up and hugged her. Ella embraced her, holding on as tightly as she could.

"You need to stay with him, Ella. Stay alive."

"Sometimes I think it might be easier if I weren't alive..."

"All the more reason to live. I need you to get me away from that evil queen." Raven lightly stroked her hair. "You know I'm in danger. Ever since you figured out Lady Tremaine knew her."

Ella stepped back at the image of the sister. She was weary, with dark circles laying waste to her blue eyes. Her hair was unkempt, and her fingers kept twitching for her sabers.

"Are you all right?" Ella whispered.

"I will be if you live and come get me." Raven turned away before pulling Ella back into a hug. "Your prince cares for you, and you know it. You hear it in the way he's trying to mend and grow a new relationship with you. But he was hurt too; you're just too hurt to see it. But if you listen to him right now, you'll know," Raven commented.

Ella was jostled from the garden as the horse jumped over something. No wonder no one sane traversed these mountains.

"We're almost out, and then I can examine the wound. Just a little longer," David whispered in her ear. "Please stay with me."

Ella knew they had gotten out of the mountains when the ground leveled out and the horse picked up speed. She found the energy to open her eyes enough to view the grassy hills before them before the blinding pain coated her vision in red.

"Get it out." She spoke through gritted teeth as each step the horse took moved the arrow piercing her.

"I need to find a clean water source, Ella," David said.

She wanted to object; she didn't need any enchantments. She just needed the damn arrow taken out. But she couldn't voice anything as the pain in her shoulder flared.

"Don't move, Ella," David said. "I need to get the arrow out, and it's not going to be easy."

Ella turned her head to the side and found a calm crystal stream before her. The mountains were on the other side. They had done it. They had crossed into Holodal. And she had an arrow in her back.

"What's...what are you going to do?" Ella closed her eyes, trying to keep her breathing steady.

"It might be better if you don't know." David cut off part of Ella's shirt to expose the entry.

"David, I'm an assassin. I think I can handle—" Ella sucked in air when she felt the cool touch of a blade on her skin before David made the cut into her body even bigger. "Some warning next time?" Ella growled, blinking back the stars.

"It's only going to get worse."

Ella felt something push on the arrow before feeling David's finger trailing along the arrow's length inside her until he hit the arrowhead. "Well, it's not stuck in your collarbone. Which means I can simply pull it out."

"Do it."

"I need your permission to put some Vivifica on it afterwards. I don't know how badly you're going to bleed."

Ella closed her eyes, shuddering at the thought. "Fine."

David smoothly pulled the arrow out while using his other hand as a guide. Ella bit into a leather strap, muffling her groans before she blacked out.

The first thing Ella saw when she opened her eyes again was David pressing a finger to his lips.

She frowned at him, wondering why they were suddenly pressed against the tall river grass. Warmth slid down her back as Ella focused on David and the panic in his wide eyes. She forgot about the blood she was losing when she heard the horses.

Border guards.

Shit. Their horse...where was he? If they saw him...Ella's eyes landed on the stallion who had somehow laid down in the river grass. They would only be seen if the border guards came right up on them; hopefully, they would stay away. Ella slapped her hand over her mouth, keeping quiet as David pressed a shirt hard against her wound, staunching the blood flow. She glared at him but found relief in the pressure. If they didn't get it to stop bleeding soon...she shook. They would get it to stop bleeding. Sweat trickled down her face as she shivered against David.

She curled in on herself and closed her eyes, listening to the horses move away from them.

"David..." Ella whispered as her eyes closed.

"Ella." David shook her gently, turning to face her. Sweat beaded on her forehead as her body heated up beneath his hands. A rash flushed across her cheeks as her breathing became shallow.

David grabbed the broken arrow and looked closer. He cursed.

Ella glimpsed the glittering red sludge mixed in her blood.

David grabbed a slim, stoppered vial and scrambled to the creek. Ella blinked, and David was back beside her. He pulled his magic to him rapidly.

David took a breath and began his enchantment. "*Stati sano cortare instauraretis.*" He repeated it over and over until the clear water turned into a glowing white potion.

Ella tried to open her eyes to see what was happening, but found she lacked the strength to do anything as her body convulsed.

CHAPTER NINETEEN

Calla

Calla flooded the stones with more magic.

Each day she siphoned it into the stone, giving it her intentions of heat. Adam hadn't returned to visit her again. She had hoped, but hadn't expected more. What would she have done in his place? She would hope she would be brave enough to see beyond the evidence given to her and trust the person she had known, but she also knew what it meant to trust and be betrayed.

Calla had lost count of how many times she had been brought down to the torture room. Each time she was presented with a new form of torture, a new form of madness ensued. But they never broke her. She supposed there was one benefit to being an enchanter right then, being more resilient to the poisons they pushed into her. She knew Raven had tested each one to make sure they were perfect, and how Raven had survived, Calla could only imagine.

The air was filled with electricity as the guards carried Calla into Morgan's torture room. Something was off...different. She could taste it on her lips, in her magic. She'd been able to keep it clamped down all this time, but it rose to the energy in the room. It slowly unwound from within, a peaceful snake ready to snap, coiled and waiting.

Morgan walked in, a smirk on her lips. Two others followed her. They were twins and dressed in the same black clothing. Their blond hair was the lightest thing about them. Their blue eyes did little to settle Calla as they walked in unison to either side of her head. They had strapped Calla to the table, only this time it was propped up, so that she was almost standing, almost touching solid ground.

"We're going to have fun today, dear." Morgan smiled viciously at her. "We're going to see what you're really made of."

Calla didn't look at her. She watched the door separating her from freedom and began counting all of the nails. One, two, three, four, Morgan came back carrying three bottles in her hand. One, two, three, one, two, one, one, Calla felt the sweat on her forehead. What was she going to do with three poisons? Surely she wasn't intending to give all of them to Calla at once? No one, no enchanter, would be able to maintain control with that much chaos in their body, literally and figuratively, for Calla saw that one of them was Chaos.

Calla turned her eyes away from Morgan and began counting again. She could do this. She did not break. She was strong. She was loved. She did not break. Calla repeated Raven's phrase over and over in her head as she turned her head to watch Morgan mix three poisons together. Morgan walked over and held Calla's nose until she could no longer keep her mouth shut. Calla spat the liquid out at Morgan the moment after it touched her lips. Morgan punched Calla so hard white spots blinded her. Before she could do anything else, Morgan poured more into her mouth. One of her assistants shut her mouth and held her nose until she swallowed.

The effects were instantaneous.

Chaos, Fenith, and Blaze charged forward, vying for dominance over Calla's mind and body. All the while Calla reigned in her magic, thankful she had pushed more into the stones earlier. Because she did not break.

She would not break over this. No matter how much it hurt, she couldn't reveal herself. If she did, she would die. Calla knew that, and she had to keep fighting. She had to stay alive for them. For Raven. For Ella. She would live for them, at least long enough to see their deaths avenged. If anything, she owed them that.

Fenith, it seemed, had taken prominence in her mind as it broke every bone in her body. Chaos kept her from escaping to her mind palace, painting hallucinations of her father and sisters that would haunt her for eternity. Calla saw her father before her, bruised and beaten. They had found him. He had tried so hard to disappear, to never be found again, but there he was, kneeling before her, staring at her through watery brown eyes.

Calla watched as Lady Tremaine did the one thing she had always threatened to do if Calla left Aumont, shackled her father and turned him over to the crown. And Calla got a front row seat. Guards flooded around them.

"Turn away, Calla. Don't watch this," her father pleaded with her. She tried to reach out to him. Everything would be okay. She would fix it. She did not break. Lady Tremaine couldn't go back on her deal if Calla didn't break. Everything would be okay. It had to be okay. He had to take care of Iris and Rose. They needed someone to care for them.

"I'll fix it, Father. I'll fix it." More men came in, chaining up Lord Marcel. "Leave him alone!" Tears ran down Calla's face as one of them punched her father to the ground. Someone screamed. She was screaming. Her bones were breaking as her father was beaten and dragged away.

Calla screamed in pain as every bone in her hands splintered and her ribcage fractured. It happened over and over, and Calla was helpless to do anything. All she could do was make sure she didn't break. Her magic would not respond to this assault. She would not allow it. She could handle it. She would not lose control. If she lost control, it wouldn't even be worth it. She would only kill Morgan, and if Calla was going to lose control, she was going to make it count.

Blaze came in last, burning through everything. Just when she felt she could feel no more, its fire licked her clean. Calla was empty; her lungs burned to ash.

"Well?"

She couldn't look up at the voice. All she knew was that the queen was there, watching her. Calla didn't care. She didn't care about anything but remembering how to take her next breath, no matter how much it ignited the fire burning in her lungs.

"No enchanter could survive without revealing themselves. She's just a common maid." Morgan gripped Calla's chin in her hand, making Calla meet her eyes. "You're just a worthless maid. You probably don't even have any important information."

Queen Lyanna sighed. "Well, at least we have some leverage over Astrid if she ever shows her face again. Keep her alive, torture her for whatever information she has, but make sure she stays alive." Then she was gone.

"You hear that? We get to have more fun." Morgan laughed so loudly it echoed for hours in Calla's mind.

Calla just continued to breathe.

She woke up in her cell. She had no idea if they had dumped her hours, days, or minutes ago. Bile rose, and Calla had just enough of her wits about her to turn her head, but nothing else. She couldn't make anything else move if she tried. At least the remnants of Raven's poisons had now vacated her body, though their effects lingered. Sweat poured down Calla's back as her body slowly put itself together and slowly realized it had all indeed just been a figment of her imagination.

"Calla?"

She couldn't move. She didn't want to see Adam. Not now. Not like this. She couldn't even form a coherent thought right now. She kept her eyes shut, waiting for the swirling to stop. Her magic was so tightly bound she felt it could spring free any minute. She had to siphon some off soon.

"Calla?" Adam seemed to yell her name as he crouched down before her. It rang in her ears.

"Shhhhh...." It was all she could muster. "Too....loud..."

"What did they do to you?" Adam whispered.

"You mean, what haven't they done to me?" Her voice was scratchy; her vocal cords were tired from screaming.

"Calla..." His voice caressed her, holding her close. "What did they..." He couldn't finish the question.

"Three...poisons..."

"Not all at once." He clarified.

Calla nodded her head. All at once.

"We'll get you out. Somehow...somehow I'm going to get you out." He was so quiet Calla wasn't sure she had heard him. She didn't let herself hope. Didn't dare let her heart bear that weight right now. If she did, and she was wrong, she would break. And Calla did not break.

Calla stared mindlessly at the bread and porridge that had been put before her. It was the only meal she would be given, and if she didn't eat it right then, it would not be waiting for her when she got back from whatever torture they had planned for her today. Her stomach rebelled at the thought, though it growled for some form of food. She ate it anyway, hoping she wouldn't lose it later. They hadn't brought her any change of clothes, so her amazing gown was now ruined beyond all repair.

The guards came too soon, and she couldn't siphon off any magic before they hauled her off the ground and forced her to walk with them. She never saw anyone when they took her out of the dungeon. If they were ever around, they knew to hide. The last time she had tried to fight back, they had punched her so hard she blacked out. Her eye was still swollen. So she went with them, head down, searching for any chance of escape. Those chances never came. No one was coming for her. They still blindfolded her. Each time they removed the hood, she was strapped to the wooden table, the enchanter smiled down at her through lips redder than a rose.

Calla turned her head to face the stone wall. She would count those stones today. One, two, three, she wouldn't look at the enchanter as she circled her.

One, two, three, four, Calla watched her move over to her worktable. She rummaged through Raven's poisons. Morgan still hadn't gotten anything from her. Though she had asked questions, Calla had refused as the poison had worn off. She would not break.

"Let's see how you handle this one," she whispered, forcing Calla's eyes open. She dropped two droplets into Calla's eyes.

Calla shut her eyes, trying to make herself cry. Not Chaos, anything but that. She didn't want to know what she would see again. But she didn't get it out in time as darkness swamped her mind, and her entire reality changed.

Calla opened her eyes at the sound of laughter.

It wasn't just any laughter, though that had Calla scrambling to clear her vision. It was her laughter...Ella's laughter. Calla twisted in her bindings, relaxing when she saw Ella.

Her friend.

She stood next to her, smiling at Calla. Her white hair flowed down her back; her uniform was immaculate. Jaq had done a great job with this one. It was perfect for her.

"Cinderella." Calla found a way to get her name past her lips. Tears welled in her eyes.

Her heart fractured as Ella lay down next to her on the wooden table.

"Hi, Belle." Ella gently brushed some hair out of her face. "I've missed you."

"You...too..." Calla choked out. She could do this. She could endure this torture. She would survive for them.

"You know you're never alone, right? You'll always have us by your side." Ella wrapped her arm around Calla, and she could have sworn she felt Ella's grip. Calla closed her eyes, tears falling down her cheeks. She shook in Ella's arms.

"I'm not strong enough for this, Cinderella. I can't do it."

"Yes, you can."

Calla looked at Ella. Something was hot and dripping. She felt it on her skin, the drip drip of something that should not be on her. So Calla gazed at Ella instead of whatever Morgan was doing to her. ,

"E—"

Ella's eyes flicked beyond Calla. Calla stopped short of saying her real name.

"Cinderella...I'm all alone. I'm not strong enough...not this time."

"You are strong enough, Belle. I know it hurts, but you must survive. Find your motivation. Use it, embrace it."

"There's nothing to fight for anymore," she whispered. The heat was becoming unbearable. What were they putting on her? She couldn't move her hands to touch it, couldn't wipe it off.

"There is. Just listen to them. Listen to how they talk," Ella whispered. Calla turned her attention away from Ella, focusing her hearing on what Morgan was saying.

"Both are responding the same way. Just laying there and speaking to someone. Neither one provided anything useful from this poison. I expected Guard Raven to put up some resistance, but I didn't expect it from a common maid."

"Do you think Guard Raven trained her?" One of Morgan's little assistants walked over to the table where she stood, making notes. Calla noted the dripping on her skin had stopped.

Ella whispered in Calla's ear, "Isn't it strange they're talking about Raven as though she's still alive?"

Calla didn't respond. If they could hear her, she didn't want to give anything away. Calla's hope sparked in her, her magic swirling to her, singing throughout her body.

"I miss you, Cinderella," she whispered, one last tear breaking free.

"I miss you too, my love." Ella pressed her head against Calla's forehead. "You are strong. You will survive them. Chaos is running out now. The pain will come in full force. Remember your motivation, Belle. Let it guide you."

"Bones of my ancestors." Calla whispered. The burning along her neck and arm intensified.

"Blood of my veins." Ella flickered out of her vision as Chaos left her, and in its wake slow ripples of burning heat flickered over her skin that deepened with each passing second until her entire body pulsed in pain.

Calla gulped back her screams. What had they done to her? She turned her head down and saw candle wax had built up on her arm. Calla shook, needing to tear it off.

"Get it off. Get it off, get it off." The words burst from her lips before she could even think to stop herself. Morgan turned to face her, smiling. Then she turned back to her worktable, ignoring Calla.

Calla's chest beat rapidly, her magic rising to meet the pain. She reined it in. She would not lose control, not in a place where she couldn't direct her magic. Calla turned her head to the side and began counting the stones.

Calla was dropped into her cell. She sat defiantly as they chained, watching them leave. The candle wax that had been spilled across chest and shoulders had fully cooled on her skin. Once the footsteps disappeared, Calla peeled the wax from her arm. She flinched as it pulled on the hairs on her arms, breaking off into pieces.

The majority of it had been poured right between her breasts so that it slowly dripped down under her gown. Her fingers shook the longer it took to remove the wax, removing skin with some of the larger chunks. Tears gathered in her eyes as she chipped away at it. She was strong. She could survive, would survive. Her hands faintly glowed as her power built to soothe her. It pushed against her, requesting release. Every day her magic grew back stronger than the day before, and every day she siphoned it into the stones, though she wasn't sure how much more power they could store.

Calla sniffled as she removed one large piece from her shoulder, squeezing her eyes shut as flesh came off with it.

"Calla?" Adam whispered. He had sneaked up on her.

She flinched away from his gaze. Adam knelt before her in the dimming sun's rays. She stared at him in silence, unable to move.

She snapped her head around when confident footsteps echoed down the hall.

"Hide."

It was all Calla could say before she would be heard. Adam stepped away, pulling the hood over his cloak as he backed away to the side and into the shadows. Calla turned her back on the bars. She didn't need to see whoever was coming down to gloat.

"Calla, is that how you welcome royalty to your dungeon?"

She stiffened at the light sound of Princess Arianna's voice. Calla didn't turn. She didn't want her to see the tears or the defeat in her eyes. She wouldn't turn around until she knew she could stand tall and face the princess.

"Here I was coming with a gift, and you're being rude to me."

"Why?"

"Well, I can't tell you why you're being rude to me. I've done nothing to deserve such a response," Princess Ariana said.

"Why did you bring me a gift?" Calla clarified.

"Well, last night in my room, Prince Adam confided in me how much he missed his home." Princess Arianna paused.

She didn't get a reaction. Calla wouldn't be moved. She schooled her features and took a breath.

"And I had to wonder if you missed your home."

"I have no home," Calla replied.

"Really?" Princess Arianna's voice gave Calla pause. She knew something, and Calla was about to find out what it was.

"Yes. I have no home." Calla turned to face the princess so she could get a better read on her.

"Not even this one?" Princess Arianna asked.

She held out a mirror the size of a book in an ornate golden frame and passed it through the bars.

"Go on, take it; it's not a trick." Princess Arianna assured as she shook the mirror.

Calla reached out slowly and cradled it in her hands. A small cabin sat on the edge of some trees, with a mill attached to it and the river running beside it. The sun was setting around the cabin, casting it in an orange hue. Calla tilted her head. She had never seen this cabin before.

The door opened, and two girls, young women, she realized, ran outside. Their dresses were plain but well cared for. Their curly long black hair whipped around their faces.

Calla's heart stopped as she gripped the mirror tightly.

"Now you see your home," Princess Arianna said, her voice filled with malicious glee.

Calla's fingers hovered over the mirror, as though she could reach through and grab them.

"Iris...Rose..."

"You see, Lady Tremaine sent some information to us about you. And it turns out you have a family. Your sisters, what are they now? Ten?"

"Twelve."

"Twelve." Princess Arianna stood and looked down at Calla. "You should know that this is not a memory scry. My enchanter is there right now, sending this to you."

"Your enchanter..."

"Yes, like I said earlier, I wanted to give you a gift. And what better gift to give than a reminder of family?"

Calla looked down at the mirror of her sisters. Sisters she hadn't seen in eight years. Hadn't dreamed of seeing for fear of Lady Tremaine's retribution. And there they were, smiling, laughing...did they even remember her? They had only been four when she left.

"Now, give me the mirror." Princess Arianna stuck out her hand, waiting.

Calla handed it back as the mirror dimmed, and the image of her sisters vanished.

Calla's heart thundered in her chest, her magic pushing against her to be unleashed. She pulled it back, balling it up. She was strong. She was loved. She did not break.

She did not break. Calla repeated it over as Princess Arianna walked away.

They had found her sisters. Her innocent sisters, who knew nothing about who she was. Who probably thought she had died. They had found them and...Calla tore at the wax pressing into her chest, the weight suddenly becoming too much to bear.

She held back what remained in her stomach as it tore skin. Better to experience the physical pain than the onslaught she felt inside as her power continued to crescendo.

"So you never lied to me?" Adam stepped back into the setting sunlight.

Calla swirled around.

"How could I have been so stupid?" Adam asked. He walked up to the bars, his hands gripping them. "Every time I try to believe you, you throw it back in my face."

"Adam —"

"You told me you didn't have a family. You said they died."

"I was protecting them, Adam," Calla said. She walked up to him, the chains pulling her arms back as she got as close to him as she could.

"Well, that worked out marvelously, didn't it?"

"What would you have done, If you were me? You saw...she all but threatened their lives the moment she discovered their existence." Calla's face crumbled, saliva coated her mouth as she tried to calm herself. "I have nothing without them..."

"Then tell Queen Lyanna what she wants to know. She'll let you —"

"The only way I am getting out of here is in a coffin. To think otherwise is foolish, and if you think I will trade any information for the lives of people I love, then you really know nothing about me. "

"Well, if parading your sisters in front of you didn't get you to talk, then nothing will."

"Princess Arianna didn't do that to get information out of me. She did it to let me know she can do whatever she wants to them."

"Well, you know what they say, 'all is fair in love and war'."

"No, it's not," Calla snapped. "Love is worse."

Adam stepped back from her. Calla pulled on the chains until they shook with the strain.

"Love is pain, anger, and a passion so deep it has the power to shred your soul into a thousand pieces." Calla tried to get closer as she locked eyes with him. "But love is also beautiful, compassionate, and precious. Love makes your heart fly so high you never want to stop feeling something so raw and pure. War is war. It's hateful, bloody, and disgusting. There is nothing to gain from it but pain, death, and some fucking land. War is war, and love is love. And they are never fair."

Adams' arms dropped to his side before leaving.

Calla didn't see if he looked back as she turned around and focused on the remaining wax stuck to her skin, ignoring the way her vision blurred. Eventually, Calla gave up. Her heart and her body were exhausted, and she needed as much rest as possible before whatever torture they had in store for her tomorrow.

CHAPTER TWENTY

Mira

"Prince Adam." Mira stepped back in surprise from her door. She was about to head out to locate Calla.

"Princess Miraya, can we speak?"

"We're speaking now, aren't we?" Mira leaned against her door frame, arms crossed, denying him access.

"Can it be in private?" Adam whispered. His brilliant green eyes were wide as he fidgeted in front of her.

Mira kept her face expressionless. "What did you want to speak about?" Mira remained by the door, resisting the urge to count down the minutes this took from her. Why did he, out of anyone, have to be here? Besides, what could he possibly say to her after all these years?

"I'm sorry."

Mira's arms fell to her sides. No one, let alone Prince Adam, had apologized to her before for what had happened.

"You're...sorry..." Mira leaned against the wall as she watched a formerly angry prince pace in front of her, twisting his hands.

"I should have apologized years ago...only recently have I realized..." Adam stopped talking as he walked over to her and held her hands in his.

She gazed into the only pair of eyes that had ever equaled her own in beauty, ignoring the rough callous's on the hands that firmly, yet gently held her own.

"I'm sorry I told our fathers about you kissing that servant, and for everything that happened afterward with our engagement." Prince Adam bowed his head before her. "I'm not asking for your forgiveness, but I needed you to know how sorry I am, especially for everything that happened after I left."

He stepped away from her, head downcast.

Mira was glad he couldn't see her face. It gave her the time she needed to compose herself. She didn't need him to see the fear that struck her at the mention of what happened...after...after Prince Adam and his father had left...after her life had been blown apart like a tropical storm tearing through a village. No...he didn't get to see the trauma that still lived in every bone of her body, worming its way through her until some days she wasn't sure she could exist in a world where she didn't feel it.

"I have to admit, Adam, I never expected this from you. What made you change your mind? Surely not finding out what happened to me, that could have been a simple letter," Mira commented.

"I may have been told by someone that I was a self-entitled prick who never took responsibility for the things I did."

Mira laughed. "Who had the courage to say that to the likes of you? I know it wasn't precious Princess Arianna."

Adam blushed. "No one important," he muttered. "Well, not anymore. She's just as bad as the rest of the liars at court."

"Well then, we must concoct a plan to take her down."

"NO!"

Mira raised her eyebrows at him.

"I mean, you can't. She's not at court anymore. She...left."

Mira cocked a hip but let the poor white lie go. She would figure out who it was, eventually. She just wasn't sure if she would rather kiss the girl, or sink her into the depths of court politics.

"She must have been very special if she could be so candid with you." Mira pushed off the wall and moved over to her bed.

"She was...no one else had been that open with me, or I with them since...you," Adam said just loud enough for her to hear his confession. He sat down on the chaise under her window and hung his head in his hands.

"We were quite a pair." Mira paused as she bit her lip. "I'm sorry too, you know. About what I did. I didn't want to get married to anyone, and I guess...well, I always enjoyed pissing off my father."

Adam winced. He must know a lot then, Mira mused. She was surprised by that fact. Of course, when they had been courting, she had told him about her life, but that particular event...well, her father had done his best to keep those events contained.

Adam nodded his head.

"So..." Mira paused until he looked at her. "What are we doing to get you out of this arranged marriage?"

"Nothing."

"Adam —"

"Nothing. We...I...can do nothing." He turned away from her.

"They have something over you."

Adam flicked his eyes to her and away, turning his attention outside her window.

"Don't worry about me. I'm not worth saving, Miraya."

Mira got off her bed and walked over to kneel in front of him. She took his hand and squeezed. "Everyone is worth saving."

Mira walked down the hall in a dark green gown. It was so dark it appeared black. She couldn't wear sneak suits like the others. Not in her role. She had to always have a good reason she was somewhere she shouldn't be, and she usually found that wearing something beautiful and seductive worked just as easily as being a shadow.

Adam had left shortly after their conversation ended, informing her of the imposed curfew. Mira thanked him and promptly ignored his comment. She could get around just fine and had no worries about talking herself out of trouble, should she be caught.

She had never walked through a palace that had a curfew. The empty halls and dim candles created minimal light and sent a shiver down her spine. She had been in plenty of weird places in her work. Courtesan houses were not always a beautiful sight. While you could count on them to be discrete, it did not always mean they were clean or void of spiderwebs. Her first objective was to get a better sense of the palace's layout. Its twisting hallways seemed to go in directions that made little sense, and informed her that there was probably a hidden series of tunnels for her to find.

Candlelight poked out from several doors as she padded through the palace. Voices could be heard in hushed tones where the noblemen lived, while the servants' quarters were only slightly more boisterous. This is where Calla had lived, Mira realized. She wondered which room had been hers and if she could search it without being caught.

Mira approached the north wing of the palace. It was worn down and horribly kept. But scones lit the way. Mira raised an eyebrow as she continued down the empty hallway. These rooms had been truly abandoned by their occupants. Mira stopped when she came to a wall. The hallway ended directly against a wall with nothing to indicate why it would dead end. Mira tilted her head.

"Excuse me, there's a curfew. Get back to your room."

Mira paused as his voice hit her. She turned around and came face to face with Bastien. He stopped in his tracks and turned to his partner, a handsome guard with curling brown hair and charming blue eyes. Bastien whispered to him, and the other one stepped back to have a view of the crossing hallways as Bastien approached her.

"Apologies, I got lost looking for the kitchen."

"The kitchen is closed," Bastien replied.

"Damn. I'm really craving some excellent bread. I guess it can wait until morning. Maybe one of the other royal guards can show me to my room?" Mira pointedly stared at the other guard.

"I could —"

"No," Mira snapped. "Literally anyone but you. Even that disgraced guard would be better than you."

"Princess Miraya —"

"No. You don't get to say anything to me. Not after everything that happened because you needed to climb the ladder in front of my father. I'm happy to see you've continued that trend here. I heard that the former guard was quite impressive. I'll bet you couldn't stand that a woman was outshining you. Tell me, did you sabotage that guard and frame her for treason?"

"I wouldn't." Bastien took a step towards as he lowered his voice. "I wouldn't betray anyone like that, especially Raven."

"So, it's only me you don't mind betraying," Mira said. She looked around the hallway and swallowed the nausea that roiled in her stomach. She blinked quickly to get the image of Bastien six years ago barging into the horse stalls out of her mind.

"I wanted to —"

"I've had enough apologies tonight," Mira said. She worked up a sob. It came to her more easily than she had expected. "I hear that that guard may have had an accomplice or others helping her, and I'm lost, and I just want to get to my room." She let the tears fall down her cheeks.

"If you would like my partner Charles to take you to the correct wing, he would be more than capable," Bastien said softly. "And don't worry about her accomplices. The only one remaining was captured and thrown into the dungeon. She's not going anywhere."

Mira sniffled. She looked around Bastien to Charles. "You sure you don't mind being separated? It's not breaking any rules?" She raised her voice.

"It's not." Bastien stood stiffly.

"Good." Mira waved Charles over. "Do they..." she paused, feigning a sob again, "does anyone know you're from Grecia or that you served in my house?"

"They know I'm from Grecia." He motioned to his red hair. "But not that I know you."

"See that it stays that way." Mira sniffled once more, rubbing a tear as Charles reached them.

"Guard Charles, if you wouldn't mind escorting Princess Miraya to her room, I know she would be most grateful."

"Of course," Charles replied.

Charles walked down the hallway, leading Mira back to her room. As she followed him, she planned out her next move.

"How was your journey here?" Charles asked in a stuttered Grecian.

Mira rested a hand on his shoulder. "It was utterly boring," she replied in Evrotian. Charles smiled at the kindness. Truthfully, she was impressed he had tried speaking her native language at all. She wrapped an arm around Charles, slowing him down to her speed. "I'm hoping to find more entertaining distractions here. Any suggestions?" She squeezed his arm playfully.

"If you search in the right places, I'm sure you'll find it."

"Might you be able to help me?" Mira ran a hand up his arm.

"If I might offer a word of caution," Charles said. "Recent events have made a lot of us cautious. So you might find everyone less inclined to be the type of distraction you're looking for until everything settles down."

"I thought everything was settled when the traitor died," Mira replied. Had something else happened to Raven?

Charles stopped walking and stood in front of her.

"If you haven't heard yet, no one within the palace may leave until the traitor is found and brought back for justice."

"What do you mean? What happened?"

"The traitor escaped —"

Mira tried to focus on everything else Charles shared with her, but she couldn't get past those three words. Raven was alive.

"Are you okay, Princess Miraya?" Charles gently touched her shoulder.

"Yes. Should I be afraid the traitor will come back?"

"You have nothing to worry about. Everyone is on high alert, and no one can leave until she's dealt with."

Mira ignored the churning in her stomach.

"You don't think she'll return for her accomplice?"

"She doesn't know we have her. And Astrid...Raven wouldn't dare come back here after everything that happened."

Astrid? Mira ground her teeth. Sir Conrad knew nothing, and she only had more questions than answers. By the time Mira got out of her thoughts, Charles was stopping in front of her door.

"Guard Charles, thank you for the escort."

"I am at your service." Charles stepped away from her.

"Guard Charles, might I ask, the traitor's accomplice, there's no chance she'll escape?"

His eyes softened. "None. She's in the dungeon's basement, chained to the floor. Not even the traitor had escaped her jail cell."

Mira figured out where the dungeon and Calla were, and she was going to take advantage of this curfew while she could. She had spent the previous night wandering the halls, listening for Charles and Bastien until she found the dungeon's main entrance. She knew she couldn't go that way without someone seeing her. But given the location of the dungeon and north wing, she had a feeling there was another way in there; she just had to find it.

It was in the old guard's wing that was now vacant due to the queen's inability to keep her guards fully staffed. She slipped in easily now that she knew the way. For how cruel the queen was, Mira expected the dungeon to be swimming with citizens, and while there were some, including a woman who had begged before the queen that morning, it was mostly empty.

Mira didn't ponder for too long if it was a bad thing or a good thing that the dungeon didn't seem to hold prisoners. She hoped it meant that the guards chose to release them after a short while instead of what she assumed was the reason. Moisture dripped down the walls as Mira got farther into the dungeon. Moss and mildew grew in the crevices. She could see her breath in the air as she pulled her cloak tighter around her. Mira's torch flickered, granting her desperate heat.

She found Calla huddled in the middle of her cell.

For a moment, all Mira could do was stare at her. Her precious flower was curled up in what had to have once been the most beautiful gown. Mira had never seen anything quite like it, and she wished she could have seen Calla in all her splendor dancing in it.

Then Mira saw past the shredded gown and noticed everything else about the woman she cared for the most in the world. Calla's hair was tangled and stuck out at all angles around her, and she shook on the floor as she held herself.

"Calla?" Though she whispered, her voice seemed to shout as Calla's name slipped through her lips.

Calla turned to face her, and that once innocent face she loved was now burdened with the reality of their life. Her dark skin appeared dry, and her lips were cracked and bleeding. Mira stepped close to the bars and reached out a hand to her.

"Mira?" Calla croaked. "How?"

"I felt something was wrong, so I got on the first ship I could find."

"You traveled from Rairene on a hunch?"

Mira almost laughed at Calla's rationalization of her insanity, but it was true. All she'd had when coming here was a feeling that something was wrong. Ella had encouraged it even, now she knew why.

"I did. I had to make sure my flower was okay." Mira knelt down to be at eye level with her. "What happened? I've barely been able to get a glimpse —"

"Everyone is dead." Calla broke into tears as her entire body seemed to release itself from all of the burdens it was holding. Her hands flickered with power for a moment before it was gone.

Mira tried to reach out to her, but she was too far away. "Calla —"

"All our friends...killed...and I don't...I can't...Mira, what do we do?" Her speech was garbled as she spoke through her sobs while crawling over to Mira.

"Flower, take a slow breath." Mira took one herself. She exhaled calmness. This was already information she knew. Information she couldn't process until Calla was on the right side of her cell. "Again, another deep breath," Mira said as she pressed herself against the bars to grab Calla's hand. It was frighteningly cold and rough with calluses.

Calla squeezed her hand back and didn't let go.

"Let me ease some burden. I already know about Ella." Mira's voice caught when said Ella's name. She would never...no...she couldn't focus on that. Calla was here now, and she needed her. Mira squeezed Calla's hand as she looked at her through blurry eyes.

Calla's head fell as she took another breath. They could do this. Together, they could get through this. "Jaq died too."

"I know you cared deeply for him." Mira squeezed her hand. She had cared for Jaq as well, but she had barely had any interaction with him. Whenever she needed something enchanted, she went to Calla or Gwylan, her very discrete friend.

Calla gripped Mira's hand. "Raven is dead." She spoke so fast Mira almost missed what she said. "At least, I think she is. I heard of her execution, but my torturer refers to her in the present tense, so I'm uncertain."

"Raven escaped. I don't know how. It involves another guard and Prince Aleksander, from what I can tell," Mira rushed. She continued gripping Calla's hand.

"You're sure?" Calla sniffled.

"I'm sure." Mira smiled. "Snow is alive, and being called Astrid?"

Calla huffed. "She's the long lost princess of Evrotia."

Mira's jaw dropped.

"I think that's what happened when I found out," Calla said. She sniffled again, but she was smiling.

Mira adjusted herself into a more comfortable position. "How?"

Calla launched into everything that had happened over the last few months. Mira continued holding her hand, using it as her anchor to the world. It was an anchor she needed as Calla revealed everything Lord Conrad couldn't or wouldn't share with her.

By the time she left, the sun was lightening the sky, but Mira didn't care. All she did care about was the knowledge that she had to get Calla out.

CHAPTER TWENTY-ONE

Drea

Six Weeks Before Drea's Accident

The dinner was a more intimate setting than Drea had expected. It was in a private dining room with the king, Prince David, Princess Celeste, Princess Lena's entourage, and several of the king's advisers. They sat at a long table, and having a private conversation with anyone would be nearly impossible. Luckily, Drea and Liam were of little importance and had been relegated to the end of the table, far away from Princess Lena.

"What's the most exciting thing you've done since coming here?" Liam asked as they began their first course.

"Well, I don't know if anything can be as exciting as the horse races back home, but I would have to say the winter balls are the most exciting," Drea said.

Even Liam was not allowed to know who she was or what she did in the night. He couldn't know her genuine answer was repelling down the side of a stronghold wall from four stories up after defeating several guards. Or that she enjoyed the challenge of horse riding with a bow and arrow during shooting practice, and that her stepsister Ella always proved to be her biggest challenge with knife fighting.

"What makes the winter ball so exciting and why haven't we come to it yet?" Liam asked. His blue eyes were full of mirth and curiosity.

"There's something about being under the stars with the crisp air touching your skin while dancing with someone."

"The winter ball is outside?" Liam questioned.

"Definitely not. But I always find my way outside, and sometimes I have someone there to dance with as we cool down —"

"Or heat up." Liam winked.

"Well, when you get cold, you need someone to help you heat up," Drea murmured.

"Maybe one day I can experience dancing under the stars with you."

Drea smiled, turning away to hide the blush rising in her cheeks.

"Do you still race your horse?" It was the only topic Drea felt was safe to mention. She'd been courted before, but not by anyone she knew so well.

Liam smiled at her. "Every year. Though Aleks has been getting better and will probably win this year."

"Well, only if Cai allows it," Drea commented before she could stop herself. Prince Cai was well known for his brash and controlling personality. However, Liam....

"He's only behaving in a manner befitting his station, Drizella," Liam replied. "I know he can be abrasive, but it's what he's been raised to do."

"You're right. I was out of line in saying that. I apologize." The last thing Drea wanted to do was cause an incident between Rairene and Trudel over her judgment of a prince.

Liam accepted her apology with a brusk nod and went back to eating their second course of a delicious thick stew filled with potatoes and chunks of beef. Throughout the rest of the dinner, the two of them spoke on lighter topics, reminiscing about the time Drea had lived in Trudel. It was just the two of them at a table filled with people. Their small corner of the room felt private as they talked and ignored the rest of the surrounding people.

"Let's move to the lounge," King Matthias proclaimed.

Drea looked up in surprise. Had dinner ended already? She turned her attention to the rest of the room to realize they had gone through all of their courses and were relocating. She got up to follow at the end of the train of people, Liam beside her.

"Come with me," Liam whispered. He grabbed her hand and pulled her down the hallway.

"Where are we going?" Drea asked as they continued to walk down the hall.

"You'll see," Liam replied, smiling back at her as they hurried away from everyone else.

Liam finally seemed happy with what he found as he slowed down, straightened his tunic, and squared his shoulders before opening a door that led to the gardens. The cool night air washed over Drea as she sighed. Liam turned to face her with that charming smile back on his face. He gently took her hand and pulled Drea in close before leading her in a dance that had her magic unraveling under the touch of his fingers on her skin. She stared at Liam, his blue eyes locked on her.

"Have I mentioned yet how much I missed seeing you?" Liam asked, stepping close enough that he was just a breath away from her.

"Not in so many words, but I missed you too," Drea replied. She kept her eyes locked on him until they became perfectly still, wrapped in each other's arms. "Liam..."

He cut her off with the gentle brush of his lips against hers, all thoughts of protest vanishing as she leaned into him.

Her heart fluttered as Liam's arms wrapped around her waist to press her against him. She responded in kind, her hands twisting through his hair as she did all that she could to have them as close together as possible. Drea kept her eyes closed, diving into the moment of feeling him, memorizing the way his hands sent shivers down her spine every time he teasingly ran them up and down her back or the way his lips felt pressed against hers. The entire kingdom faded until it was only Drea and Hen...Liam.

It was Liam she was kissing.

Drea's magic continued to build inside her as guilt and joy warred for supremacy. Kissing Liam was like...nothing she had experienced before. Drea was keenly aware of how desirable she was to the men of the court, but none of them had made her feel wanted or special the way Liam had. Not even Henry had paid her this much attention.

Drea shook away all thoughts of Henry as Liam's lips found the gentle curve of her neck, shocking a gasp from her lips.

"Well, I certainly hope I'm interrupting something scandalous," Anastasia said, her voice filled with playful amusement as she stepped into their private part of the garden.

"We were only dancing," Drea quipped, taking a small step back from Liam.

"If that was dancing, then I need better partners."

"As always, Ana, your timing is impeccable," Liam muttered.

"You should thank me for my timing. Prince David and several members of the court are about to come out here," Anastasia replied, shooting a knowing glance at Drea.

"Why would that matter? They don't even seem to know who Drizella is," Liam said through gritted teeth.

"Her reputation could be ruined, Liam. Now be quiet," Anastasia commanded.

Liam clamped his mouth shut as Prince David, Henry, and several other courtiers' voices reached them. Prince David stopped abruptly when he noticed them standing before him.

"Lady Anastasia, Lady Drizella, and Commander Liam, I didn't expect to see you out here. Isn't Lady Tremaine heading home?"

"She is. We had wanted to go for a short walk before getting back into the carriage. We were just on our way back to her," Anastasia explained. She grabbed Drea's hand and pulled softly.

"Lady Drizella, are you okay?" Prince David asked.

Drea gave him a quizzical brow. He was never so formal with her, though she supposed it made sense with Liam and others around.

"Your hair," Anastasia whispered.

Drea felt her hair to discover it was in shambles from Liam. Not for the first time that night, Drea was ecstatic it was too dark to see how red her face had become.

"Oh, yes. I tripped on some rocks and got my hair caught in a bush."

"I see...well...make sure you're careful on your way out," Prince David said as he, Lena, and Henry began to walk away.

Drea made eye contact with Henry, shame washing over her as she felt his eyes on her. Which was silly. She shouldn't feel ashamed for having some fun with Liam. Henry wasn't courting her.

Present Day

Drea gripped Ana's hand as they approached the palace. Both of them wore black gowns as they sat side by side in their carriage. Lena had taken her own carriage behind them, claiming she wanted some time to herself. At least she got to spend some time alone with her sister.

Ana squeezed her hand, leaning her head on Drea's shoulder.

"Everything will be okay. None of them would dare say a word to you about your scars." Ana commented.

"I...know..." Drea spoke slowly. Of course, none of them would say anything to her. That would happen after...after they laughed and pretended to be friends...only then would they comment on her scars once she was gone. "I'm nervous about...her...being there."

"Her?" Ana sat. "Oh...Gwen. I can kill her if you want me to."

Drea smiled softly at her sister's reaction. "Don't do that, Ana. We can't afford anything to link back to us." Drea added quickly. She couldn't have Ana thinking she had gone soft on killing threats.

"You're right, of course." Ana sighed as she leaned back against Drea. "I'm tired, Drea. I just want everything to end." Ana spoke softly, as though she didn't want the driver to hear.

"I feel the same. Hopefully, it's soon. Any word from Queen Laila on when she wants to make her move?"

"We move when she says we move, Drea," Ana snapped.

"I know, but maybe we could plan a fun trip. Just you and me. We could go visit Trudel in the summer?" Drea asked. While a trip did sound divine, she wanted to see what her sister knew and wasn't telling her about the queen's plans. How much was being kept from her?

"That sounds nice. Maybe we can go back with Lena? We won't have a reason to be here anymore by then, anyway." Ana shifted, wrapping her arms around Drea's waist. "Unless, of course, a certain Prince's Champion has started to pursue you again." Ana teased.

"He's engaged, besides, per mother, I'm still not supposed to see him. I feel like I've betrayed her from just those two instances, and those were approved by the queen." Drea vented.

"You could still see him, Drea. I don't think the queen knows about Mother's rules, and I wouldn't say anything." Ana whispered as she hugged Drea.

Drea leaned her head on Ana's. "Thank you..." She spoke softly as tears choked her. "It still doesn't solve my 'he's engaged' problem."

"Go meet her then. Determine how much of a threat she is, or show her that Henry belongs to you and that she needs to give him up."

Drea chuckled.

"I'm being serious, Drea. Take her to that cafe you love and assess her." Ana sat back up as the palace came into view.

"I'll think about it. Maybe after tonight we'll have a better idea about her," Drea replied. She rested her head on the soft, cushioned wall of the carriage and closed her eyes. Her magic was a disaster at the moment. It fluctuated and twisted against the dance she tried to get it to perform. While she wanted it to spin in a slow waltz, and it wanted to pound the earth and dance to drums. It was a beautiful rhythm she couldn't control. Drea spun her magic round and round until it found its way back into her slow, steady beat.

As the footman opened the doors, Drea stepped out with her magic in control and her hands firmly clutched together around her cane. Stairs were still proving to be a nuisance throughout her training, and the ones in front of the palace had always been daunting. Drea gripped her cane and took a few steps, not bothering to wait for Ana or Lena. Both of them would outpace her before she could get halfway. She paused after a few steps and assessed her leg. So far, so good. Drea took a few more, testing her legs' endurance each time by taking more steps between breaks. A flicker of a cramp twisted her leg for a moment when she was five steps away from the top. Drea willed it gone, blinking against the twinge and moving through it as she reached the top.

Ana and Lena waited for her there, both deep in conversation.

"What did I miss?" Drea asked as she reached them. Ana was smiling as Lena whispered something to her.

"Lena was giving me a status update on the search for Luca. We might have him," Anastasia replied.

"Wow, really? Where did he go into hiding?" Drea did her best to hide her complete shock. She truly hadn't expected that answer, especially since she had heard nothing about Luca since handing over his portrait to Henry.

"Well, that and Ana was telling me about her master plan to have you meet Gwen and threaten her away from Henry. I think it's a wonderful idea," Princess Lena interrupted.

"I told Ana I would think about it more after tonight," Drea responded. "Shouldn't you discourage me from courting Henry?"

Princess Lena sighed dramatically. "Our mothers are stuck in the past. I think a woman should be able to enjoy herself while also honoring her oaths. I know you wouldn't tell Henry anything. If you were going to, it would have been back before...everything..." Princess Lena said. Drea once again schooled her features as Lena surprised her with her views.

"Besides, nothing says you can't spy on him at the same time. I actually think you would get more information from him that way. I'm shocked your mother didn't have you do that; it would have been such a simple thing to accomplish."

Drea remained silent. Lena was correct, of course. It was astounding her mother hadn't thought of that. Though her mother also knew Drea could never betray Henry either, something Drea would need to keep from Lena.

"Let's go, shall we? The sooner we get through this dinner, the better. I don't know how much more grief and wallowing I can take from Princess Celeste or the king."

Drea followed Lena and Ana in silence. Her cane thumping on the floor was the only sound as they walked through an empty hallway. The palace had gone silent since the news about David being hidden had spread. All balls would be canceled. All feasts postponed. The palace was frozen, waiting for its prince to breathe life back into its depths.

"Princess Lenaria, Lady Anastasia, and Lady Drizella, your majesties," the palace crier announced.

Drea walked in behind them to a dining room that was small compared to the typical banquet hall they feasted. King Matthias sat at the head of the table with Celeste beside him. Both of them wore smiles plastered on their faces as they stood and walked over to Princess Lena. King Matthias hugged her with one arm, while Celeste did the same before they went back to their seats with Lena seated on King Matthias's left. Drea surveyed the room and spotted Lord Andrew and his wife, along with another visiting diplomat from Grecia. The red-haired woman turned, and Drea could have sworn Mira sat in front of her. The princesses eyes were the same shade of emerald green, with a smile that matched. Her gown was in the traditional Grecian style of light, flowing fabrics dyed to match the varying colors of the sea. However, she was also adorned with armor on her shoulders and several loose gold chains that dropped in layers around her bust and back. Her outfit was made formal by a sash going across her body and another wrapped around her waist to pull the loose fabric into shape. The crown on her head was gold and barely discernible amongst her fire colored hair.

"I hope you don't mind, Princess Lena, that Princess Maliah is visiting us. She'll be in port for a few days before going down to Evrotia, and I didn't want her to dine alone in her chambers," King Matthias explained as Princess Maliah smiled at Drea.

"Of course not. I haven't seen Princess Maliah in years and have always enjoyed her company. Wasn't there some type of scandal the last time I visited?" Princess Lena asked, her voice pitched higher than normal.

Drea looked at Princess Mahliah, noticing the way the features on her face shifted just slightly at the mention of a scandal before going back into place. She took a seat beside Henry, opting for that instead of being forced to sit near Princess Lena.

"There was, but it's been handled," Princess Mahliah responded with poise as she cut into a roasted carrot and ate it, blatantly ignoring Lena.

"Do you have a sister? You look just like a friend of ours," Anastasia said, leaning forward.

"I have six, and we all look similar, though I'm not sure how you could know any of us. None of them besides me has ever left Grecia."

"Well, besides that *one*..." Princess Lena offered.

"Is she in Evrotia? Is that why you're going there?" Anastasia asked, her eyes large as she got closer to Mahliah.

"No, and frankly, my reasons for travel are none of your concern," Princess Mahliah snapped.

Anastasia leaned back at the chastisement. She primly grabbed a fork and took a bite of her roasted potatoes. Ana promptly turned a shoulder towards Princess Mahliah.

"Lady Drizella, how have you been? Is there anything the palace can do for you and any funeral arrangements?" King Matthias asked a few minutes later.

"Preparations are underway, Your Majesty. I think we'll be having her funeral in Trudel, but I thank you for your kind offer. We're all doing as well as expected in our circumstances," Drea answered as she did all that she could to not stare at Anastasia.

"Please let me or Lord Andrew know about any assistance you need, no matter the request. We both want to ensure you and Lady Anastasia are well taken care of."

"We will." Drea slightly bowed her head in thanks. "How are you doing?"

"I hope we can have David back home soon. Though how he'll do with Eleanor's death...I'm not sure." King Matthias slumped in his chair. "I have some good news to share. Lord Andrew's men informed him they're close to discovering Luca. To think we allowed him into our home to guard David only to have him be the one to murder our dear Ella and your mother." King Matthias pounded his fists on the table.

"I'm sure that once caught, he'll be brought to swift justice," Princess Lena remarked. "Henry, are we going to be graced by your charming fiancée? I would love to meet the woman who has captured your affections." Lena turned the conversation once more away to safer waters.

"Unfortunately, Gwen had to stay home tonight. She passes along her apologies to the king," Henry said, turning to the king for the apology.

"I'm starting to think Gwen isn't real, Henry. That or she's doing all she can to avoid me," Princess Lena teased, though the edge in her voice suggested otherwise.

Henry's face lightly flushed as he took a bite of chicken. He chewed slowly before responding, "I can assure you, Princess Lena, that Gwen means no offense. She's not one for social events, and sometimes her nerves get the better of her."

"She must have been quite the match to have nerves that afflicting, yet still remain engaged to one of the highest ranking members of the court. I can only imagine how many social engagements you might have to attend on your own." Princess Lena commented.

"I know I would rather be at home reading a good book near a fire right now," Drea retorted.

"Yes. You would, and yet..." Princess Lena let the end of her sentence hang in the air.

Drea, of course, knew the end of the sentence, and yet she hadn't been enough to secure an engagement to Henry. She knew it. Everyone in the room, excluding Princess Maliah knew it. Drea held her gaze with Lena, begging her to drop it. So what if she hadn't met Gwen? She didn't matter in the scheme of things. Henry was too loyal to David to have any leverage with her. Gwen was a useless pawn in their game and should be left alone.

"Lady Drizella, what book are you currently reading? I find that I have too much time on my hands while sailing," Princess Maliah asked.

Drea flushed. "Um, well, it's a —"

"What my baby sister is trying to say is that she reads romances," Anastasia interrupted.

"I love a good romance," Princess Maliah said, her voice rising an octave.

"You do?" Anastasia practically sneered.

"Really?" Drea asked as she leaned forward. "I'm currently reading a book about a girl who's been locked in a tower her whole life with magical hair that she can never cut. There's a prince who found her, and he visits her by climbing the tower using her long hair."

"I've read that one. The ending is utterly delicious." Princess Mahliah practically squealed. "What's one you would recommend?"

"Have you ever read the book called 'Beauty and The Beast'?"

Princess Maliah shook her head.

"Well, it's about a young woman who sacrifices herself to save her father from a hideous beast and goes live with him. Only she learns that he's not actually —" Drea stopped herself. "I don't want to spoil it. But I will gladly lend it to you."

"Thank you." Princess Maliah shifted in her seat as she cleared her throat.

Both of them turned away from each other to find the rest of the table staring at them.

"It's a great book," Drea said.

Everyone went back to their meals, all conversation about Gwen, Princess Lena, and David forgotten. Drea turned back to her food, focusing on pulling her power back in. *Shhh*....it was longing for Henry. She could feel all of it pressing against the left side of her body, begging to dance with Henry. Drea shook out her hand, pulling her power back with the flick of her wrist. But it wasn't enough.

Drea cracked her neck and straightened her shoulders as the pressure built. Drea closed her eyes and took a calming breath as she pulled her magic back into her core. She didn't even let it dance. She spun it into a tightly wound ball and shoved it deep.

"Everything okay?" Henry whispered. He leaned close to her.

The smell of metal and mist covered grass breezed around her, and Drea almost lost all of the progress she had made on her power. She nodded her head stiffly as she finished regaining her composure. Henry reached out a hand and gently held hers.

Drea maintained her control as she slowly removed her hand from Henry's. Her magic howled in protest, fluctuating around her fingers. When she moved her hand back to Henry's, her power settled, allowing her a moment to rein it back in. Somehow, Henry's presence stilled her power in that moment. His hand was a soothing balm to the fire that threatened to consume her. Instead, because of Henry, her power allowed her to spin it back into a dance that slowly swayed within her.

Drea lingered back a moment after dinner finished, watching Lena and Anastasia walk ahead without a thought spared for her. She didn't mind, not right now, at least. Let them forget her.

Drea stood in the hallway, waiting for Princess Maliah. She walked out, standing tall beside King Matthias. Drea hadn't realized how tall the woman was until confronted by her standing just as high as the king. It also wasn't until that moment that Drea noticed she was wearing some true armor and had the physique of a trained warrior. Her arms weren't just slim, but well defined with muscles that were used to holding a blade. Drea wondered what King Matthias thought about that, or if he even knew.

"I'll leave you two to finish discussing your books," King Matthias said, smiling as he patted Drea on the shoulder.

"What can I do for you, Lady Drizella?" Princess Maliah's voice softened as she walked down the hall with Drea.

Drea held her cane in one hand, moving slowly. Princess Maliah slowed her pace until there was enough distance from them for no one to hear.

"I do have a copy of that book if you would like it?"

"I would love to borrow it, though I have a feeling there is something else you would like to discuss?" Princess Maliah questioned.

"Yes. Without causing offense, I truly think I know your sister. Is her name Mira?"

Princess Maliah stopped, her hand holding Drea's wrist. Somehow she stood taller as she turned Drea to face her. The woman before her was no longer a fellow romance book lover. Instead, Drea was gazing at the future queen of Grecia in all her righteousness. She had heard rumors about Princess Maliah. She was kind and fair to her subjects, and while she didn't inherit her father's endless anger, she knew how to be just as terrifying.

"I command you to tell me how you know about Miraya. King Matthias claimed no knowledge of her, yet this is the kingdom my father sent her to," Princess Maliah ordered with passion in her voice and fear in her eyes.

"I'm guessing your father sent her to a finishing academy for young women?"

Princess Maliah nodded.

Drea looked around to make sure no one, especially Lena or Ana, was around. "If you're able to contact Mira, you should. But you should know that she wasn't sent to a finishing school."

"What do you mean?" Maliah stepped closer.

"I can't tell you more, but we can try to meet in a few days if you would like?"

"I leave in a few days."

"Have Lord Henry bring you into Riset tomorrow morning. He'll know where to find me."

Princess Maliah nodded before parting ways. Drea walked slowly back to the front of the palace, taking her time to process what little information she had just learned about Mira. The palace hummed softly around her as servants worked on getting the palace ready for the night.

"There you are," Anastasia exclaimed, snapping Drea out of her solace. "I was worried sick. I thought your leg had cramped up, and I wasn't there to help you." Anastasia continued to ramble on as she approached Drea.

"You waited for me?"

"I'm going to do my best to not be offended by that question," Anastasia replied as she took Drea's left hand and wrapped it around hers.

They walked in silence all the way to the carriage, where Princess Lena awaited them.

"Thank you for waiting," Drea said, curtsying slightly to Lena. It was an unexpected gesture from both of them.

"Of course." Lena got inside first, facing backwards as Drea and Anastasia got in and sat beside each other. "I hope your leg is okay."

"It is, thank you. I was checking with Princess Maliah on that book I was telling her about."

Princess Lena made a noise while Ana shifted beside Drea.

"I didn't appreciate your behavior tonight, Drea. The way you spoke to me was not how I expect people of my court to conduct themselves," Princess Lena snapped.

"You were clearly making Henry uncomfortable, and Princess Maliah was getting mad with your questions about Mira."

"I was right," Anastasia exclaimed.

"Yes, and Princess Maliah knows nothing about us or her sister. So, the less attention on us, the better," Drea replied.

"How are you certain she knows nothing?"

"She told me as such. I told her I would explain everything about her sister in two days. Which I'll use to misdirect her about Mira." Drea added before either of them could get more annoyed with her.

They hadn't truly wanted to wait for her; she realized. They'd wanted to yell at her.

"What do you think King Matthias meant by 'make sure we're taken care of'?" Anastasia questioned.

"He and Lord Andrew are probably trying to figure out if we're complicit in any scheme," Drea replied. Though she knew King Matthias was being genuine, she needed to play along with Anastasia and Prince Lena. "I might add, Princess Lena, that your behavior was unbecoming of a princess. If you want to make sure the king and his champion remain free of suspicion from us, the least you can do is not behave like a child."

Princess Lena crossed her arms. "I was only having fun. You sound like my brother, Aleks. He was supposed to come on this trip, you know, to 'keep me in line'." She rolled her eyes.

"I missed out on getting to see Prince Aleksander?" Anastasia pouted.

"Mother sent him on some other assignment. I'm sure he's bored out of his mind in Evrotia."

"You don't think there's anything connected between him, Raven, and Calla, do you?" Anastasia asked.

Drea almost laughed; that had to be part of what was happening over there. "For his sake, I certainly hope not." Drea snorted. "That would be a lot of opinionated women to handle." Drea turned back to Princess Lena. "I apologize for my behavior tonight. I want you to know that everything I do is in the best interest of our kingdom, and I would hate for King Matthias to suspect us now, while we're so close."

"Thank you, Drizella," Princess Lena replied. She folded her hands together on her lap while gazing out the window.

Their ride continued in silence. Anastasia held Drea close, her head leaning on Drea's shoulder. Drea closed her eyes and did her best to ignore the feel of Princess Lena's eyes examining her. The only thing she could have done differently was to have done nothing at all. Drea wasn't sure which one was more suspicious. She just hoped she had done enough to continue Anastasia's trust in her. If she had that, then she had Lena's.

CHAPTER TWENTY-TWO

Ella

The sound of crackling wood was the first thing Ella heard as she regained consciousness. The first thing she felt was the warmth of a sturdy blanket wrapped around her. She opened her eyes slowly, blinking when she saw plain wooden walls and a thatched roof over her head.

Ella rolled onto her side, grimacing at the pain. Right, she had been pierced by an arrow, a poisoned one. Ella searched around for her daggers. She wasn't about to wander around unarmed in Holodal. She lay down when the door rattled.

David walked in.

Ella sighed, relaxing into the bed.

"Good, you're awake."

"How long have I been asleep?"

"A day." David stood over her with narrowed eyes.

Ella chewed the inside of her cheek. What could she have possibly done while sleeping to upset him? "How uh...how did we get here? Where is here? I don't remember anything." Ella sat, rubbing her head.

"Can I check your wound?"

Ella nodded and lifted her tunic.

"The arrow was coated with poison. I had to use Solacium on you, but you would have died." David ran his hand gently over her injury. "Once you stabilized, I got you on the horse and rode away, looking for shelter. I was lucky enough to find the home of our host. She's letting us hide in her shed until you're better."

Though his voice was rough and angry, his hands were not as he finished examining her. Why was he upset? Nothing he said would indicate why he was annoyed.

"Thank you...for taking care of me, again," Ella whispered.

David harrumphed. "Here, I found this." He tossed her pendant onto her lap.

Ella clutched it. "Where did you find it?" She had been so careful to make sure it stayed securely tucked away in her pocket.

"I found it in the creek bed after it had fallen out while you convulsed."

She had been convulsing? Ella stared at the pendant instead of David. She didn't want to acknowledge the crack in his voice.

"Care to tell me why you weren't wearing it?"

"I didn't want it to get dirty," Ella mumbled.

David moved to kneel in front of her. "Ella, this pendant has the power to protect you, even from dangers you may not see. It's your shield. If you had been wearing it when you fell over that tripwire while saving me, the arrow wouldn't have pierced you. You wouldn't have almost died. Please promise me you will always wear it. Never take it off." David held the pendant in his hands before clasping it around her neck.

"I promise." Ella touched it, too ashamed to look at David. This was her fault, well partly her fault, and now they were behind. "So, where are we?"

"Near a small village. I haven't been able to get any supplies. It's too risky, and I feel bad asking our hostess to go in for us. She doesn't know who we are, and I don't know how much danger she'll be in."

David quieted as Ella sat up higher, her eyes wide. He had heard it as well. Footsteps. Fast approaching. David didn't even need to see Ella to know to toss her the daggers as he grabbed his sword. Ella summoned the strength to stand as the door to their shed opened and two figures came in, weapons drawn.

The larger one moved on David, while the other faced Ella.

She lost her grip for one second on her dagger before maintaining her hold. The woman before her was one she would never forget, and it wasn't just because of her beauty or her presence.

"Shen?" Ella's mouth dropped as she saw Luca's childhood friend.

Shenzali's accent was thick as she spoke Holodalian, asking Ella a question she didn't understand. Shenzali didn't wait for Ella's response before attacking.

"It's Ella..." Ella held her daggers, holding in a groan as her injury pulled. "We met in Rairene." Ella grunted as she deflected Shenzali's sword.

Shenzali gave her a quizzical look.

"Luca is my friend." Ella was pressed against a wall, the tip of the sword close to her neck.

"Luca?" Shenzali pressed her harder against the wooden wall. "What do you know about Luca?"

"We've met before, please, Shen." Sweat broke out on Ella's skin as she tried to keep the blade back. All she needed was for Shenzali to get away from her. Before Shenzali could move, she was thrown backwards, the pendant glowing on Ella's chest. The man engaging David broke away and ran to Shenzali's side as she staggered to her feet, clutching her chest.

"Who are you?" Shenzali stared at Ella and the pendant.

"I'm Luca's friend...the one you told to not hurt him. I was wearing a wig, that's why you don't recognize me." Ella stepped closer to them on shaky legs. Her vision blurred as fatigue washed over her.

"What are you doing here?" Baako moved towards her, stopping when David touched her elbow.

"Looking for answers." Ella leaned into David.

David helped her back to bed. She did her best to ignore his furrowed brow. "You've done too much; you need to rest," he whispered.

Ella's vision darkened, stars shining in her eyes. "I thought you gave me Solacium."

"I did; it's why you're alive. You still need rest. The poison might be gone, but you still suffered an injury," David said.

Ella mumbled unintelligibly. "I need to talk to..."

"Now that we're not under attack," David glanced at Shenzali and Baako for assurance, "you can get some rest, and I'll talk with our guests."

Ella slowly sat, letting her body adjust and her mind remain clear. Voices filtered to her as Ella got off the bed and walked over to the door. No wonder Raven always took longer to get back to normal after testing a poison. She'd barely had a taste of it with this one, and she was knocked to the ground. At least it hadn't been enchanted, just lethal. She opened her door slowly to find David, Shenzali, and Baako sitting around a small table.

"How are you?" David got up and pulled out a seat for her.

"Slightly foggy, but better." Ella scrunched her face, trying to shake the cobwebs free of her mind. "Are we sure there was only one poison on that arrow?"

"Where were you attacked?" Shenzali leaned back in her chair.

"We were in the river near the border."

"Ah, the loaded crossbow. You're going to take a while to recover," Shenzali said.

"What was on it?" David growled. His hands rested under the table, gripping the armrests.

"We are under no obligation to explain ourselves to a nobody knight or the person he is protecting," Baako replied. "Especially someone not from Holodal."

"I am perfectly capable of taking care of myself," Ella ground out, gripping a butter knife. In response, Baako raised a brow and smirked.

"What are you doing here, anyway? I'm surprised Luca let you out of his sight," Shenzali said, examining her nails.

"Why?"

"How much do you know about him? Did he tell you about Naomi?"

Ella nodded. She knew all about Luca's former flame, who had left him for his brother.

"Then you know Luca can get very jealous, and he would never send you away from him with someone who looks like your handsome knight." Shenzali smiled at David as she gave him a very appreciative undressing with her brown eyes.

"Maybe I came to speak on Luca's behalf." Ella sat taller. "He didn't believe Baako's story that his father wanted him to come home, so he sent me to verify its validity before walking into a death sentence." Ella didn't dare turn to David. His grip next to hers was telling enough.

"Luca wants to come home?" Shenzali leaned forward, her eyes lighting up.

"Only if I can verify what his father claims. If you let me into the palace to speak with the emperor, I could see if his father is telling the truth and that the emperor did rescind his banishment."

Baako and Shenzali's mouths dropped for a second before they quickly recomposed themselves. They crossed their arms.

"Luca didn't send you, why are you really here?" Baako commanded.

"He did." Ella crossed her arms in defiance. What had she said wrong? Ella ran through Luca's story in her head. The emperor had banished him after killing his brother. Now, years later, his father sent word that the emperor had allowed his banishment to be undone. She hadn't misspoken.

"You do not know who Luca is, so he didn't send you. Tell me why you're here." Baako ordered.

Shenzali remained quiet at his side, though Ella noticed the slight twitch of a smile on her face.

"Only if you tell us why you think Luca didn't send us," David negotiated. "Our journey has two missions, one of which we have told you about; the other will remain with us unless you agree to our deal."

"You first." Baako smiled.

"No," Ella retorted. "We've already told you something."

"I don't have any incentive to tell you anything Luca hasn't willingly shared with you."

"Ella, aren't these the guards whose help you wanted to seek when we got here?" David said gently.

"Fine," Ella huffed. "We need to locate someone who said he was coming here to call in a favor. Does the name Jason or The Huntsman mean anything to either of you?"

Both guards froze.

"You do know him." Ella contained her excitement. Finally! They were getting somewhere. Someone knew him.

"It would seem our answer to Luca is more intertwined than you might think." Shenzali began. She was methodical in her words, speaking slowly.

"It would appear that way," Baako added. "I'll tell you how we know Luca didn't send you, but then I have more questions about why you're looking for Jason," Baako said. He turned a ceramic cup in his hands, waiting for them to nod their agreement.

"You said you wanted to speak with the emperor about Luca's father's claims that he was no longer banished." Baako waited for Ella to nod her head. "I need you to understand I'm only telling you this information to save you the embarrassment, as I don't believe Luca would ever intend that for you. Your conversation with the emperor would be very interesting and awkward, given that Luca's father is the emperor."

Ella laughed. "That's…that doesn't…he would have told me." Ella sobered. He would have told her. Right? He had told her everything else about himself. Why keep that a secret?

"Our prince is very private about his life. The fact that he told you so much speaks of his trust in you," Shenzali said. For the first time, Ella saw kindness and understanding instead of jealousy staring back at her.

"And the story about his brother? How he killed him in a…a…what's the ceremony again?" Ella fumbled to talk as her mind processed a set of information she had not been prepared to handle.

"A martakan, yes, all true. However, it is also true that his brother is still alive and remains the heir-apparent to the throne of Holodal," Baako supplied. "It was only discovered after Luca's banishment to be an elaborate ploy by Prince Malik to remove Luca from succession. He faked his death with an enchantment. He and Naomi went underground for a month before resurfacing. The emperor was livid and almost banished him. As soon as he realized his eldest was alive, he sent out guards to find Luca, but it had already been so long. It took years to find Luca. Jason had been…hired by us," Baako exchanged a glance with Shenzali. "We wanted to make sure Luca survived, so we hired Jason to get Luca out of Holodal and hidden away. We just didn't think he would do such a great job."

"So his father…the emperor…wasn't setting him up to be killed? He really wants him back home?" Ella looked between the two guards for any lie and found none as they nodded. "And he thought it was a lie because it took so long to find him."

"Correct. Now, why do you need to find Jason?" Shenzali asked, shifting the topic.

"He has information we need. We're hoping someone saw him when he was here a little under a year ago."

"You'll have to speak with the emperor to get any more information. He was very cautious about who knew he was even here. He seemed to be running from —"

"My step-mother, and a queen who wants to start a war." Ella stood slowly, waiting for the rush of dizziness to pass before she went outside to think.

For the first time in a day, she stepped outside and drank in its beauty. Grasslands sprawled before her, covering the land in waist tall grass with short trees for shade that led up to towering rocky mountains. The dense forest was far behind them. A desert of red rocks and gorges lay before her. She couldn't even see the village she'd been told was nearby. The home they were in was tan and short, blending into its surroundings with a thatched roof creating the perfect disguise. This land was where Luca had grown up, and it took her breath away.

Ella sank to the ground and leaned against the home. Luca was a prince. He was a prince, and he hadn't told her. Why hadn't he told her? If anyone would understand what it felt like to be shunned from their family, it was she. Ella laid her head against the house, grinding her teeth. Luca was a prince, Jason had helped him years ago, and his father, the emperor, wanted him home.

None of them seemed to know Luca was on the run for 'killing' her or David. They didn't even realize who David was. How could the relations between their kingdoms have failed so spectacularly? Ella hung her head between her knees, closing her eyes. She could do this. They could do this.

"Potion for your thoughts?" David sat beside her.

"Luca is —"

"I know."

"Jason helped —"

"I know."

"They don't know about —"

"Nope. They don't. Baako seems to think I'm a knight sent to protect you. Who do they think you are?" David rested his arm around her shoulders, tucking her close.

"I was dressed as a noblewoman. Clearly, they also don't know what Luca does…did." Ella leaned on David. "Why is it every time I feel like we're getting somewhere, we just end up ten paces backwards?"

"Apparently the gods are out to make our lives entertaining," David chuckled.

It was nice to feel his chest rumble against hers. "That's only slightly funny. You would think they would give us some hints along the way." Ella yelled at the sky, mockingly raising her fist at the gods.

"Well, let's use what we know to our advantage. They don't know who we are, but we know who Luca is." David's hand slid a piece of hair out of Ella's face. "Ella?"

Ella's eyes fluttered as she gave her most valiant effort to not further lean into David.

"Whatever was in the poison must have some long term —"

Ella missed anything else David said as the poison took over.

"Oh, you're here." Ella almost went back into the room when Shenzali pinned her with her brown eyes.

"Is there somewhere else I should be?" Her accent was thick and her voice deep as she spoke in a language she wasn't used to.

"Don't you have to guard the emperor or something?" Ella wrapped her arms around her waist as she walked over to a pitcher of fresh water.

"No." Shenzali smiled. "That's not my job. My job is to protect my kingdom from foreign invaders who would harm it or its leader. Are you going to harm a member of our royal family?"

Ella paused as she formed her response. It would take a fool to not notice Shenzali was in love with Luca. "Of course not. I would never intentionally harm someone from the royal family."

"If you'll recall the last time we spoke, I made you a promise if you hurt him."

"That's not a promise you'll need to uphold." Yet, Ella added to herself. Gods, she hoped Luca was okay. They hadn't been able to talk to Henry in days, and were as blind about their kingdom as apparently Holodal was.

"Where's Baako?" Ella searched for the brooding soldier.

"He had to retrieve something. Please sit; you must still be exhausted." Shenzali pushed a chair out with her foot.

"What's in the poison on that arrow and why won't you tell us where Baako is?"

"Aside from the fact that I don't know entirely myself, it would be treason to my emperor to tell a foreigner how a poison has been twisted to have lasting effects," Shenzali said. "Do not think it's a mistake there was no pure water nearby when you were hit."

Ella nodded in understanding, hoping David could make more sense of it later when she told him. Both sat in silence for several minutes, drinking water that ran colder than she expected it to. Ella lightly touched the water with her finger and found it room temperature. She frowned at Shenzali.

"It's going to be a few days before you're back to normal."

"A few days?" Ella growled. "We don't have a few days to sit around and do nothing."

"So then learn about Holodal." Shenzali shrugged.

Ella looked up at the sound of footsteps to find David leaning in the doorway.

"What's wrong with her?" David moved to Ella, placing a hand on her forehead. "My potions are strong. Strong enough to defeat any poison."

"I know; it's how she's still alive." Shenzali got up and walked around the room.

David took Ella's pulse and examined her. Shenzali moved before Ella could voice a warning. But David had been ready; he rolled away from Shenzali, withdrawing a dagger in one fluid movement.

"Can I help you with something?" David asked.

"How dark is your mark?"

"What, no dinner first? Just straight to dessert?" David kept a steady breath as his eyes darted between Ella and Shenzali, who currently had a sword very close to Ella.

"I do like my sugar." Shenzali repositioned herself closer to Ella.

Ella may have been fighting off a poison, but she still withdrew her own blade without drawing the guards' notice.

"I'm not going to tell you how dark my mark is. Your enchanters are treated just a bit better than slaves. I'll not become one to your emperor."

"Then you better wait a few days for Ella to recover. No one has survived that poison before. We'll have to tell him it was a bad batch if you wish to keep your skills hidden."

"You would help us?" Ella asked, tucking the dagger out of the guard's line of sight.

"For Luca, we would, and Baako and I know something is happening in your kingdom, and we want to help. That's why he's not here."

"So he's not bringing more guards to detain us?" David asked.

"Bringing guards?" Baako laughed as he walked in. "I needed to grab something Jason left with me." Baako held out a piece of parchment.

Ella saw David relax and get out of his fighting stance as Baako sat down across from Ella. Shenzali also relaxed and shifted her feet.

"What's on the paper?" Ella leaned back, trying to not show how badly she wanted to reach over and snatch it from him.

"I have no idea what it means, not sure if you will either," Baako replied as he handed it over.

Ella opened the parchment and stared. "Shit." She balled it up and tossed it to the other side of the room. She ran her hands over her face, groaning.

"What did it say?" David picked it up and scrunched his lips as he read it. "What does 'what's our place' mean and why is it written in Evrotian?"

"It means I have to scry my friend." Ella rubbed the bridge of her nose.

"I thought you missed Snow White; this will be good, right?" David sat beside her.

"You know that poison I told you about? The one that was pure darkness?" Ella waited for David to nod. "She made it after Jason broke her heart."

"Oh." David looked at the parchment that barely held a clue, with only one person in the world to know the answer.

"I'm going to need somewhere private." Ella slowly stood and went into what she now deemed to be her room.

David followed her closely, going to her pack when she motioned for it. As Ella searched through her pack, she told David what Shenzali had told her about the poison running through her.

"I don't want to wait for it to be gone. I'll be fine, and we don't have the time." Ella shrugged. "We just need to make sure we get an audience with the emperor...ha," Ella exclaimed as she pulled out a small compact mirror. It was her only link to her friends, and luckily she wouldn't need David's magic to make it work. Ella opened it and thought of Raven. Her curling black hair and brilliant blue eyes that held more scars than anyone deserved to bear. Then she thought of her loyalty, love, and passion to do the right thing. Ella continued to picture her friend. Nothing happened.

She should have answered. Raven knew this mirror was only used in emergencies, and this qualified.

Ella closed the mirror. She should have been able to connect with her. The hairs on Ella's arms rose as her heart raced at the implications. Before she could let her mind get too creative with the status of Raven's life, Ella opened the mirror again and pictured Calla. Calla had enchanted all of their mirrors for all of them, so all they had to do was think of who they wanted to reach and it would connect to that owner's mirror.

So, Ella pictured her friend's dark curly hair, hazel eyes, and a smile filled with so much kindness you couldn't help but love her. Ella continued to think about her, hoping she would answer. If Calla didn't answer, then something was truly wrong, and she would be too far away to do anything.

Ella's jaw dropped when Raven came into the mirror. Her hair was so long and messy, and her normally bright eyes were dark and clouded with anger.

Sn—

Ella? She was so quiet, Ella wasn't sure she had heard her correctly. *You're alive.*

Of course, Ella leaned forward, trying to see around her sister. Where was she? She was outside, and she appeared filthy. Why hadn't she used their code names? Who was around her that she didn't want to go by Snow White?

Of course? What do you mean, 'of course' Raven yelled so loud Ella had to pull back the mirror as she winced.

I sent you a letter. Didn't you get it? Ella bit her lip. *Mira didn't get it to you?*

Mira? Raven's eyes glowed with pent up rage and confusion.

That's not important right now. Ella sighed. *Hi.* She tried to smile as she stared at her friend and waited. But the Raven she had known hadn't been capable of smiling for a long time, and now Ella had to make it worse. *Is Calla nearby?*

Raven's brow furrowed farther, her lips pursed. *No, why?*

This is her mirror. I couldn't connect to yours, so I thought of her.

I see. She's not around. Did you need her?

Nope, just you. Ella twisted a piece of hair between her fingers. *I miss you.*

I miss you...more than... Raven's voice stopped when it hitched. Ella narrowed her eyes, wishing she could reach through the mirror to her sister. Raven seemed to want to reach out to her as her eyes assessed Ella. *Are you okay? You don't look —*

Oh, just some minor poisoning —

Minor poisoning? Raven's voice grated on Ella's ears.

I'm fine. I'm recovering, I promise.

Did Jaq convince you to take a potion? Raven leaned in close, trying to analyze her further.

Jaq's uh...he died, Raven... Ella whispered, unable to say anything else.

Oh, Ella. Raven's voice soothed over her, and it was all Ella could do to not cry. *I wish I were there.*

I wish you were here too. Ella couldn't stop the tears that welled. Every emotion she had been keeping shoved down flew to the surface at the sound of Raven's voice and the feel of her love. Her absence had been harder than Ella had realized.

Raven wiped her own tears. *What did you need to talk about?*

I want you to know I did everything I could to not have to reach out to you about this. Ella started, watching Raven straighten and become Snow White, cold and distant. *I traveled to Holodal to try to avoid it.*

Just spit it out. There was the Raven Ella had come to know.

I need to find...Jason, Raven. He left a codeword in Holodal for me to say when I find him, and I need the answer, but you're the only person who will know it. I'm hoping at least that you're the person to know it.

What do you need from him? Raven stared down at Ella through the mirror. Ella didn't think it was possible to pull off that gaze through a mirror, yet there she was, regal in her command. Unyielding in her desire to show no emotion. Not now. Not while talking about him.

He has information that will help me and Prince David take down the Queen of Trudel for the war she's trying to instigate. With that information, we'll not only be able to stop her, but we'll also be able to come home and be protected.

Raven glanced away from the mirror, her gaze assessing. Someone else was there. Raven was deciding whether they could be trusted with what Ella had said.

Let me see him. Raven ordered. *The prince.* Raven added when Ella didn't move.

Ella turned the mirror to face David, who waved awkwardly, his mouth slightly open at the sight of her friend. Of course, he would find Raven beautiful. She was, even while covered in dirt.

I hate that I have to open this wound.

Raven nodded.

It's a codeword. The question is, where is 'our place'?

Raven shuddered, and Ella saw her struggle to contain all she was feeling. Raven closed her eyes as she spoke. *It's a place in northern Rairene. We had discovered it after escaping on one of our missions.*

Ella took it all in, listening to her friend's story and watching her shrink in on herself as a light glow began to form around the mirror. She was close to losing control.

Raven had to stay in control. She was in Evrotia, and if anyone saw...Ella closed her eyes against the thoughts. She would be fine. This was Raven. She would be fine.

Thank you, Ella whispered, knowing the cost she had exacted from her friend. *I love you. You're stronger than what happened.* Ella spoke just for her, hoping that whoever was around her couldn't hear. Raven nodded tersely.

Ella waited for Raven to close her mirror, not wanting to leave her friend. She hadn't seen Raven so upset in a long time, and she could only hope this time the same thing wouldn't happen again.

"Well, at least now we have the codeword. The only problem is—" David said.

"We need the emperor's blessing to meet him."

David nodded.

"And he'll want to know about his son and if he's safe." Ella added.

"Which we can't guarantee."

"Sounds fun."

Ella had never been more grateful to have been caught than she was when Shenzali and Baako found them. The guards were able to swiftly bring them across the grasslands and gorges of Holodal, with Ella staring at the surrounding landscape. She had only ever seen green, snow capped mountains and forests stretching for miles along the sandy coast of Rairene. She had never seen barren red rocks that towered over her, jutting out of the ground to be quickly filled with grasslands around the creeks that ran throughout the land. The trees were short and stumpy, providing just enough shade for one person. And it was beautiful.

The palace sat atop a large plateau of red rock, overlooking the valley below it that was filled with grass and wildlife. Several times their stallion had been startled by some wild herd running nearby. But Shenzali and Baako's horses remained calm and carried on.

The Kalareshi Palace was a large stone building showing its age with the sandy walls. But it was extravagant nonetheless, with four stories and dozens of what Ella learned were called palm trees surrounding it.

Shenzali and Baako were waved through the gates, with David and Ella allowed passage behind them. The grounds were immaculate, with servants in loose linen clothing hurriedly going about their day. The sun had begun to crest by the time they had passed through three layers of gates and got to the palace stables.

"We must hurry if you are to see the emperor today. He is almost done seeing the public for the day," Shenzali said as she dismounted and handed her horse to a stable hand, leaving behind all of her possessions.

David and Ella didn't feel as comfortable with that and ensured they brought their two packs with them, leaving behind their satchels on the horse. Ella glanced back, wondering how long it would take for a spy to go through their items. Baako drove away from them, jogging ahead to make sure they got their audience. Shenzali kept them at a brisk pace, making sure she stayed beside them to avoid any questions from the guards who watched them.

Shenzali surveyed Ella several times, a frown forever pressed between her brows.

"Is something bothering you?" David asked.

"She is not healed yet, and you cannot, must not show weakness to our emperor. He already does not like your kingdom."

"I'll be fine. I've suffered through worse," Ella said, accepting the challenge. Her body, however, didn't fully agree. Mentally, she would be fine, but the aches and fever hadn't gone away yet.

Before Shenzali could say more, they got to a large set of double wooden doors with an epic battle carved into their grain. The entire room emptied out as they walked in, with several commoners eyeing them as they passed. Some appeared pleased; others were holding back tears. The throne room was twice the size of the one in Rairene, boasting open, windowless arches that allowed a cool breeze to flow throughout. The dais was high off the ground with a throne made of gold that shone in the setting sun. By the time they reached Baako, who knelt before the throne, the only other people who remained were the guards stationed on the perimeter and two women behind the emperor himself.

David and Ella both knelt and curtsied, respectively, before Emperor Edris of Holodal.

The emperor pounded a scepter on the ground, giving them permission to look at him.

Had Ella not been told this was Luca's father, there would have been very little doubt about it now that she saw him. Emperor Edris had the same strong jaw, golden eyes, sun kissed skin as his son. His black hair fell down to his back in thick waves, with a simple golden crown circlet inlaid with a diamond resting on his head. He wore beautiful cream silk robes that accented his body well, with a dark red silk sash crossing over his chest and left shoulder.

“Emperor Edris, we would ask permission to have an open conversation with you on behalf of the Kingdom of Rairene.”

“Unless it is to tell me you will be releasing my son, Prince Lucian, from your prison, then we have nothing to discuss,” Emperor Edris said. His deep voice rocked Ella to her core filling her with dread.

CHAPTER TWENTY-THREE

Raven

Raven closed the mirror.

Calla's mirror.

She clutched it tightly in her shaking hands.

Ella was *alive*.

Her sister was breathing and needed to find Jason, but she was alive. Raven's magic sprang to life, spinning with joy.

Raven stared at the mirror in her hands as she processed everything.

Why did she have Calla's mirror in her hand?

"She's alive," Aleks said.

Raven's head snapped to see the slack jawed look on Alek's face.

"Ella's alive." He walked around the campsite aimlessly, his hands at his sides, his head turned toward the sky.

"Why do I have Calla's mirror? She never would have handed it over," Raven questioned.

"What?" Aleks's gaze faded as he looked at her.

"Why did *you*...have her mirror?" Raven barely got the words past her lips. It had been in Aleks' bag. Though not meant for her, she had felt the call in her magic.

"I uh...I took it from her room." Aleks slowly walked backward, his hands at his sides.

"You said she had left. You said you couldn't find her." Raven's heart hammered in her chest so fast she was certain Rowan and Aleks could hear it. Her magic spiraled. She stood and paced around the campfire.

"Calla's the maid who was arrested, right?" Rowan questioned.

"She was what?"

Birds flew out of the trees as Raven's voice rose. Her entire body shook as she clutched the mirror in her hand. Her magic engulfed her core, rising to meet the emotions blazing a path through her. Ella was alive. She was alive. Calla was...Calla...

"I have to go get her." Raven went to her bedroll and frantically rolled it. "I have to go."

"What about the advisers? We have to go to them," Aleks said. He stood near her.

"Forget them. Calla can't...I have to get her out." Raven continued to shove her things into the pack. "Why didn't you tell me she had been arrested?" Raven put everything on her horse. More magic filled her to the brim before spilling out.

"Raven —"

"We could have gotten her out." Raven ran shaking hands through her hair. "Why didn't you tell me?"

"We couldn't have gotten her out —"

"Why didn't you tell me?" Raven yelled. Aleks had taken a few steps away from her.

"You never would have come —"

Raven exploded.

Her magic flared out as she screamed. It ripped through her, making it feel like her insides were being shredded as her spilled over magic illuminated her hands.

Raven growled, trying to get control. She did not lose control, *not like this*. But her magic had become too much. She had felt too much and hadn't been able to control her power's response to her grief, her anger, and her terror.

The only clear thought she had was that she needed to protect Rowan. She directed her magic towards a giant redwood, screaming as pure, raw magic unleashed itself. She flicked her eyes towards Rowan, seeing Aleks standing in front of him, an enchanted shield raised high.

A snow covered tree exploded into millions of shards, showering the forest. It wasn't enough, though. Raven knew it would never be enough to quell what she was feeling for her sister. Calla, who was probably being tortured by Morgan for information. Her sister, who was innocent and pure, and didn't fully know how to resist that kind of pain. Calla never should have been sent. Raven never should have followed them without making sure she was safe. She had failed her, and now Calla would be in pain because of her.

Raven threw her power towards another tree. And another. So much magic had gathered to pour out of her that she felt it illuminating her entire body.

Calla was in danger. She was with that *monster*. Alone.

Raven squeezed her eyes tight, blocking out the images from her nightmares as tears burned her cheeks.

She opened them to find Aleks in front of her, his ice blue eyes wide as he got close to her. Raven knew she should have regained her control by now, but it was too much. Her inner wall continued to crumble too fast. No matter how quickly she tried to mentally rebuild it, no matter how many stones she placed, she couldn't seem to build it fast enough to get her magic contained. It was exhausting. Her ability to focus at all dwindled the longer it took for her to pull her power back.

Raven screamed as it burned in her. It was here to help, and it wasn't going to be caged.

Aleks touched her shoulder, not flinching away.

"I can't stop it, Prince Charming. It hurts. I have to get it out," Raven spoke through gritted teeth.

"You are more than your power. You control it. It does not control you. Now take it back." Aleks growled.

"I can't stop. How can anyone feel this much?" Raven groaned. Her body burned. She had to get control. She would die if she didn't. She would burn out and kill Rowan and Aleks.

"Raven, you can do this."

Another tree exploded as Aleks locked eyes with her. He wrapped his hands around her wrists. She clenched her jaw and curled her hands.

"Deep breath. Take control. Put your magic back into your core."

Raven breathed with him, pulling the magic in. She gripped it and folded it back in on itself. She did it again and again. Raven landed on her knees, bringing Aleks down with her, her wrists still gripped in his hands.

"You've got this. We'll find her," Aleks said.

She growled as she ground her teeth until slowly, her magic came back until it was on the surface of her skin, then inside, traveling from her fingertips and into her center. Raven kneaded it up, and folded it tightly until she was sure it wasn't going to break free. She breathed slowly, trying to keep her focus on Aleks and nothing else until her world darkened around her and she collapsed against him.

Raven woke up next to a fire after only gods knew how long. She opened her eyes and searched around as her eyes adjusted to the dark. Raven shuddered against the cold as she pulled the blanket wrapped around her closer.

Her body screamed in protest as she tried to move into a new position. She stilled her body, checking everything. Her magic was back in control. Normally, when she turned within, her magic was a swirling mass in her core that seemed to always be pushing the edges of her skin, but now...it faintly flickered in the dark. It was going to be a long time before it grew back to its normal strength.

Raven sat up slowly, leaning against the log behind her. Aleks and Rowan sat on the other side of the fire, watching her. She shivered under her blanket.

"How are you?" Rowan broke the silence first.

"I'm...breathing..." Raven stared at Aleks. He stared off into the forest, rubbing his hands together. She remembered him helping her, getting her to a place of control. He had touched her, held her wrists. "Your hands?"

How much damage had she done?

Aleks revealed to her. Dark red lines streaked his palms like lightning. They wrapped around his arm, swollen from the raw magic that had raced over them.

"I've seen worse scars from unleashed magic," Aleks muttered.

"Um —"

"You could have told us you're an enchanter," Aleks said.

"Would you have told anyone if our positions were reversed?" Raven asked.

Aleks opened his mouth, but closed it and shook his head. "No. I wouldn't have."

"How did you hide your mark from the guards?" Rowan asked, speaking for the first time.

"The inking covers it." Raven turned around and lifted her head to reveal the raven tattoo on the back of her neck and shoulders.

"I think the enchantment has begun to wear off," Rowan commented.

Aleks stood and got right behind her. "May I touch it?"

Raven nodded curtly.

His fingers gently rested directly over where she knew her mark was, trailing down over her skin as he outlined the tattoo. Shivers raced through her, and it had nothing to do with the cool night.

"I wonder if, as your memories come back, the enchantment and thus the ink have begun to fade. It was darker the last time I saw it," Aleks whispered. His fingers still gently traced her skin.

Raven twisted trying to see it. Rowan sat hunched on a log, his head down.

"Rowan, can you tell me another good story about us as children? I would really like to have a good memory."

Rowan looked at her, a small smile on the corner of his lips. "There was this one time when Aleks was visiting where you and I snuck him out of his room at night to go watch some enchanters," he teased.

"You and I snuck him out? Shouldn't it have been the other way around?" Raven quirked a brow as she tried to associate her younger, rule-breaking self with whom she knew.

"Oh no, definitely not," Aleks said. He got up and moved so they could all sit in a circle. "Like we said, you were always the troublemaker of our group. I, of course, had no problem participating, but everything we got in trouble for...that was all because of you."

"Everything we got into trouble for?"

"Well, there was that one time you swapped the sugar for salt in the kitchen," Rowan added.

"Or the time where we let the horses out of the stables." Aleks smiled at her.

"And the time where we played hide n' seek with the servants, only they had no idea about the game and spent the better half of a day trying to find us." Rowan inserted, his smile just as wide.

"Or how about —"

"Okay, okay, I get it," Raven interrupted as she laughed. "We got into a lot of trouble." She looked between the two of them, smiling. "Rowan, why were we sneaking out to see the enchanters? It wasn't forbidden then, right?"

"We had heard some whispering from the maids that your father was working with his strongest enchanters on some new enchantment, and you wanted to watch. Mainly because everything felt so secretive, and you hate secrets. Feather even came, though he was small and a risk if he barked."

"Did we get in trouble? What happened?" Raven leaned forward, stretching out her hands to be closer to the fire.

"No, we weren't caught. We sat and watched from behind some tables. They were working on a very large mirror. Now that I think about it...it was odd. Mirrors have been enchanted before, but this one seemed different. Ten of your father's enchanters stood around it with him, all of them holding hands as they cast their enchantment. To be perfectly honest, I've never seen anything like it since." Aleks turned to Rowan. "Do you know where it ended up? Did you ever see it again?"

"Nope. It was impossible to miss. It had to have been as tall as I am now and set in an ornate golden frame," Rowan said.

"I wonder if my aunt destroyed it?" Aleks questioned. "I guess we'll never know." He shrugged as he turned his attention to the fire, feeding it a few twigs to keep the dim light going.

CHAPTER TWENTY-FOUR

Calla

Calla giggled as she stumbled sideways into the guard escorting her back to her home. “Oops,” Calla exclaimed as she leaned heavily on him. Her feet tripped her as she pushed herself away from him and landed against the stone wall. “Ow.” Calla rubbed her head as she rested against the cool surface of the rocks. Her cheeks were too warm as sweat trickled down her forehead.

Calla’s magic spun lazily within, content to swirl. She took another step, frowning as the guards blocked her path. A door was open to her. Her door. Her cell. Calla dropped to the ground like a rag doll, all energy leaving her just as rapidly.

“Do you have to put me in chains?” Calla mumbled as one of the guards clasped the shackles around her wrists.

“You know we have to.” One guard grumbled.

“Do you?” Calla leaned towards him, her mind fuzzy and floaty at the same time. Was that even possible? Calla thought. Could she be fuzzy yet floaty? She certainly felt it.

"Yes," the other guard responded. He pulled on the chains for good measure and then left, locking the door behind them.

"One day you'll forget, and on that day..." Calla's speech slurred as she wavered from side to side.

"What will you do on that day?"

Calla's head snapped up at Adam's voice. She blinked, trying to clear her vision so that she only saw one Adam, not two. "What?" She asked, holding her head.

"The day they forget to chain you. What will you do?" Adam asked again.

"I'll walk free. I'll leave this wretched place behind and never come back," Calla proclaimed.

"Are you drunk?" Adam crouched down at eye level with her, his head tilted.

"I dunno," Calla swayed again as she leaned toward him. "I've never been drunk. Never had alcohol before, what's it like?" Calla rested her head on her hands and stared at him. "You're beautiful."

Adam's mouth dropped. "You're definitely drunk. Calla, this is very important—Calla," Adam waved a hand in front of her. "Listen to me. What did they ask you?"

"Nothing important. Not that I told them anything. I'm a secret floor," Calla whispered, winking at him.

Adam hung his head. "Calla, please let me help you. What did they ask you about?"

Calla huffed, blowing a curly strand of hair out of her face. "Nothing important. They wanted to know about Ella, which I refused to talk about, doesn't matter since she was killed anyway, and then they asked questions about Raven, but I think she's alive. I love them so much. Why did they have to die?" Calla asked.

Her heart swelled as their image rose before her. Ella and Raven had their arms slung over the other's shoulder as they smiled at her. Calla reached out a hand to them, trying to hold on to them.

"Why did they have to go?" She choked on her words, saliva rising thick in her throat. Calla blinked, and her sisters blurred before her. By the time she cleared her vision, they were gone. "I'm all alone. No one loves me." Calla did her best to wrap her arms around herself. "Adam, why is that everyone I love leaves me?"

Calla curled onto her side as her magic began to spin in response. They had left her. They were supposed to stay beside her and always remind her that she was loved.

Four years ago

Calla swiped at the tears staining her cheeks. They were stupid, worthless tears. Her hand clutched a piece of parchment in her hand. She didn't want to read it again. The message was clear. Her family didn't want to see her. They had moved on, and so should she. Calla threw the ball of parchment as she screamed.

"Well, I can see Ella and Raven's attempts at training you have gone well," Mira remarked as she dodged the ball.

Calla glared at her. Mira raised her hands and continued walking over to Calla's bed.

"I didn't invite you in," Calla sniffled.

"Your tears did. Come sit down." Mira patted the space beside her.

"You have to get ready for your mission." Calla motioned to her long, wavy red hair that hung perfectly down her back, and the emerald gown that she wore was elegant for a night out in Riset.

"He can wait. Besides, it'll make him jealous that I was late due to being with someone else." Mira winked. She wrapped her arms around Calla and hugged her tightly. "What happened?"

"Just another reminder that no one wants me," Calla replied, eyeing the parchment.

"How dare you say that."

"But —"

"No. That is my dearest friend you are disparaging, and I simply will not hear another word about it. Calla," Mira gripped her biceps and turned Calla to her, "you are loved. You are loved by Ella. By Raven. And most importantly, by me. Don't you dare forget. Who cares about the family you were born into. It's the family you choose and who chooses you back that matters."

Calla nodded.

"Now, repeat after me, 'I am loved'."

"I am loved."

Mira kissed her forehead and held Calla close.

"Calla?"

Calla uncurled her body just enough to see Adam.

"You haven't been left."

Calla scoffed. Calla was just aware enough of what she was about to say that she stopped talking. "Those who are important to me have left me alone."

Without realizing it, Calla switched to Rairenian as she continued. "I wish I had never come here."

"Why did you?"

"I've already told you," Calla replied, continuing to speak in Rairenian.

"No. You've denied what Princess Arianna has said, but you never told me your side."

"You never let me say anything. You always leave me. You've been leaving me...and it hurts."

Adam opened his mouth, but Calla carried on.

"It hurts when I look into your beautiful eyes and all I can see is that wall from the first day we met. I didn't...I didn't mean for any of this...I wasn't even supposed to be your maid. By the time I got to the palace, all of the other maids were so terrified they pawned you off to me, and I...I regret it. If I hadn't been so distracted...I could have made a difference. I could have scried something, or read something that would have changed everything and saved my sister, but I didn't...and she's dead."

"What did you say?" Adam asked.

"I just..." Calla lay down on her back and stared at the ceiling. "You just wanted to know why I was here, and I told you as much as I could. I don't like keeping secrets from you." She closed her eyes as the cell seemed to be spinning around her, while she lay perfectly still.

"Calla —"

"Do you think it's possible for an enchanter to be too powerful?" Calla asked, cutting Adam off.

"I think that all enchanters are given the amount of power they were meant to wield and that no enchanter is given more than they can handle," Adam replied. He sounded far away, but the room was spinning too much for Calla to confirm her suspicion that he was leaving her again.

"I am strong. I do not break. I am loved," Calla spoke softly in Vicurian. "I love you."

If he replied, she didn't hear as the world finally stopped moving, and the darkness claimed her.

Calla jolted awake, groaning as her head protested the sudden movement. The sunlight streaming in blinded her as she blinked. Her head felt like she had been stuffed into a dress that was too small, leaving her immobile and uncomfortable. She moaned as she rolled over and lay on her back to stare at the ceiling.

She thought about the previous day's events. It had started out like any other day of torture, strapped down to the table with Morgan and her assistants swimming around her. Only this time they didn't give her poison. What was it Morgan said?

Calla closed her eyes tightly. She had said her usual methods weren't working, so she was going to try something different, something pedestrian...alcohol. The taste rose on her tongue quickly as she swallowed, the taste of sour yeast coating her dry mouth.

Morgan's assistant, Fiona, put a cup filled with dark, cloudy liquid in front of Calla. Calla scrunched her nose as she remembered the smell. It was horrid. Fiona didn't wait for Calla to willingly open her mouth. She forced it, pouring the contents down Calla's throat. She spat out what she could; her face contorting at the taste.

But then they had plied her with more until the whole room seemed to sway around her. Only then did they ask their questions.

Calla tried to remember what they had asked her. She was certain she hadn't given up anything. She wouldn't. Even drunk, she would never betray her friends.

Multiple footsteps echoed down the corridor, pulling Calla out of her memories.

She sat when ten guards stood before her cell.

What had she said? Calla thought as one of them opened her cell and they funneled in to encircle her. Calla's magic began to unfold, rising to meet the surrounding threat. Only once all of the guards were around her did her true visitors come in.

Queen Lyanna walked in wearing one of her least ornate gowns, a simple grey with twisting black details on the hems and waistline. She smirked as she gazed at Calla. Two guards moved in unison with their spears, crossing them behind Calla's neck and pushing her forward.

Calla's magic rose, coming to the surface as it flickered within, ready to unleash itself. A third guard pushed aside her hair to where her enchanter's mark rested, his gloved hand pressing onto her scalp.

"It's just like the royal guard, covered by the inking of a wolf," the guard explained. He removed his hand and stepped back from her. But the other two guards and their spears remained.

"Well then, we won't take any chances," Queen Lyanna replied.

Calla looked through her hair at the queen as she motioned for someone to come in. Morgan's voice reached her first as she cast an enchantment. The moment Morgan came into view, the guards pressed down harder, pushing Calla's chest into her bent legs.

"No," Calla bucked against the spears.

As Morgan got closer, the obsidian shackles glowed in her hands.

"No, please, don't do this." Calla moved, trying to find a way out of the spears. She got her legs out from under her.

Two more guards held her down.

"Please." Calla felt tears rise in her eyes as she thrashed against the spears. Her arms were currently pinned under her, with the chains pressing into her skin.

"You should have told me what I wanted to know," Morgan said as she stopped her enchantment. "Lift her; I need her arms."

The guards gripped her, their hands bruising as they hauled Calla to her feet.

Calla's magic rose, her hands illuminating with the threat. She would not be parted from her power. It pressed against her skin, expanding outwards. Calla gave herself over to it. She wouldn't fight her magic anymore. At least this way, her death would have meaning.

"Morgan, shackle her. Now." Queen Lyanna's voice ricocheted in her head.

But it was too late.

Calla closed her eyes as her power consumed her.

Calla soared on her power, joining with it as it sang the song she had been keeping it from. She basked in its warmth as her core seemed to become enveloped in radiant light. She saw and felt everything; the rough stones grounded her, the body heat from the guards fueled her with their own fear, the currents of the air flowed around her and mingled with her magic. It streamed around her, extending her awareness in a way she had never known could be possible. So...this was what it felt like to lose control.

She wondered why she hadn't done it sooner.

The light consuming her shut off, plunging Calla into a well of darkness.

She opened her eyes and peered out through sparkling vision as her magic fluttered through her vision.

Two obsidian shackles had been placed on her wrists.

Followed by two more.

The light she had felt glimmering in the darkness got softer.

Shackles were placed on her wrists up to her elbows.

The internal glimmer was gone. But her magic was fighting. Her vision remained coated in it.

Two more sets of shackles were placed on her biceps.

The power in her eyes disappeared, and she clearly saw the room around her. The guards had taken several steps away from her. Queen Lyanna was now on the other side of her cell, and Morgan was before her, enchanting the shackles as she placed each one.

"Would you like me to place any other obsidian on her?" Morgan asked as she took a cautious step away from Calla.

"Have you ever seen something like that before, Morgan?" Queen Lyanna's voice quaked.

"No," Morgan whispered.

"Do it," Queen Lyanna commanded.

Morgan nodded as she motioned to Fiona. She carried a small cloth in her hand. Calla eyed it as Morgan flipped over the cloth and pulled out a thin slab of obsidian that was chained to another thin slab. The pieces were raised over her head and settled on top of her chest and back. Morgan began enchanting under her breath, using two bands of obsidian to fully merge the pieces together on top of her shoulders.

Calla sank to the ground, her knees digging into the stone as her connection to her power all but vanished. Calla wrapped her arms around her waist, curling in on herself.

Calla was left with her thoughts for the rest of the day. Outside of food being delivered, she was alone. Mira didn't come. Adam didn't come. Calla sat in the afternoon and stretched her arms, adjusting to the weight. The obsidian stone wasn't as heavy as she had always assumed, but it did make her muscles ache with the weight. It was thin, smooth, cool to the touch, and shone like glass in the sun's rays.

Instinctively, Calla reached for her power to read it. She had never come across enchanter's shackles before, and she wanted to know their history. Her magic didn't even flicker at her summons. It wasn't empty, but more like a wall was between her and the power she had felt her entire life.

For the first time since she was eight, the weight of her power wasn't pressing against her skin, demanding to be set free. Calla tilted her head at the sensation. Her power wasn't thrumming in the back of her head or through her veins. It was simply contained, and she felt...free. Calla's shoulders relaxed in relief.

She was strong. She did not break. She was loved.

CHAPTER TWENTY-FIVE

Drea

Drea shifted back and forth as she rubbed her arms under her cloak and waited. She had *been* waiting in the cold night air ever since Henry scried her to inform her he was coming to her and he wasn't going to be alone.

Drea had found reasonable attire in her dark room as quickly as possible before grabbing her cane and stealthily walked through Aumont. Henry said it wouldn't be possible to meet in the garden, so she found herself walking through the maze with only the moon's light to guide her. Drea muttered to herself as telltale signs of cramping in her leg started in her knee. She needed to get to their meeting place. Fast.

So, here she was, waiting for Henry and his mystery guest while her leg cramped. Drea shifted her weight again and pushed down on her cane.

A branch snapped.

Drea turned as Henry and Princess Maliah stepped out from behind a hedge.

"Sorry for the delay, one of the sentries here almost saw us," Henry said.

"I thought we were going to meet in the morning, not the middle of the night." Drea looked at Princess Maliah.

"My father has ordered me to leave in the morning, and your message seemed important enough to warrant a rendezvous," Princess Maliah replied. She stepped closer to Drea, allowing Drea to see how wide her eyes were and how concerned she was. "Please, tell me what happened to my sister. She doesn't have anyone to protect her."

"Mira isn't as helpless as you think," Drea said.

Maliah snorted. "My little sister is a sassy girl who loves to get into trouble without thinking about how to get out of it."

"Then you should know the training she had here made her a very capable person, both mentally and physically."

"I need to explain in direct sentences, Lady Drizella. Enough of this side stepping bullshit. How much danger is my sister in?" Princess Maliah gripped Drea's arms.

Princess Maliah held Drea so that she was not only off balance, but completely dependent on Princess Maliah to keep her standing. But Drea didn't care because she felt the worry in how Maliah's arms shook, the flexing of her fingers, and the fear in her eyes. Drea understood everything and if the roles were reversed, and it was Ana...she would probably be doing much worse to find her.

"What I'm going to share with you is not known by many, and for the safety of others, I ask that you don't share it with anyone."

Maliah nodded and then let Drea go.

"Mira has been trained to seduce men and women to get information out of them. She was also trained on how to defend herself. She is incredibly smart and knows how to infiltrate anywhere. A few weeks ago, she went rogue and left to help someone she loves."

"Why would she be trained to do these things?" Maliah asked. She paced around Drea and Henry.

Henry remained silent, staying in the background.

"Because it's what my mother was ordered to do by her queen."

"Your mother, the ambassador to Trudel..." Maliah continued to pace. "I don't like my sister being involved in your mothers political warfare. Do you know where she went?"

"She didn't say in her letter, but if I had to guess, I would say she's in Evrotia."

Maliah tugged on her cloak and wrapped it tightly around her. Drea watched the future queen of Grecia straighten her back and comb her hands through her long hair and braid it. It was the same thing Mira did whenever she was trying to solve a problem.

"Is there anything else you can tell me?"

"No," Drea said. "What are you going to do?"

"Well, my father has ordered me to return home. But he didn't say I couldn't stop anywhere along the way." Princess Maliah smiled tightly. "Evrotia is an ally of ours, so Mira should be treated well there." She nodded more to herself than anyone else. "Thank you, Lady Drizella for this information. It seems my sister and I have a lot of catching up to do."

Drea nodded as Princess Maliah gave her a firm nod before leaving.

"Thank you for bringing her," Drea whispered.

Henry grimaced. "I'm not sure it helped anyone, but you're welcome."

"At least she can try to help her sister. It's what I would have done."

"But would she have done the same for you?" Henry asked.

"Of course," Drea snapped. Of course, Ana would do the same. They would always have each other's backs.

Drea spun around as she dived away from Gus's sword. The impact vibrated up her leg as she landed on the wood floor. Drea gritted her teeth and maintained her composure as she kept her defensive stance and got her guard up in time to block Gus's attack. He pushed her back, but her leg held up, and Drea began to push back.

She switched from a defensive hold to an attack with her blade, forcing Gus to retreat.

Their sparing continued for several minutes, with both of them getting through the other's defenses.

Drea yielded when Gus knocked her to the ground, leveling his blade at her throat.

"Better," Gus said as he dropped his sword and helped her.

Drea swiped her hair out of her face, blinking against the sweat as she caught her breath.

"Thanks to you." Drea stretched out her muscles as they debriefed.

"You've done the hard part; you should be proud."

"There's still a long way to go," Drea commented as she sat down and massaged her thigh.

"Perhaps, but don't discredit how far you've come. It's the small steps in the big picture that matter. Remember to celebrate them," Gus said.

Drea nodded, keeping her eyes downcast. "I'll try." She glanced outside the room as the sun began to rise over the gardens. They had started practicing earlier in the mornings when Princess Lena had continuously started their meetings early in the morning. Earlier than even Drea thought was acceptable. But Anastasia had yet to complain, so Drea certainly couldn't.

"I better get washed up before everyone else wakes." Drea headed for the door.

"Drizella." Gus paused. "She isn't...Ella isn't really dead, right?"

Drea turned to him. He twisted his hands together before crossing and uncrossing his arms. He watched her from the corner of his eye, the barest flicker of hope in their brown depths.

"Gus —"

"I know you were here," he whispered. "The rest of us had been sent to the ball, so everyone but you and Jaq were gone...I need to know. She was more than my pupil and partner; she was my friend. If you're protecting her, I understand, but I...please..." Gus's voice cracked.

Drea's magic soothed her as her heart raced with the desire to tell him the truth. To tell him everything. But what if that was the goal? Ella had trusted Jaq, and everything unraveled because of it.

"I saw her wounds, Gus. They were fatal."

It was the first time this lie had hurt her. Every other time was to fully protect Ella, and if she was being honest, it gave her a certain level of satisfaction to lie to the princess, but right now, she was causing genuine heartache.

"I understand." Gus's shoulders fell as he walked over to the prop weapons rack. "I should get ready for the other lessons."

"I'll see you tomorrow?"

Gus nodded once in confirmation, his back turned to her.

Drea opened the door, freezing when Anastasia stood directly outside.

"Let's go; we have our meeting," Anastasia said, holding out a lightweight dress to her.

"How did you know I would be here?"

"I had a feeling you had started training again when you didn't come to our meetings with tea anymore. I haven't told her." As if to reiterate her point, Anastasia shook the dress in front of her again. "I don't see why you haven't told Lena, but it's your information to share." She shrugged her shoulders as she walked with Drea towards one of the changing rooms.

"Thank you, I'm still doing strength training, so I didn't want to say anything until I was useful again."

"I wish you wouldn't say that about yourself." Anastasia huffed.

Drea turned around as she laced the dress and raised her eyebrows.

"You're not useless, Drea. What you do here matters."

"Tell that to Princess Lena," Drea laughed.

"I do. All the time. So will you stop fighting me in front of Lena?"

"I'll try." Drea smiled at her big sister. "All set. Do I look like I've been sweating while getting my ass handed to me by Gus?"

Anastasia tilted her head before tucking a stray hair behind Drea's ear. "Perfect. You would have no idea that Gus just kicked your butt." Anastasia winked.

The two walked arm in arm, with Drea's cane lightly tapping beside them down to the meeting room. The novices were starting to get up and move throughout the house as they approached the room. For the first time since Ella had blown up their plans, the room was empty of everyone but them, Lena, and the Queen.

Have we heard from...what's her name, that girl we sent out a few weeks ago? Queen Laila asked.

"Tressa." Anastasia supplied for her. "We haven't heard from her. She was supposed to check in every few days, but hasn't recently."

She should have reached her suspected location by now. Lena, what's your plan of action to recover her?

"I think she did find Ella, and that something happened. I'm going to send some of our men out along her route to find her," Princess Lena replied. She squared her shoulders and sat before her mother.

Do we think this is a failed mission?

"Not yet. I want to find her first," Anastasia cut in.

"Might I add something for consideration?" Drea asked.

Ana flashed her a glance as the queen motioned for her to continue.

"Let's say Ella is alive, and that Tressa found her...what if we haven't heard from her because she killed Ella when you explicitly said to bring her in alive."

"You're entertaining the idea Tressa would be able to defeat Ella," Anastasia replied.

"If we think Ella got away while fighting off who knows how many enchanted poisons, then I have a feeling Tressa would be able to stand a chance against her," Drea replied.

"Are you saying you agree with me now?" Anastasia questioned.

"I'm saying I'm open to the idea that I'm wrong and that we need to plan for whatever outcome," Drea replied. She turned toward her sister, waiting for her response. She had to know Tressa would go after Ella, and if she did...well, Drea knew Tressa never stood a chance, no matter Ella's condition.

"If Tressa has gone after Ella and perished, then it's her own fault for not keeping us informed as we had ordered. If Ella is alive, then we know which plans we've discussed to move forward with. I would say it's a win-win. Tressa had become increasingly annoying, especially after Lucifer's death." Anastasia waved a hand.

Drea bit the inside of her cheek to keep herself from arguing. She had told Ana she would work on supporting her, and she would.

Well, do we have any good news today? What about Luca? Did we get to him first? Queen Laila questioned.

Princess Lena shifted in her seat.

"No. Lord Andrew beat us to him," Princess Lena mumbled.

How? Where was he hiding?

"Some house within the borders of Riset," Lena grumbled.

How did we miss it?

"More importantly, how did the palace figure it out before us?"

"Well, all but those for Holodal," Drea conceded.

Why? Queen Laila commanded.

"Our kingdom has never had a good relationship with them. There has been almost no diplomatic communication with them since the king came to power. It never seemed to be at the top of mother's list," Drea answered.

Queen Laila muttered something under her breath. *Fine. Let's try to get someone in there to talk to Luca. Drea, maybe you can?*

"Me?" Drea turned her full attention to the queen. Why her? What could she possibly have that Ana or Lena didn't?

Yes. He worked for you and, as Ambassador, it is within your right to speak with him.

Drea nodded in understanding. Ana tensed beside her, but she wouldn't say anything, not in front of the queen. Their meeting ended shortly afterward, with Lena keeping both of them after the queen left.

"Do we have anyone else in our employ from Holodal?"

Anastasia and Drea shook their heads. They hadn't even met anyone from Holodal before Luca knocked on their doors all those years ago. He had come in the middle of the night, soaking wet, and carrying a single pack. His boots had been worn to the ground, and his clothes had been covered in filth. But her mother had recognized him somehow. Drea still never knew how her mother knew who Luca was, but she let him in with a gleam in her eye that Drea hadn't seen for years. The spindles were turning as her mother churned on ways to use Luca like a pawn. And now Drea had to go visit him in the palace dungeons.

"Well, let's figure out where Luca's been and go from there. There must be other people from Holodal living here." Princess Lena began walking down the hall. "Ana, while Drea does that, I want you to follow up personally on all leads about Tressa. Let's find her and figure out what happened."

Anastasia nodded, turning around quickly to go upstairs. Drea assumed it was to investigate Tressa's room before potentially heading out on her own to track her onetime friend.

Drea didn't waste any time going to see Luca. The queen had commanded it, and she was nothing if not loyal to her kingdom. She didn't warn Henry or the palace of her arrival. As Ambassador, she wouldn't. As Ambassador, she could show up at any time and make the demands befitting her title, and she was going to see how much allowance she got because of it today.

Drea's cane lightly tapped the stone floor of the palace as she walked with determination down to an office she barely dared to enter; Lord Andrew's. His was a room she had avoided at all costs. Not only was he the king's champion, but he was the Master of the Guard, and the Spy Master and Head

Enchanter both reported all movements to him. She always half expected to find a book with her name on it sitting on his desk, waiting for her confession.

That was not what she found when she was granted access to his office. Walking through the door, Drea was greeted by the smell of musty books and too much clutter. Lord Andrew stood before towering bookshelves overflowing with scrolls, documents, and other leather bound books.

"Lady Drizella, I have to say I was surprised when my assistant came in and said you wished to speak with me," Lord Andrew said as he walked over, a stack of documents in his hand.

"I heard you found Luca. As his former employer, I would like to speak with him."

"That is within your rights, and as Ambassador, it is also within your rights to request for him to be transferred into your dungeon before being moved to Trudel to face punishment there. Of course, I say, request. We may refuse it." Lord Andrew clarified.

"That won't be necessary right now. But thank you for the information. Would you mind if your assistant showed me where the dungeons are?"

"I can take you. I need to go down there on a different matter."

Drea followed Lord Andrew as they walked deeper into the palace. In truth, Drea knew exactly where the dungeon was located. She knew the palace kept a rotation of guards on it day and night, and that there were several layers of security throughout it, including several well-placed enchantments that would make a person forget themselves. But as a lady of the court, knowing where the criminals were kept was none of her concern.

"Have you gotten anything out of Luca yet?" Drea asked as they began their descent. The dungeon was kept in the basement with only a small stream of light through the bars to guide them.

"No one has questioned him yet. You'll be the first. I'll be curious to see what you learn, if anything, from him," Lord Andrew replied.

He lit a torch and held it out in front of them as they approached the first set of guards. They parted before them without a word, opening the door to the lower level with four more guards behind it at a small circular table. A single locked door stood behind them.

Lord Andrew removed a metal ring filled with keys. He flicked through several before getting to the correct one. They went farther into the dungeon, each level presenting a new layer of guards and locked doors.

It was one way in, and one way out.

Drea hugged herself, rubbing her arms as they reached the deepest level. The air was dry and crisp as they continued past the cells. Some held men and women, but the majority were empty. Several guards stood out in front of the final cell where Luca was being held.

Luca sat in the farthest depths of the cell, covered in shadows. Chains clinked as he shifted. His once lustrous black hair was dirty and tangled. His clothes were in good condition, though currently a layer of dust had settled over them. He sat on top of a thin mattress that was beside a small plate of food and some water. He stared at her and watched all the guards leave, with Lord Andrew remaining by her side.

"I certainly wasn't expecting Lady Drizella to be my first visitor," Luca said.

For some reason, Drea had expected his voice to be raspy from dehydration or exhaustion. But it was completely normal, as though he hadn't been in hiding for the last three weeks.

"As the new ambassador for Trudel, and your former employer, it seemed only right I come see you," Drea said. "Where were you hiding?"

"I wasn't hiding. I was staying with some friends," Luca retorted as he got up and stood in the middle of the cell.

Drea fiddled with her fingers. She would have to be very careful about what she said.

"After all we did for you, taking you in, giving you a job, and you try to kill Prince David? Why?" Drea asked.

"It wasn't me." Luca tried to cross his arms, but was stopped by the shackles.

"There were witnesses," Lord Andrew inserted.

"I was at Aumont." Luca stared them down.

"That will be for the king to decide," Lord Andrew replied.

"Well, I look forward to meeting with him," Luca said. He turned his back on Drea and sat down.

"Come on, Drizella, you won't get any answers from him about Eleanor," Lord Andrew said. He gently began to lead her away from Luca's cell.

"What about Eleanor?" Luca asked.

"Your arrow killed her." Lord Andrew approached the bars as Luca remained sitting, his head slightly turned. "That arrow you shot at Prince David was coated in poison, and it killed her," Lord Andrew's voice rose as he gripped the bars. She hadn't seen the King's Champion lose his composure since Queen Charisse's death, and even then, it had been but a slip in his stoic facade.

"What poison?" Luca twisted around so fast Drea barely had time to track him as he lunged for the bars. "Ella can't be dead."

"Was it jealousy? After all, you were her personal guard. Did you fall in love with her and then decide to kill the prince when you realized you couldn't have her?" Lord Andrew carried on, standing just as tall as Luca.

Luca's brown eyes were large as he stared at Drea. "What poison?"

He didn't know. Drea watched him as his eyes darted between her and Lord Andrew. She had never seen him that night. He had simply vanished. Maybe he didn't know anything. If Luca wasn't in on the plan...Drea swallowed.

"The arrow that was used in the attempted assassination of Prince David was coated in a lethal dose of Frost," Drea whispered. She monitored every twitch Luca made as she told him that the love of his life was dead.

"No," Luca backed up.

"According to Henry, Ella already had several other injuries and didn't survive them," Drea added.

"That wasn't....she was fine." Luca spoke through gritted teeth. His knuckles were white as he vibrated with emotion. "She was...she was hurt when I saw her, but she was fine."

"When did you see her?" Lord Andrew demanded.

Luca paused, relaxing his hands as he widened his stance. "I got them safely out of the palace."

"Well, apparently that wasn't safe enough." Lord Andrew snapped.

"Drea, she can't be dead. Tell me she isn't dead." Luca turned all his attention to her.

Drea evaluated him. He was clueless, and Drea couldn't tell if it was because Ella didn't trust him or because he had been in hiding. She couldn't tell him anything. Not even a hint. If Henry didn't trust his father with the information, she couldn't trust Luca.

"I don't see why Henry would lie about seeing his close friend die." Drea said quietly.

Luca wilted down to the cell floor. He lay down on his side with his back to her, a blanket pulled over him as he shook.

Drea turned to Lord Andrew, motioning for them to go. They walked in silence back through the dungeon, their steps echoing around them. Drea didn't stay around to see if Henry was available. She parted ways with Lord Andrew and headed for her carriage. Lord Andrew had pulled himself back together with every step he took as they had left. He had even smiled at her and patted her shoulder as he thanked her for getting Luca to place himself in the palace, as though that had been the entire purpose of their visit. Maybe it was for him. Drea hoped she hadn't broken Luca and that somehow, he knew Ella was alive.

CHAPTER TWENTY-SIX

Raven

Raven stared at Calla's mirror. It was a simple one that matched the rest of their set. They wanted to make sure no matter where someone was, they could pull it out and use it without someone questioning them about it. So they had settled on plain golden painted mirrors that would appear elegant, but not expensive. She turned it over in her hands as she thought about what she was going to do. She had to know about Calla. She didn't care that her magic was still flickering in the darkness. She would have to maintain absolute control over her emotions. She had to.

Raven strengthened her resolve, built some walls, and calmed her mind as she opened the mirror and, with the smallest of touches, pulled on her magic. She pictured his face with his cute dimples, unruly brown hair, green eyes, and a healing scar that faintly trailed a path down his face, with an arrogant personality to go with it.

Please, please don't close the mirror, Prince Adam, Raven said in Evrotian. She wasn't sure how he would respond if she had spoken to him in Vicurian. She really couldn't afford to have him close the mirror. She wasn't sure she would be able to form the connection again.

The prince stared at her with wary eyes. Dark circles lined them, his scar contrasting against his skin.

Princess Astrid, this is dangerous. His voice was rougher than usual, as if he had been yelling...or crying.

I know. I just...is Calla— Raven stopped as she spotted a woman in the background. It was too dark to see her clearly as the sun had just begun to rise, and Raven had thought he would be alone. *Who's that?*

The woman stood and walked over until she was beside Prince Adam.

Raven did all she could to keep a blank expression as Mira stood beside him.

Adam, who is it? Mira leaned over his shoulder, locking eyes with Raven a glint of mirth in their green depths.

Raya. Prince Adam's voice tightened.

Mira rolled her eyes. *Fine, I'll leave. I need to get ready anyway. You're going to love my gown, Adam. It's such a *beauty*, I just have to make sure it's still safe and not harmed from the journey,* Mira said as she sashayed away, closing the door behind her.

Raven reeled her emotions in before her magic had a chance to respond. Somehow, she maintained her composure as realization dawned on her...Mira was there...Mira was making sure Calla was okay and mostly unharmed if she had understood her correctly.

Apologies about Princess Miraya, she can be a lot...but I promise she won't tell anyone about this conversation, Prince Adam said.

Raven frowned as she tried to put everything together.

What can I do for you, Princess Astrid?

Uh, Princess Miraya? Raven couldn't stop the question from tumbling out. That was a new trick for Mira to pull off, though how, Raven had no idea.

Yes, from the Kingdom of Grecia, Prince Adam said. He raised his eyebrows at her.

Calla, your maid...is she okay?

Prince Adam turned away from her, his brow furrowed. *I don't understand. Why are you reaching out to me? Surely this just confirms her guilt — that she was part of your plot.*

Part of my plot? Raven tilted her head. *What plot?*

What does it matter? You'll just deny it—

All I care about is that Calla is okay. That she's not being tortured...not how I was tortured. That that horrid woman isn't taking her to her special room to get her secrets from her—

Worried she'll give up all of your secrets? Prince Adam snapped. It was then she noticed Prince Adam's green eyes were red, and his hair was more unruly than usual.

She took a moment. He was upset, tired, and unsure of whom to trust.

Can I tell you something about Calla? Raven waited for an objection. None came. *When I was eleven, I went into the library at the house I was trained in to get a book when I found someone crying in a corner surrounded by books. You see, this person was bullied often by some of the older students, and the library was her escape. She was always afraid of something going wrong, so she made herself small. When I asked her who had hurt her, she denied it. Refused to tell me. Instead, she told me she was crying because the book she was reading was so beautifully written. She was eight years old and had already read more books than I could dream of.*

What's your point? I already know she loves to read, Prince Adam muttered.

My point is whatever they've told you about her...it's not true. Whatever they told you about me...is probably true. Raven attempted a smile. *But Calla...she's as sweet as they come. She's not an assassin, or part of any plot. She was only there to help me with my assignment to find the late king's advisers. So, back to my original request. I need to know she's okay. I'm coming to get her out, but I just...I have to know.*

Prince Adam nodded his head. *You realize I should report this to the queen?*

I do.

Then why tell me?

Because I know Calla trusts you. So, I'm trusting you.

Prince Adam looked away, his eyes staring down.

She's...okay. I haven't gotten to see much of her. The sooner she can get out, the better. Prince Adam said.

Raven nodded her head. *I'll get there as soon as I can. You need to work on a plan to help me.*

He nodded in acceptance. It was more than she could have hoped for from him. He must really care for Calla.

I won't scry you again unless absolutely necessary. It's better for you to reach out to me. Raven paused as she observed him. He stood straighter now than he had when she'd first reached out to him. His eyes were glassy as he blinked rapidly. *She deserves more from the world than you'll ever be able to give her.*

I know.

Raven closed her mirror.

She gazed into the stormy blue eyes of Aleks.

She shoved the mirror into her pocket, wiping away a tear before it could fall free.

"That was risky," Aleks stated.

"I had to." Raven replied as she got up and began to exercise her muscles. She had to be ready to get Calla out. She looked over at Aleks as he worked on the fire. "Aleks, does the name Princess Miraya of Grecia mean anything to you?"

Aleks rubbed his head. "It does...why?"

"Her name was mentioned in passing." Raven crossed her arms.

"I'm going to just walk past that very obvious lie. It's not a good story," Aleks said as Raven stopped stretching.

"I only met her a couple of times, and it was..." Aleks paused. "The last time I saw her was six years ago, before everything went to hell. I'm not entirely sure what happened; they kept the scandal well covered. But she was caught up in something when she was thirteen. Her father, a scary man, was livid from what I heard. Whatever she did, he sent her away to some academy and ended her engagement to Prince Adam, actually. Why?"

Raven took a moment to form her thoughts. Mira was a princess, and she was in Evrotia. Raven frowned, trying to piece it all together.

"Raven?"

She turned back to Aleks. "Prince Adam mentioned her when I scried him, and I was curious," Raven replied, shrugging her shoulders. How had two princesses ended up in Lady Tremaine's care? Raven thought.

"Uh-huh..." Aleks paused as he fiddled with the fire. "If I tell you a story about Ella, will you tell me one about her living with you?"

Raven watched him as he remained crouched on the forest floor. He stared at the fire, his knuckles white as he stirred the flames.

"I only met her once, when she was five," Aleks said as he gazed at Raven. "Her mother had just died, and she and her father had sailed over with the body for the funeral. I was eight, and my family..." He turned his attention towards the sky, pulling his blanket around him. "Well, we've never been in a good place. All my siblings and I have known is ice from our mother and indifference from our father. We gathered together in front of the palace to welcome them. The horses pulling my aunt in her crystal coffin arrived first. I had only ever heard stories about her from my mom, tainted with anger."

Aleks sighed, his eyes distant. "I remember my older brother, Cai, being particularly mean that morning. He kept pulling on my clothes and hair so I would be unkempt, something our mother wouldn't tolerate. Though that morning, when I glanced at her in fear of the reprimand I would get for my appearance, she was absolutely still as the coffin went past her. If it hadn't been for the tears I saw, I would have thought her truly frozen. It was the most emotion I had ever seen from her. All I had ever heard about my aunt Laila was how she had ruined my mom's life. I thought my mom hated her, but if those tears were full of her hate, I have to wonder what tears full of love looked like from her. A carriage pulled up after the coffin, stopping before us. A man stepped out of it, holding a little girl with hair as white as mine." Aleks ran a hand through his, grimacing at it.

"As soon as the formalities were done, my cousin, Ella, jumped out of his arms, walked over to me and smiled the biggest smile. Then she grabbed my hand and asked me to go play with her. It didn't matter that we didn't have any toys around; she was content running through the courtyard, laughing. I had looked to my mother for permission to play with her, and I know she almost didn't let me. I saw it in the small twitch of her lips, one final way to get back at the sister she so despised. She was going to say no, but then she nodded her head, and I was free to run. The rest of their visit was just like that. Running through the halls, chasing each other and our imaginary villains. Laughing when we startled Lena, or going riding on horses." Aleks leaned back, smiling one of the most genuine smiles Raven had ever seen.

"It may have been just one time, but those memories...they got me through some bad ones. Until Ella, I hadn't realized someone who looked like me could demonstrate any amount of kindness or warmth. Meeting Ella and her dad showed me that just because I was born into my family didn't mean I had to be like them. She doesn't even realize the impact she had on my life, but I hope one day I can tell her in person."

Raven shifted on the log. Aleks's story of Ella was beautiful, and while she had many beautiful memories with Ella, none of them would be worthy of that.

"The Ella I know hasn't lost that spirit, but she has changed. Her carefree bliss was extinguished in her a long time ago—"

"She seemed okay in the mirror."

"She was." Raven confirmed. "But...she went through a lot, Aleks. She's determined, loving, and fiercely loyal to the crown she defends. But to become that person, to become one of the best assassins—"

"Assassins? Ella is an assassin?"

"Yes," Raven replied.

Aleks nodded. "Well at least it means she's just like you, capable, smart, and probably more of a badass than my sister is expecting."

"Absolutley," Raven commented. It had been a shock when Ella and Prince David had revealed that information and that they were on their way to get proof. The Snow Queen was going to end up on the wrong side of a war, and Raven wondered which side Aleks would choose. "So, what story do you want to hear about Ella?"

"What was it like growing up with her?" Aleks leaned forward, his blue eyes wide.

"It took a bit for Ella to form a bond with anyone, let alone me. She didn't know who to trust. But she learned how to survive. There were days where we would lie on her bed and read or talk about different killing techniques we had learned. We have two other friends, Siren and Belle. The four of us would go on adventures in the back of the house or train together." As Raven talked, she sank into her memories, languishing in the happiness they brought up. "The thing Ella and I loved the most was racing our horses. She grew up on them, and I guess I did too. We would host tournaments when we were younger, back when there were just a few of us." Raven smiled.

"It sounds like the two of you are really close," Aleks murmured.

"We're sisters," Raven stated. "Mira joined us a few years ago, but she's been a perfect fit." Raven thought about Mira going to Evrotia, protecting Calla. She had joined their group seamlessly. Raven hoped she knew what she was doing. Queen Lyanna would not hold back if she realized exactly all that Mira was.

"I wish I had gotten to choose my family." Aleks wrapped himself tighter in the blanket.

"We did choose each other, I guess. I can't imagine my life without them. I would give anything to protect them."

"Careful now, that sounds like a weakness," Rowan teased, lightly nudging her.

"It would be if I knew they couldn't take care of themselves. Calla is the only one I worry about, and that's because she's not trained to fight." Raven pinched the bridge of her nose.

"Then why was she sent?" Aleks grumbled.

"That's a question I've asked myself every day," Raven whispered. "What about your family? You make them sound even more charming than you."

"My family..." Aleks adjusted how he sat, shaking out his shoulders. "Where to start? My oldest brother, Cai, heir to the throne, and an arrogant prick to go with the title. Just like our father, always trying to prove he's better than everyone else."

"Sounds lovely." Raven grimaced. She rubbed her arms, pulling her cloak tighter.

Aleks rubbed his head. "I have a half brother, the family pawn. He's...interesting to have in the palace at times. Lone wolf, black sheep complex. Consistently forced to prove himself as a way of ensuring he remains in the palace until my mother throws him out. She's only allowed him to live this long in the palace because he doesn't have my white hair and can therefore move about without being noticed."

"My sister Lena has always desired power, and my mother raised her to rule Rairene, instilling an ego as large as a throne. Though Prince David has never liked her, I can guarantee you Lena won't go down without a fight. She's vindictive and cunning, but won't boast about it like Cai. Cai lets you know upfront what he's going to do, Lena works in the shadows luring you in with a trap you don't see coming until it's snapped."

"Your family sounds delightful." Raven commented. Even though the sun was still rising for the day, a chill had set in, and she had to wrap her blankets tighter around her shoulders.

"I'm sharing this so if you ever meet my family, which hopefully you won't, you'll still know what to expect from them. My youngest brother, Joseph, is the only one not fully corrupted. He loves to hide from his fighting instructors and would rather live life surrounded by his books and scholars.

He's smart, though. He convinced my mother his time was best spent learning about warfare and strategy."

Raven shuddered. "It's freezing, don't you feel it, Rowan?" Raven's teeth chattered.

"It's warm." Rowan rested a hand on her forehead. "You're burning up, Raven." Rowan stood and walked over to Aleks. "Both of you, what's wrong with you?"

Aleks curled on his side, shivering under his blanket. "It's an enchanter's flareout sickness. Rowan, we need to get to an outpost village. It's a day's ride away, but soon..." Aleks glanced at Raven, "probably sooner than we would like, both of us will fall into an enchanter's sleep and most likely hallucinate, to only name a few of the side effects."

"How am I supposed to get you there?" Rowan looked at the horses.

Aleks stumbled to his feet, collapsing in front of Raven before getting back up. "You're going to have to tie us to our horses." Aleks's teeth chattered.

Raven had curled into a ball, trying to find an ounce of warmth where none existed. Aleks's assessment had sent ice shooting through her. She had only ever heard of the enchanter's flareout sickness. It only happened after an enchanter lost control, and was their body's way of recovering from the loss of magic. She'd assumed that since a day had passed, she was in the clear. Lady Tremaine had instilled in her the desire to never lose control and had hung not only enchanter's shackles over her head to keep control but also this sickness. First were the chills, and a never ending freeze through her body. Followed by hallucinations, an unbreakable sleep, and fever dreams. Some would last for a day or so; others would last for weeks. Raven had a feeling hers would last a lot longer than a day.

She knew she had to get up. Even told her body to do so. All she had to do was unfurl her legs, push out her arms and push off the ground. But her muscles wouldn't listen to her. They refused to respond. It was as if they had become glass and rocks at the same time. Too fragile and heavy to move. Still, she tried. She tried until she felt tears falling down her cheeks.

She could do this. She would make it to her horse before the hallucinations started. She could do that. Had to do that.

"Whoa, easy, Raven." Rowan was beside her in a blink, keeping her upright.

Had she stood? She must've.

Raven opened her eyes as she felt her horse's coarse mane in her hands.

When she opened her eyes again, she was tied down to her horse. When did that happen?

"Rowan?" Raven swung her head around for her partner. "Rowan, why am I tied up? What's going on?" Raven resisted closing her eyes again as her eyelids weighed her down. Saliva coated her throat as her heart pounded. Raven slipped into Rairenian. "What's happening? Why are you doing this?"

Rowan sidled up next to her, resting his hand on hers. "I don't know what you're saying, Raven—"

"What's happening?" Raven asked in Rairenian.

Rowan shook his head as he squeezed her hand. "You're sick. You're tied to your horse so you don't fall off. We're riding to a village outpost that Aleks uses as a safe house. It's not too far. We'll get you help there. I hope that helps you."

Raven mumbled again in Rairenian before her eyes won the battle and forced her to sleep.

CHAPTER TWENTY-SEVEN

Raven

Raven was racing on horseback with Ella beside her, laughing as they ran through the forest behind Aumont. She didn't know why they were racing, and she didn't care. Ella was alive, and she was running free with her.

"Isn't this great?" Ella yelled over the wind, her white hair unrestrained as snow fell around her.

"I've missed it!" Raven hollered back. She had missed it so much. Ever since she'd enchanted that poison after Jason left her, she had been different. But not now. Now she felt the blood rushing through her veins, her magic thrumming softly throughout her.

Raven glanced around at the snow. It had never snowed there so close to the coast before. Raven's horse labored beneath her, as though he had been running for hours, not minutes. His coat glistened with sweat.

"Ella?" Raven asked, turning towards her sister.

"Something's wrong," Ella whispered, her eyes wide.

Raven cast a glance behind her, the blood draining from her face at the army of men chasing them. Shadows of men rode after them, chasing them into the black forest. The snow fell harder around them, blinding them.

"Just over this ridge, Raven, and we'll be safe. We'll be at the outpost." Ella yelled, fear coating her voice.

"The outpost?" Raven scrunched her face. They were going to an outpost? She glanced ahead and then back to Ella, except she had vanished. Ella was gone, her horse vanishing into the darkness. "Ella!" Raven twisted in her saddle.

"Raven, please stay still." Rowan's voice grated through her skull.

Raven opened her eyes, the snow covered ground staring at her as she was jostled. A horse came up beside her, the rider reaching over to adjust the ropes tying her down.

"It's okay. We're almost there," Rowan said.

Snow blanketed the mountains as ice slowly crept into Raven. The sun had begun to set, and the last thing Raven saw was the purple sky before darkness consumed her once again.

The bindings loosening around her wrists were the first thing she remembered as she opened her eyes. The next thing she noticed was her cloak was covering her face. She tried to remove it, only to have someone shove it back down.

Raven's mind cleared just enough cobwebs to realize it would keep anyone from seeing her. Smart move Rowan. Strong arms lifted her off her horse and carried her somewhere warm. She opened her eyes long enough to see a large man lift Aleks off his horse and carry him over his shoulder. A woman followed behind, her black cloak obstructing her features.

"Rowan," Raven croaked. "I think I have enough energy to make it to a room. You look as dead as I feel."

He set her down instantly, keeping an arm around her waist.

"Thank the gods, I wasn't sure I was going to make it," he whispered. Sweat rolled down his forehead.

"Let's get to the room and never wake up again." Raven tried to smile. Both of them leaned on each other to get up the last steps to the third floor.

They stopped short when they reached the top and came face to face with a beautiful, dark-skinned woman. Her hazel eyes were calculating and fierce as she observed them. Her hand rested on a hip, one eyebrow raised.

"Well, I certainly hope you're worth it; you don't seem like much. You two are staying through that door." She motioned to the door on her right before sidestepping the two of them and heading downstairs. "Rowan." They turned to her. "I'll take the watch tonight. You've worked yourself to the bones, it's no wonder I was able to sneak up on you." She winked at him.

"I still beat you, Daciana. But thank you," Rowan mumbled before shuffling Raven through the door.

"Who was that?" Raven stumbled into the small room until she sat on the bed, the room spinning beneath her feet.

"She works for Aleks. Outside of that, all I know is we wouldn't have made it here without her."

"How are you doing?" Raven asked, her hands shook as she tried to undo the clasp on her cloak before giving up.

"I'm okay." Rowan walked over and unclasped Raven's cloak.

Raven hugged him. "Thank you. You've been through a lot...all because of me...I don't think I can tell you enough how grateful I am for you."

"I'll always be here for you," Rowan said as he hugged her back.

Raven took stock of her body as she blinked. Her muscles ached, and when she tried to move her arms, they protested, the movement causing enough pain she dropped her arms back to her sides. She shivered, wishing she could pull the blankets tighter around her. Raven turned her stiff neck to the side to find Rowan sleeping, wrapped in blankets, his boots and cloak removed.

The room only held the necessary furniture for a room to function. Two beds, two wooden chairs, one armoire, and one small table. At least they seemed well kept, Raven noted. The blankets were hefty, despite the chills and aches that refused to leave her body.

"Good, you're awake. You need to take a bath."

Raven frowned at the woman who leaned in her door frame, examining her nails. She was dressed entirely in black, though that didn't hide the multitude of weapons on her. Her black coiled hair was tightly braided back on the left side of her head, leaving the rest loose and falling down past her shoulder.

"Who are you?" Raven tried to remember her name, but she could barely remember how she got up the stairs the night before.

"Daciana. I work with the prince." She jerked a thumb over her shoulder, where Raven assumed Aleks was. "You'll feel better if you take a bath." She smiled.

"That bad, huh?" Raven groaned.

"Yes." Daciana tossed some towels to her. "Bath's down the hall. Let me know if you need help getting there."

"I think I should be okay." Raven carefully forced her legs to move before standing. She bent her knees and stumbled, catching herself on the fireplace before collapsing to the floor. "I'm okay," Raven shooed her away when Daciana got to her side.

She grabbed the towels and found a way out of the room, leaning heavily against the wall as she dragged her body down the hall. She trembled as she saw the bath filled with hot water. Raven bit her lip, her knuckles turning white as she clutched the door frame. She could do it. One small step at a time. Raven approached the tub as she would a mark, silently and slowly. She didn't bother removing her clothes as she put one foot and then the other into the tub. Her legs shook so much she fell into the water, her head ducking under. She resurfaced, blinking when she saw Morgan and Queen Lyanna stood before her. Both of them laughed as they poured more water over her head. She squeezed her eyes shut, convincing herself it wasn't real. She would open her eyes, and they would be gone.

Raven lifted her head and surveyed the empty room.

She glanced down at the black water in the tub, grimacing. She was that filthy? She emptied it and refilled it with clean, hot water. She supported herself with shaky arms as she got back in. Her vision blurred as it darkened around the edges.

A hand lightly touched her cheek, startling her from wherever she had gone in her sleep.

"What the fuck?" Raven's mind told her body to spin around, but her body ignored the order as it continued to lie there, unmoving.

"You fell asleep. Prince Charming, as you call him, thought you might need some help. He sent me to check on you since he's unable to get out of bed and wanted to make sure you hadn't drowned," Daciana said as she looked Raven over.

"How very charming of him —"

"It is."

"I'm being facetious," Raven snapped. "Calling him Prince Charming is not a good thing."

"Oh, I know. I love it. I can't believe I didn't think to call him that myself." Daciana started to wash Raven's hair, pouring hot, clean water over her scalp and massaging her head.

"What poison did you give me?" Raven could barely twitch her fingers, and the cold in the tub had sunk back into her blood.

"I didn't give you anything." Daciana moved to sit in front of Raven.

"Then why can't I move?" Raven ground out. Her eyes began to close again. She had to stay awake. She had to see what Daciana was doing to her, and she couldn't do that if she kept falling asleep.

"It's the enchanter's sickness, Raven."

Raven longed to turn around and see him.

"You!" Daciana stood fast enough to knock over the stool. "Get back to bed. You can barely stand."

"You can't order me around. I'm *your* superior."

Even Raven, in her state of mind, could hear the exhaustion pulling on him, the weight sinking in.

"If I touched you, would you fall over?" Daciana asked, glee coating her voice. Raven decided right then she liked her. She didn't have to move to know what the scene behind her looked like. Daciana would be towering over Aleks as he leaned heavily in the door frame, sweat on his brow as he himself tried to stay conscious.

"Please knock him over," Raven called. She could lean her head back just enough to see them. To see that Aleks did look like shit, and that she was probably worse. "Aleks, please leave so that I can get some sleep."

Aleks grumbled something incoherent before Raven heard the door close.

"I brought you a change of clothes. Your old ones are disgusting. How long have you been wearing them?" Daciana held them, her nose wrinkled.

"A month? I've lost track of time." Raven glanced at the clean clothes beside the tub that seemed very far away. Oceans away in her current state. She gulped her pride and stared back at Daciana. "You don't think you could help me, do you?"

Daciana smiled gently before putting Raven's old clothes down and helping her get out of the tub, dried off, and get dressed. Daciana didn't say a word as she saw Raven's naked body and the scars that painted it.

CHAPTER TWENTY-EIGHT

Mira

Mira felt tingles shoot down her left thigh. She paused in the hallway, making sure she hadn't imagined it. In all her years since leaving home, she had never felt the gentle sensation of that enchanted mirror calling her. Though the silence hadn't kept her from keeping it in a pocket everywhere she went.

Mira turned back and darted for her room. She had to get there before the enchantment faded.

The pinpricks in her leg increased to a crescendo.

She sprinted to her room, not caring if someone saw.

She slammed her door behind her and ripped the mirror out of her pocket.

It was a minuscule, single-sided mirror plated in gold with a decorative trident. Mira gripped it in her shaking hand and gazed into it.

The moment the enchantment in the mirror saw her, the surface rippled and a face she hadn't seen in six years appeared before her.

Mira stared at a golden skinned woman with deep red hair pulled back high in a ponytail. The emerald eyes of the heir to the throne of Grecia and Mira's eldest sister stared back at her.

"Maliah," Mira whispered as her fingers touched the edge of her vision in the mirror.

Hey, little fish. Maliah's voice washed over her like a refreshing tide that gently caresses you in the early morning sun.

Tears welled instantly as Mira covered her mouth. She stared in awe through blurry eyes at the sister she held closest to her heart.

"I don't know what to say. How are you?" Mira asked. Her arms ached to wrap her sister within them.

I'm well. I miss you, little fish.

"I miss you so much," Mira replied. She aggressively whipped away the tears. Mira took a breath and asked a question that twisted her gut. "Did something happen?"

Why are you in Evrotia?

Mira frowned. How could she possibly know?

Queen Lyanna scried me. She wanted to verify father had sent you to her court under the correct pretenses and to not break our alliance with them, Maliah said. She raised an eyebrow. *So, I'll ask you again, why are you there and not at the academy learning how to be part of the court?*

Mira blanched. "I'm here because of the academy. I had no choice but to say where I was from."

We both know that's not true. I was in Rairene. I went to get you. Let me bring you home.

"It doesn't matter. Not anymore," Mira replied.

If I'm going to lie to a queen and an ally, I want to know what's happening.

"I'm here to help a friend."

Well, you need to leave. I didn't like how the queen was talking —

"I can't, Mali —"

You can, and you will. This is an order from your future queen.

Mira bit her lip. "Lili...I can't. You don't understand, and I won't leave —"

Miraya, come home, Maliah whispered.

"What do you mean?"

Come home to me.

Mira blinked tears away. She had waited years to hear those words. "I can't." Mira spoke through a throat swollen with pain.

I am commanding you, Princess Miraya of Grecia, to return home. Maliah's voice was stern as she stared Mira down.

"My home is the friends I've made over the last five years, and one of them is in trouble."

Mira pressed her hand over the mirror, destroying the connection before her sister could see the tears beginning to well in her eyes. She had waited so long, and she had to say no. She had to save Calla, no matter what. She was more important. Mira shook herself, pulling her emotions back in and flicking away the lone tear that escaped. She walked out of her room and almost ran into Morgan as she raised a hand to knock.

"Oh, hi, Morgan, right?" Mira took a small step back as she smiled.

"Hi. I was wondering, um, would you like to walk with me to court?" Morgan asked.

"That would be great. I got lost the other day trying to find the kitchen." Mira stepped out of her room and followed Morgan. "I haven't seen you in a few days at dinner with everyone else."

"I've been trying to locate some information for the queen, and it's proving difficult, so I've been too exhausted to attend court," Morgan replied.

"Well, I hope you find it soon."

Mira glanced down and noticed fresh burns on Morgan's skin.

"What happened?"

Morgan put her hands behind her back. "Accident. I burned myself with some candle wax while getting said information. Nothing I can't handle. You should see what I spilled the candle wax onto."

"Did it damage the table? How much wax was there?"

"I'm hoping it's not too bad, but sometimes you never know how deep the burn can go. The queen didn't care, so that's all that matters." Morgan shrugged.

Mira turned away and watched how they were getting to the queen's throne room. It seemed like there was always a new way to get there.

"Do the walls feel off to you?" Mira asked.

Morgan gave her a quizzical gaze.

"They feel off to me. In Grecia, my great-grandfather had built a series of small tunnels in selected sections of our palace that he could use to escape if anyone should surround it. Is that the same thing here?"

"I never thought about it. There could be." Morgan didn't add to Mira's theory. "Tell me about Grecia. It's one of the few places I haven't traveled to."

"Why not?"

"It always seemed too far, I guess. I don't know, actually."

"Well, if you're able to manage being on a ship for a month, I highly recommend it. The beaches are like nothing you've ever seen. The sand is pure white, and when you squish it between your toes as the warm water rushes over you..." Mira drifted off as she thought about it. "There's nothing that can describe the power of the ocean at the tips of your toes. It's hard to believe sometimes that something so turbulent and powerful as an angry ocean can also be so calm that you want to drift on your back for hours in its depths."

"I've often found the most powerful people are like the ocean, powerful and terrifying when they need to be, but calm and reassuring when they're called to lead."

Mira nodded. She agreed with Morgan, noting she said powerful people and not powerful rulers.

"What's something fun you would do there?"

"I don't know if I would say it's fun, but I loved collecting seashells. There would always be different ones, and it became a scavenger hunt with my sisters to see who could find the best one that day."

Morgan laughed. "Is there anything you don't miss?"

"The moisture in the air. You see, I'm a vain person and I love my hair, but it does not look like this at home with its tame glossy curls. It's an effort to control it, and I usually have to have it in a braid."

"You're beautiful with your hair braided." Morgan remarked.

"Thank you." Mira spoke softly.

"I have to check on someone before court starts, but maybe I can see you later?" Morgan asked.

"I thought the queen frowned on tardiness." Mira tilted her head.

"She makes an exception for me."

"That must be some important information."

"You could say that. I'll see you inside." Morgan left before Mira could say another word. Mira thought about their conversation as she took her spot in the middle of the crowd of nobles. Morgan walked with a confidence she had only seen in Ella and Raven. She would bet her crown Morgan was at least a spy, if not more, for the queen.

She gazed around the room. The area roped off for commoners remained empty. So long as the palace was closed, no one could complain to their queen. Mira wondered how long it would last. The people would begin to demand answers, and the servants would need to see their families. It had been over a week; surely she didn't think there was any chance of Raven being caught?

Mira didn't even know why the queen was holding court today. There was no reason for it. The house staff was here as well. Mira glanced around as she worked on getting to the edge of the throne.

Prince Adam walked beside her.

"Any idea why we're all here?" Mira whispered.

"None. Princess Arianna was in a good mood."

“So, it’s bad then.”

“Most likely.” Adam stiffened as the doors slammed open.

Mira was about to say something snarky when Calla was brought forward, wrapped in chains.

CHAPTER TWENTY-NINE

Ella

Ella processed Emperor Edris' claim that Luca was in a dungeon in Rairene...that he had been caught.

"Your Majesty, we are not here on behalf of your son, though his capture is not something we were aware of. I'm afraid we come with more dire news—" David said.

"What could be more dire than a prince of Holodal being held for crimes he did not commit?" Emperor Edris's voice echoed around them as he walked down from his throne to stand a foot taller than David.

Ella stared at the emperor and swallowed. Now she understood why Shenzali had been so concerned. Ella didn't think he would hesitate to kill both of them if they did not explain themselves. Immediately.

"Emperor Edris, if you would give us leave to explain our mission, I think you will find our answer will intertwine with Luca...Prince Lucian's current detainment," Ella rushed, hoping the emperor would stop staring at David like his next kill.

The emperor nodded briefly before walking back to his throne and motioning for them to explain.

Ella poured out their story about the Queen of Trudel attempting to instigate a war, making sure she left out some key components of their story. He didn't need to know she was an assassin, or that David was the prince Luca had been charged with attempting to murder. She also made sure to keep Luca's status as an assassin as downplayed as possible, focusing on the work he did as a guard for Lady Tremaine. As she spun their tale, the sun had fully set and torches had been lit around the room. A servant had even brought in a meal for the emperor. By the time Ella finished, her throat was dry, and she was certain she had walked a trench into the ground from all of her pacing.

David stood behind her, arms clasped behind his back.

"That is quite the tale, Lady Eleanor," Emperor Edris said once Ella was done talking. "Why, then, have you come here?"

"We would seek an alliance —" Ella began.

The emperor laughed. "You hold my son prisoner and make this request? Tell me, why did the great King Matthias send a Lady and a nobody knight on this important journey? Does he think I am so gullible to be honored by the mere idea of an alliance that I wouldn't be insulted by the gesture?" Emperor Edris banged his scepter on the ground again.

"King Matthias meant no disrespect, I promise. The Kingdom of Rairene sees the value of an alliance with you —"

"He sees the value my army can provide. Tell me, would it bother him that half of my army is composed of women?"

Ella stood taller. "Not in the slightest." Ella's veins thrummed with excitement at getting to see his legendary warriors.

"I do not believe you. Your king dishonors me by sending me someone who cannot negotiate fully for his kingdom, and based on your backward ideas, I don't believe he'll accept his men fighting beside women."

"The king means no disrespect." David inserted.

"How would you know, knight? Did King Matthias tell you, 'make sure the emperor of Holodal knows I mean no offense when sending you'?"

"My name is Prince David, heir to the throne of Rairene, and I have come to seek information and an alliance with our neighbors. Long have we let the relations between our two kingdoms dwindle away to the point that neither kingdom is able to recognize when a prince is before them. As the crowned prince, I am seeking to rebuild what was lost and create an even stronger bond between our people to make sure both of us are protected. I can promise you the Queen of Trudel will not stop at my kingdom and will turn to Holodal next should she be successful in her attempt at winning a war with mine." David stood tall in front of Ella.

Ella did her best to hide her rage as David revealed himself.

"Tell me what we can do to make an alliance start to grow," David said, transforming into the regal king he would one day become.

"Release my son. Clearly, you and Lady Eleanor are not dead."

"I cannot do that. My champion is the only person who knows we are alive. The Trudelian Queen was thorough in creating her web of spies, and my champion is the only person I trust. I can guarantee your son's life and safety while he is held there. Lord Henry will not let anything happen to him. That is all I can offer in regard to Prince Lucian's current status."

"Is what your Lady says about you being able to accept our female warriors true?" Emperor Edris leaned forward. "It is strange to us that you keep these ideas that women are not just as capable as men. My women have proven to be far more effective and vicious fighters than my men. You are not a worthy ally if you refuse to use half of your population in battle."

"It would not be an issue, we have some female fighters." David spoke calmly. The hands clasped behind his back shook as he pleaded their case.

"Prove it."

"What?" David's arms dropped to his sides.

"Prove it. One of my warriors will take on one woman from your kingdom. If she can beat her, then I will forge the alliance you seek."

"Lady Eleanor is the only woman present from my kingdom. Anyone else would cause a delay."

"Then I guess you better hope she can fight," Emperor Edris snapped.

David paused.

"Is there a reason she can't fight for her kingdom?"

David would either have to let Ella fight or reveal he was an enchanter and risk the emperor seeking to keep him as a prize.

"No reason, Your Majesty. The Prince is simply protective," Ella said as she stepped forward. She stretched her muscles, then braided back her hair and unclasped her cloak and pendant, handing both to David. "I'll take on whichever warrior you wish." Ella looked at Emperor Edris through the waning sunlight. He grinned down at her. It was so eerily similar to Luca she could have sworn it was him before her.

"Takani, you will fight Lady Eleanor." Emperor Edris called forth one of the women who stood guard behind him.

She stood as tall as the emperor, with black hair tightly braided to the middle of her back. A gold nose ring glinted as she looked down at Ella. Takani wore loose fitting linen pants that were snug around her hips and ankles, but still full of fabric that allowed for easy movement. Her tunic, however, clung to her, with bracers and pauldrons gracing her shoulders and arms. She removed them as she walked down the steps, letting them clang to the ground. Ella backed up until they were directly before the emperor.

"Lady Eleanor, I'll let you choose the style. My warriors are masters of all."

Ella huffed to hide a grin. She had grown up learning about the warriors of Holodal. The emperor was accurate when he said they were elite and ruthless. Each one trained from birth to fight. It was rumored that the moment they could walk; they were given a staff. Now was the moment Ella got to discover if that was true.

"Hand to hand combat," Ella said. If the rumors were true, the last thing she wanted to do was give the warrior an extra weapon. Her body would be enough of a challenge to defeat.

Takani smiled as she dropped her spear beside her and got into an open fighting stance. Ella shook out her shoulders as she assessed her opponent.

She was strong, her entire body seemingly made of muscle. She was also taller, and Ella could almost guarantee, faster than her. So, all she had was the element of surprise.

Ella got into her own stance, pointing her feet incorrectly and tentatively raising her fists before her.

Then she waited.

She was not going to make the first move.

Takani grew impatient and attacked first with a rapid fire series of punches directed at Ella's face and torso. Ella made sure to miss blocking one and took a punch to the stomach. Ella gasped for breath as she doubled over. Before Takani could react, Ella swung up and slapped her hand over Takani's ear, disorienting her. Ella knew she couldn't hold anything back in this match. She jumped into action, not giving Takani a moment to recover from the hit.

However, Takani quickly found her footing and forced Ella into a defensive move when she wrapped her arm around Ella's neck and applied pressure. Ella wrapped her hands underneath and threw her entire body forward, flipping Takani over her head. She was on her feet in an instant, charging Ella and knocking her to the ground. The two grappled on the ground, each using the strength of their bodies to try to gain the upper hand.

Takani pinned Ella on her back, her thighs pressing into her hips. Ella pulled Takani forward, throwing off her balance. This allowed Ella to push her off and scramble to her feet.

Ella took the moment to catch her breath. She had to win. She had to prove herself to this pompous emperor, who in any other scenario she would have been glad to agree with. But right now she hated him for putting them in this position. The fate of her kingdom hung in the balance. She couldn't let Rairene down. Couldn't let David down. And most importantly, she couldn't let any other little girl who dreamed of training to be a knight down.

Takani came at her with a series of punches and swipes, forcing Ella to get defensive and evade her assault. The two continued to dodge and evade each other's attacks. Sweat trickled down Ella's forehead and into her eyes as the room darkened and the temperature remained hot in the throne room. What she wouldn't give to be wearing the linen clothes Takani wore instead of her own thick clothing.

Ella blinked.

Takani was directly before her.

She barreled into Ella, wrapping her arms around the back of Ella's thighs. She pushed Ella onto her back.

In one swift movement, Ella was vulnerable, and Takani had the kill shot.

"Yield."

Frustration and tears gathered in Ella's eyes as she glared at the warrior in defiance.

"Yield." Takani stepped in closer.

Ella grunted, withholding the scream that built in her throat. Takani held out her hand to Ella, lifting her off the ground.

"You fought well," Takani said softly.

Ella nodded as she stood beside David and faced Emperor Edris.

"Thank you for entertaining me tonight. We will talk more tomorrow. Shame you couldn't beat Takani; I was curious about an alliance. For now, Shenzali will show you to the guest suite." Emperor Edris dismissed them.

***

Ella swiped at her eyes the moment they were outside the throne room. She followed Shenzali in silence, grateful the guard was in front of her.

David reached out for her, brushing his hand against hers.

Ella pulled away.

"There are fresh baths in each room and some loose clothing. Trust me, you'll want it while you sleep. I'll see you in the morning," Shenzali said as she stood in the doorway to their suite of rooms.

"Thank you, Shenzali," David said softly.

Ella stood in the entrance, staring into the distance.

"You did well, Lady Eleanor," Shenzali said before closing the door.

Ella scoffed. She had lost. *Lost.*

She had lost before.

But not when it mattered.

"Ella —"

"Not right now, David. Please." Ella requested as she left the living space and walked to the closest room on the right. The washroom was lined with black stones and held a filled tub in the center with fresh clothes on the sink. Ella striped off her clothes and stepped into the tub without a second thought.

She sat in silence until the water became cool and the breeze brought gooseflesh to her arms and neck. The loose linen nightgown hung to her knees and was the lightest material she had ever worn. No wonder they moved with such ease. Ella thought.

Ella brushed her hair before she lay down on her stomach, preparing herself to ride the wave of emotions she felt approaching in the back of her mind.

They developed like a thunderstorm, thick and heavy with the weight of her failure.

Her only mission was to protect her kingdom, and she had failed.

The moment it mattered...she'd blinked, and now...

"Ella, can I come in?" David asked.

She gave a noncommittal noise as she turned her head to the doorway on which David leaned . He wore a loose linen tunic and pants, his hair dripping droplets on the floor. She turned her head away from him as another thunderstorm gathered.

She had failed in front of him. They had been making progress, and she...Ella closed her eyes as the tears pricked the edges of her eyes.

A sob rose too quickly to stop.

A hand gently rested on her shoulder.

Ella sniffled as she turned her head and found David sitting beside her. She turned until she found eyes not filled with anger or hate, but with something far worse…understanding.

It was the kindness in his eyes that undid her.

Ella turned her head into the blankets as unwelcome tears broke free.

David gathered her into his arms, holding her against his chest as she buried her head in his shoulder.

"You were…" David started.

"Horrific."

"Wondrous."

Ella shook in his arms as she tried to contain the sobs that refused to be restrained.

"You fought one of the most elite warriors I have ever seen, while recovering from a poisonous drug, and you held your own. Do you know how inspiring you are, Ella?" David whispered to her. One arm held her tightly as the other gently ran through her hair.

"I lost *everything*."

"No. You are the most amazing warrior, and I have been a fool for ever believing you should be put on the sidelines when you are the person we need leading the charge. I'm sorry it took me until this night to realize that."

"Please, I failed at acquiring the alliance we have to get. I am the last person who should be leading anyone."

"Your kingdom is proud of you, Ella. No matter the outcome, we're proud of you. I'm proud of you," David confessed. He rested his head on Ella's and held her close as she felt the steady rhythm of his heart and did her best to not give in to the darkness.

CHAPTER THIRTY

Drea

Drea landed flat on her back.

Gus crouched over her, a smile spreading across his face. "That was better." He held out a hand and helped her.

She dusted off her trousers and tightened the strap holding her hair. "Whatever you say. We both know I would have never failed that spectacularly three years ago." Drea paced around on the mattress, limping slightly on her left leg. She paused for a moment to rub out the cramping.

"You're right. Three years ago, you could have wiped the floor with me. But you can't continue to compare yourself to who you were three years ago. First of all, I've improved through training all of you. Secondly, you aren't able to fight the same way anymore, and you need to learn how to use that to your advantage now. You have years of knowledge and experience in that stubborn head of yours, and while you're frustrated with your perceived limitations, I would challenge you instead to see how you can apply your knowledge to your new body. Who knows, maybe you'll be better than who you were three years ago." Gus lectured.

Drea gave an incoherent mutter. He was right, of course. She just hadn't been able to find a way for her leg to not be a weakness anymore. For now, all she could do was focus on her training and hope that when it mattered most, her leg wouldn't betray her.

Gus had her work on more strength training for the rest of their time, pushing Drea's leg to the limit. By the end of their session, Drea collapsed onto the mattress and lay down. She stared at the wooden beams in the ceiling.

"You are improving," Gus said as he lay down beside her.

"I know. I can feel it. Sometimes I think I could go all day without my cane."

"Hopefully, one day you can."

Drea got quiet as she closed her eyes. She had to go have her morning meeting with Princess Lena and Anastasia, but right now she wanted one more minute where politics weren't on her mind. She focused on her magic, tuning into its steady waltz as her heartbeat slowed to a normal staccato. She felt like a leaf on a lazy river, floating along its currents.

"Do you know why the princess has asked me to increase everyone's training?" Gus asked, shocking her out of her peace.

"What kind of increase?"

"She wants all of the novices ready for anything in the next month."

"A month?" Drea sat on her elbows and gazed at him.

Gus nodded his head slowly. "I can see she didn't tell you about this."

"I knew we would be increasing, I just wasn't aware the timetable for our plans had been moved. Did she give you any indication about why?"

"No. She only said they needed to be ready."

Drea stood and straightened her clothes. "Thank you for that information. How close are they to being ready?"

"To be ready for anything? If I had them every day for twenty hours, I would still need about three months at least with them. Some of them joined us only a month ago."

Drea nodded her head and left to get ready for whatever meeting she was about to have with her sister and Princess Lena.

***

Drea paused outside her mother's office as she twisted her hands together. Her magic began to unravel, dancing offbeat. Drea tightened the ribbon holding back her hair before shaking out her fingers. Though she tried to contain her power and ease back into a calm cadence, it refused. Drea grabbed the dagger from her hidden shirt pocket and held it before her.

"*Interficiam per os sicut filum*," Drea whispered. She called on her power, pulling it out of its anxiety and into focused purpose. She thought about her training with Gus and how it felt to move with speed again. "*Interficiam per os sicut filum*." Drea zeroed in on her intent to harm. She thought about...him...truly focused on how she wanted to take the cool metal in her hands and shove it through his heart while watching the light fade from his dark blue eyes. Her magic trilled in her veins, rushing forward to fulfill her wishes by imbuing the blade with a sharpness that would deliver a fatal blow with a featherlight touch. "*Interficiam per os sicut filum*." Drea sealed the enchantment, her power flaring out and around her hands before twisting into the blade.

Drea breathed softly as she tucked the blade back into her pocket. Her magic danced once more to a soft tune as she opened the door and stepped into the meeting. She didn't allow herself to pause when she noticed several instructors had joined the table as well today. Queen Laila looked at all of them through the mirror, a thick fur cloak wrapped around her shoulders. Drea took her seat on Princess Lena's left, across from Anastasia.

I've had Princess Lena summon each of you so that we can discuss an important subject. Queen Laila paused as each person in the room straightened their backs.

Drea took the moment to survey them. Gus sat near the front, his brow furrowed. He looked at her, motioning with a simple turn of his head that he had not known about this meeting before their training session. Their weapons master was present, along with their stable master and their master thief. Drea's mind churned as Queen Laila continued.

Each of you brings a specific set of knowledge I need in order for our mission to be successful. We have one of our own out in the field right now confirming Lady Anastasia's hunch, but I cannot wait for that validation to continue making our plans. That is where each of you comes into play. We need to make several plans for how to eliminate Lady Eleanor should she be alive, and then other plans of attack should she in fact be dead, as Lady Drizella claims.

Drea turned to face the queen. Where she had received pure anger from Anastasia, she found only open consideration from the queen.

"What do we offer?" Gus asked. He stared at the table, his hands in his lap.

Each one of you directly oversaw Ella's training. You four know her the best in the aspects, I have been told, that she excelled at. Your insights into how you created her will be essential in her downfall, Queen Laila said. *Outside of that, the four of you are the most respected masters in Aumont and offer the best opinions on how to get our novices ready while also ensuring our other pupils remain loyal to me.*

Drea kept the smile off her face as the four instructors shifted in their seats.

"What do you wish to know about Lady Eleanor?" Madame Dauphine, a renowned master thief, spoke first. Her blond hair, which usually sat twisted on her head, hung in loose waves down her back, giving her a younger appearance.

Drea wasn't surprised she spoke. Madame Dauphine had come to them out of necessity after gambling away all her money and escaping King Matthias's prison. She had never left Aumont since joining their list of instructors.

Everything, Queen Laila replied, steepling her fingers in front of her as she leaned forward and began asking her questions.

Anastasia and Princess Lena remained relatively silent throughout the meeting. Ana would give a validating head nod or shrug whenever the queen flicked a glance at her as the masters spoke. Their stable master noted Ella's love of the horses and how he felt Ella embodied their strong spirit and steadfast loyalty. Madame Dauphine seconded this sentiment in how she observed Ella with her friends, while noting that Ella was cunning and had been her best pupil, so much in fact, she would have Ella instruct their newer recruits. The weapons master also echoed Ella's skill with a blade and how easily she took to mastering her glass daggers.

Gus was the only one to remain silent.

Master Gustavo, do you have anything to add to your colleagues' opinions? It's my understanding you are the closest to her and have even gone on some assignments with her.

Gus turned to the queen. "I can only agree with the sentiments provided by the others."

If you do think of anything, it is your duty as someone sworn to me to report.

Gus nodded.

Well then, let's begin discussing different ways we can nullify Ella before she ruins my plans.

Drea made a point of ignoring Gus as the conversation continued. Queen Laila and the others all agreed Ella's loyalty was her greatest weakness —

Do you have something you wish to add, Lady Drizella?

Drea snapped her head up.

"You grunted in disapproval," Ana said.

Had she? She hadn't meant to. Drea looked between the queen and her sister. "I think everyone is forgetting Ella's strongest trait. She only wanted to train out of a desire to protect the crown and those whom she loved. She is more loyal to the crown than she is to her friends or lovers. Take Luca for example, Anastasia thought that giving him up as the killer would flush her out of hiding, and it didn't. So, I wouldn't lean on just her loyalty. If she had to choose between protecting Prince David, herself, or another friend, she would choose him. Every time."

You're right. Thank you for that reminder, Lady Drizella. I'll think about our alternatives with that information in mind. Queen Laila glanced at someone on the other side of her mirror. *I have some important business to attend to. Thank you all for your insight.* Queen Laila severed her connection with a dismissive swipe of her fingers, leaving the mirror black.

As everyone got out of their seats to leave, Drea was left with a tingling sensation that crawled up her back and clung to the base of her neck.

***

Drea wandered around Riset's third circle until she arrived at The Bird and Mouse. The morning rush was beginning to fizzle out, and the idea of a cup of tea was too good to pass up. Albert smiled as she approached him and his nearly empty pastry display.

"You're going to have to expand your shop soon," Drea said, smiling as she noticed all of the people savoring his craft.

"All thanks to you and Lady Eleanor, may she rest in peace," Albert replied.

"All we did was tell others. Your work speaks for itself." Drea made sure no one was close enough to hear. "Albert, I have an opportunity for you that I think would make your business triple."

Albert chuckled. "What could possibly make my business triple?"

"The best tea of your life. Are you able to step away for about thirty minutes?" Drea asked.

Albert grunted and walked over to a young woman, who nodded before he followed Drea out the door.

"Just where is the best tea of my life?" Albert asked as they walked through the merchant's square and past all of the other cafes, pastry shops, and vendors.

"You'll see soon enough." The corner of Drea's lip quirked as they walked in companionable silence. The people around them bustled by, each one wrapped up in their daily lives. Eventually, the crowds passed, and they walked through the gates leading to the fourth circle. Albert's head turned on a swivel as the houses and roads became rundown.

"Lady Drizella —"

"Let me do the talking," Drea said, interrupting him as they approached a home Drea would never forget. She knocked three times and stepped backward, wondering if the door would fall over.

The door opened cautiously. Liza stuck her head out, grinning when she saw Drea.

"Liza, who is it?" Danielle called from within. "Oh, Drizzie, I didn't think I would ever see you again."

"Well, I had to check in on my favorite assistant," Drea said, hugging Liza. "How's your hand?" Drea motioned to see the burn.

"Completely healed. Thank you...for what you did." Danielle spoke softly, holding her hand close to her heart as she opened the door. "Please come in."

Drea squeezed her shoulder as she walked through. "I'm glad I was here to help. Do you have a few minutes? I brought a friend with me, if that's okay?" Drea asked, her face flushing with her rudeness. She hadn't thought about what she would do if Danielle said no.

"I can spare some time." Danielle motioned to their dining table.

Drea took a seat and motioned for Albert to do the same. Though he hadn't picked his jaw up off the floor yet, and it took everything within her to not kick him. Apparently, it had been quite a while since Albert had been down in the fourth circle. Liza raced around them, pulling out the chairs. She was excited to see Danielle already had a kettle over the fire.

"My apologies for the mess. I would love to say it's a rare occasion it's this messy, but frankly the rare occasion is when it's clean," Danielle said as she sat across from Drea and Albert. "What can I do for you?"

"It's more about what I can do for you. But first, you wouldn't happen to have any of that tea brewing in that kettle, would you?"

Danielle smiled. "Of course I do. I would be more than happy to share it."

"May I pour it?" Drea asked. Danielle nodded as Drea stood and grabbed four teacups from the rotting cabinet shelf.

As Drea poured the tea, Albert asked Daniella how she knew Drizella. Drea made sure to have the tea in front of Albert before Danielle could ask who he was.

"Give it a minute to fully steep," Danielle commented before either of them could savor it.

Both lifted it to their noses, inhaling the scent of her delicious spiced tea. Albert's eyes widened as the spices and mild floral notes hit his nose. Drea grinned as she blew on it, her impatience getting the better of her.

"Have you thought more about my idea from the last time I was here?" Drea asked.

"I have, and I'm not sure I even know where to begin or have the time for such an undertaking." Danielle fidgeted with her light shawl, wrapping it tighter around her boney shoulders, pulling on the frayed edges.

"What idea was this, Lady Drizella?" Albert asked, leaning forward. He still held the cup in his hands as they both impatiently waited for it to cool.

"To sell mother's tea," Liza exclaimed, startling all three adults.

Drea frowned as she spilled some of her precious drink.

"And now you can see why I don't think I can do that. I can barely keep this home together with Erik's support. It would take me away from Liza too much."

Drea took a sip of her tea, testing its temperature. Perfection. She closed her eyes as the spices hit her senses, transporting her to a place filled with books, cozy blankets, a wood burning fireplace, and Henry. Her shoulders slumped as she leaned forward on her elbows, taking another blind sip.

"What if you could have someone watch Liza here while you made your tea?" Drea asked.

Danielle let out a broken laugh. "I know you're from a noble family, Drizzie, but even you are not so naïve to think I could afford that."

"I know," Drea whispered. "But I want to give you the opportunity to not have to worry about Erik's job or your security."

"How would you do that?" Danielle mumbled.

"By having you supply me with your tea," Albert inserted. "I think Lady Drizella was being coy by not mentioning who I am, but I own a cafe and pastry shop, and it would be my honor to serve your tea to my customers."

"What?" Danielle's mouth opened.

"And I want to invest in both of you. Danielle, I will cover all expenses of your home for a year, in addition to whatever payment plan you negotiate with Albert, and Albert, I will invest in you as well to expand your shop, while also making sure Danielle can afford a wage that can support a life in the third circle."

"The third circle?" Danielle couched on her tea. "Drizzie —"

"I accept those terms," Albert replied, enjoying another sip of his tea.

"This is...too much..."

"I disagree; it's entirely too little for what you deserve, but we'll discuss our partnership later," Albert said.

"Partnership?" Danielle looked between the two of them.

"Yes, I would like to partner with you. I'll come by tomorrow so that you can process and come up with a list of demands for our business venture."

"I can help," Drea said. Smiling, she handed over a piece of parchment to Danielle, who could only stare at it as Drea set it down on the table.

"Can I add that every month we open up a small shop to give away pastries and tea to the residents of the fourth and fifth circles?"

"My dear, I'm pretty sure you could ask for the palace and I would do all I could to grant it," Albert said.

"Why are you doing this for me? I haven't..." Danielle turned to Drea. "All I did for you was have my daughter probably bruise your hip and then brew you some tea while burning my hand. You've done more for me than I could ever —"

"Life shouldn't have to be about earning good things. You deserve more than what you've been given, Danielle. So does Liza, and so does Erik. You have a recipe that's magic, and I have the funds to make your dream possible."

"Drizzie, why me?"

"Because there needs to be more kindness in this world," Drea whispered. She leaned forward and gripped Danielle's hand, squeezing it. "Think about it."

Danielle nodded, sipping her own tea. Before she left, Drea made sure to leave behind a large coin pouch filled with the funds Danielle would need for at least a year in the third circle. Whether Danielle took Albert up or not on their plan, Drea wanted to ensure she was able to take care of her family.

CHAPTER THIRTY-ONE

Raven

Raven woke up with swollen eyes and a headache so fierce it felt like daggers were stabbing into her skull. She closed her eyes, tears leaking from the edges as she attempted to find some pitiful relief. The only position she found a modicum of release in was lying flat on her stomach, with her head turned to the left and her eyes closed. Every time she moved, her muscles continued to tighten, and she begged for their release.

The only time she opened her eyes, she saw Rowan and Daciana carrying Aleks between them before laying him down on Rowan's bed.

"It'll be easier to care for both of them this way," Daciana muttered. Raven caught movement in the corner of her eye, but couldn't make it out.

The next time she opened her eyes, Daciana, and Rowan had left. She peered over at Aleks. His white hair was stuck to his head; his breathing was laborious, and his clothing was slick against his body.

"You look like shit," Raven rasped.

"So I look like you then," Aleks whispered. Suddenly he was wracked with endless coughs. Aleks curled in on himself with two thick wool blankets, shivering as he huddled within them. "Daciana." Aleks swallowed, his vocal cords straining. "Daci—" Aleks's voice cut off.

"Daciana," Raven called, her own voice protesting.

"What's wrong?" Daciana threw the door open, blades drawn. She relaxed once she had finished observing the room.

"There's a flower...I need you to find it," Aleks said. "It's called blooming poison. It's—"

"I know it." Daciana interrupted. "I'll go find it."

"When you come back..." Aleks stopped as he coughed. "Crush the entire flower, petals and pollen, and mix it into any tea. But crush up the *entire* thing." Aleks closed his eyes and rolled onto his back.

Raven watched him as she heard Daciana stampede down the stairs.

"What's blooming poison?" Raven asked softly.

"It'll help us recover."

"How do you know that?" She asked, blushing at her own ineptitude.

"How do you..." Aleks stopped his question. "It's part of the education most enchanters get on the perils of losing control and what to do if you survive." Aleks turned to face her. "What were you taught?"

"My instructor was more focused on teaching me how to do enchantments. He said flare outs weren't worth teaching because if you did flare out, then he didn't want to instruct you anymore." Raven turned away from Aleks. "So, I maintained my control...at all costs. No matter what happened, I did not lose control."

"So when you felt a strong emotion, you —"

"Balled it up and shoved it down. I shoved them down so far, I couldn't feel a thing."

"I'm sorry your instructor educated you through fear instead of reality," Aleks said.

Raven curled in on herself, pulling the blankets around her tighter.

Rowan opened the door, blinding them with daylight. "Daciana filled me in. While we wait for her, is there anything I can bring you two?" he asked as he went to the fireplace and stirred the fire.

"Some soup and bread. We need to try and maintain some strength." Aleks replied.

Rowan nodded as he left.

"Why is this happening to us?" Raven whispered.

"What did your terror of any instructor tell you would happen?"

"He said only enchanters who weren't worthy of being enchanters lost control. So as long as I and the others maintained control, then we would be worthy."

"I see." Aleks's face turned red. He took a deep breath. "What's happening is a normal response to have as our bodies recover from the loss of magic. When we lose control, our bodies' ability to keep us alive rapidly deteriorates. It pours itself into keeping us alive while we lose control, and eventually, if we survive, we pay that price. Right now, our bodies are attempting to build back what was lost. That means blood, depleted organs, tissue, bone, anything you can think of. I've seen enchanters lose control before. It's terrifying, and rarely do they come back from it. I've never seen any last as long as you did and still survive, Raven. Those who did lose control for that long...died...so your mark...it must be very dark to withstand that."

Raven arched an eyebrow as she searched for the lie he was spinning to get information out of her, but she saw none. His sweat covered face was open and honest, something she realized she had rarely seen from him. The only other times had been when they were in bed, rolling in the sheets. Or when she was tucked within his arms and they lay under the covers, content with where they were. Raven shook the memories away.

"Why are you so affected?" Raven asked.

"My magic rose rapidly to meet your challenge when I gripped your wrists. I must have fed some of it into yours, and in my fight to help you, I guess I used more than I thought. Enchanters are at their most dangerous when they lose control. Every ounce of our actual life force is poured into it. So when another enchanter tries to help one who's losing control..." Aleks paused, slowly running his fingers down his face and massaging his temples. "I knew the risks. Most of the time, if an enchanter goes near another losing control, both lose control and die in the process."

"So...you tried to help me, knowing it would most likely kill you." Raven looked into his bright blue, fevered eyes and tried not to fall into them. If her entire body hadn't felt like sludge, she would have found a way to get to him and kiss him.

"Well, I —"

Rowan walked into the room, carrying a tray laden with food. He propped both of them up with extra pillows and set a tray on each of their laps. They cautiously sipped some stew and chewed fresh bread in silence.

"Rowan, how did Daciana find us?" Raven asked.

Rowan sputtered on his stew, coughing. His face turned bright red as he found the air to breathe. Raven glanced sideways at Aleks to see he had also leaned in to hear Rowan's answer.

"It's not that important. What is, is that she found me right in time. I was about to become lost due to that snowstorm."

"Why won't you tell us?" Raven asked as she took another sip. The stew Rowan had brought was delicious and filled her insides with a warmth she desperately desired.

"Because it doesn't matter." Rowan crossed his arms.

Raven was about to prod for more when she began to sway in her bed as though she were on a boat at sea.

"Rowan. Bucket." Raven clapped a hand over her mouth as she tried to push her tray away with the other without spilling anything.

"Well, I guess the beef stew was too much for your stomach. I'll get a light broth." Rowan left as Raven heaved into the bucket between her legs.

Raven hoped Daciana would be back soon; she didn't know how much more she could handle.

Two days passed with no sign of Daciana.

Neither one of them had made leaping improvements. Both could barely keep broth and bread down. Raven couldn't stop sweating, while Aleks was perpetually in a state of freezing with a headache that paralyzed his entire body.

On the third night, Raven was startled by Aleks having a nightmare. She stumbled out of bed, crashing hard onto the floor. Her muscles burned as she tried to get to him. On hands and knees, she crawled the five feet to him, spurred by Aleks's whimpering.

"Raven, please," Aleks whispered. "Raven, Raven, no..."

"Aleks, wake up." Raven gently touched him, her fingers shaking from the fear in his voice.

"Raven! No, Cai, no! Raven," Aleks's voice strained as his body thrashed under the blankets.

"Aleks." Raven shook him harder, gripping him tightly. He whimpered. "Aleks, wake up."

His eyes flew open, his chest pumping up and down as he turned to her.

"Are you okay?" Her eyes had adjusted enough to see Aleks's eyes were almost entirely black with his fear.

All he could do was stare at her, his arm raising to gently cup her cheek. She sighed, holding it close. Though she had no access to her magic, she found she didn't need it to feel the spark of fire from him rush through her veins. Instead of asking any further questions, Raven delicately lifted his blankets and crawled in beside him. Her muscles relaxed for the first time in days as she lay in bed with him, wrapped in his embrace.

“Well, look at what the wolf dragged in.”

Raven felt Aleks flinch beside her at the voice that carried down the hall.

“You have to get to your bed,” Aleks said. He twisted around to face her, his hands gripping her biceps.

“Aleks—”

“Get. Out.” He shoved her until Raven found herself on the hard wooden floor. If she had had the strength to punch him, she would have. “Get into your bed.”

If Aleks’s eyes hadn’t been wide, she would have thought him embarrassed to be found in bed with her. Instead of arguing, which would come later, Raven moved to her bed as quickly as possible, her legs shaking with each step. By the time she got into her bed, Aleks had sat himself up and attempted to tidy his hair. She had just gotten the covers over herself when a man opened the door; the bang ricocheted through her head.

“Don’t worry, little brother, you’ll feel better in no time.”

“Cai.”

Raven took a longer look at Aleks’s big brother, and heir to Trudel. He dominated the entire room. His white hair was cut short, and his jaw was just as sharp as the ice blue eyes shifted to her. He wore warm traveling clothes still freshly dusted with snow. Daciana stood to the side, head hung low. She looked at Aleks through wide eyes, a million apologies etched into her brow.

Prince Cai grinned at them, his fisted hands on his hips. “I brought you a present, aren’t you going to thank me?” Prince Cai’s deep voice, that she would normally find entrancing, slid unpleasantly down Raven’s back as Prince Cai held up the bag filled with the blooming poison flower they needed.

"Thank. You. Brother." Aleks spoke softly, his hands gripping the blanket at his side.

"You're welcome. Now, Daciana, go fetch some warm water; we need to get these two back on their feet."

Daciana moved fluidly, grabbing the bag from him before leaving.

"Brother, you must introduce me to your friend and explain how you became so ill." Prince Cai crossed his arms and leaned in the doorway. "That's an order."

"This is Raven. We were ambushed by an overzealous enchanter who was out of his depth. He lost control of his magic, and the two of us had to intercede. We must have held on for too long because both of us got sick."

"An enchanter and a woman grab onto an enchanter, losing control, sounds like the beginning of a bad nursery rhyme. You're both lucky to be alive. Especially you." Prince Cai pointed at Raven. "Just who are you to my brother?"

"I'm really not important," Raven replied. She stared Prince Cai down. She'd seen enough men like him to know that cowering before him would only make him worse.

"Really? So you're not the royal guard who escaped my aunt's clutches and somehow got my brother tangled up in this mess with you?" Prince Cai moved slowly around the room until he sat at the end of Aleks's bed.

Raven didn't say another word, waiting to see what else he knew about her.

"Aleksander, you wouldn't believe the luck I had in finding you and your *friend*." Prince Cai gripped Aleks's foot through the blankets.

"I don't care—"

"There I was, waiting for you to pass through your normal discreet route, which, by the way, isn't discreet, when I find your lapdog spy with a bag of blooming poison?" Prince Cai roughly tapped Aleks's leg.

Raven crossed her arms as she watched the exchange.

"Cai—"

"Hold on, I'm not done." Cai patted Aleks's foot. "She almost got away from us, but my wolf, well, he likes a good chase."

Raven held in a shiver at the smile that crossed Prince Cai's face.

"We caught her up a tree. Once I had her, she did as she was told and led us straight to you. Do you know how much trouble you've caused by your little stunt, Aleksander?"

"It's so good to see you, brother. I would hate to continue to keep you from your princely duties, you should get back to them. We'll be fine from here."

Cai laughed as he continued to grip Aleks's foot. "You, little brother, are my princely duty right now. Bringing you and your mistake to mother is my job now." Cai smirked at her, as though he could undress her through the layers of blankets.

Before Aleks could respond, Daciana came into the room with two large mugs in her hands. Prince Cai stood, disappointment and glee on his face as he surveyed his brother one last time. "I'll let you two get better. We'll stay for a few days, gather provisions, and then you'll get a royal escort home," Prince Cai declared as he left.

Daciana leapt to Aleks's side, handing him a mug. "Prince Aleksander, I'm —"

"I don't blame you, Daci," Aleks mumbled as he sat, slumped back in his bed. "He would have found us one way or another —"

"I should have known better than to go on that route, but it always has the blooming poison. At least now we know he's watching and has figured out one of your routes. I'll inform the others in the network to find new ones."

"You two sound as though you're talking about a hostile enemy," Raven croaked as Daciana brought a mug to her.

"We are when Prince Cai is concerned," Daciana whispered. "Make sure you drink all of it, and trust me, you'll want to drink it while it's still hot." Daciana smiled at her before going back to Aleks.

He grabbed her hands and clenched them. "I do not blame you. As you said, if anything, this has forced him to reveal information, and now our people can adjust to continue moving without detection." He let her hand go and took a large gulp of his drink, grimacing at the taste.

Raven followed suit, gagging on the rotten flavor. "This is reason enough to not lose control."

Aleks lightly laughed. "You and I get to drink this for the next few days. Thankfully, we should start to feel its effects within hours." He raised his mug in a toast to her. "May we never have to drink swill again."

Raven raised hers back to him, taking another long gulp.

Daciana stayed in the room, writing at the table on dozens of parchments. Raven assumed they were memos to be sent to Aleks's other spies. Questions rose to her lips, but each time she was about to ask something, Aleks caught her eye and shook his head. So, the questions piled up in her mind as more worry and doubt built in her heart. Who was Daciana to him? She was clearly important, and Raven had witnessed the affection for him from her. She wasn't sure why she cared. They weren't together. Even though they had spent the previous night wrapped in each other's arms, it hadn't meant anything. They were simply two friends finding comfort in the other.

Right as Raven began to nod off, Daciana got up and left, nodding to Aleks as she took all of the memos with her and left the inn through the window next to Raven's bed.

"How —"

Raven sat and peered around her room. She grinned when she saw the Inn had built a trail into its wall out of ledges that were just wide enough to place a foot on them, but not wide enough for anyone walking through the narrow alleyway below to notice.

"There's a reason I always get this room." Aleks smiled momentarily.

"Aleks —"

"I know you have a lot of questions. I probably can't answer them, or I would have to lie, and I really don't want to lie to you. Not anymore," Aleks said quickly. He stood and walked over to her. He sat heavily on her bed as though the weight of the blanket wrapped around his shoulders bore the weight of a kingdom.

Raven nodded her head. "Once we're on our way, I expect some answers."

"I'll try, but Raven...I'm not sure that will happen now."

Raven sat, balling the blankets in her hands instead of punching them into Aleks's face.

"I. Am. Going. To. Rescue. Calla," Raven spoke with as much confidence as she could muster, though her heart sputtered at the pity she saw in Aleks's eyes.

"Raven," Aleks grabbed her hand and closed his eyes for a moment. When he opened them, Raven could have sworn he was about to tell her Ella had died again. "I can't disobey him."

"No —"

"I can't," Aleks whispered.

He reached a hand toward Raven's cheek.

She pulled back from him. "Don't."

"I wish I could change everything, I wish I could have brought Calla with us, and that I had been able to break you out of those damn dungeons sooner, and that I hadn't pushed you away, and I'm sorry for all of it. But I can't deny him. You could ask anything of me and I would do it so long as it didn't go against my mother's wishes, and she sent him to get me, and I can't turn on her...I can't."

Aleks's wishes fell on deaf ears as Raven stewed.

"You can't stop me from running away."

"I can't, and I won't, but you'll die right now if you go out there. Let me help you as much as I can. Stay here until you're better, and the first chance you get when we're on our way, you run. I'll have Daciana pack your bag with extra supplies, whatever you need, and you run."

"You really fear him, don't you?" Raven asked.

"Yes."

Raven paused. She hadn't expected him to answer with honesty.

"I told you I didn't want to lie to you." Aleks ran a shaky hand through his hair. "Cai is not one to reveal a weakness to. I have seen a lot of horrible people commit horrible acts, myself included, but Cai relishes the terror he causes. He lives for inflicting pain on others, and his favorite pastime is torturing someone you love in front of you."

"So...no weaknesses." Raven gulped. She did her best to not read into what he said about love. She wasn't sure if it was about her, and she didn't think her heart could take it if it wasn't.

"No weakness. Cai will exploit it. You can't show any deference to anyone. Not me. Not Rowan. Not even Daci."

"I understand." Raven affirmed.

"You don't yet, but you will." Aleks rubbed his face. "The only advantage we have is that he doesn't know you're the lost princess. Either my aunt didn't disclose that information to my mother, or my mother chose not to tell Cai. I'm not sure which one I prefer," Aleks said.

Raven couldn't help but notice the sinking in her stomach at either option.

For the first time since getting sick, the sunlight breaking through her window didn't make her squint in pain. Smiling, she gently rubbed her temples as the pain in the back of her eyes and head receded.

"You must be feeling better." Rowan walked into the room carrying a change of clothes. "I haven't seen you this content in weeks."

"Well, I no longer desire to rip my eyes out of my head," Raven said.

"That's good; your eyes are your most attractive feature," Aleks commented, turning to face her.

Raven gestured rudely at him. "I thought you said other parts of me were my most attractive features."

"I don't know which is worse, you two fighting, or sleeping together." Rowan grumbled.

"Definitely fighting," Daciana commented. She had come back a while ago and taken up residence at the table. "I assumed." She smiled. "I'm glad you two are well enough to verbally spar with each other."

Rowan walked over to Raven's side and felt her forehead. "You don't seem to have a high fever anymore."

"Though disgusting, the tea has helped —"

Prince Cai swaggered in through the entrance, not pausing for permission. Though Raven assumed he had never needed it before. He smiled as he looked them over.

"Let's get these two downstairs for some food. I'm sure they would love a change in scenery," Prince Cai commanded as he hauled Aleks out of bed before he could form any type of protest.

Daciana moved quickly to Raven's side. She lifted Raven gingerly out of bed, keeping her body between Raven's and Cai's. Rowan was on the other side. They walked carefully down the stairs. Raven discovered that though she felt better, her legs were refusing the cooperate as quickly. The more movement Raven got, the more her head cleared. She knew it would be a few more days still before her bones didn't ache with exhaustion, but at least they could support her.

The inn they were in boasted a nice pub and living area at the bottom of the three levels of stairs. The bar was in impeccable shape, with a barmaid who seemed like she could lift an ox and not be bothered in the slightest. The chairs were well crafted, and none of them were crooked. For being in the middle of what felt like nowhere, this location was very well financed. Though Raven supposed, it didn't hurt that a prince used it as an operations post when necessary.

Prince Cai directed them towards the living area that encircled a large fireplace. Several boisterous men sat at a table playing cards. All of them instantly stopped, waiting for Cai to instruct them. Aleks settled on one of several plush, high back chairs in front of the fire. The barmaid carried over a tray laden with soup and bread. Raven's mouth watered as her stomach gurgled at the smell.

As soon as Daciana sat Raven down, she grabbed a plain wooden chair and sat in a dark corner. Smart. Daciana would soon be forgotten, allowing everyone to speak freely around her. Rowan sat near Raven, and she couldn't help but remember Aleks's warning about showing any type of emotion, especially as Prince Cai took the other seat near her. But right now, all that mattered was inhaling the food before her. Aleks had the same idea as he shoved food into his mouth.

Prince Cai leaned back in his chair and ran his eyes up and down her body. She was dimly thankful for the fresh clothes Rowan had brought in for her. While it wasn't her uniform, the simple black cotton tunic and pants fit her well enough. The fur lined underclothes made all the difference to her comfort, and even though Prince Cai wouldn't know, it allowed her to hide some of her knives. However, no matter how many layers she wore, Raven still felt like prey being assessed by its predator. She stared back at him through bites of her meal, not flinching, not backing down from his gaze. He needed to know she would not be something for him to boss around or play with. The sooner he learned that, the better.

"Tell me, brother, what could you have possibly been thinking in keeping this creature from being killed? I mean, she's beautiful, but there are plenty of beautiful women who would gladly share your bed."

"I was in the process of recruiting her to work for me. Someone found out and framed her for a crime she didn't commit." Aleks leaned back and mirrored his brother. He waved a dismissive hand. "It's been a huge inconvenience, but I protect those who help me."

Raven quickly glanced over at Aleks. This was a new mask for him. The boredom oozing from his mouth even gave her a flicker of doubt about her importance. He was cold, uncaring, and dismissive. Nothing like the witty man she knew...

"You were going to recruit one of our aunt's royal guards? That's ballsy, even for you. I didn't know you had it in you." Prince Cai rubbed a hand over his mouth, mulling things over.

"Well, if not now, then when?" Aleks turned away from his brother.

Raven waited to see where Prince Cai wanted to lead the conversation. She was curious to see what his next move would be. Prince Cai pulled out a pair of shackles. Her shackles. Raven stiffened.

"Come here like a good whore," Prince Cai crooned.

"Fuck off," Raven said, the corner of her lip curling into a snarl.

Prince Cai blinked at her as Aleks covered his mouth to hide a small smile.

"You're a royal guard who committed treason, and you will obey me; you don't have a choice." Prince Cai stood to tower over Raven as he glowered at her.

She stared at him in defiance.

"Cai, she saved my life." Aleks tossed out. He continued to sit in his chair, his head resting on a hand.

Prince Cai snorted. "You had to be saved by this woman? You've been gone far too long, brother."

Prince Cai lunged towards her, shackles in hand.

Raven twisted away, withdrawing a dagger.

"You will not put those on me. I won't run off. I promise." Raven spoke calmly, trying to remember what Aleks had said. Still, she had to pause to gather her thoughts. If he put shackles on her, it would be an inconvenience to pick them without detection. She assessed the surrounding room, trying to hide the shake in her hand and the exhaustion that pulled at her. A few of Prince Cai's men stood, awaiting his command.

"Your word may be good enough for my brother, who deals in shadows, but it's not for me. I don't trust a royal guard who turns on their ruler." Prince Cai stalked closer to her, forcing her to put the chair between them.

"If you put those on me, I swear on my sisters' lives I will kill you—

Prince Cai laughed. His eyes burned with hatred and glee in the firelight as he prowled.

—But not before I made you see things you'd never believe while making you feel so much pain you'd beg me to make it go away," Raven hissed. She thought of each poison she'd pour down his throat and envisioned how he would react. She smiled at the thought. A large smile filled with her own malice.

The rest of Prince Cai's men stood at her comments, each one watching her.

"Brother, trust me." Aleks rolled his eyes as he examined at a fingernail, not once looking at Raven. "She speaks the truth. On top of being a former royal guard, she's a trained assassin. One of the most feared, apparently," Aleks shrugged.

Raven held her breath as her heart sputtered at Aleks's reveal. She did her best to not show any emotion. Not one ounce of fear or anger could cross her face in front of this man, who had the cruelest eyes.

Prince Cai hesitated at Aleks' claim. "What's your name then?"

Aleks scoffed. "Good luck. She won't tell anyone."

For a second, Raven couldn't help but wonder if Aleks had revealed her to see if it would force her into telling him who she was. Raven dismissed the thought. Even if it were true, it didn't matter right now.

Raven crossed her arms. "All you need to know is I keep my promises and my threats." She leveled her dagger at him, waiting for him to sit down before rejoining the circle of chairs.

CHAPTER THIRTY-TWO

Calla

Two new guards arrived at her cell that morning. Calla had never seen them here before. The guards shoved her forward, forcing Calla to stumble over her feet. She froze again. She couldn't go there. People died in that room. She wouldn't go there.

The guards shoved her again.

Calla fell forward, hitting the hard stones.

Both guards picked her up under her arms and continued forward.

"Please don't take me there."

"We're just following orders," the guard to her left muttered.

"But you don't want to. You know what she does to people in those rooms. I've done nothing. I'm innocent, and you're taking me there to die," Calla pleaded.

"Maybe you should have thought about your innocence before helping Rav —"

"Charles," the guard on Calla's right chided him, Charles, into silence.

"You were Raven's unit."

"What's left of it. No thanks to her and Rowan, if we want to stay alive, we cannot do anything that would be seen as traitorous, which on some days, is simply existing," Charles said. He wore a face of determination, but his dark brown eyes betrayed him. Calla didn't need her power to see that Charles was not only angry, but that he missed Raven and Rowan, and probably wished he had found a way to go with them.

"So, Raven really did escape?" Calla asked. She would never doubt Mira, but the confirmation from Raven's unit would be reassuring.

Charles nodded just enough for her to notice. Bastien, who had to be the other guard, remained silent as they approached the throne room.

"Do you know what's going to happen to me?" Calla whispered.

"Nothing good, though our queen is mad enough that she'll want to keep you alive for as long as possible. So stay alive until someone rescues you," Charles whispered.

"No one is going to rescue me," Calla replied. She didn't want them to think that Mira was already working on a plan. Better to let them think she was harmless; maybe they would pass that along to the queen.

The throne room doors opened on squeaky hinges. To Calla's dismay, it was filled with people, mostly nobles, and all of the other palace maids.

"Your Majesty, we've brought the traitor's accomplice," Charles called. They had yet to fully enter the room. Instead, it appeared the queen had wanted her paraded through a silent crowd.

"Bring her to me," Queen Lyanna's voice was light and playful, a bad omen if ever there was one.

The room parted before Calla as Charles and Bastien gripped her shoulders to push her forward. Several of the nobility nearby wrinkled their noses as she got closer to them. Maybe the queen would torture her with a nice bath, Calla thought. She didn't dare search for Adam or Mira. She wasn't sure if she could handle whatever was about to come in front of them.

The loss of her magic was odd as her heart beat heavily in her chest. It was always there, ready for a fight, unfolding in her, waiting. But now...there was nothing there, and she felt naked without her power coursing through her veins. She was defenseless. So, Calla stood as tall as she could, wearing her dirty and tattered ball gown before what appeared to be the entire noble class and some servants. She didn't even want to imagine the state of her hair after all it had been through. She was sure it would take her several washes to fully untangle it back into something manageable.

"What is your name? I want everyone here to know who you are," Queen Lyanna commanded.

"Calla." She narrowed her eyes at the queen. What was she doing?

"How long have you been under my generous care?"

"A few months."

"A few months. You see how quickly they were able to infiltrate and enact a potential coup? A coup that was only stopped by me because of my good judgment, not any of yours." The queen pointed an accusing finger at those in front of her.

She turned back to Calla.

"When were you planning on killing me and my family?"

"There was no plan," Calla replied. "I haven't done anything."

"Liar." Queen Laila strutted down from her throne to be at eye level with Calla. It was only then Calla realized how short the queen truly was.

"I'm not lying." Calla spoke calmly, staring directly at the queen, hoping against all hope the queen would believe her.

The queen nodded to someone.

"Please, I'm not lying. I promise I was never involved in a plot to kill you." Calla's voice rose when her magic couldn't meet the panic that fluttered through her.

Someone grabbed her wrist, and before Calla could form any type of response, she was shoved to her knees and her hand was pressed onto a tree stump that had been placed beside her.

"I haven't done anything." Calla whimpered as they forced her hand to remain open.

"What was the plan, Calla?" Queen Lyanna hissed. She stepped closer to Calla until their feet were almost touching.

"There was never any plan."

The queen nodded, and the guard who held her hand took out a small mallet from his belt, and before Calla could process or prepare, he struck a finger.

Calla couldn't help her response.

She screamed as her small finger was broken, quickly followed by the finger next to it. Calla cried as she struggled to rip her hand away from the guards that held her down. But they remained firm in keeping her on her knees in the center of the throne room.

Queen Lyanna smiled at Calla.

"I'm not involved in any plot to overthrow you or kill you." It was true, of course. That had never been their objective. But as Calla gazed into the queen's light blue eyes, she knew that wouldn't matter. The queen was going to make someone pay for Raven's transgressions, and Calla was the only one who was adequate.

"I'm going to get the truth from you."

"You already have."

Calla turned away. Her eyes briefly landed on Mira. She was on the side of the throne room, at the front of the crowd. Her hair was pulled back, allowing Calla a glimpse of the full horror written across her friend's face. Mira bit her lip, and Calla could tell she was debating something brash. Calla shook her head once, trying to signal to Mira to do nothing. To say nothing and remain a shadow. She would survive this.

"Tell me, Calla, if that really is your name, is there anyone else working with you?"

"No." Calla kept her eyes trained on the queen. "I'm not working with anyone, nor have I ever worked with anyone. I got a job as a maid here. That's all. I swear it."

Queen Lyanna looked at the man behind Calla and nodded.

"No, I promise I'm not lying, please," Calla begged.

But it didn't matter. The man broke another one of her fingers. This time, the men holding her down released her. Calla fell against the cold, hard stone and clutched her hand to her chest as she whimpered.

"That's enough for today. Charles, Bastien, take her back to the dungeons."

She was lifted by two men, causing another yelp when her hand was jostled. She glanced at one of them through tear stained eyes and found Charles looking at her with grim determination.

They walked Calla out of the throne room on hurried feet. Once they were out and the doors were closed, both guards dropped her arms and stood still for a moment. Calla grabbed part of her dress to wipe her eyes, dropping it when Charles held out a handkerchief to her. She nodded her thanks as she wiped her tears away. They took their time walking back to the dungeons. They didn't force Calla to move at a normal pace, instead allowing her to shuffle her feet over the cobblestones.

"You should just tell her what she wants to know," Bastien whispered.

"Did it occur to you I'm not lying? That I am, in fact, unable to tell her what she wants to hear?" Calla snapped. "I'm not some masterful liar who won't break under pressure. Your queen just doesn't care."

They left her chained to the floor, cradling her hand against her chest.

Calla eventually pulled her shaking hands away from her chest. How could she ever enchant again? A distant internal pang echoed throughout her body as her power fought against its cage. It denied the thoughts that she could never enchant again. None of that mattered, though, as she tried to examine her hands. Calla blinked to clear her vision and lifted her shaky hands with tense muscles. Calla held back the vomit as she stared at fingers bent in unnatural directions and swollen. She didn't even try to bend the others for fear of the pain it would cause. If only she could take some Solacium.

Footsteps treaded softly down the hall. Calla couldn't scurry back fast enough before her visitor approached. She relaxed when Adam came into view, her throat constricting at the sight of him.

"Adam." It was all she could say before her voice caught on the saliva flooding her throat.

"How could they do this to you?" Adam fell to his knees before her. He reached a hand through the bars to cup her cheek.

"I'm an enchanter," Calla whispered. "I think I told them when they got me drunk. I don't know how else they could have known, but they did, and that's why I'm shackled and why today happened."

Adam stilled. Calla opened her eyes to look at him, and she wondered what he was thinking. She was no longer keeping anything from him.

"I wish I had told you sooner. I hope you understand why I didn't," Calla whispered.

Adam nodded. "I brought that salve you used on my face. Would it help your hands?" He held it out to her.

"Not for this. It's only for external wounds. Though...could you put some on my burns?" Calla asked.

"Your burns?" Adam leaned closer, bringing a torch down to see her.

"Morgan...she uh..." Calla couldn't talk as fear rose to the forefront of her mind. "She melted wax on me."

"I'll kill her," Adam snarled. He rubbed a thumb over Calla's cheek.

"Not if I get to her first," Calla whispered. It was the only time she had allowed herself to verbally admit she wanted to do someone harm.

"What do you need me to do?"

"How much is left?"

Adam opened the jar, wrinkling his nose as he showed her. "I forgot how horrible this was to smell."

Calla examined the contents. There was only enough for a thin full coat over her burns, or a thicker coat on the worse parts. Either way, it wasn't enough to completely heal her.

"Can you spread some onto the burn on my chest first? And we'll go from there."

Adam nodded as he used his fingers to scoop some out. Rage flickered in his eyes as he saw her burn marks. While rage warred on his face, his hands were kind as they applied the cooling salve. Calla exhaled as the pain instantly diminished to a low throb. She got as close to him as she could to make it easier.

"Can I assume, since you're an enchanter, that this healing salve is your creation?" Adam locked eyes with her.

Gods, she could get lost in the depths of his emerald eyes with slivers of gold. Her fingers twitched to reach out and touch him, but then the movement turned to blinding pain. Calla blinked her eyes as she nodded to answer him.

"It's ingenious. I can't believe no one else has done it. What made you think of it?" Adam asked as he spread more over her marks.

"An...acquaintance almost died."

"An acquaintance?" Adam smiled lightly.

"She's not a friend, really, but she had gotten hurt." Calla gulped. She didn't like to think about that night with Drea. "She's also an enchanter, but she was dying, so I...I forced her to take Vivifica to save her. She didn't get addicted, but she could have, and it would have been against her will." Calla thought about those moments with Drea. She had begged Calla to let her die, but Lady Tremaine...Calla shook herself. Drea was fine.

"So you created this?" Adam prompted.

Calla nodded. "It took me months and was an accident when I got it to work."

"Well, I know I'm thankful you created it," Adam said. He grabbed the last remnant of the salve and finished coating her burns. Adam leaned against a bar and gently rested one of her hands on his. Calla winced as her bent fingers tried to move.

"Adam..." Calla took a breath. "I don't know how much longer the queen is going to put up with me, and I need you to promise me something."

Adam nodded.

"I need you to promise me you'll leave. Don't marry Arianna. No matter what happens, you don't deserve to be with someone who won't appreciate who you are. You are not a beast," Calla confirmed for him. "You are intelligent. You are brave. You are kind, and most of all, you are loved, and anyone who is loved the way you are shouldn't force themselves to suffer a punishment like Arianna over vanity," Calla confessed. "Even if you don't go home, go somewhere. Any life has to be better than one with her."

"I promise," Adam said. "But only if you come with me into this brave new life."

Calla smiled. "I promise."

CHAPTER THIRTY-THREE

MIRA

Mira watched them from the depths of the shadows. She had gone to Calla as soon as she could after the events in court that day. If it hadn't been for Adam's hand wrapped around her wrist, she would have probably ended up in a dungeon cell next to Calla. How he had restrained himself...she didn't know, especially as she witnessed Adam in front of her with Calla. If she hadn't seen it herself, she wasn't sure she would have believed it. Prince Adam, the most vain and pretentious man she knew, was crouched down in front of Calla, and he stared at Calla as though the world began and ended with her. Mira felt a crack in her heart when Calla looked at Adam the same way.

Now she understood why Adam had changed. Somehow, Calla had come into his life, and Calla, being the wonderful person she was, changed the beast into a true prince.

The moment he left, and she was certain he wasn't coming back, Mira walked over. Calla searched around with wide eyes when Mira revealed herself.

"I won't say anything." Mira smiled as she sat down directly in front of her.

Calla flushed.

"What did he come for?"

"He brought me my healing salve. I had used it on his facial wound and had left what remained in his room."

"So you've been in his room." Mira prodded, wiggling her eyebrows.

Calla's face turned scarlet. "I was his maid," she muttered.

"Uh-huh." Mira grinned. She saw him applying the salve to Calla. It was mostly well done. "Do you have a way to cover the salve?"

"No, but they won't know what it is. They don't have it here. They'll just think it's horse manure or something." Calla shrugged. She flinched at the motion.

"Let me see your hands," Mira commanded.

Calla held them out delicately. Her fingers were bent and swollen.

"I brought things to wrap them. Is that okay?"

Calla nodded her head. "Let's put strips from my gown on top of them."

Mira gave her a dubious stare.

"That way I can try to tell them I did it. Otherwise, they're going to want to know who helped me, and it could expose you...and Adam."

"Good idea. I don't like it since they're not clean, but I'll do it anyway." Mira pulled out the dagger strapped to her thigh and tore some strips off the bottom of Calla's gown, what was left of it, anyway.

She reached through the bars as far as she could to ease Calla's arms as she worked around the constraints of the shackles.

"How are you feeling about those?" Mira motioned to the enchanter's shackles that covered Calla.

Calla glanced down at them, her expression conflicted. "For the first time since I was eight, I'm not afraid of losing control. I'm not sure which one scares me more, the idea that I want to keep them, or that I don't know who I am without my power."

"You are the smartest, kindest, and gentlest person I know. No power gave that to you. Don't let your identity get tied into what it does for you," Mira said.

"Mira," Calla paused long enough that Mira looked at her. Tears began to form as Calla gazed at her hands.

Calla sucked in a breath as Mira continued to slowly wrap her fingers together. It was the best she could do. She couldn't put a support in them to set them correctly. All she could do was try to find a way to alleviate the pain.

"What will happen to my powers if my fingers don't heal correctly? All of us channel through our hands, and our fingers...they're the last piece of that intention. They direct it...if my fingers are twisted..." Calla choked on a sob.

"Look at me," Mira ordered. She finished wrapping the last one. It was a pathetic attempt, and she didn't know how it would impact Calla's enchanting. She waited for Calla to face her with golden hazel eyes swimming with pain. "We will cross that bridge if it happens together. You will never be alone." Mira rested her hand on Calla's cheek and rubbed a tear away.

"I don't know what I would do without you."

"You'll never have to know." Mira reassured her. "Now, I brought you some food as well." She brought out a few dinner rolls that she had been able to stuff into her pockets, along with some small minced meat pies.

Calla cradled the roll between her hands and took a bite. Mira stayed as long as she could, making sure Calla ate and drank some water.

"Both of us need some sleep," Mira said as she stood. "I am going to get you out. I've been flirting with this one woman, who I know is close to the queen; I just can't figure out how."

"Who?" Calla asked.

"Her name is Morgan —"

"No." Calla's voice rang throughout the dungeon.

"Calla —"

"Please, Mira, I am begging you, leave her alone. You don't want to get in her way." Calla stood and walked up to the bars. Her eyes were wide as she stared at Mira, her hands shaking. "Please."

"Why?" Mira leaned on the bars to truly see all of Calla. "Who is she?"

"She...I can't tell you." Calla backed away from Mira. "Please trust me; don't get any more involved with her."

"I do trust you, but I also know when something's wrong, and I want to know why. She's clearly important to the queen, and if I can use that, then I will." Mira watched Calla step away and pace. She had never seen her so agitated at the idea she was getting close to anyone.

"You can't, Mira, please."

"I need better than that, my love."

"If I tell you, you'll go after her."

"That's an even better reason for me to know, Calla. Who is she?" Mira pressed.

"Mira, please, I can't lose you too." Calla stopped pacing.

"You won't —"

"You don't know. With the things she's done, I can't...I can't imagine you going through them because of me." Calla's hands flexed in front of her, as though they were trying to enchant. "You can't, you can't, you can't."

Mira noticed she seemed to be saying that more to herself than to Mira as she walked in a circle throughout her cell.

"Calla, you are worth more to me than you could ever know. If this woman has done something to you, then I need to know, and I will happily bear the cost of whatever comes my way if it means I am a step closer to saving you," Mira confessed.

"I can't lose you!" A spark of magic swirled around Calla's hand as it cracked a shackle. Her power continued to swell as the crack grew. "I can't lose you, Mira."

"You won't."

Another spark crackled around Calla's right hand.

"Everything I have suffered has been at her hands," Calla whispered.

Another spark crackled.

"Same for Raven. She's the one torturing me," Calla replied.

"*She's dead,*" Mira growled.

"No." Calla stumbled over as far as she could go towards the bars. "No, you can't. You will be killed, Mira. She's an enchanter, and she's not to be underestimated. Promise me you won't do anything rash."

A small spark crackled, but Mira wasn't afraid. She reached through to Calla, who had power crackling in her eyes, turning them purple, and rested her hands on Calla's shoulders. "I promise I won't do anything rash."

Calla's shoulders slumped under Mira's hands before she lay down on the cold stone below her. She would keep her promise to Calla. She would not do anything rash. But she promised herself Morgan would suffer for every scar, burn, and injury she had bestowed upon Raven and Calla. No matter what.

CHAPTER THIRTY-FOUR

Raven

A snowstorm rolled in quickly and fiercely. Aleks claimed it wouldn't delay them more than a few days and that the mountain passes would be okay, if not slightly icy for their journey. Daciana moved into Raven's room, and Aleks back to his. As the morning passed by with flurries outside their window, Raven settled for getting to know one of Aleks's most trusted spies.

"You know, Rowan refuses to tell me how you found him," Raven said as she took a bite of her breakfast.

The two of them were in their room, keeping as much distance between them and Prince Cai as possible.

"Oh?" Daciana glanced sideways at Raven as she leaned back in her chair next to the fire.

"Will you?" Raven did her best to not get excited. The woman was hard to read. She clearly cared for Aleks, though Raven didn't think it was out of anything but strong loyalty.

Daciana smiled, her brown eyes lighting up as she leaned towards Raven. "I had heard about what Aleks, did to save you. I knew Queen Lyanna would send someone to retrieve him, so I diverted off my current assignment to try to intercept him. Luckily for me, a trail of mountain men was left for me to follow."

Raven grimaced. She motioned Daciana to carry on.

"I found Rowan and tracked him through the forest for about an hour, waiting for my best opportunity. Granted, at the time, I didn't know who Rowan was. For all I knew, he was the person who had killed all of those men and currently had my prince, unconscious, tied to a horse, with another body beside him."

"I'm surprised you didn't outright kill him," Raven cut in.

"Well, I wanted to. But Aleks always told me that not everything is as it seems at first glance and to always make sure I'm certain before I act. So I waited, and I watched. He cared for both of you, but it wasn't clear enough for me to realize he was genuinely caring for a friend and not a prisoner. A snowstorm began to race through the mountains, and I knew my time was approaching." Daciana got up from her chair and sat down beside Raven.

"Rowan mentioned you saved him from getting lost."

"Really?" Daciana tilted her head as she smiled. "I don't see it that way. I snuck up on him, or at least I thought I did. He had sensed me in the trees above and was ready for my attack. He and I sparred, fighting through the whiteout snow. It was just the two of us there with the horses just feet away. I got my leg behind him and was able to trip him, forcing him to the ground in a flurry of powder. He stopped struggling when I pinned him beneath me and pressed my blade against his neck." Daciana paused as she recalled the memory, her fingers frozen in her curled hair. "I will admit I was about to pull my dagger across his throat when I made the most devastating mistake of my career."

Raven leaned forward.

"I saw his face. Most importantly, his deep hazel eyes, which have flecks of gold shimmering in their depths." Daciana stared off into the distance, a small smile pulling at her lips. "The next thing I knew, I was the one with my back on the ground covered in snow, with Rowan pinning me beneath him, his blade pressed to my throat. He whispered, 'I've had a really long day. If you don't tell me who are and what you want, I will slit your throat.'" Daciana slid down in Raven's bed to lie on her back, her hands clasped over her stomach. "Have you ever had someone do that to you? Completely disarm you and command you with such confidence that you can't think straight and do as they say?"

Raven smiled. "Can't say that I have."

"I don't know how you can look at those eyes and not lose your train of thought. I've had to avoid him ever since." Daciana pouted.

"I've never noticed Rowan's deep hazel eyes with flecks of gold shimmering in their depths before." Raven was beaming inside. She was certain she could feel a flicker of her magic at the pure joy that surged through her. "I'll have to make sure I look next time I see him. If you need my help to get him to notice you—"

"No." Daciana bolted up. "No...it's okay, I know how to catch my men," she said as she blushed.

Raven chuckled. "Well, if you ever want to talk about him or men in general, you know where to find me." She lay down on her side of the bed and wrapped her arms around her stomach.

"Speaking of men...you and my prince?"

"What about me and your prince?" Raven closed her eyes, awaiting whatever emotions would begin to surface within her.

"He cares for you. He's a private person, but I saw a shift in him when it was just us here. I've never seen...'Prince Charming' before."

"Any tips to share with me?"

"I'm not at liberty to share any information about him," Daciana said sadly. "All I can say is here in Trudel, he's known as the Prince of Ice."

Raven absorbed the name.

"And Prince Cai?"

"He's the Prince of Fire. He burns everything in his path."

"Why do you hate him? Surely your loyalty is to the Crown?"

Raven couldn't help but think of her own loyalty, and how that had ruined her. She should have questioned Lady Tremaine more. Should have forced her to explain herself. But Raven had blindly followed the person who had been a surrogate mother in more ways than Raven was willing to admit.

"My loyalty lies with Prince Aleksander alone. Prince Cai is cruel and vindictive. He's not someone deserving of the loyalty Prince Aleksander has earned."

"How did he acquire such dedication?" Raven hunkered down in her blankets.

"He cares about those who work for him. We're not blank faces that bring him information. He knows us and ensures our safety. He doesn't choose to be cold, but it's forced upon him. He tries to show kindness when he can."

Raven's grumbling stomach at midday had her questioning how long she could put off going downstairs. It hadn't passed her notice that she and Daciana were the only female fighters, and that the surrounding men stared at them. But as she continued to recover, she couldn't do anything that would hinder her healing. With Daciana by her side, the two of them ventured down to the large gathering room to get their food.

She had intended to grab their food and go back to their room, but when the men glowered at their interruption, she had a change of mind. Raven sat down in her chair, smiling at all of them. Aleks was near the fire, sharpening his sword. He hadn't left Prince Cai's side since his arrival. Aleks barely spared her a glance, while Rowan moved closer to her. Strategically, Raven understood. Emotionally, she knew it hit her harder than she had anticipated.

Raven's examination of them was cut short, however, when Prince Cai swaggered over and sat in the chair next to her.

"How important are you to my little brother?" he inquired, resting his head on his hand. The other hand loosely held a dagger in his hand.

"I'm not important to anyone." Raven huffed.

"Cai," Aleks said at the same time. He continued to sharpen his sword, not once looking up.

"So, if I took her and showed her what it means to be with a real man, you wouldn't have a problem with that?" Prince Cai spoke so nonchalantly, so at ease with the idea, that Raven knew he would try, and Aleks wouldn't be able to intervene without revealing himself.

Not that she needed him to intervene. She was strong enough now that she would be able to handle anything he tried.

"No problem at all." Aleks continued to examine his blade.

Prince Cai stood and grabbed Raven's biceps.

"Let. Me. Go." Raven spoke from deep within her chest, a low growl following.

"You're coming with me."

"The fuck I am." Raven ripped her arm free. "I am no one's possession. No one's 'thing' to be traded."

"I don't care what you think." Prince Cai reached for her again, hauling Raven out of the chair.

Raven fought him. She grabbed his thumb and pulled it back hard enough to break his hold on her, but not enough to break his thumb. Raven hip checked him and put her leg behind his, easily pushing him to the ground. As Prince Cai blinked in shock, she rolled him onto his stomach, pinning his arm behind his back as she pressed her knee into his lower back. Prince Cai tried to rise, but Raven tightened her hold on him, pushing his arm to the breaking point.

"I said I wasn't going anywhere with you." Raven hissed as her chest heaved. "Now, if you want to keep this arm, and your precious man bits, I suggest you leave me, and any other woman who doesn't willingly want the pleasure of your company alone."

Prince Cai grunted, nodding in agreement.

Raven stepped off him as the barmaid came over with her tray of food and handed it to her.

"Daciana?" Raven motioned towards the stairs, hoping she would come. That way, she could lock their door and push a dresser in front of it.

Raven did her best to keep the tray of food from shaking. She tightened her hold on it, making sure she remained in control. What little magic had returned thrashed at its leash, begging for release. Raven walked up the stairs, glancing back only once. She saw Aleks sitting in his chair, sharpening his sword.

Prince of Ice, indeed.

Two days later, the storm relented. Raven walked through the inn, ignoring Prince Cai's men as she went to the washroom. She wouldn't let them intimidate her, especially where a bath was concerned. Gods, she needed one. Raven relaxed into the steaming water, giving in to the warmth. Her magic had grown stronger by the day and was a consistent hum in her veins now. Her muscles loosened in the heat, all stiffness disappearing. Walking back to her room, she found Daciana ready for the day, wearing a new uniform.

"You have new clothes as well." She motioned to Raven's bed. On it lay a brand new change of clothes in varying shades of white. "The princes agreed that stealth would be necessary, along with discretion. We will be traveling as quickly and stealthily as possible to the palace to avoid any more ambushes by mountain men," Daciana said in response to Raven's raised brow.

"They seem to be a problem here."

"Not usually. Typically, they pick off merchants dumb enough to travel through the passes without guards. But recently, they've become more brazen," Daciana conceded.

"Any reason why?"

"Do they need one? They're outcasts from their kingdoms. Most were criminals at some point in time. Or they used to be in the military and left…eleven years ago…"

Raven turned away, putting on clothing that in any other situation she would have avoided at any cost. The white pants were thicker than she was used to, as they were lined with fur. She stretched in them, getting a sense of her range of motion. Raven tried on the plush, fur lined calf high boots with thick soles that would make traversing the snow and ice much easier. She got help from Daciana with the enchanted corset next, lacing it to give her a comfortable level of support. The panels weren't as thick as the corsets worn by other women. It couldn't be in order to allow for better movement, but it served its purpose with enchantments of protection. Next was a thick tunic, followed by an even thicker wool sweater. While Rowan had been unable to grab her sheaths, he had ensured he brought her most prized belongings with them; her curved blades. She secured them in her pack, unable to display them. But that didn't stop her from strapping a few daggers to herself through a wide leather belt wrapped around her waist and another on her calf, hiding within her boot.

Before pulling on white gloves, Raven braided back her hair and slung the pure white fur lined cloak around herself, clasping it with the Trudelian insignia of a howling wolf. It was so similar to Calla's tattoo that Raven did a double take before moving on. That was a question to ponder another day.

"How do you move in all of this and still fight?" Raven twisted and stretched, adjusting to her outfit. "I thought my uniform in Evrotia was cumbersome, but this is a very different type of restriction."

Daciana shrugged. "You get used to it. You'll be thankful for all of those layers later. Trudel is only pleasant for a few months of the year. The rest of the time, it's cold and icy."

"Why does anyone live there then?"

"Because those few months of beauty...they make the rest of it worth it." Daciana left the room, her belongings packed into a single satchel. Raven packed her small belongings and slung them over her shoulder.

Aleks waited outside the door, his mouth opened slightly as she walked out. He quickly closed it. She hadn't spoken to him since he had left her room.

"You've seen me naked, and this is what makes you speechless?" Raven cocked a hip.

"It's just a shock to see you in anything but black. I remember being just as in awe of you when you wore that incredibly beautiful red dress to my aunt's ball. I couldn't wait to rip it off you that night," Aleks whispered as he got close to her. He lightly touched her arm, trailing his fingers up to rest on her shoulder.

"Don't," Raven whispered. "Aleks, please. This is hard enough. I—"

"I know. I'm sorry." Aleks removed his hand from her, and she nearly pulled his hand back to her.

Raven closed her eyes as she pulled her power in tightly.

"Remember what I said. The moment you can escape, you take it. No matter what."

"Aleks—" Raven peered into Aleks's ice blue eyes to find them hardened with determination.

"No matter what, Raven. I don't care if one of us is dying, you leave. You may not agree with me, but you're the most important person here." Aleks held her hand and pressed it to his lips before walking away.

Fresh snow crunched under Raven's boots, its crisp smell biting her nose. Birds chirped in the stillness, bringing life back to the surrounding mountains. Raven gazed out at her surroundings for the first and last time.

Behemoth mountains stood out in stark contrast to the sky covered in dark gray clouds. They appeared endless before her, stretching beyond her vision to form the borders between three great kingdoms. Vicuria lay to the south, bordering the eastern side of Evrotia, while Trudel captured the northern border and the rocky terrain that remained impassable for the majority of the year. At any other time, Raven would have tried to stay for several hours, soaking in the beauty before her. But she wasn't allowed any respite as men continued to move and gather around the inn and its stables.

"Where are the horses?" Raven glanced around at the men, each one carrying a large pack and stomping their feet.

"They're going to the palace a different way," Daciana said as she stood next to Raven, hands on her waist.

"Why?" Raven couldn't hide the shock. Without a horse to carry her, her chances of escaping and being successful at avoiding capture dwindled rapidly.

"Because Prince Cai has deemed it so. He wants to throw anyone else who might have cause to follow us off our trail." Daciana rolled her eyes.

"No one is going to find us."

"Unfortunately, they disagree. One of Prince Aleksander's birds brought a warning that some mountain men want revenge for the death of some of their people. That wouldn't sound familiar, would it?" Daciana smiled as Raven grimaced. "Come on, let's join the group," Daciana sighed. She straightened her back while slightly loosening her blades. Raven quirked a brow, making sure hers were all easily accessible.

"How long is this going to take?"

"Five days," Aleks said. He hefted his own pack onto his back. "Be prepared for anything, Raven," he muttered before leaving her side.

CHAPTER THIRTY-FIVE

Raven

Raven noticed, for the second day in a row, white smoke trailing through the sky. They were being followed, and whoever it was, they weren't amateurs. She had almost missed it herself as the white smoke mixed into the gray clouds.

But she didn't say anything. Hopefully, these mountain men were smart enough to put together a decent enough ambush so that she could flee. Raven chewed her lip about whether she should warn Daciana or not. She had come to enjoy her company. Daciana was witty, funny, and knew when to speak up, though Raven could tell she always wanted to have more input.

Raven knew they would attack today. They had gained distance on them, and this would be one of their last chances to attack before some large crossing. Prince Cai kept being cryptic about it, not wanting to reveal more secrets. She had simply rolled her eyes and carried on walking. She loosened her hidden daggers and tried to pull on her magic to enchant them with strength, but her power only flickered inside her, dimly lighting up before going back to her core.

They approached a large grouping of trees with shadows that stretched long before them in the lowering sunlight.

"Can we take a short break?" Raven asked. This would be the perfect location for an ambush if only they could stay long enough. Hopefully, these assailants had enough men compared to their eight. Prince Cai had sent the majority of his men away with their horses, leaving them with just three of his men.

"We can establish camp here for the night," Prince Cai replied, dropping his bag and sitting down against a tree. He never helped them set up camp and insisted on overseeing it instead.

Halfway through the setup, Raven went to find a suitable spot to take care of some womanly matters, signaling to Daciana where she would be digging their latrine for the night. It was as she pulled her trousers back up that Raven heard the clash of metal on metal.

She cursed as she approached, needing her pack in order to escape.

Ten men wearing large gray furs had surrounded Raven and Prince Cai's men before engaging everyone in a fierce battle. These were not mountain men. Their prior attackers had been poorly dressed, living off the land. These men were warriors. Raven grimaced at her gamble as she withdrew her blades and joined the fray. Prince Cai's men were either knocked out or dead; she couldn't tell. Hopefully dead. Rowan seemed to be okay, having disarmed at least one of them. Prince Cai was engaged in a battle of two on one. Daciana was holding her own, but Raven noticed the stress in her furrowed brow. She knocked out her opponent and jumped to Daciana's side, putting their backs to each other.

Raven knocked out and killed two of the men when she noticed Prince Cai lay on the ground unconscious, and that his opponent was coming for her.

She saw him in the corner of her eye during the skirmish. While not the largest man, he was the most skilled and carried himself in a way that relayed to Raven that he knew he was the best.

Well...he hadn't faced her before.

He carried a large silver sword that screamed wealth. As he approached her, he discarded his furs and outer clothing, a luxury Raven envied.

Raven adjusted her clothing, not removing her cloak. She found that it helped hide her intentions, and she would need every advantage she could take against him. Her opponent moved just as well as her. He had probably been training to fight since the day he could walk. His black hair was tied back from his face, giving her a clear line of sight at his handsome face.

A gust of wind blew back Raven's hood right as she swung her curved blade at his neck.

Or at least where his neck should have been.

Raven kept her blade raised, ready to attack.

He had dropped to his knees, sword before him, sticking out of the snow as he...bowed?

Was he bowing?

All of his men quickly followed suit.

"My queen —"

"I'm no queen," Raven cut in. She glanced around. The only person still conscious from their party was Daciana, who was currently restrained between two warriors. Rowan lay nearby, but was waking up, holding his head. Aleks was...she spun around trying to locate him.

She saw a tuft of white hair and went to it, flipping the body over. Aleks breaths were shallow; the surrounding snow stained red.

The lead warrior stood, towering over her. She stared at him to find his blue eyes wide as he said, "You are Queen Astrid. My men and I were sent to find you after you escaped and bring you back to my father, Lord Nikolaus."

"You're the Commander." Daciana's face twisted with hatred. "He's a rebel, Raven, don't listen to him. He'll tell you anything."

Raven turned away and stared at Aleks as he groaned.

"Raven?" The Commander crouched down to her level. "You're the guard who sent a letter to my father."

Raven glanced at Daciana. The spy had calmed down, situating herself into a relaxed stance between the two warriors.

"So what if I'm the guard? That doesn't make —"

"A portrait of your family still hangs in my father's home. I would recognize the daughter of Queen Regina anywhere."

"I don't want the throne." Raven spoke in hushed tones. "I sent that letter before I knew who I supposedly am."

"Come with us, Astrid—"

"Raven." She corrected him. She stood and placed a hand on her hip. Looking at him again, she memorized his tall height, broad shoulders, and strong legs. His jaw was chiseled, and his blue eyes were more calculating than friendly. "What's your name, anyway?"

"Willhelm, but everyone calls me Will." He tried to smile, holding out a hand to her.

"Well, Will, I—" Raven paused. This was the perfect time to escape. She could be long gone before the others regained consciousness and be on her way to Calla. Raven turned back to Daciana. She nodded once in understanding.

"I'll take care of them," Daciana replied, motioning to Aleks and Rowan.

Raven nodded her thanks before turning to Will. "I'll go on one condition."

Will raised an eyebrow.

"We have to save my friend Calla first from Queen Lyanna."

Will didn't hesitate as he held out his hand. "I've been wanting a reason to knock down her doors."

Raven smiled. "Let's get out of here before they wake up." She followed Will and his remaining six men into the woods without a sound.

Will took off running through the eerily silent forest. All Raven could hear was her breathing and the beat of her heart as her muscles did their best to carry her through the snow. Raven knew she was strong and capable of running long distances. She had done it plenty of times, but nothing could have prepared her for the cardio and endurance needed to run through knee deep snow. Raven couldn't be bothered to ask questions when several men broke off in different directions, leaving her with three of the eight men. They continued jogging until Raven thought her lungs had burnt to a crisp. She collapsed onto the snow, sighing at its cold embrace. She didn't even care that this was probably the most undignified thing a princess could ever do.

"I'm impressed you kept up," Will said as he pulled her back to her feet.

"I didn't have much of a choice," Raven said. "Besides, we needed to get as much distance between us and Prince Cai."

"Hopefully, I knocked him out long enough for this to have made a difference," Will replied. He paused to search their surroundings.

Raven noted the thick trees and dense foliage as well. They would be hard pressed to find a secure resting spot here. They would have to take shifts and be ready at any moment to leave.

"We'll set up here and wait for my men to rejoin us, then we'll continue on after they've rested."

"Where did they go?" Raven asked.

"To muck up the trail. I want to at least try living up to the reputation I've built for myself," Will said.

"What reputation is that?" Raven asked.

Will and his men paused to stare at her. The other two went about establishing a perimeter and sourcing some wood for a fire.

"You truly don't know who I am?" Will walked about the makeshift campsite he was clearing to give them a place to sit down and rest.

"I didn't know I was this long lost princess until a few weeks ago. Would you like to tell me all about your reputation?" Raven asked as she crossed her arms and cocked a hip.

Will flushed. "It's nothing, really." He turned away from her as he dug through his pack.

"He's the leader of our rebel army, ready to serve you, Your Majesty," one of the men said. He was shorter than Raven, with shaggy brown hair and blue eyes. Raven assessed that he couldn't have been much older than sixteen.

"What's his reputation, though?" Raven asked, trying and failing to not be impressed by Will.

"He's been a constant thorn in the side of Queen Lyanna and Queen Laila for the last two years by testing their defences and recruiting more people to our cause...your cause...and..." The man trailed off as Will walked over to them.

"And I make sure that the men know how to survive and do their chores before stopping to talk to pretty women," Will said as he shooed the boy away. "That's Daniel. He's new. Talented fighter, but new, so he doesn't know when to keep his trap shut."

"It's fine. I appreciate being treated like a normal person."

"Don't get used to it where we're going," Will replied as he sat down. He patted the ground beside him.

"You should know, before we get any farther, I have no intention of claiming my throne. I want to rescue my sister and then find a small cottage in the woods where I can spend my days baking and doing absolutely nothing else."

"Your sister? We're saving Princess Arianna?" Will's face wrinkled.

Raven chuckled. "Gods no. My sister, Calla. She's not my sister by blood, but by spirit."

"I see. Well, I think by the time we get to my father and the other advisors, they'll convince you that taking the throne is your destiny."

Raven snorted. "I doubt the men who disobeyed a direct order from my father and left me behind will be able to convince me of anything." Raven leaned back against a log and stared at the sky. The sun was beginning to set, casting pastel pinks across the sky.

"Is that what you think happened?" Will asked.

"It's what I was told." Raven straightened her shoulders. Lord Cenric had had no reason to lie to her. He hadn't known who she was at the time of his confession to her. He had been genuinely angry at what the others had done by abandoning his father to face the wrath of Queen Lyanna alone.

"What if I told you King Stewart had changed his plans the night before he was murdered?"

"I would say I need proof. All I have is heresy, and frankly, I'm more inclined to believe my source right now as I barely know you."

"You're right. I apologize. I simply don't want you to think my father and the other men of King Stewart's council didn't honor their word to the man they devoted their lives to. What would you like to know?" Will gazed at her with open blue eyes and an expression that told her she could ask him anything and he would answer it.

"How do you know me?" Raven whispered. Now, more than ever, she wished for her memories. Her gut told her she could trust Will, but her mind urged caution as she evaluated The Commander, the man who was, in theory, in charge of the army she didn't want.

Will opened his mouth and closed it for a few minutes. His eyes bounced back and forth as he took his time responding. "I don't think you would remember me. You were always running around, getting into trouble with Guard Rowan, and I was busy learning how to be the future leader of your armies."

"That young huh?" Raven grunted.

"My father was your father's commander, so he wanted me to be prepared to take on the role," Will explained. "Despite that, though, we really didn't interact much as children."

"How did you find me? I wrote that letter a long time ago, and I don't know how you knew where to search for me."

"The mirror showed me."

"The mirror?" Raven raised her eyebrows.

"Your father had a large mirror enchanted to reveal your location so long as the right person with the right intentions used it."

"That sounds like a very complicated enchantment." Raven shifted on the forest floor. She didn't very much like the idea of a special mirror being able to reveal her location to anyone who knew how to ask.

"It is. It took seven enchanters, including your father, to do it. The mirror has very specific enchantments in it, and until three weeks ago, no one had been successful in finding you, and believe me when I say I've seen those men try every day for the last eleven years to find you."

"So, what changed?"

"I saw you in bed, suffering from the enchanter's sickness. I was dispatched with a small group of men immediately to save you."

"I never asked to be saved. I just wanted your father to raise his banners to help the princess reclaim her throne from Queen Lyanna," Raven muttered.

"And now that you know the princess is you?"

"I don't know," Raven whispered.

An hour later, the other five men returned, and all of them rested as the sky turned dark. They nodded to each other as each one checked in with Will before getting some food and sitting down around the small fire.

"What's your report, Gregory?" Will asked.

Gregory, a bulky man with muscles to spare and a thick black beard, looked from his bread and dried meat. "I circled back to make sure they lost us. They were still tending to their wounded and establishing a base camp. Prince Cai was screaming at the men as they set up camp. I think he yelled at the queen," Gregory said in a deep voice.

"He'll come after me, if only because he doesn't like to be bested," Raven commented. "We should move out as soon as everyone is rested and make our way to Queen Lyanna's doorstep."

"We will." Will stretched out as he ate.

The other men followed his lead as they settled in and ate. Raven observed them together. All of them communicated in hushed voices and quick hand gestures that were too dizzying to follow. Will watched them too before turning his attention to their surroundings. He got up and tapped one of his men on the shoulder to go eat, as Will took watch. Though they remained quiet, the men seemed relaxed and happy as they rested.

Could she really take over as their queen? Raven rested her head on her arms as she contemplated what it would be like to be queen of these men. She pictured herself sitting on Queen Lyanna's black throne with the seven pointed crown atop her head. It would blend in with her hair, becoming one with her visage. All the power would be hers. She could take that gauntlet and drive it through a commoner's heart, and no one would be able to stop her. Or she would have a starving woman and her children before her, begging for mercy as they failed to pay their taxes. They would turn to her for guidance on all matters of the kingdom. Raven shuddered.

"You don't look like a queen." A young boy plopped down beside her. His ash brown hair hung limply around his face, obscuring what appeared to be wide brown eyes.

"Watch that tongue of yours, Michael," Gregory grumbled as he pointed his sword at him.

Raven smiled. "What does a queen look like?"

"I don't know. I've never met one. Maybe scarier?" Michael asked. He shrugged his shoulders and turned to the others.

"So your leaders should scare you? Does Will scare you?" Raven questioned.

Michael laughed. "No..." Michael glanced at Raven. "Should he?"

"No, he shouldn't." Raven turned to watch Will for a moment. "So, if our leaders shouldn't scare you, what else about me isn't worthy of being a queen?"

Michael tilted his head. "You could use a bath and some finer clothes. Maybe then — OW." Michael rubbed his head after Gregory smacked it.

"She may not seem like it, but if Will says she's our queen, then she's our queen, and you best remember your manners around her."

"I may not be your queen," Raven mumbled. "I may not want to be queen."

"You'll make whatever decision is best for you. I'm not one to judge," A man with a refined voice and manner of speaking walked over and sat down. "I'm Thomas, and because I know these plebeians haven't introduced themselves, I'll do it for them," Thomas said as he pointed to each man. "You've met Gregory, Michael, and Daniel. So that leaves Colin, the brooding one in the corner. Riann is our tracker over there." Thomas pointed to a man wearing a black outfit with blond hair and blue eyes. "And last, but certainly not least, we have Andrew, our resident enchanter." Thomas motioned towards the man beside Will. He was taller than all the others, with his brown hair tied back in a low ponytail.

Raven nodded her thanks to Thomas as he remained by her side.

"So is this your way of making sure I don't run, or do all of you just naturally sit this close to people you don't know?"

"Neither, my dear, you just so happen to be beside the fire and we'll all take what precious little warmth from it that we can before it's put out for the night." Thomas explained.

Raven's cheeks flushed as she turned away from him. Of course, there was nothing nefarious happening. She shook herself as if it would do anything to help her feel better. Raven stood and walked over to Will. A chill raced through her body as she left the cocoon of warmth, her teeth chattering.

"You should have some furs on, Your Majesty," Will commented as he removed his own.

"Please don't," Raven said as she held out a hand.

"Don't give you my furs?" Will glanced between her and his outstretched hand.

"Call me 'Your Majesty'. I don't want the title, so please don't call me something I'm not," Raven requested.

Will made a noise that Raven took to mean he was agreeing with her request. She took his fur cloak and wrapped it around her shoulders. Before Raven could sit down, Daniel had brought a new cloak over to Will.

"Tell me why the advisors left me," Raven whispered.

"You want to talk about this now?" Will asked.

"If everyone wanted me to be queen so badly, why did they disobey their orders?"

Will huffed. "I've thought about that day for a long time. All of them have over the years. The day King Stewart was killed, there was pandemonium everywhere. King Stweart had prepared for a different kind of betrayal. He knew his wife would do something, but I think he had always thought it would be directed at you. So, he didn't plan for what would happen should he die. Every safeguard created was done for you. All of it was to keep you alive, and some of those plans meant not knowing where you were. It's why he had that mirror enchanted," Will explained. "So...when he died, the advisors did what they had planned for...save you, even if it meant losing you. Your mark being covered by that raven, for instance, was part of the plan. They knew if you lost your memory for a little bit, you would be protected."

Raven listened to Will talk about how the advisors had ensured she was safely tucked away with Rowan's dad before coming to the queen, but by that point, Queen Lyanna had claimed her throne. Lord Robert, Lord Cenric's father, had sacrificed himself, and it was too late. Their lands and titles were gone and replaced by other men. The generals who commanded their men were either bought or killed, and the coup that Queen Lyanna had plotted for years came together in a matter of days.

By the end of Will's story, Raven didn't know what she believed. It was easier to believe Lord Cenric's story that they had scampered like whipped puppies to the hills. It made it easier to hate them, to not want to become the queen they wanted her to be.

CHAPTER THIRTY-SIX

Ella

Ella left her room in Holodal's palace the next morning and walked into a large open air room with floor to ceiling columns to her right. Thin white curtains drifted in the air that blew in through the open air windows. She hadn't noticed any of this last night when she had sulked off to her room. David's room was on the opposite side of the living area, which held a large cushioned settee in the center around a large stone table already set with fresh fruits and meats. The dry air swirled around Ella, bringing with it the smell of campfires long extinguished and a hint of spice that reminded her of Luca.

Her own bedroom was spacious with a large bed and a wild assortment of pillows that could have swallowed her within their depths.

"Hello sleepyhead," David said. He sat on the settee, a book in one hand, a piece of fruit in the other. He wore a new set of linen clothes that hung perfectly off his broad shoulders.

"You're a ray of sunshine this morning," Ella grumbled. She sat down, grabbing some meat and fruit.

"I'm not giving up on this alliance. Even though we don't agree on a lot of things, I still believe there is common ground for us to find a way forward," David said. He was so confident Ella almost believed he would make it happen.

"Don't do that," she whispered.

"Do what?"

"Don't give me hope. Our entire mission…our kingdom depended on me, and I let them down. So you don't get to give me hope. Hope is powerful, and it is crushing." Ella paced around the room. "I've seen what happens to those who have hope. They're happy, confident, and disgustingly optimistic that it will all work out." Ella began to raise her voice as she threw her hands in the air. "And then it doesn't, and you see their soul die. You see it happen. It's the saddest thing you will ever witness, and I refuse to be one of those pitiful people who fell for a dream and gave into hope," Ella said. She turned away from David, her heart racing. "I refuse to be weak."

"Ella —"

"Stop. I can't…I can't take that kind of goodness into me. It will die in there, and I…I won't survive it. I'm not strong enough, David. You saw me last night."

David walked over to her, pity in his eyes.

"I'm not like you or Henry…I can't be…I have to remain strong so that you can be kind and full of hope." Ella's voice cracked as she kept back the emotions that threatened to overtake her again.

A knock on the door was their only warning as Shenzali walked in with Baako quickly trailing behind. Ella leaned back on the settee as David stood to greet them.

"Emperor Edris requires your presence; we are to escort you now," Baako said.

"I'm not dressed —" Ella swiped at her eyes.

"You have ten minutes. The emperor is a morning person and, as such, expects everyone to be available to him before the sun rises over his throne," Shenzali said. Ella didn't miss the slight shudder that went through her when mentioning the emperor's early morning demands.

Ella moved towards her room to try to find a decent set of clothes. Shenzali cleared her throat, giving Ella pause.

"We have been sent with these so that you do not have to disrespect the emperor by wearing such inferior clothing again." Shenzali coughed to hide a smile as she held out a pile of clothes to both of them.

Ella grabbed them and went to her room as she grumbled about the peculiarities of Emperor Edris. The clothing she was given was exquisite and light in design. The deep red fabric didn't wash out her pale skin as it hung perfectly on her body. The sleeves broke off at her shoulders to flutter down her arms to her elbows. The top of the gown scooped across her neckline with delicate gold filigree embroidered along its edges. The dress hung to the floor with the same pattern of filigree on its edge. But the true marvel was in the lightness of the gown, which consisted of the same linen she had slept in.

Ella walked out with two minutes to spare as she braided her hair. David walked out wearing a pair of clothes that matched her own. Both of them followed Shenzali and Baako down the halls as fast as they could. Ella continuously glanced over at David, who had groomed his hair back and wore his sword at his hip.

The sun began to crest the edge of the throne room as they walked in, the early morning light washing the room in a beautiful hue of pink. Takani stood behind her emperor with one other warrior beside her. Both of them bowed before him as they came to the stairs below his throne.

"Your Majesty, thank you for allowing us to stay in your beautiful home," David said as he got out of his bow. "If we could continue —"

"No. I will not hear you grovel before me for an alliance."

"Emperor Edris —"

The emperor raised a hand to David. He closed his mouth, his cheeks turning red.

"I do not wish to have you grovel for something I will not be moved on. However, I will say these next two things without interruption. First, I was impressed by Lady Eleanor and will therefore give you access to Jason. Secondly, if you return my son to me unharmed, I will enter into negotiations for an alliance. But it is conditional upon Lucian's return to me."

David opened his mouth, but closed it.

"Enjoy the win, young prince. I am not often impressed by anyone." Emperor Edris smiled gently at Ella.

Ella curtsied, hiding the smile blooming on her face. She hadn't completely failed.

"I will, of course, do all I can to secure Prince Lucian's return to you —"

Ella stepped forward, interrupting David.

"Emperor Edris, I would prefer to make an adjustment to that request about Luc...Prince Lucian."

"You tread on shifting sands with my generosity."

"Of course." Ella curtsied again. "My request is simple. So long as we release Prince Lucian and allow him to go wherever he pleases, then you will meet with us to negotiate an alliance."

"You would dare make such a request —"

"I would." Ella lifted her chin. "Your son is a dear friend of mine, and I know his history. He may not wish to return, and I will not send him from one prison to another for the sake of an alliance with an emperor who banished him."

"Lady Eleanor," David whispered. "You cannot make that —"

"Fine. I agree to your terms. I will not force my son to return, though please let him know he is missed," Emperor Edris said. "Shenzali, escort the prince and lady around our city. Make sure they are well fed and get some more suitable clothing before sending them on their way. It'll be a few days on horseback before you reach Jason."

Ella curtsied once more before leaving with David and Shenzali. She wanted to make sure he wasn't given time to change his mind.

Four days later, they walked toward a cottage on light feet. If anyone ever wanted to get away from any form of life, this was the spot to do it. The road was completely exposed, while the back of the cottage was against an imposing outcropping of trees at the base of the mountains. She couldn't have chosen a better spot to hide. The closer they got, the more hairs began to rise on Ella's arms. She loosened her daggers, fingers twitching. Her ears strained to hear any sound. Any indication of movement. He may have left Aumont two years ago, but Ella knew better than to think Jason the Huntsman would have let his skills dull. There was a reason he owned his name. It wasn't just anyone who could be in the open and not be seen, who could use a bow with such deadly accuracy. There was a reason his departure left Aumont shaken. What could have possibly led him to abandon everything...to abandon Raven. She was about to find out.

Ella heard the shift of his clothing right before the arrow sang in the air. She shoved David to the ground before sprinting for the man. He was only thirty feet away, yet as she saw him reload another arrow, she had only moments before he let it fly again.

Ella rammed her body into him, pointing the arrow toward the sky as he let go.

They rolled, falling down a hidden hill.

She freed her dagger and tossed their bodies until she landed on top, pressing the blade to his neck. Rapid breaths left Ella's body as she looked down at one of her former teachers. His green eyes stared at her with defiance. His face, which had once been so good at hiding emotions, was open as anger and fear flickered in his eyes.

Ella took a breath and relaxed her dagger as she leaned back to sit on him.

"Huntsman," she said. Ella listened for any other signs that he had a trick up his sleeve.

"Cinderella."

"You're slipping, old man. Time used to be I wouldn't have heard you move before taking your shot."

"You've become more paranoid," he asserted.

"Probably." Ella squinted against the sun as she adjusted her positioning, not giving him any wiggle room.

"So, she finally sent someone to kill me."

Ella's head snapped.

"Given our history, I would be the last person she would send to kill you...well, one of the last. No, Huntsman, I need your help." Ella stood and helped him to his feet. She looked at David, who was approaching, sword drawn. "We need your help."

Jason hung his head and started walking towards his home, motioning for them to follow. Once inside, a much different story was told than Ella had expected. Toys were scattered around the floor, clothing lay folded on the couch, and the sink was piled with dishes.

"I didn't realize having a family was something you wanted," Ella commented as she walked around. That had been what he'd told Raven, at least.

"Don't be rude, Ella," David said.

Ella stuck her tongue out at David as he sat at the wooden table.

"Please sit, Ella, and tell me what I can help with."

"Are we going to be interrupted? The last thing I need is for anyone to know we're here."

"Considering you had to get permission from the emperor to see me, don't you think it's hard to find me? Besides, aren't you supposed to be dead?"

"Yes, and I need it to stay that way."

"It will." Jason sighed. "It was quite a shock to learn who you really are, *Lady* Eleanor."

"Well, you weren't the only one shocked. I imagine Raven was —" Ella stopped abruptly, her cheeks flushing.

"Well, that didn't take long," Jason replied. He leaned back in his chair as he watched her. "You may be good, Ella, but diplomacy and finesse were never your strong suit."

"At least not when it comes to those I love," Ella retorted. She crossed her arms, turning away from him.

"I'm not going to lecture you. You're no longer my student." Jason walked around his cottage, gathering the toys. "How is she?"

"I don't know —"

"How couldn't you know? You two are thick as thieves —"

"Why do you care, Jason? You left, remember. For no reason we could fathom, I might add."

"Raven knows the answer," Jason asserted. "I would have never left without telling her. At least give me that much decency."

"Will you two stop? There are more pressing matters at hand than the love quarrel between Raven and Jason," David said as he stood and paced.

Silence poured over them as Ella regained her composure.

"We need your help, Huntsman. One of Ella's cohorts, what's his name, Ella? James? Jon?"

"Jaq," Ella said softly.

"Jaq told her to find you right before he died," David said, collapsing into an old chair.

"I'm sorry for your loss, Ella." Jason rested a hand on hers, lightly squeezing it. "But I don't know what he meant. I haven't had any contact with any of my former connections. I let my entire web die when I left."

"Why did you leave? And how?"

"You'll hate me —"

"I already do, Jason, so how could it hurt?" Ella asked as she twirled a dagger on the table.

"Fine...I got my target pregnant." Jason held up a hand to silence Ella.

She kept her mouth shut, moving to the window to avoid him.

"I didn't know for months...not until six months later when I was sent by Lady Tremaine to kill her. I didn't have any qualms about it at first. It was my job; I had done it before. It happens sometimes that a mark who was previously thought to not be dangerous is a while later. This time was different, though. It felt different when she handed the assignment to me. I could see in the slight glimmer in her eyes that she knew I was going to be ruined. I had everything lined up. I was hidden in her garden and was about to shoot when she turned and I saw her stomach. I knew it was mine. She was innocent enough to have not been with anyone else while she was with me."

Ella turned to him. Jason stared at the floor.

"What did you do?" Ella asked as she surveyed the house in a new light.

"I confronted her. She confessed everything to me. She had been shamed by her family for getting pregnant by a man who had simply vanished."

"What did you tell Lady Tremaine when you went back?"

"I didn't come back for a few days. I need to plan."

"That makes sense. She would see straight through your lies. How did you get away while making sure she didn't kill you?"

Jason ran a hand over his face.

"Tell them, Jason."

Everyone glanced at the woman standing in the front door with a little girl in her arms.

"Lady Abigail." David stood and walked over to her. "My mother was sad to see you go."

She nodded her head. "I was saddened to hear about her death, Prince David."

"Lady Abigail was one of my mother's ladies-in-waiting. She came on after..." David trailed off. "Please take my seat."

She sat as Jason took the child from her.

"I'll tell you what I know, but you need to know if you use this information too soon, it could backfire...Lady Tremaine could —" Jason said,

"You should know I killed her. Any danger she posed to you is gone," Ella interrupted..

Jason sat straighter, his face visibly slackened as he took in the information.

"Jason...does that mean..." Abigail whispered.

"We can go home," Jason replied, his mouth left open. "This changes everything. I can..." Jason paused, his eyes darting back and forth. "The most important thing you need to know is I'm actually the youngest son of House Everett and a sworn knight of Rairene."

Ella sat in silence as she absorbed Jason's story.

"I was recruited by Lord Andrew when I was twenty. I had just returned home from a diplomatic mission to Vicuria with him, and he had a task for me. As he put it, I was perfect for the assignment because I was a forgotten son of a nobody house that wouldn't be missed."

David winced beside Ella. "Lord Andrew is nothing if not direct."

"He was right. My father didn't question Lord Andrew. I had never been in Riset as a nobleman's son, so no one there would know me. He needed someone with my fighting skills to infiltrate an assassin guild that had recently taken residence in Riset."

"Lord Andrew knew —"

"He knew a guild had been formed. He needed me to find it and get it. He had no idea, and still doesn't know, it was Lady Tremaine running it."

"That's how you got out. You told her," Ella muttered.

"I did. I told her I would expose everything if she didn't let us live and leave."

"You risked the entire kingdom for your life on the whim of a woman who could have changed her mind at any moment," Ella accused.

"Why do you think we ran away from everyone we knew and loved? We banished ourselves so that she could never find us," Jason replied.

"How could you choose one person over the fate of our kingdom? Does your oath mean nothing to you?" Ella stood and towered over Jason.

"Ella, that's enough," David said.

"No, it's not. All of this could have been avoided if he had just done his duty."

"Your oath isn't real, Ella." Jason spoke through gritted teeth.

"You're right; it's not. But the one you swore as a knight is very real." Ella condemned him. She sat down with her arms crossed and glowered at Jason.

"I know you don't understand, but I did what was best for Abigail and our child. Nothing else seemed to matter. Surely, in matters of the heart, you can understand?"

Ella grumbled, holding herself tighter. She did understand. If she had truly been tasked with killing David for the betterment of the kingdom...she couldn't have done it. She would have done everything...did everything within her power to save him. She stared at Jason in silence, refusing to make the confession.

Jason stared out the window. "I'll tell you everything I know. I'll even return home with you to deliver the news to King Matthias."

"Thank you, Knight Jason," David said. "We'll leave at first light. I need to go tell Henry."

"Don't you want to know what I have first?"

"If it frightened Lady Tremaine, I'm sure it's damning information."

"Well, I need to hear it," Ella said. "I need...I need to know."

Jason turned towards her and told her everything. He explained how he had joined the house and quickly became one of Lady Tremaine's lackeys. His priority was to gather intel about the kingdom and any secrets that weren't public knowledge. The assassins did mostly focus on horrible people. She had to make sure no one realized her true strategy. Since Anastasia and Drea were still in court, they couldn't risk their cover being blown by a failed attempt. So, most of those political kills belonged to Ella or Raven.

"I know it's not what you want to hear," Jason added.

"No, but I need to. I need to know what role I truly played in order to face down Queen Lyanna."

"All I could gather about her was she was obsessed with claiming Rairene. Especially after her other sister succeeded in marrying the newly widowed King of Evrotia."

Ella straightened her back. She squeezed her eyes shut, trying to pull all of the pieces together. "I need some time. David, do you mind talking to Henry without me?"

David shook his head, leaving Ella and Jason in the room alone as Lady Abigail left as well.

"I still love *her*," Jason whispered. His hands were pressed together between his knees; his head bowed. "Not a day goes by I don't wonder if Raven's happy, if she's found someone."

"No one like us truly finds someone, Jason. You know that. Why do you think...you weren't there afterwards. You didn't have to try to pick up the pieces of what you left behind. I did." Ella leaned towards him. "She was devastated, Jason."

"Leaving her...seeing her...it was the hardest thing I've ever had to do. I would have stayed there forever with her, no matter what happened. Lady Tremaine said breaking her...ripping out her heart...lying to her about why I was leaving...was the only way she would let me leave."

"Well, you succeeded."

"Will you...when you get home, will you tell her how sorry I am?"

"No." Ella stood and turned her back to him. "I would never do that to her. Besides, I don't know if I'll see her again. Lady Tremaine made sure to separate us with an ocean."

"Where is she?"

"Evrotia." Ella turned to Jason. He had gone as white as her hair.

"No..." Jason whispered. "She can't be there. The queen will kill her when she finds out who Raven is."

"What does that mean?"

"Raven is the heir to the throne of Evrotia."

Ella laughed. "She would have told me."

"She doesn't remember who she is, Ella. But Lady Tremaine knew who she was. It was one of the things I discovered during my investigation."

"Ella," David poked his head into the room.

Ella stared at Jason. Why hadn't Raven said anything to her when she had scried her? What was more important was why Lady Tremaine had sent Raven to the kingdom she was meant to rule?

"Ella?" David said. This time he was directly in front of her.

"Hmmm?" Ella looked up.

"Henry said to come home with Jason. He practically fainted when I told him everything."

"He did seem stressed the last time I saw him."

"He appeared worse now."

"Then it's a good thing we're coming home with good news." Ella replied.

CHAPTER THIRTY-SEVEN

Raven

Raven stomped through the snow, and not for the first time on this journey, she was grateful for the thick fur lined leather boots she had gotten at the inn. While the rest of her forgot the meaning of warmth, her feet at least remained temperate in the snow. Thomas walked beside her that morning. It felt as though the men were taking turns keeping her company, with Thomas consistently drawing the short sword.

"Tell me about this friend we're saving," Thomas said.

"She's one of my closest friends and the most gifted enchanter I've ever met," Raven said.

She told Thomas all about Calla and who she was, and what Calla did for her. Raven didn't notice half the day had passed with Thomas asking more questions and carrying on the conversation. By the time they stopped for a midday break, Raven's voice was raspier than usual, but she couldn't help but smile. They were going to save Calla. She had absolute faith this eight man crew could pull it off.

Raven searched for Will. She needed to talk strategy with him. "Thank you for letting me talk your ear off, Thomas."

"It has been my pleasure." Thomas bowed to her before walking away.

Raven turned on her heel and ran after Will before he could disappear. She caught up to him as he gathered some kindling.

"Shouldn't we keep moving? We need to get to Aslar as soon as possible." Raven said as she followed him around.

"We won't be getting Aslar for over two weeks at least —"

"Two weeks?" Raven's voice began to rise. "What do you mean, two weeks? That will mean Calla's been in Queen Lyanna's dungeon for over a *month*. Do you know what happens in those dungeons? Because I do, and Calla...she won't last that long."

"Well, I hope she does. We have to get down from this mountain and then resupply in the nearest town before sneaking into Aslar without any back-up or inside person assisting us. It's a tall order, one my men and I are prepared to carry out for our queen, but it means we have to be methodical. We cannot simply waltz in there and fumble our way through it like a boy becoming a man for the first time. So, apologies, your majesty, but it will be two weeks."

Raven stood with her mouth open as she watched Will walk back to the others. She followed him, stumbling over a hidden tree root, and landing face first in the snow. Thankfully, no one saw it happen as she stood and straightened her clothes. Raven rejoined the group with her arms crossed as she looked at Will. He ignored her, walking around his men and checking in with them. Raven rejoined them, standing beside Gregory. He was quiet, and right now Raven wasn't sure she could handle Thomas's inquiries or Michael's novice enthusiasm.

Gregory turned to her and gently brushed her hair. Raven watched snow fall out, her cheeks flushing. Gregory winked at her before turning back to the men. Raven remained by his side, unwilling to glance at the others to see if they had noticed the exchange. Based on the silence, she assumed they had.

They continued shortly after, walking through the snow covered mountains until the sun began to set. Raven found herself between Michael and Daniel. Both of them were just two years younger than she was .

"Why did you decide to follow Will?" Raven asked them. They were the youngest on the team by several years and still had eyes full of joy and wonder.

"I've known Will my whole life. Saw him go from page to knight to commander. All of us live in the same hidden village, training and preparing for your arrival," Michael said.

"All of you?" Raven asked. She looked at the eight men. Surely they hadn't devoted their lives to a dream?

"Our parents all served King Stewart and have continued to do so until your return," Daniel added. "When Will chose us for this squad, it was the greatest honor of our lives."

"Haven't you ever wished to have led a different life? One where all you have to do is run your land and keep food on the table?" Raven questioned.

"That sounds mighty boring. I much prefer adventure and saving ladies." Michael winked.

"You wouldn't know how to save a lady if she stood before ya," Colin said from behind them.

Michael flushed as Daniel laughed. "You wouldn't know either," Michael retorted as he shoved his friend.

Raven laughed as the two chased each other while tossing insults. She ended up walking beside Andrew, the squad's enchanter. He hadn't approached her in the days they'd been together. He barely spoke to any of them outside of enchanting their armor, weapons, and occasional potions.

"Did you train at the academy in Rairene?" Raven asked.

"I did not. I studied at the Vicurian University for Enchanting," Andrew replied. "What about you? You are an enchanter, if my memory serves correctly."

"I am, but I didn't get official training. The place I grew up in after...everything...was an academy for assassins. They had enchanters, but I'm not so sure now that their methods were the best."

"How do you mean?"

"Would you ever train an enchanter to only know how to enchant poisons?"

"*Only* poisons? No. They would also need to know how to enchant healing potions to balance out the intentions of the poisons. If you only ever enchant poisons, you'll become affected by them. Did that happen to you?"

Raven nodded.

"I see. Well, what you should do is focus on enchanting weapons for strength and defense, and creating enchantments that make you think of loving intentions. Healing is the best route. I think if you do that, you'll find yourself feeling more yourself."

"Thank you, I appreciate that insight," Raven replied. "How long does it take for your full power to come back after losing control and suffering from an enchanter's sickness?"

"My dear child," Andrew caught himself. He wasn't too much older than her, though Raven supposed he could have been at least over a decade older. "Your Majesty, my apologies." Andrew bowed his head to her. "That is a lot to go through. I'm afraid it depends on how strong an enchanter you are. The stronger you are, the longer it will take to be fully restored. Until you are, you are at a greater chance of flaring out again as your magic is more wild. I would caution you against enchanting until you feel full again. Once you are, if you would like, I would be more than happy to start a formal education with you."

"I would like that, thank you," Raven replied. She twisted her hands together at the idea of getting a formal education. "Is there anything you could tell me now?"

Andrew laughed. "Of course."

He launched into a long discussion about enchanting and the importance of intentions. It was all topics Raven understood and could implement, but hearing Andrew's baritone voice explain them felt as though she were learning them all over again.

By the time they stopped for the evening, Raven's mind spun with new information and more questions about Lady Tremaine. Why hadn't she ensured they got this training? Surely she would have wanted her enchanters to be safe and fully educated? But now, Raven was seeing it was quite the opposite.

As the night darkened, the men all sat around the fire to keep themselves warm as they ate, with Will sitting outside the circle watching the forest around them. Raven pulled her fur cloak tighter around her shoulders as they ate bread, cheese, and dried meat.

As the meal finished, Colin started to sing a low folk song. The men were not surprised by this sudden gift from Colin. All of them leaned in and listened as his voice melodically wrapped around them. Raven found herself drifting off at his voice, fully entranced by its beauty. She knew her voice was pretty good, but it would never compare to Colin's.

Once he was done, she got up and walked over to Will, joining his watch with him.

"I'm not worth it, Will," Raven whispered.

He turned to her. He had let his black hair fall loosely down around his shoulders with his hood down to let him hear better.

Raven shifted beside him. "I don't deserve this devotion from the men. I'm no fated leader who's going to change the kingdom. I can't even enchant properly, and if people knew what I was trained to do..." Raven trailed off. "I'm not worthy of being a queen."

"I think anyone who thinks they're worthy of anything is usually the last person I want in charge. Anyone with a good head would flee from being a ruler," Will replied as he nudged her shoulder. "But your history doesn't make you unworthy."

"I'm not this queen all of you have envisioned protecting. I don't even need protecting," Raven said.

"I know. It makes my job a lot easier knowing you can take care of yourself. Besides, who said we have this grand idea of who you're going to be?" Will asked, leaning closer to her.

"No one," Raven replied. "But all of you have been training since my father was killed for me to supposedly come back and lead our people to victory against Queen Lyanna, and I'm not worthy of that devotion."

"Oh, so you're just scared."

"I am not." Raven straightened her back.

"All I'm hearing is you're scared that complete strangers have been preparing for their queen to arrive and that you don't deserve it because you won't compare to the dream they've built around her. Well, we didn't know it was *you* we were planning for. All we did was continue living as King Stewart would have wanted, which was making sure our people and an army were at your beck and call should the day arrive where you wish to reclaim your throne," Will said.

"Maybe," Raven muttered. She folded her legs against her chest and wrapped her arms around them.

"I'm not pressuring you to become our queen, but I will continue to treat you as my queen, as is your birthright. But the decision is yours on whether you'll claim that birthright, and no matter what I do, that decision will remain yours alone."

Raven bolted awake when hands shook her. She opened her eyes as Thomas held a finger to his lips. The rest of the men were up and ready to leave. None of them spoke as they hefted their packs on and began to rapidly descend more of the mountain.

"What happened?" Raven whispered as Will moved to her side.

"Riann spotted some troops a few hours behind us." Will replied. He placed his hand on her back, guiding her over some large boulders.

"Troops?"

"From Trudel."

"How did they follow us?"

"I don't know, but we need —"

Will stopped when an arrow flew past his head and struck a tree in front of them. Raven removed her sabers and prepared for the fight that was to come. Will pulled out his sword right as dozens of men fell from the trees above them. She didn't wait for permission or for them to attack. Raven soared through the air as she leapt onto one of the men and pierced his back with both of her blades. She pulled them out and moved onto the next in a flurry of movements.

"Interficiam per os sicut filum," Raven enchanted her blades, focusing on sharpening them to slice through metal. *"Interficiam per os sicut filum,"* Raven spoke under her breath as she summoned her power. A trickle of the roaring river she was used to streamed forward to her fingertips. It was all she had available to use. Raven broke the enchantment. She couldn't risk needing it later when her blades were plenty sharp now.

Raven spun around and cut down another man before he could shoot his arrow at Will. The men were impressive as they took on multiple opponents at once. Each one held their own, even Michael, as he deftly wielded his short swords. Riann shot opponents from the tree he had climbed, and Colin and Gregory were a pair of giants smashing their way through the ambush, clearing a path for them.

Raven drew enough of Will's attention to show him there was a way out of the melee. He nodded, following her as the others fought their way through. Raven sliced her way through multiple men, each one falling before her, painting the snow red.

Daniel and Michael fought in front of her, while Colin and Thomas took the rear. They were close. She could feel it. Their attackers had grown weary and were starting to slow down. Raven increased her attack, putting more on the defensive as she gained ground.

Will grunted beside her.

Raven turned in time to see Will remove a dagger from his shoulder.

Thomas growled in front of her, dropping to a knee.

Raven did a quick spin, searching for her men... *Will's* men, she corrected. Somehow, more troops had descended upon them. That's when she saw him, Prince Cai, on a horse, in the back, letting his men do the dirty work.

"*Queen Astrid*," Prince Cai's voice rang over the battlefield. "Yield, and I will spare your men."

Raven didn't believe it for a minute. Prince Cai did not strike her as the type of person to let someone go.

"Our queen will never yield to a coward like you," Daniel yelled.

The men echoed his sentiments as they charged forward. Raven hesitated for a split second as she watched men who barely knew her risk their lives for her.

And...she couldn't do it.

She couldn't watch them die. For her.

"Stop," Raven yelled. She charged forth as the clashing of swords and grunting men grew too loud for her to be heard.

Raven cut through anyone who approached her, wincing as some of them got lucky shots, slicing her arms and legs. She had to get to Prince Cai. Raven located his horse and froze.

He was charging for Will, and his back was turned to the prince. Raven didn't hesitate this time.

She sprinted for Will, dodging any blades that came near her, not sparing a single thought to engaging her assailants. Will still hadn't noticed her or Prince Cai, as he was engaged with two other men. They were pushing him backward, and though they slowed down from exhaustion and injury, they carried on.

If they killed Will, then her father's army would die with him.

Raven used the body of one attacker to launch herself off his shoulders and land between Will and Prince Cai. As she dropped, Will dispatched both of his attackers. Raven didn't glance behind her to make sure Will was unharmed as she faced Prince Cai and his charging steed.

"I said, stop," Raven commanded.

Prince Cai halted his horse and raised his arm. Silence greeted Raven as the men stopped and the forest stood still.

"I'll go with you," Raven spoke through gritted teeth.

"I have to say, I didn't expect this from you," Prince Cai remarked. "I assumed you would rather die."

"My queen, please don't do this. We can take them," Will whispered behind her.

"I have no doubt," Raven replied to him. "But I do not wish to have anyone's blood on my hands. Especially not when..." Raven trailed off. She couldn't say 'not when she didn't want to be queen'. It was her leverage right now, and Prince Cai would leap at the opportunity.

"How do I know you won't kill her the moment we leave?" Will asked. He stepped closer to her, his body heat pressing against her.

Raven's magic sparked within her at Will's presence. She gently kneaded it in. The last thing she needed was for her tiny amount of power to be wasted over excitement.

"My mother has sworn that Queen Astrid will not come to harm so long as your army stays away from Trudel and Evrotia," Prince Cai said, sighing as he rolled his eyes. "It's very boring, in my opinion."

"I want to hear it from Queen Laila herself," Will demanded.

Prince Cai rolled his eyes again as he pulled out an enchanted mirror and opened it. "They wish to hear your terms from you," Prince Cai said before turning the mirror around and handing it to Will.

Raven had never seen Queen Laila before, but she had no doubt believing this woman was the ruler of a kingdom. Her pure white hair and ice blue eyes were so similar to Ella, it was as though she was seeing a future version of Ella.

The word from the heir to the throne of Trudel is not enough for you? Queen Laila asked.

Raven held still as Ella's voice came out of the mirror.

"You will forgive me for not trusting the nephew of our usurper."

And my word, as her sister, is different?

"You are a queen and are more beholden to your promises."

Raven snorted.

Queen Laila ignored her.

I promise your 'queen' shall remain unharmed so long as your army remains where it is and does not make a move to rescue your queen, or to reclaim her throne. If you break those, I will kill her.

Will gazed at Raven. She wasn't sure if she was impressed by him or now filled with anxiety at her decision. She couldn't leave them. She needed to go with them. They were going to save Calla.

"Are you sure about this?" Will whispered. "I still think—"

"I'm sure," Raven said, though her heart raced and her magic tried to flare. She nodded for more reassurance.

"Raven."

"I promise, I'll be okay. Try to save her for me?"

Will nodded in understanding before turning back to the mirror and Queen Laila. "We have a deal." Will snapped the mirror shut before Queen Laila could respond.

"Let's go, queenie," Prince Cai said. He tossed down a pair of manacles.

Raven looked at them, their cold metal biting into her skin. She could do this. She could willingly sentence herself to prison to protect these men. Will stood in front of her, holding his hands out for the manacles.

Raven gazed at him, locking her eyes with his as he placed one on her wrist and then the other before locking them.

"We will always be there when you need us," Will whispered.

He rested his hands on her shoulders before running them down her arms. Her magic sent a shiver down her spine at his touch. Raven nodded as she felt his hand drop something into her pocket. She stepped away from Will and turned to Prince Cai.

"Let's go," Raven said as she walked over to him. Two of his men lifted her onto the back of Prince Cai's horse, and a different shiver raced down her back as they tied her shackles to the pommel of his saddle.

"Your men need to leave first," Prince Cai said.

"No. Your men need to leave first. I will not have my men turn their backs on your little squadron."

"Your men, huh?" Prince Cai asked as he smirked at her.

"Have your men leave," Raven ordered, ignoring his comment.

Prince Cai motioned for his men to turn and leave back into the forest. She watched all of them before turning back to the others. Will stood in the middle of them, sword drawn, waiting for her to change her mind. She could have. She could have ordered those eight men to surrender their lives in an effort to free hers, but that wouldn't be just or fair, and she would never live with herself if Colin didn't get to sing another ballad late in the night, or if Michael and Daniel didn't get to meet a pretty lady because of her. She stared at all of them, swallowing when she caught Thomas's eye and he nodded. He, out of all of them, would be missed the most. Raven nodded to each one before locking eyes again with Will. He nodded first with his hand fisted against his chest as he bowed.

CHAPTER THIRTY-EIGHT

Raven

Raven shifted in the saddle for the hundredth time in the last hour. Prince Cai had not stopped his horse from the moment they had left Will and his men.

"Can we stop? I need to examine my wounds," Raven said. She hadn't noticed them for a while, but they had increasingly become more painful the longer they went unattended.

"My men got some shots in?"

"I was too focused on saving my men to give them any level of my attention," Raven snapped. She would not give him the satisfaction of thinking his men had bested *her*.

Prince Cai stopped his horse and allowed her to dismount, though he still held her chains. He followed her down and dug through his pack for his healing kit. Prince Cai tossed it at her and went to tending the horse. She was grateful he didn't try to insist on examining them himself. She could make do on her own.

Raven lifted her shirt and found three shallow cuts along her torso. She dug through the contents of the healing kit, searching for what she needed. Raven froze. A bottle of Solacium shone in her hands. She swallowed, gripping the bottle. Raven watched Prince Cai as he continued grooming his horse. She could take it.

Raven shook herself. *No.* She would not put herself through that again. Raven put the bottle back, grabbing out some clean fabric strips and alcohol. She poured the alcohol on her injuries, groaning as it burned her before tightly wrapping the wounds.

"Let's go," Prince Cai said.

She didn't argue. Though she had more injuries to tend to, they were small scratches on her arms and could wait until they rested for the night. Prince Cai grabbed the healing kit from her and stowed it away before mounting his horse. Raven scrambled after him.

"How did you get all of those men here so quickly?" Raven asked as they took off again.

"I always have a squad nearby when I'm sent on a mission. Unlike my brother, I don't like to leave things to fate," Prince Cai remarked. "They're two days ahead of us, but if we're lucky, we'll get to them before the river crossing."

"I see." Raven surveyed the towering trees and silent mountains.

"I can see why my brother withheld who you were from me." Prince Cai twisted to glance sideways at her.

"Oh?"

"He wanted to ensure he held all the glory of bringing the long lost princess of Evrotia to our mother."

Raven snorted.

"You disagree?" he asked.

"That doesn't sound like Aleks."

"Then you must not know my brother very well. Prince Aleksander will always do what's in his best interest."

Raven laughed.

"Something funny?"

"He said the same thing about you," Raven said.

"Our mother did raise us correctly."

Raven glanced behind, hoping to catch a glimpse of Will or Riann. Would they follow? Would he be there when she needed them? Though she barely knew them, Raven had a feeling they would be nearby. The squad Prince Cai had brought dispersed, going back to their post.

"Aren't you curious about the condition of Prince Aleksander? When you were 'taken' he was in bad shape." Prince Cai asked. His voice lifted to a mocking tone that told Raven all she needed to know. Prince Aleksander was fine.

"No."

Prince Cai tsked. He turned his head forward and didn't say anything else as they rode. It was a rough two days, even by Raven's standards. Prince Cai pushed them until his horse couldn't go any farther. Sometimes he had them dismount and walk with the horse to give it a different break. Raven never got to examine her injuries. It was either too dark or they didn't rest long enough for her to make sure they remained uninfected. Throughout all of it, he barely spoke to her. It was a complete shift in how he had treated her at the inn when he had thought her nothing but a lowly royal guard.

On the second day, he began mumbling to himself about some big crossing, and how Aleks and everyone were supposed to meet up with him on this side.

"If they crossed without us..." Prince Cai trailed off.

"Cross what?" Raven asked.

The sound of a distant waterfall reached her. Far off to the right, she could make out a towering cascade of water. That's when she stopped. They had come to a large, frozen river.

Semi-frozen Raven amended.

She could see water running beneath the thick layer of ice. She shifted in the saddle, searching for the bridge. There was a bridge, right? There was no way she was going to cross that. Absolutely no way anyone was going —

"The mighty royal assassin isn't afraid of some water, is she?" Prince Cai questioned. He turned to grin at her.

"No." Raven spoke through gritted teeth so he wouldn't hear the quiver in her voice. She clenched her hands so he couldn't feel them shake in the shackles. "Where is everyone? You don't think they crossed the river already, do you?"

Raven and Prince Cai dismounted and surveyed the ground below them.

"I do, actually. We're an hour behind schedule, but they should have waited." Prince Cai paced back and forth along the edge of the river.

It was mostly frozen, but Raven could hear the water rushing underneath. Prince Cai looped a rope around Raven, tying it to her and then to himself.

They were not...Prince Cai stepped into the ice.

Raven's hands violently shook. If she had been holding a potion in her hands, it would have shattered. She could do this. She had done so much already. What was one river? With rushing water in its depths and a waterfall to fuel it...

She stepped onto the ice in the exact same spot as Prince Cai. The ice crunched under her, shifting beneath her weight. Then she moved again, hearing it softly crack. But nothing happened. It was the ice absorbing the pressure of her foot. Raven breathed again, taking another step, and another. She kept her eyes locked on her feet, always watching for Prince Cai's footprints. Her grip on the rope was firm, and she was glad she had gloves to protect her skin.

Raven turned at the sound of her name. Aleks and the others were on the other side of the river. Prince Cai yelled something at them as they walked across the river. Raven couldn't focus on what he said as she glanced down and could no longer see where Prince Cai had previously stepped.

Raven searched all around her without moving a single leg muscle, but it all looked the same. She couldn't see a footprint, and Prince Cai was still moving. Raven was yanked forward, stumbling. She caught her balance, and her foot landed hard on the ice.

Spiderwebs splintered out from beneath her.

She froze.

So did Prince Cai.

Both of them looked at her feet as the ice continued to fracture.

"Don't. Move," Prince Cai ordered as he turned to face her.

CHAPTER THIRTY-NINE

Drea

Three Days Before Drea's Accident

Princess Lena was leaving in four days.

Though Drea had thankfully not been forced to interact with her much, it did mean her time with Liam was ending. It had been two weeks since her fight with Henry, and she hadn't been able to speak with him since. Between her life at court, training in the house, and her own assignment, she had had very little time to even attempt a conversation. Last night had been especially brutal. She had finally got into the gambling den. It had taken her longer than she had expected. Apparently, a pretty face wasn't enough to sit at the top table. But she had done it. The lord had been so impressed with her skills that she had barely said hi to him before he invited her over.

His life was over shortly after. She would have preferred to make it as long a death as possible, but she didn't have the time and she didn't want anyone to suspect torture. It was simple. He would overdose on the same enchantments he peddled. So, maybe a bit of pain would be involved. Drea had forced him to swallow several at once. None were as potent as Raven's or hers, but they would still put his body into a state of hyper-awareness that would gradually shift into pain that would burn him from the inside out. It would appear to be a bad batch of enchantments to anyone who investigated.

As he died, Drea had searched late into the early morning for his stash. She had found more than she had bargained for.

"Drizella?" Liam's hand waved in front of her, snapping Drea out of her reverie.

She had gotten home as the sun rose, giving her about five hours to sleep before a maid came knocking. Not only had the lord been peddling enchantments, but he had also been selling weapons and slaves. That had been the biggest shock for her to stumble upon. They were free now, and she hoped, going to a better life. All she could do was let them out and hope they wouldn't mention her. "What were you asking?"

"It's not important anymore." Liam shrugged.

Drea stepped closer to him on the dance floor. She hadn't realized until then how many people were on the floor. The ball was to honor Princess Lena and her impending nuptials to Prince David, as well as to say goodbye to the princess for another year. The palace buzzed with excitement, though it had nothing to do with the wedding.

A pair of dancers bumped into her.

Drea turned her head at the error.

The woman turned scarlet at the faux pas. "Lady Drizella, apologies, I lost my footing."

"Mistakes happen. Maybe stay on the edges until you've mastered the dance," Drea recommended, doing her best to not snap at her.

"Or a better partner," Liam grinned as he drew Drea's attention to the man.

It was Henry.

Of course, it was Henry.

"I believe you two were too distracted to notice the dance had changed," Henry snapped. "Lady Miranda was being polite in taking the fall for your error."

The dance had changed? Drea focused on the music and realized, to her horror, that it was a different dance.

"My apologies, Lady Elizabeth. You are too kind," Drea whispered.

"Like I said, I lost my footing." Lady Elizabeth smiled before moving on with Henry.

Drea turned back to Liam and motioned for him to escort them off the floor.

"What was that about? Lord Henry was unusually rude, even for him," Liam observed.

"It's nothing." Drea didn't want to bring any more attention to her tenuous relationship with Henry. He didn't need to know. "Are you almost ready to leave?"

Liam didn't appear convinced by her dismissal but moved on when he nodded his head. "For the most part, though I do have some unresolved items to take care of."

"Anything I can help with?" Drea asked.

Liam smiled. "Are you so desperate to be rid of me?"

"No!" Drea blushed. "I don't want...I'm simply...I just wish to spend more time with you."

"There's something we could do so that you can continue to spend time with me," Liam replied.

They had reached the balcony now, and the night sky seemed to pulse with her magic as she felt it grow within her. Drea stood close to Liam as the cool air wrapped around her. The stars weren't as bright tonight, though she didn't seem to care as Liam wrapped his cloak around her. The scent of pine and fire circled her, relaxing Drea as she breathed it in. She stepped close to him and wrapped her arms around his waist. She was going to miss him. More than she had thought possible in such a short time.

Liam gently touched her chin, tilting her head.

He brushed his lips over hers until she returned the gesture and deepened their kiss.

"Come with me," Liam said between gentle kisses.

"What?" Drea murmured, certain she had misheard him.

"Come home to Trudel with me," Liam repeated as he nuzzled her neck. The sensation did wild things to her magic. It seemed to scatter everywhere as her senses were heightened by the gentle touch of his lips on her neck and his fingers on her back.

"I...um...can I think about it?" Drea spoke through ragged breaths as her chest heaved.

Liam's shoulders slumped just enough for her to notice as he pulled back.

"Of course. I won't pressure you to decide now. But hopefully you know before I leave in four days." Liam tried to turn it into a joke as he ran a hand through his hair.

"I'll think about it. I promise."

Drea would think about it. Henry may have suggested it in anger, and she may have never thought it possible, but in that moment, a life without Liam...seemed dimmer. She would have a lot to think about.

Present Day

Drea opened her door right before Anastasia could knock on it. "Do you realize how early it is?" Drea asked. The sun had barely begun to rise, which was normally the perfect time to train with Gus.

"Early," Anastasia yawned. "I can't check in with you? You did see Luca yesterday."

"Ah." Drea motioned for Anastasia to come into her room. Guess she was going to be late for training. "It was fine. You'll be interested and happy to know Luca didn't see Ella alive and struggled when I told him Ella was dead."

Drea didn't see the point in hiding anything from Anastasia about their conversation. There really wasn't much to hide. Either Luca had no idea what they had been planning to tell everyone, or he hadn't been there.

Ana made a noise of excitement.

"Any updates from Tressa?" Drea asked. She didn't want to tell Ana her former lover was in pain over the idea Ella was dead.

"No. It's why I've come, actually. I have to go out and find her. I won't be gone for more than a few days." It was then Drea noticed that Anastasia wasn't dressed in her usual gowns, but rather in her sturdy travel clothes.

"What do you need me to cover while you're gone?"

"Nothing. Lena has it all covered." Ana reassured her. "Though there is something I think you should do about a certain prince's champion and his intended." Anastasia smiled coyly.

"Oh?" Drea sat across from her sister.

"You need to meet her. I know I've said it before, but I truly believe you need to see her. Determine how much of a threat she really is to you and Henry being together."

"Ana, they're engaged. I'm not going to intimidate her into leaving him."

"Of course not. But once she meets you and sees how perfect you and Henry are for each other, I'm certain she'll see that she shouldn't be the person to get between you two."

"Why are you so keen on me meeting her and ruining her relationship with Henry?"

"Because Henry was yours first," Ana snapped. "I never agreed with mother's opinion about Henry. I know you can keep the two lives separate. I have always supported your being with him, and I always will. So, now it's your turn to fight for you two and win your man back."

Drea watched her sister calm down from her speech. "Fine, I'll meet her." Drea slouched against her wall. She didn't believe for a second her sister's sole motivation in pushing this was her desire for Drea to be with Henry. No, Ana and Lena wanted to see if Gwen could be a puppet, and they were going to use Drea to do it.

"Perfect! I already arranged a meeting with her today at that favorite cafe of yours," Ana exclaimed as she stood. "It's midmorning. I'll be unable to attend, but do have a croissant for me," Ana said as she got up and walked towards Drea's door. "I'll be back in a few days." With that, Ana was gone, a black cloak and large pack slung over her shoulder. Drea wasn't sure what her sister was more excited about, getting to go back into the field or Drea's tea time with Gwen.

Drea had to skip her lesson with Gus as she prepared for her meeting with Gwen. Or rather, tried to prepare. It was just tea and probably scones. Nothing fancy. She perused all of her gowns and found that none of them met her needs of being flattering, beautiful, and not overtly fancy. They were either made for a ball or were for cleaning. She hadn't had a reason to go out for tea with someone in years. Drea ran her hands through her hair, which was only going to make it frizzier. She removed her fingers from her tangles and crossed them.

What was she going to wear? Her magic twisted itself into knots as her anxiety rose. She had to find a gown from somewhere, and she knew the perfect person. Mira.

Drea walked as briskly as she could down the hall to Mira's room near the end of the hallway. It had remained unlocked since her sudden departure. Mira had left behind a note saying she was returning home, that she would be back eventually, and she had taken only what she had deemed necessary for her trip. Granted, five trunks full was more than Mira could physically carry, but she had still left behind quite the wardrobe.

Drea walked into the depths of Mira's closet and began her hunt. She went through multiple gowns before landing on the perfect one, which was simple and elegant. She slipped into the form fitting dark purple dress that flared perfectly from her hips. The bodice was traditional for Rairene, with flowing sleeves and a neckline that wrapped around her shoulders. Silver embroidery detailed the edges of the gown, trailing down around the bodice with leaves and flowers.

Drea went back to her room before anyone had the chance to see her. It was the novice's relaxation day, which meant all of them slept in. Drea let her hair fall loose around her as she put on the final touches with some cosmetic powder and a little bit of rouge before grabbing her cane and walking down to the carriages.

The stable master had been given a warning and already had one of the footmen up and ready to go as Drea walked outside. It was only once she was in the carriage that she had time to think. Leave it to Ana to put her in a state of emotional decisions and be unable to contemplate if this was the right move before it was too late. Of course, she could just never show, but Drea knew Henry would have something to say to her about that. So she let the carriage rumble on into Riset. The entire city was bustling as the morning began to ease into midday.

Drea had the carriage stop at a stable house close to the cafe so that she could walk the rest of the way. Though she still carried her cane with her, Drea kept it tucked in the corner of her elbow, walking as far as she could before any cramping began.

None did.

Drea walked a full ten minutes without the aid of her cane and knew she could go farther still. Smiling, she walked to The Mouse and Bird. A crowd of patrons had gathered outside the shop. All of them, it seemed, were clamoring for Danielle's tea. Drea grinned.

"I had heard this shop was popular. I guess I didn't realize just how popular." A young woman stood beside Drea. Her blond hair fell in perfect waves down her back. Her pale skin was rosy in the early morning air. Her dress was perfectly simple, with enough embellishments to tell others she was well off without making a thief wonder if they should bother picking her pockets. She was classically beautiful with her demure posture.

"The owner partnered with a woman who makes the most delicious tea you'll ever have," Drea said. She searched for Gwen as she continued to wait in line.

"Well, I'll make sure to order some when we get to the front." The young woman held out her hand. "I'm Gwen; it's nice to finally meet you."

Drea shook her hand as she reassessed everything she had noticed about the woman. She appeared to be everything Ella had feared becoming. A quiet, docile lady of the court who was there to be beautiful and nothing else.

"It's nice to meet you. I apologize that I didn't recognize you." Drea added.

"Oh, you wouldn't recognize me. I prefer to stay at home with my books or in the kitchen baking than out at court."

"Not even the balls could tempt you away from the books?" Drea asked. She had to have been at at least one ball.

"Nope. I find that the worlds within those pages tend to be more interesting than the surrounding one," Gwen said. Her voice was soft as she stared off at the cafe with a look of wistfulness Drea knew well.

"Well, I —"

"Lady Drizella!" Danielle waved her hands in the air from the front of the cafe. She motioned for them to come to her.

Drea got out of line and pulled Gwen along with her.

"You never have to wait in line. Come sit here with your friend," Danielle said as she pulled out two chairs from under a small table. "Shall I grab you both tea and two croissants?"

"Yes, please. Thank you, Danielle." Drea smiled at her as Danielle bustled off.

"Who was that?"

"Danielle is the one who makes the tea, and the rest is a long story."

"Well, I have the time. I would love to hear about it." Gwen scooted her chair closer to Drea as Danielle came back with their order and some extra scones.

Drea gave Gwen a timid smile as she launched into how she had met Danielle. The two of them sat beside each other and watched the other patrons as Drea relayed her story. The cafe only grew busier as the patrons visiting as the day turned into lunch. Erik and Liza seemed to bring out an endless supply of chairs and tables.

"I really could just drink this tea every day. It pairs so well with the scones and croissants." Gwen leaned back in her chair. "I think I speak for all of Riset when I thank you for making this partnership happen, and that Liza ran into you."

"It was nice to hear something about you that wasn't directly from Henry." Gwen added as she shifted in her seat once more.

"I'm surprised you've heard anything about me," Drea blurted.

Gwen snorted. "I've heard about you for years. Not directly from Henry, of course, but from the court. You were always the belle of the ball, and from what I have gathered from the small events I've been forced to attend, you were always a courtier to be reckoned with."

It was Drea's turn to snort. "I was not that influential at court."

"Maybe you didn't realize it, but everyone at court talked about you, even after you left." Gwen affirmed. She looked Drea directly in the eye, not flinching away from her face. "Why did you leave? No one seemed to know. One person said you had gotten married to a foreign beast of a prince, another said you went back to Trudel, and many others said a myriad of other reasons."

"If I were as influential as you claim, do you think the court would still have accepted me as I am now?" Drea asked. She lightly referenced her face as she turned her head away from Gwen to watch the crowd. She could tell Gwen was being genuine and kind in her words. But hearing that everyone had thought of her as important and that they had then simply accepted her disappearance as mere gossip...well...Drea wasn't sure how she felt about that.

"If they would have judged you or tormented you for surviving something painful, then that's a court I wouldn't want to be a part of. There would have been some, but I know the majority would have welcomed you back."

"I think what you're trying to avoid saying is that they would have treated me with pity, and that would be worse than what I experienced."

"Perhaps." Gwen conceded. She sipped more of her tea and began to nibble on the meat and cheese that had been brought out to them.

"What book are you reading right now?" Drea asked, desperate to switch the topic.

"I'm currently at the climax of a book about a girl who rides these creatures called wyverns, and she's on a quest to save her kingdom from ruin. It has a delicious romance with an enemy prince and a plot to kill her."

Drea leaned forward, intrigued to hear more. The two of them continued to talk about their love of books as they finished eating their lunch. Danielle even joined them for a few minutes, with Liza sitting on her lap.

"I can't thank you enough, Lady Drizella. Without you...none of this would have happened."

"I'm happy it worked out so well. It seems like you and Albert will have to expand your business soon." Drea said.

"We've already started searching for a bigger space," Danielle whispered.

Drea leaned over and hugged her tightly. Finally, something was going the right way.

"Lady Drizella." The footman from her carriage approached her table. "Princess Lena is requesting your return to Aumont."

Drea nodded as she stood. "Duty calls. Thank you for agreeing to meet me, Gwen."

"It was a privilege. It's not everyone who gets to enjoy a meal and some laughs with you. I can see why Henry holds your friendship in such high regard."

"Henry is one of the best men I've ever met." Drea added.

"He is," Gwen mumbled. "Drizella, if you —"

"You don't need to worry about me. I'm not in the habit of making friends into enemies." Drea curtsied to Gwen before following her footman to the awaiting carriage.

By the time she got home, Princess Lena was pacing in the foyer in Aumont. "Where have you been?"

"I was meeting with Gwen. Wasn't that what you and Ana had planned?" Drea frowned. Anastasia rarely did anything without Lena's approval.

"It is. How did it go?" Lena asked as she motioned for Drea to follow her.

"She's very nice and very beautiful."

"Hm." Lena turned away from Drea. "So she's not competition for you with Henry then."

"I wouldn't say that."

"We all know Henry is in love with you. All you have to do is let him know." Lena sat down behind Lady Tremaine's desk.

Drea ignored Lena's comment. "What can I help you with while Ana is gone?"

"With Luca captured, the threat to David is gone. I expect to hear from the king that he'll be returning any day now. With his return, our plan will be in action once more."

"Which plan are we going with? The one where you marry him or the one where we kill him?"

Princess Lena gazed at the ceiling. "It depends on if Ella is alive or not. If she's alive, then we'll kill him. If not, I'll finally get to be the future queen of Rairene."

"That's a lot to plan for." Drea sat back in her chair as the different plans spun through her head.

"I know that with your support, we'll be successful." Princess Lena leaned back in the chair. "Do I have your support, Drea?"

"Of course. There is nothing I would like more than to see you in your rightful place here and to serve our queen," Drea said. She leaned forward, waiting for Lena to tell her more.

"Good, I can't tell you how happy that makes me. At the end of all this, I'll either be declared future queen as we welcome back our future king, or Prince David will finally be taken out."

"That's truly what you want? You don't want to find a way to force him away from Ella and become queen if she is alive?" Drea questioned. Of course, even their original plan hadn't counted on Ella being alive.

"No. Ella will always be a threat. So if she's alive, I'm going to find a different way to accomplish mother's goals."

"Anything you need from me?" Drea asked.

"Find out when David is coming back. Now that they have Luca, there really isn't any reason for him to not return." Lena waved her hand.

Drea got up and walked out as several other assassins walked in. They had worked for her mother for a few years, each of them skilled with a sword and not much else. They were great at following orders and assisting with ambushes, but none of them were very bright. Drea watched them sit down at the table before the door was closed.

Drea walked through the halls, her cane thumbing loudly on the stone floor. Everyone moved around her with purpose. Aumont had recovered during the last few weeks. The novices trained with renewed vigor under Gus's training, and the other instructors seemed to be pushing their pupils harder.

Drea went to her room and eased down onto her plush bed. The soft wool blankets would be changed soon for lighter covers as the air continued to warm. She ran her hands over them, focusing on the texture of the fabric rather than the endless thoughts spinning through her head.

Her small compact mirror lit up on her vanity. Her magic responded to the small tug of power as the mirror called for her to open it. Drea pulled on a stream of power and opened the connection between the two mirrors.

"Ana." Drea rushed over. "What's wrong?"

Nothing's wrong. I wanted to check in with you about your meeting with Gwen, Ana said. She shifted back and forth in her saddle.

"It was fine. Gwen is very nice," Drea answered once she got over her shock.

I was hoping she was a bitch. Ana rolled her eyes. *Well make sure you do your best to not feel bad when you break them up.*

"I'm not going to break them up, Ana," Drea reiterated. Drea sat down at her vanity and began brushing her hair.

All you have to do is tell Henry you love him, and he's yours.

"Ana, I won't repeat the behavior of our mother or queen."

Suit yourself. At least you know he's with a good person.

"Where are you right now?" Drea observed her sister's surroundings. Towering redwoods seemed to surround her.

I'm almost to a small town Tressa should have come across. Hopefully, I'll find some information there; she's pretty hard to miss.

"Let me know if I can do anything for you from here."

Ana nodded before closing her mirror. Drea changed into a comfortable dress and sat down in her window nook, rested her head on her knees, and closed her eyes. She was so close to everything coming to an end, she could feel it; she just wasn't sure which way it would go. Her first step at least was easy; she would find out when David was returning.

CHAPTER FORTY

Raven

Raven tried to hold still as the ice continued to crack. Her entire body shook with the effort, which only got worse as her foot sank farther into the ice.

Her focus was on the way in which her heart fluttered, and how her magic whispered in her veins, rising slowly. She pushed it down. Now was not the time for her power to come back.

"Raven." Prince Cai called to her, but she didn't respond.

She couldn't move.

She couldn't do anything. If she did...

"Raven."

"Charming." Raven couldn't look up when Aleks said her name.

"Aleksander, go back, that's an order," Prince Cai said.

"Raven, look at me."

She flicked her eyes up. Aleks stood nearby. He was directly at the edge of the cracks. If she moved...at...all...the ice would break. She was certain. It could crumble and take all of them under.

"Raven, I need you to grab my hand."

"I can't." A tear froze in the corner of her eye.

"Raven. Move. That's an order." Prince Cai stood taller.

"You're feeling extra bossy today," Raven snapped. She crouched down, unable to see beyond the ice and the blinding terror as she tried to breathe. Just breathe.

"Just one more step to me."

"If I stand, all of it will shatter. I can feel it, Aleks." Her voice trembled at the certainty of her situation.

She glanced at Aleks. He was glancing back at the other side of the river, where Rowan was. All of them had gotten together and anchored themselves with their rope. She watched Prince Cai, whom she could see was calculating his losses. His ice blue eyes were set in their decision. He would save Aleks over her. He would cut their rope and not spare a second thought about her.

She stared at Aleks right as he grabbed the rope and pulled.

Raven fell forward, her heart lurching as she crashed into him.

The ice fractured beneath them.

Aleks grabbed her hand and pulled. All three of them ran, not caring to look for safe spots anymore. They bolted until they reached the other side.

"If you ever pull a stunt like that again..." Raven blurted.

"It was nothing," Aleks snapped.

"Are you okay? The last time I saw you—"

""I was lying in the snow bleeding?" Aleks asked.

Raven nodded.

"I'm fine." Aleks replied. "All wounds have been tended to." Aleks stepped closer to her. "I'm glad you tried to run. I wish you could have seen his face when he realized you were gone." Aleks smiled.

"Me too." Raven smirked. She did her best to pull her cloak tighter around her shoulders. The shackles jangled against each other.

"Brother, what is this?" Aleks asked. He gripped the manacles and showed them to Prince Cai.

"I will explain this once, and only because you were unconscious from your wounds. Princess Astrid is a prisoner of war. Her life is dependent on her father's army staying away, and she should remember that if she tries to flee, not only is her life forfeit, but so are the lives of her men," Prince Cai said. "You really left me no choice, brother. Once mother found out we had her, and had promptly lost her, it was her orders to secure Princess Astrid by any means necessary and deliver her to the palace."

"Raven won't run. If she promised mother she would come, then she'll come."

"She already ran once, Aleks. Now that I know who she actually is, I'm not letting her out of my sight. You may have wanted all the glory of capturing her, but that will belong to me now." Prince Cai retorted as he pulled on Raven's chains.

She had watched the exchange between the brothers, knowing it was useless to interrupt. Aleks wouldn't win, and neither would she. Not yet anyway. She would bide her time until there was enough distance between them and Will. Will and his men would be fine, so she wouldn't let that threat impact her. No, she would go like the 'princess' she was and wait for the perfect time to strike.

Luckily, she wouldn't have to wait long; the Tarntan Palace was one day away.

CHAPTER FORTY-ONE

Raven

"I could kill for some caffeine right now," Raven said. Everyone turned to her. "What? It's a figure of speech…I wouldn't actually…kill someone…" she huffed.

As they walked out of the forest, Raven paused at the sight before her. A tall, lone mountain towered over them, capped in snow. Halfway up its ridge sat one of the most beautiful palaces Raven had ever beheld. The palace had been built in front of and into the mountainside, hiding its true size from enemies. Countless towers pierced the sky. Its white stone shone fiercely over the land. Huge farmlands led to the base of the mountain, where a steep path awaited them.

"We have to climb that?" Raven's legs melted at the thought. It would take them at least two hours to traverse the mountain, if not longer. No wonder no one had tried to take out this monarchy; you would be dead upon arrival.

"It's not too bad, I promise. Though I've only ever climbed it on foot once." Aleks scratched his chin. A beard had started to grow, the white stubble covering his sharp jaw.

Raven had to catch her breath once they got to the top. It had taken them almost three hours to reach it, but she had to admit the view was spectacular. She stood next to the stone wall that was the only thing separating her from falling twenty feet to the road below. The mountain palace of Tarntan overlooked all of Trudel as far as she could see. Valleys and mountains formed a tapestry of beauty below, with peaks and valleys slowly transforming from white to green. Her magic spiked for a moment as Aleks approached her. It swirled in his presence, wanting to reach out to him, to touch him, to hold him. She clamped down on her magic. Not now.

"It's beautiful," she said, her eyes remaining focused on the horizon before her.

"Yes, it is."

Raven glanced at him to find him staring at her.

"Let's go, little brother," Prince Cai summoned.

Raven watched him shift. For a moment he had allowed himself to relax around her, and now he was the Prince of Ice...again. Here, nothing would crack the surface.

The palace was as beautiful as its kingdom. The stone walls remained white despite their age. The front of the palace Raven saw was only the beginning. It was the size of a small city, and the place all members of Queen Laila's court called home. All had their own residences, separated by courtyards and training grounds. Spires circled until they vanished into the sky. Each courtyard seemed to serve a different purpose. One had a water fountain in its center, where courtiers gathered to gossip, while another had a grass yard where children played. Raven took it all in with wide eyes. She had only been to Trudel once before. It was a quick assignment that was strictly information retrieval and nothing else. She had been in and out of a small, nameless town in one day and hadn't been able to stay and enjoy the scenery.

While she didn't have to feign her awe, it didn't keep her from tracking every turn and twist. She noted which way they went and when Prince Cai led them in a circle. She took it all in with silent wonder. Let him think she couldn't find her way out. She knew exactly how to escape should the need arise.

The throne room was near the front of the palace, making their thirty minute jaunt pointless. The back of the throne room faced the front of the palace, overlooking the main entrance and kingdom through five floor to ceiling windows comprising the entire back wall. Raven's magic grew at the threat before her. Her power was almost back to full strength, and she welcomed the comfort of her power like an old friend gone too long. It gave her strength she hadn't realized she had needed. Several people were gathered in the throne room, all of them moving aside as the large double wooden doors opened and Prince Cai and Prince Aleksander were announced. They strode forward together, Aleks a single step behind his brother. Raven and Rowan followed with Daci and the remaining guards close behind.

As they walked, Raven counted the exits. One was behind her, along with one on each side of the throne room corners. The room smelled of fresh snow and a hint of metal. Nothing like Queen Lyanna's room, which was dominated by metal and blood. Raven quickly found her gaze transfixed on the woman at the top of a flight of steep black stairs that led to the throne.

If Raven hadn't already known Ella to be related to Queen Laila, she would have had zero doubts after meeting the queen. Queen Laila and Ella could have been twins, despite their age difference. Queen Laila's pure white hair cascaded down to her waist, with sections braided back to highlight the silver crown atop her head. It was twisted to appear like reindeer antlers, with the two points coming together and pointing down on her forehead. She was perfect, and Raven's stomach dropped at the blood red lips that smiled down at her with ice blue eyes so similar to Aleks's, with one difference, where he showed kindness. Hers only revealed hate.

"You know, I can't believe my sister didn't throw you in the dungeons the moment she laid eyes on you. You're the spitting image of Queen Regina," Queen Laila commented. She descended from the throne before anyone could utter a word. Her emerald gown trailed behind her, its edges covered in gold floral embroidery. A gold chain hung around her hips, with a dagger attached.

Raven found herself paralyzed before her. This was a queen.

Queen Lyanna was only pretending, while Queen Laila had clearly been born to rule.

"When I sent my son on his mission to find the Princess of Evrotia, I didn't think he would be successful. Of course, he had brought me rumors you were alive, but I never believed them. The guard had been very convincing. Aleksander didn't believe them either, couldn't of course, though for very personal reasons." Her lips tweaked to the side as she glanced between Raven and Aleks.

Aleks, Raven noted, had gone as still as a statue before her.

"I guess he wouldn't want to believe that his betrothed was indeed still alive after all this time."

Raven was fuming. *His betrothed?* Her magic, which had so desperately wanted to feel his touch, now wanted nothing more than to pierce his soul. Betrothed? They were engaged? Raven remained facing forward, arms casually at her sides. Her feet were spread just enough that no one would think she was in a fighting stance.

"Mother," the Prince of Ice warned.

"I know, I know." Queen Laila fluttered a hand at her son before resting it on his shoulder.

"What do you mean, betrothed?" Raven asked.

"You don't remember?" Queen Laila asked. "You two have been betrothed since you were born. Pity we'll have to sever that now that you're not going to rule your kingdom. I can't have my son married to a kingdomless princess."

"Mother, stop."

"Why? Do you care for her?" Queen Laila spun towards Aleks. "Have you become so blinded by her beauty that you've forgotten she's an assassin and one of the most dangerous enchanters?" Queen Laila walked around Raven, looking her up and down.

Raven faced forward. She examined the stone throne, staring at the black stone it was carved from. It was an impressive throne, intimidating in its beauty. One of the guards stepped near her, a rope in his hand.

"I haven't forgotten," Aleks ground out.

"Guards, bring in the shackles." Queen Laila ordered. She turned to face Raven. "I may have promised to not throw you in the dungeon, but I will not have you roam about my home freely.

Four guards approached her cautiously. Behind the guards walked a palace enchanter, her hands glowing as she pulled on her magic. Raven's magic cowered as she saw the enchanter's shackles.

"Charming —" Raven began.

"Mother —"

"I'm not going to use ordinary shackles, love." Queen Laila laughed. "She's an enchanter and will be restrained as one. Now, if I remember correctly, Astrid's mark is dark. Very dark. So it won't be simple wrist shackles."

The guards pulled out obsidian cuffs.

Raven tried to back up.

"Mother, be reasonable —"

"I am, Aleksander. You are the one becoming emotional."

"Raven, run," Rowan yelled. He grunted when Prince Cai punched him in the stomach.

"I will kill him. He is no one," Queen Laila hissed.

Rowan wasn't no one. He was her friend. She would not leave him to save herself from this fate. Raven locked eyes with the queen as the guards clasped obsidian cuffs around her wrists and continued up her arms until they reached her biceps. The enchanter was next, resting her hands on the shackles, speaking her enchantment of imprisonment and awakening the other enchantments in the cuffs as their inscriptions glowed red.

Raven's power flared against the intrusion.

She had just gotten it back.

It whirled around in her, screaming its indignation. They couldn't do this to her. She had sworn she would never wear these shackles again. It would not be contained. Her power continued to rise, and it was like losing control all over again. It pushed past her skin as it arched around her in a beautiful array of shimmering light. She could have sworn she heard its screams echoing through the throne room.

"Please! You're making me lose control," Raven said, unable to do anything. She had no control over her powers. All of it rested in the hands of the enchanter, putting her in a cage.

The enchanter's eyes widened as she gripped Raven's wrists, pushing her power into the obsidian. Raven sank to her knees as the enchanter continued to hold on. Her power dwindled until it was back inside her, and then...numbness started in her fingers and toes. The sensation crept into her arms and pushed into her body. With each inch that her power was forced back, a crack splintered within her core.

"Please stop," Raven begged. "Please."

Her magic was shoved farther behind a thick wall that had encircled the core being of her power. With each stone set in place, they weighed her down until she couldn't move her arms. Raven bowed her head, her hair covering her face as the light of her soul was striped from her. Yet the enchanter didn't stop.

"You've taken enough...please..."

"Mother," Aleks called from somewhere.

"Please..." Tears ran down Raven's face as what had to be hours passed by. The cuffs seemed to gain weight, pulling her down to the floor.

"Please stop. Make it stop," she begged. But the enchanter continued on, enchanting every cuff on her arm. The wall had shut her off. Not a sliver of power could escape.

Raven lay limp on the stone ground, unblinking. She watched sideways as the enchanter left the room with the majority of the guards. Their footsteps were a resounding thud that echoed around the room.

"Raven." It was so soft she almost didn't hear it. "You need to stand." Hands gently gripped her, pulling until she was sitting. Aleks was beside her.

Raven closed her eyes, focusing on her body. Did it know how to work without magic? She had thought being depleted had been the worst feeling, but now...this was a complete loss of her entire self.

Raven stood on wobbly legs and stared at the throne again. She couldn't look at anyone. Couldn't even glance at Rowan to make sure he, at least, was okay now.

"I wonder, my love, did she ever tell you her codename?" Queen Laila rested her hands on Raven's shoulders. Her knees buckled for a moment before she regained her composure.

Aleks, she saw, stood off to the side now, Rowan next to him. Aleks stared at his mother. Raven remained stiff. Of course, Queen Laila knew who she was. If Queen Lyanna knew, it made sense for Lady Tremaine's closest friend to know as well. Queen Laila lightly tapped her fingers on Raven, dancing them over her shackled arms. Raven quivered under them.

"I don't care about who she was as an assassin." Aleks spoke low, his voice choking off.

"So that's a no, then."

Raven shuddered at the mischief in the queen's voice.

"Tell me, how many assassins do you know that are also enchanters?"

"I don't care. So, just tell me." Aleks raised his eyes to the ceiling before glancing back at them.

"Astrid, would you like to tell my son?"

Raven remained intent on memorizing the throne. She would not respond or be baited into satisfying the queen's request. Clearly her name would mean something; what that was, Raven didn't know. But she would not participate in this family drama. Raven chanced a glance at Aleks. His hands remained clenched, his arms crossed as he stood in a defensive position, eyes dark with anger.

"No?" Queen Laila circled her again. "You're not brave enough to tell him?"

"No." She glanced at Aleks, hoping he saw she was just as clueless about this as he was.

"Such a pity." Queen Laila patted Raven's hair, grimacing at the dirt. "Well, Aleksander, since your formerly betrothed refused to be honest with you, I will be the one to tell you that Princess Astrid or Raven," she waved a dismissive hand, "is the enchanter and assassin known in the kingdoms she hunts in as Snow White." Queen Laila turned to Raven with a cheshire grin on her face. She was beautiful in her cruelty.

Then she turned to Aleks and Raven followed.

His hands fell to his sides, his mouth open just enough to relay the shock he felt.

And then he left.

Aleks turned around and left her in the throne room, shackled and captive.

Raven stood in shock.

Rowan glanced back and forth, meeting Raven's eyes. He motioned with his head towards Aleks, a question in his eyes. Could he follow his friend? Raven nodded her head slightly to give her approval.

Once they were alone, the queen gave her a pitying smile.

"Well, shall we?" Queen Laila shook her head at Aleks's departure before motioning for the guards to make Raven move..

Raven collapsed halfway to her new room.

The two guards had to carry her the rest of the way. She hung her head in embarrassment. She hadn't even realized she was falling until the ground tilted under her and the stone floor was kissing her face. Queen Laila had laughed at her as she was hauled off the ground.

The thick wooden door to her room eased open. As she surveyed her surroundings, she noticed that everything around her was muted. The wood beneath her feet was cold, but she couldn't sense its coarse core. The fabric on the bed was some of the finest she had seen, but it didn't pulse beneath her hands. After the guards had left her in the room, she had walked around, touching everything from the wooden bedframe to the soft rug beneath her, and she felt...nothing.

Raven stared at her arms as she lay down on her new bed in her new cage. So...this was what it was like to live a life without magic. Before, she could sense every part of herself, feel everything within her that her magic touched, and now it was as though someone had stripped her of all sense of self. She couldn't hear, smell, or feel anything in her body.

Raven curled on her side, holding herself close. Her one current consolation was that at least she had a bed, and though it was a different type of dungeon, at least her room was clean and comfortable.

"Ella, Calla." Raven's horse spun around, trying to find them. "Mira." Raven pushed her horse to keep going. If she could get out of this storm, she would find them. She had to find them. They were in danger, and she needed to be there for

them. Why couldn't she find them? Raven screamed at the storm as it tightened its hold on her, refusing to let her go.

Raven woke in the freezing night air. The obsidian shackles were freezing as she tried to bury herself under her thick blankets.

"Raven?" Rowan whispered through her door.

Raven opened her eyes, letting them adjust to the darkness. "Rowan?" She got up and opened the door, moderately surprised to see it wasn't locked from the outside. "What are you doing?" If he were caught...actually...she had no idea what would happen. He wasn't a citizen of Trudel. Did he have some type of protection?

"I needed to make sure you were okay. May I come in?" Rowan asked. He searched down the hallway.

"I'm peachy." Raven replied as she opened the door farther for him to walk in. "Is it always this cold or is it from the shackles?"

"I'm guessing it's always this cold." Rowan frowned at her.

"Do I look that bad?" Raven let out a low, raspy laugh, stopping when she saw his frown deepen. "I'm just glad I'm in an actual room. It's more than I got in Evrotia."

"You should have had —"

"Rowan." She stopped him, a look of pity on his face. "She thought I was a traitorous spy that she wanted information from. My comfort was not high on her list. In fact, the more uncomfortable I was, the more likely it was that I would break."

"I didn't know...I would have brought you something."

"Well, you didn't visit after that fun trip with your dad."

Rowan grimaced.

"I don't blame you for not visiting. How could you? Plus, I imagine you were processing all of the lies you had been told." Raven said as they walked towards the fireplace in the room. She sat down on the large wingback chair as Rowan built a small fire.

"Something like that," Rowan muttered.

"How are you doing with that? We haven't really gotten to talk about it." Rowan sat down opposite her.

"I'm still processing. I know why he lied to me. I just don't...I feel cheated somehow. As though if I had known, maybe I could have done something from the inside to help."

"That is exactly why he didn't tell you. He knew you would do something stupid like try to start a rebellion or something," Raven said. "I actually like that you didn't know who I was."

Rowan leaned forward.

"It meant you got to know me as Raven, as who I sort of am, at least who I let you see. Which, to me, is better than any preconceived notion of how Princess Astrid is supposed to be."

"Plus, I got to see you kick Aleks's ass. I don't think he would have even fought you if he had known who you were."

"That too. All of you would have been prim and proper, and it wouldn't have been fun for anyone." Raven smiled. "Speaking of Aleks..." Raven turned the torch in her hands, watching the flames dance. "Do we know why he uh...walked out when he learned I'm Snow White?"

This time she turned to him, wanting to gauge his reaction to hearing her name again. She'd been too preoccupied the first time to watch Rowan.

His face remained contemplative. There was no disgust or horror at hearing her name.

"I don't know, Raven, truly. I can find out if you'd like?"

"Thank you." She milled over her name and why it could mean anything to Aleks. "You know you don't have to stay here anymore. Go live your life, Rowan. Go find your dad and start over somewhere. Get married, have a family, or become a pirate."

"A pirate?" Rowan tilted his head.

"Yes, a pirate. I can see it now, Rowan the Raider! Or Rowan the Defender! Be a noble pirate." Raven laughed before sobering. "Seriously, Rowan, I don't want you to get hurt."

"I'm not going to abandon my queen when she needs me."

"You sound like Will," Raven muttered.

"Good, maybe between the two of us we can show you that you are our queen."

"Rowan, I'm not. I don't want it," Raven whispered.

"You are. You may not want it, but you are to me. So, I will stay and protect and help my queen. But I am also staying to watch my partner's back. I won't let you down again, Raven. I promise." Rowan wrapped his hand around hers and squeezed.

Raven gave him a shaky smile. She was unworthy of such a man protecting her. Both he and Will gave her too much credit. Rowan got up and stretched out his back. Raven stood as well to walk him to the door.

"Thank you, Rowan...for everything," Raven whispered.

Rowan nodded as he left. He paused at her door. "I just realized..." Rowan squeezed Raven's hand. "Happy birthday, Raven."

Her jaw dropped as he left.

Today was her birthday. She was nineteen and stuck in a glorified cage. At least she would be warm on her birthday.

CHAPTER FORTY-TWO

Raven

"The next time you want an answer, ask me yourself," Aleks said. He sat in one of the chairs beside the dying fire. His voice shook with barely contained rage.

Aleks was before her, one hand gripping her chair so tightly his knuckles turned white, while the other was clenched around the pommel of his sword. His white hair was in shambles, his blue eyes dark with fury.

"Are you here to kill me?" Raven asked, staring pointedly at his sword.

Aleks stood and paced around her room, avoiding the furniture like it was second nature to him.

"If you want information, just ask me next time. Don't send my friend to trick the answer out of me. I thought you were better than that." Aleks stopped before her, shaking. His hands began to glow, his magic unraveling.

"Control yourself, Prince. You're losing it," Raven rasped. "What did I do?" Raven questioned.

"Rowan was trying to very evasively ask me why you being Snow White had such an effect on me. You know he's not capable of that. You know he's a good person who just wants the best for everyone. Why would you put him in that—"

"I didn't. I simply asked him to find out. I didn't think he would try to trick it out of you. Plus, I wasn't sure you would talk to me again, for whatever it is I did..." Raven said. "I deserve a lot of things...but I don't deserve this treatment...at least until I know what happened."

Aleks stepped back, crossing his arms. "I'm sure someone of your caliber is able to figure out who Snow White is to me." Aleks said.

Raven blinked slowly as she tried to think about why Aleks would despise her. She had only been to Trudel once, three years ago.

Raven walked off the ship with a small pack slung over her shoulder. She hadn't needed much, not with how quick the assignment was going to be. Jason walked off behind her, smiling as he took her hand and kissed it. She wrapped an arm around his waist as they walked off the ship and into the small port town of Keld. It was the first time they got to venture outside of Rairene.

She looked around at the town that was small enough to host a modest port and bring in enough income to keep the homes and shops together. The stone roads were even and clean. The people were loud and well fed, and all of them wore clothes that were well made. None of them appeared to suffer. Maybe she and Jason could relocate here once they left Lady Tremaine. It was a fleeting thought. She had been having more of them recently, though. Thoughts of the future, what they might do together, how they could live together.

They walked through the town's marketplace, looking at shops and buying a few trinkets. All the while observing their target. He was a nobody, and she didn't understand why Lady Tremaine had sent two of her best assassins out to interrogate him. He was Raven's age, tall and lanky, with brown eyes that still held some innocence. Raven felt a small twinge of regret at being the one to remove that innocence.

The boy was the son of a merchant, and today was his last day in the market before he journeyed back with his father to their home in the mountains. She and Jason had found him at his wood carving stall, selling their craft. Raven had to admit it was beautiful. The dark woods had been skillfully carved. Jason even talked to him, purchasing a small carving of a raven from him. While he was distracted, Raven slipped over to the flask he had filled with water and dropped the smallest amount of poison into it. It wouldn't kill him, but Fenith would act quickly, and then they would act. While he suffered, she would ask him her questions, promising to give him the antidote, which she would, after a while.

It worked.

A few minutes later they came back to find the young man hunched over in the alley behind his stall, the poison wreaking havoc on his body. They grabbed him and pulled him farther into the alley. Raven questioned him while Jason stood guard. He resisted at first. Then his back started to break, and she held the antidote in front of his eyes, and he answered her questions. He told her about the hidden trade routes in the mountains and how one could slip between borders unnoticed. Then she was done. She had her information, and after a few more minutes of begging, Raven tipped the antidote into his lips.

"Snow White, we have to go."

She glanced at Jason and his tense position.

Someone was coming.

She left the boy in the alley, ensuring his breathing had evened out before grabbing Jason's hand. They walked out together, hand in hand, stepping into a doorway to kiss, hiding their faces as the boy's father and companion called for the day.

She and Jason spent the rest of the day touring the small town. Jason gave her the wooden carving he had purchased, a raven in flight, its eyes so lifelike she was certain it would fly out of her hand at any moment. They grabbed some food and stocked up on supplies as the day began to wane. The last thing they did was write down what the boy had told her and leave it as requested, with the innkeeper at the Oak and Sail. Together, they boarded a different ship and hunkered down together in bed.

Raven bit her lip, wondering how that could have hurt Aleks. They were just a bunch of secret trade routes, and surely they would have changed by now? If something had happened because of that information, she was never going to figure that out. No, it had to do with the boy; what was his name?

Light footsteps floated down the hallway towards Raven's ears.

"Raven, are you okay?" Daci whispered.

Raven jumped out of bed and let Daci into her room.

"I've been better...but...I've also been worse," Raven replied.

"Is there anything I can do for you? Anything you need?" Daciana peered at her.

"Aside from breaking out, getting these shackles off, food, a bath, my wounds tended to, and a way home to my family?" Raven said.

"Well, yes, anything else?" Daci laughed.

"Who's Ian?" The name came to her suddenly. The boy she had interrogated all those years ago.

"Who?"

"Ian, does that name mean anything to you? I think it meant something to Aleks."

"I don't know who that is." Daci's eyes were sincere, confusion in her brow. "But I promise to start on those other requests. Do they need to be completed in the exact order you gave me? Or can I start by tending to your wounds?"

Raven laughed as she walked over to her bed.

"Why didn't you tell us you were injured?" Daci asked.

Raven stripped down to her breast band and underwear. "I think I was so cold I couldn't feel them until I lay down on a real bed." She shrugged. "I was able to at least tend to the ones on my ribcage."

"That's some solace, I suppose. Though I don't know who will be more upset, me, Rowan or Aleks, at the fact that you didn't tell us."

"Well, it can't be you since I'm asking you to help me," Raven said.

Daci sighed as she grabbed some clean linen, a sponge, and filled a bowl with water. There were more cuts on her shoulders and thighs than Raven had anticipated, though luckily most were too shallow to have a lasting impact.

"This one is bad, Raven. I'm going to have to open it and cleanse it." Daci pointed to one on Raven's shoulder that had scabbed over and begun to change color.

"Do what you must," Raven replied. She braced herself as Daci got out a knife and went to work. Raven closed her eyes as Daci reopened her wound and seemed to dig out her entire shoulder. At one point, Raven blacked out, coming back as Daci worked on tightly wrapping her bandage around her chest and shoulder.

"I think that was the worst. Do you want me to do the rest?" Daci whispered.

Raven nodded, blinking against the spots in her eyes. "Tell me about what happened after I left to distract me."

Daci chuckled. "Prince Cai was livid. I thought he was going to kill someone once he found out why they took you. Apologies for not being able to hide that from him. I couldn't think of a reason fast enough, and Prince Aleksander was still unconscious. I figured the truth would be the best option."

"It was going to come out at some point."

"Once he scried Queen Laila, he set up camp for everyone and began strategizing how to find you. He was concerned about Prince Aleksander. He would never show it, but he kept returning to the makeshift tent we had built over him to see if he had woken up. I think he was waiting to leave until Aleks became conscious, but too much time was passing."

"How bad was Aleks?"

"It wasn't horrible, but it did take him a few days to be able to travel again." Daci lowered her voice. "When he learned what was happening, he almost went after his brother to try...to be honest, I don't know what he would have done to stop him."

"I guess we'll never know," Raven said. She winced as Daci cleaned the wounds on her sides and legs. As each one was tended to, the better she felt, and not once did she want to ask for a healing potion.

"Well, I don't know about unlocking those shackles or running away, but can I get you some food?"

Raven laughed. "I would love that."

Daci got up and left, her cloak trailing behind her.

Raven closed her eyes, her mind spinning, trying to determine what to do and who Ian was.

"I can tell you who Ian is," a woman said as she stepped out of the shadows of Raven's closet.

CHAPTER FORTY-THREE

MIRA

"Princess Miraya." Prince Adam opened his door, wearing a loose tunic and trousers.

"Care to go for a walk with me?" Mira asked. She wore a thick black cloak and a simple gown that covered her feet.

Adam nodded, leaving with her, his own cloak in hand. She marveled at the work Calla had done with the scar on his face. It must have been truly gruesome if her serum hadn't been able to completely heal him.

"Where do you want to go?" Adam asked as they continued walking through the halls.

"You'll just have to wait and see." Mira smiled. She had spent several nights traversing the grounds, making sure she avoided Bastien at all costs, and finding all of the holes in the queen's security.

Adam followed as they walked through several hallways in the early morning. She had not gotten any sleep and had instead spent the whole night figuring out how to take down the queen, Morgan, and rescue Calla. And a lot of it depended on help from Adam. He had access to the queen in a way she didn't. Plus, now that she knew Adam was emotionally tied to Calla, he would be more motivated to get her out. Mira took them through the kitchens that she had finally located, out the back into the gardens, and through a small gap that appeared in the wall behind them. It didn't lead directly into Aslar, but it did lead them to an empty space of ground that, from what Mira could ascertain, was hardly patrolled by the guards. A gate sat there unmanned and ready to be picked by Mira's tools.

"How do we —" Adam stopped talking when he saw Mira pick the lock in under thirty seconds. "Where did you learn that?"

Mira held a finger to her lips and smiled as she walked through the gate. She locked it behind them and walked farther away from the palace wall before talking.

"There's a lot you don't know about me, Adam."

"I can tell." He looked at the gate as they walked.

They walked for a few more feet before their hidden path turned into an alley made of barely cobbled together stones.

"I'll explain everything to you, I promise. But first, I wanted to apologize as well for what happened between us. I want you to know it had nothing to do with you. I simply didn't want to marry —"

"A man?" Adam asked.

"Well, yes, but also no. I just didn't want to get married. There's nothing wrong with men. I've been with plenty, and have always had a good time. But that's beside the point." Mira diverted the question. This conversation was not about her love life. "I'm sorry it ended that way. It seems we both got bad deals out of it."

Adam sighed. "I did this to myself. I refused to marry anyone who wasn't as beautiful as you, and did you know, until recently, I found no one to be as beautiful as you?" Adam confessed. He paused as they walked past some citizens. "My own vanity landed me here as a last ditch effort by my father to make an advantageous alliance."

"Well, it seems like maybe things might have been fated?" Mira asked.

Adam raised his eyebrows at her.

She switched to Vicurian before she continued speaking. "I saw you with Calla."

Adam stiffened. "How?"

"I was going to see her too," Mira said.

They continued on in Vicurian as more people walked around them. They had reached one of the many market squares in Aslar and had begun to peruse the items being sold. Neither one of them was concerned about someone overhearing them.

"You know my former maid?" Adam whispered.

"I told you, there's a lot you don't know about me," Mira replied.

She told him everything. Last night had shown her that she could trust him with this information. He loved Calla; she was certain, and she would use that to her advantage, even if it meant exposing herself.

"That's...you came all the way out here to save her?"

"Now that you know her, would you have done anything less?" Mira asked. She bought a sticky cinnamon roll, a dessert she thought she would only ever be able to get from Raven. It didn't taste as good as Raven's rolls, but it was close.

"I would have gone anywhere for her, but I love..." Adam didn't finish the sentence. "Mira, are you and she together?"

"No." Mira whispered. "And we never will be. So don't worry about that. Calla's heart is firmly settled on you." She smiled at him as they continued walking.

"Why are you telling me all of this?"

"Because yesterday showed me that I need to get Calla out of the dungeons sooner than I had planned, and I need your help."

"Whatever you need, I'll do it. Do you have an idea?" Adam responded before Mira could even begin to lay out her plans to him.

"I know I can't rely on my usual sources for help, so I'm thinking it's going to just be the two of us." Mira launched into her thoughts with Adam. She would continue to flirt and play with Morgan and get as much information out of her as possible. Mainly, she would get Morgan to take her to the dungeons. She had only been able to sneak in through the back, and Mira wanted to make sure she knew all the entrances and exits that were available to her.

"What about the lock?" Adam asked.

"What about it?"

"It's enchanted. The moment you touch it with anything but its key, it will burn you," Adam explained.

"Then I guess I need to get that key from the guards," Mira said.

They continued walking through Aslar, spreading some of their funds as much as they could among the vendors. They discussed any bumps they might come across and how to solve them. By the time they got back to the hidden gate, they had a plan laid out for rescuing Calla by the end of the week.

"Can I ask you something, Adam?" Mira asked as they walked back into the hall.

He nodded, glancing around the hallway. Mira continued to speak in Vicurian.

"You mentioned when I first got here that you had been betrayed by someone important. Was it Calla and who she is?"

Adam nodded. "I didn't take her true identity revelation well. She'd been sent to kill me —"

Mira laughed, sobering when Adam looked at her. "Oh, you're serious. You thought our sweet, mild tempered, couldn't hurt a rat woman would be able to even try killing you?" Mira watched as he struggled to say no. "Wow, you must really struggle to have any relationships. She could never do that to you. She doesn't have it in her. She can't even enchant a potion of strength or speed because it involves an intention she's not capable of. If you must know, her mission here was merely to support Raven in her assignment to spy on Queen Lyanna. No one was meant to die, not even the queen," Mira explained.

"Thank you for that clarity. She had tried to tell me, but I refused to listen."

"That's because when you care about someone and there's the smallest inkling of a chance they've caused some slight against you, you run in the other direction, Adam," Mira said.

"I'll try to work on that," Adam replied. He crossed his arms and continued walking through the palace.

"Princess Miraya," Morgan called to them.

Mira and Adam turned together to watch the woman walk over to them. She was beautiful, but Mira couldn't stop seeing her standing over Calla, laughing as Calla twisted in pain. She remembered the burns Morgan got from the wax 'accident', but given the burns she had seen on Calla...rage built in Mira as she watched Morgan walk over to them. She couldn't do anything with it yet, so Mira let it continue to simmer in her heart. Unlike her father, she didn't lash out on instinct. She was methodical and would wait for the perfect moment to seek her retribution.

Mira smiled as Morgan walked over to them. Mira kept her hands behind her back, clasping them together to resist the urge to slap Morgan. "What can we do for you, Lady Morgana?" Mira asked.

"I was hoping I could borrow your time, if the prince doesn't mind? I'm sure Princess Arianna would enjoy his company," Morgan said.

"Of course. Prince Adam, it has been wonderful catching up with you. I'll see you tonight at the ball?"

Adam nodded before walking away. Mira waited until he was out of earshot before she turned to Morgan. She had waited to make it appear that she was being secretive with Morgan, but in reality she needed her pulse to slow down.

"Are you okay?" Morgan questioned.

Mira tilted her head to the side.

"Your heart is racing, and you seem a little flushed."

"Oh, well, that's because you're here. I can't help it." Mira gave her a coy smile as they began walking away from Adam. It was Morgan's turn to flush as they walked. "What can I do for you?"

"I was wondering if you would save a dance for me at the ball tonight."

"Is that allowed?" Mira asked before she could stop herself.

"Oh yes, Queen Lyanna is a very tolerant ruler," Morgan answered.

Mira made a small noise of surprise.

"Plus, I was hoping I could talk to you more about Grecia, if that's okay with you?"

"Are you planning on moving there?" Mira joked.

"I like to keep my options open; you never know when you might have to quickly make an exit." Morgan didn't look at her as they wandered through hallways bustling with servants and noblemen alike.

"Oh? Is something going to happen? Do I need to do the same?" Mira asked. She made sure she spoke low with the perfect tinge of fear in her inflection.

"No, you're okay." Morgan stopped walking and stood in front of Mira. She rested her hand on Mira's shoulder with a kindness Mira no longer believed from the torturer. "You're a princess after all; no one would ever try to hurt you."

"Then why are you searching for a way out of the kingdom?" Mira resisted the urge to rip herself out of Morgan's hands.

"It's just a precaution. Besides, I hear that this beautiful princess lives in Grecia, so I might want to visit one day." Morgan smiled. She ran her hands up and down Mira's before releasing her and continuing on their walk.

"What did you want to know about Grecia?" Mira asked a few minutes later.

"Which city is better, Amarta or Savila?"

"It depends on what you're looking for. Amarta offers an environment similar to Aslar. There's a lot of merchants coming in with their ships, vendors selling their wares, and it's where I live with my father. However, if you want something a little smaller and peaceful where you can wander through wide cobblestone alleys, eat fresh fish off the docks, and lie on the beach, then Savila is where you would want to go."

"Savila sounds wonderful. How long has it been again since you've been there?" Morgan wrapped her arm around Mira's as they walked through a stream of people getting the palace ready for the ball celebrating Princess Arianna's fourteenth birthday.

"Years. I miss it greatly," Mira replied.

"What's the first thing you'll eat when you get there?"

Mira grabbed Morgan's arm and squeezed as she replied, "Lalagia. It's the simplest food made from an easy dough that's cut into strips and fried in fat over a fire. It's the most delicious treat, and I would die if I got to have one again."

"It sounds a lot like a sweet treat we have here. It's also a fried dough that's been cut into triangles or squares. Once fried, we cover it in snow sugar."

"Sounds heavenly. Does the kitchen ever make it?"

"No." Morgan slumped. "Queen Lyanna doesn't enjoy it, so the chef stopped making it."

Mira nodded in understanding. "Well, I don't know about you, but it always takes me hours to get this face ready for a ball."

"Princess Miraya, you could have no cosmetics on your face and you would still be the most beautiful woman in the room."

Mira smiled.

"We have a portrait of you with your family, and it did not accurately portray your beauty."

"You have a portrait of my family?" Mira asked. That was odd.

"Yes, your father sent it several years back, I believe. I'm not sure when. The queen moved it to the west wing several days later."

"Ah, it must have been the one sent out for my engagement to Prince Adam. It would have been put away because it ended a few days later." Mira explained.

"Ah, well." Morgan rocked back and forth on her feet. "I'll see you tonight?"

Mira nodded.

"And you'll still save me a dance?"

Mira nodded before shutting the door.

She leaned heavily on the door as she stared into her room. Her possessions had quickly exploded over the room as she lived out of her trunks. Gowns and clothes were strewn over her chair and the floor. The bed had remained clear of the disaster, though she had still requested ten pillows be brought to her room. Mira kicked off her boots and let her cloak fall to the ground by her door as she walked over to the vanity and stared at herself.

Mira had grown up being told she was beautiful. Out of all her sisters, she was the one who had been her father's crowning achievement. The one who could secure any match with appearance alone. Her sisters were still pretty; Maliah, for instance, was also beautiful. But Mira had been a point of pride for him. That was probably why everything had happened the way it did that night.

She delicately touched her cheeks, jaw, and the general profile of her face. It was still *her* face, but after...there had been some changes. It had genuinely shocked her that Adam had even a glimmer of what had occurred that night. After Adam and his father had left, it had been just her, Maliah, her father, and a few guards in the throne room.

That was when the real rage had been unleashed. Everything prior, all the posturing and yelling at her, that had been a show, a reminder to never step out of line of your king's wishes. Now, it was time for the punishment to be delivered in private.

She should have died that night.

Her father's fury was unrivaled, and he had held it in until he could show her the true scope of his feelings. The first punch, surprisingly, wasn't the most painful one. He hadn't given her time to recover before punching her farther to the ground. That was usually when it ended. Two punches. She would be 'grounded' and sequestered from court life until the bruising left, and then she would come back into her father's good graces.

That was how it *always* went.

But not that night.

That night, her father didn't stop punching her.

All Mira could do was lie on the ground and take the beating from her father. She had kept her eyes closed for most of it, counting the seconds between each punch. She couldn't bear to take his hits and see the disappointment in his eyes for making him punish her.

Then, the punches had stopped.

Mira opened one eye as far as she could and saw Maliah standing over their father, who was somehow also on the ground. Maliah said something to him before she got to Mira. The next thing Mira remembered was waking up in her room. An enchanter was there, pouring a healing potion down her throat. She made her swallow the entire bottle. Maliah had sat by her side in the bed, arms wrapped around her as Mira cried.

A week later, Mira was sent away on a ship with her most prized possessions and a new face. It was still her face, but the healing potion...it had enhanced her features from beautiful to someone who could get away with anything with a simple eyelash bat and a smile.

Mira threw a tunic over the mirror and walked away to get ready for the ball.

CHAPTER FORTY-FOUR

Calla

Calla had counted the wood panels for the hundredth time since her capture. She was on the table again, and Morgan was laughing with someone. Calla had stopped caring long ago about who Morgan brought to her torture chamber. It was always the same. They plied her with alcohol now, got her tipsy or drunk, asked her questions, increased her level of pain, then did it all over again.

"Calla," Morgan's voice washed over her.

Calla looked sideways when a hand gently brushed hair out of her face. Morgan was dressed in a beautiful gown as she smiled down at Calla.

"I have to go to a ball with a beautiful woman. Which means I'm inviting someone else to have some fun and watch over you while I'm gone. Do make sure you don't divulge too much to him; you wouldn't want to make me jealous. Though I must warn you, his methods are a bit different from mine. Maybe you'll be more pliant after some time with him." Morgan smirked as she stepped out of Calla's field of vision to show her who this mystery guest was.

Calla's stomach dropped as Lord Edouard stepped forward. Sweat broke out on her brow as he continued to get closer. She couldn't even beg Morgan to stop him. It would only make him happier and reveal how truly frightened she was of him.

"Don't have too much fun. Remember, I'm doing this as a favor and that the queen does still expect you to make an appearance, Lord Edouard."

He nodded as his smirk grew. Morgan left, and Calla glanced around to notice it was just the two of them.

Her heart rate accelerated as she watched him.

"You know, if you had only allowed me to have you that first night on the ship, this would have been done and over then, and we wouldn't be here." His deep voice dripped like sludge down Calla's back as he circled her.

She remained silent. It was the only course of action she could take.

"I barely had to ask a favor for this one. Morgan was more than happy to let me have my fun with you." Lord Edouard came to stand directly in front of her, pressing both hands down on either side of her face. "The main question I have is what to do first? Do I play with you, torture you, or both at the same time?"

He brushed one of her curls out of her face as Calla did everything within her power to not squirm away from him. Any signal and he would pounce on her.

"I want to take you somewhere more private, though. Your cell, perhaps?" Lord Edouard asked.

He grabbed the keys and unlocked her. This was her moment. As soon as the door was open, she could take it. Calla would rather die than have to suffer a punishment at his hands. Lord Edouard didn't know what they did to transport her every day, and Calla was about to use that to her advantage.

He swaggered around her as he unlocked the other two. Calla stood still, feigning meekness as he surveyed her. She kept her head down, peering out from under her lashes to see when he opened the door. Glancing over, she saw the potions on the counter. It was now or never.

Calla grabbed the potion bottle, with what seemed to be Fenith swirling within. Calla opened it and poured the entire bottle's contents over his face.

Lord Edouard screamed as Calla jumped around him and bolted down the hall.

She scrambled to a stop when a wall reared up in front of her. They always went straight when they brought her here. There should not have been a wall, and yet...there it was.

Calla changed her trajectory and went left, sprinting down the hall only to come to another stop. She turned around and ran back the way she had come.

"I'm going to bring you so much pain you'll wish you had died," Lord Edouard yelled as she passed him. He was clutching his face, but had still found his way out of the room.

Calla made it to a door, throwing it open to find the stairs that they always carried her down. She sprinted, getting to the door at the top. Something wrapped around her ankle and yanked her down. Calla kicked him and ran back to get out into the fresh open air. Calla ran in the only direction she knew, towards the ballroom.She didn't take the time to soak in the sights, sounds, and smells that surrounded her. Surely at the ball, someone would protect her. Someone would see that this wasn't okay and intervene.

A body tackled her to the ground.

Calla screamed as she fought against him.

Lord Edouard punched her head, and Calla saw white spots dance in her eyes as the stones beneath her seemed to tilt and then drop out from under her as Lord Edouard picked her up and hefted her over his shoulder.

"I'm taking you somewhere I can keep you chained down."

CHAPTER FORTY-FIVE

Mira

Mira arrived fashionably late to the ball. At least, that's what she would say if she were asked. She wouldn't tell anyone she had let herself cry three hours ago, or that she had snuck off to try to see Calla four hours ago. At least she had arrived before Princess Arianna. Mira had opted to continue wearing gowns in the fashion of her home. Somehow, the wispy fabric and airy sway of the sleeves made her more confident than the constricting bodices with their elaborate decorative armor of traditional Evrotian gowns. However, Mira did have to admit they were beautiful.

The gown she wore was her favorite one. She tried to never repeat a dress, but she consistently went to this one on important nights, and tonight was important. She had to get Morgan to reveal more of her work and then convince her to bring Mira down to the dungeon. So, she wore her emerald dress with gold thread shimmering along its edges and throughout the gauzy fabric. The embroidery was elaborate along the neckline and waist. She wore her hair partly up with multiple braids twisting together on the back of her head, with the rest hanging in perfect waves down her back. She rested a necklace with a pearl hanging in the center around her neck, and a gold crown encrusted with diamonds and a single emerald in the center.

By the glances she got from the entire room as she entered the ballroom, all of them thought she was gorgeous too. Good. Mira got to her spot near the throne as Princess Arianna and Prince Adam were announced. The princess was stunning in a dark red gown with silver decorative armor forming the bodice. Had Arianna been Mira's age, she would have thought of her as competition, but Mira didn't bother with getting jealous. She could have any man or woman in the room twisted around her finger within an hour.

Princess Arianna and Adam opened the party with a waltz. Adam had always been a beautiful dancer, but Arianna needed some practice as she continued to glance at her feet and not follow Adam's lead. They made it through the dance, though, and once their duty for the night was done, they both separated and went in opposite directions.

Mira did a circuit around the floor, listening to the gossip and watching the dancers. Everyone was talking about the princess and her birthday. Some people spoke in hushed tones about Raven, wondering why she hadn't been caught yet, or how much longer they were going to be expected to stay in the palace.

"You look...wow."

"I look wow?" Mira asked as she turned to face Morgan.

Morgan stood slack jawed.

"Careful, you might not remember how to close your mouth," Mira said. She smiled as she walked over and gently pushed Morgan's mouth closed. "But thank you for the compliment. I had hoped you would like it."

Morgan smiled as she continued to look Mira up and down. Morgan had dressed in a beautiful black gown with green embellishments. Her silver hair was down for the first time, falling in loose curls to her shoulders.

"Shall we dance?" Mira asked when Calla's tormentor remained silent. She had to remind herself that no matter how much she had enjoyed flirting with Morgan, she was a mark, and she was hurting the woman she loved. Mira led them both onto the dance floor and took the lead.

"How was your afternoon? Do anything fun?" Mira asked as they entered the first bridge of the song.

"I actually did. My current assignment is proving difficult, and it's always better for me when I have to work for it." Morgan smiled.

Mira kept down the bile rising in her throat.

"Yourself?"

"Oh, I spent the entire time getting ready. But I would love to hear about you. I feel like you know so much about me, and I know so little about you. What's making your current assignment a challenge?"

Morgan stepped closer to Mira so they were an inch apart. "Can I tell you a secret?"

Mira nodded.

"It's not really a secret, I guess. Most of the people in this room know what I do."

"What is that?"

"I assess threats and interrogate them until I am satisfied that they are no longer a threat to our queen."

"That sounds incredibly important. Does that mean..." Mira stepped so that there was no distance between them. She ran a hand through Morgan's hair and gently rested her head against Morgan's. "Are you the one who interrogated that traitorous guard?" Mira whispered.

Morgan nodded as she ran a hand through Mira's hair. "I'm also the one ensuring the safety of our kingdom by interrogating her accomplice."

Mira's entire body wanted to recoil at the glee coating Morgan's voice.

"You mean the one that was brought before the court a few days ago?"

"Yes. She's my challenge. No matter what I do, she won't break."

"Wasn't she just a maid?" Mira questioned.

"That was her cover. She is clearly very well trained and potentially a greater threat than the guard."

"You're torturing her?" Mira swallowed more bile.

"Hmm, that's why we're switching things up. She's going to be in my office for the next few days until either I or Lord Edouard can crack her."

"Lord Edouard?" Mira had never heard of him.

"Yes. Apparently, she had been on his ship when he was sailing from Rairene and became obsessed with her. He's been lusting after her ever since, so now he'll get to take out some of his rage on her after she embarrassed him at the servant's ball."

"I see." Mira said. She couldn't think of anything else except the idea that Calla was being tormented right now as she was fucking dancing and flirting with the woman responsible for that pain.

"I tell you all of this to let you know that you have nothing to fear from her. She may be an enchanter, but she is well handled."

"That's a relief." Mira fought every instinct she had to sprint off the floor and locate Calla. She could do this. She could hold firm and pretend to enjoy everything Morgan was telling her. Each piece added a log to the fire simmering in Mira's dark green eyes.

"Excuse me, Princess, but the Queen needs Lady Morgana for a moment," an usher spoke softly, interrupting their dance.

"Of course." Mira stepped back from Morgan.

Morgan gave her an apologetic smile before following the usher to the queen.

Mira left the dance floor and headed for the doors leading to the balcony outside the ballroom. The cold air blasted her like a fresh sea breeze. Mira rubbed her arms as she walked to the ledge and glanced down at the dimly lit city below. A flicker of candles burned in the windows as the night darkened. Mira vomited the moment she was out of sight of everyone in the ballroom.

"Mira?"

"Go away." Mira heaved again into a bush.

"Are you okay?" Adam was beside her, rubbing her back and pulling her hair out of the way.

"I'm fine." Mira stood straight and folded her arms. "Calla is with some Lord Edouard. Do you know anything about him?"

"Lord Edouard? You're sure?" Adam gripped her shoulders.

"That hurts."

Adam's eyes were wide as he released Mira from his hold. "I have to get to her. She can't be left with him. He's already stabbed her once."

"You can't go, Adam." Mira stood in front of him and held him still.

"The hell I can't." Adam broke free from her and ran along the balcony towards a side entrance.

"You foolish man." Mira hiked her dress, pulled off her heels, and chased after him. If he did something, everything would be ruined. Morgan had told her in confidence, and this would blow up in her face.

She caught Adam and tackled him to the ground.

"I have to get to her, Mira," Adam said. "You don't understand what he'll do." He struggled beneath Mira as she pinned him between her legs.

"I'll handle it," Mira spoke through gritted teeth.

"We need to get to her now." Adam shoved Mira so hard she almost tumbled off him.

"I know." Mira punched Adam in the head, knocking him out. "But I will handle it."

She stood and shook out her dress as she got off Adam and walked back toward the palace. As she approached the ballroom, she put on her heels, fixed her hair, and straightened her back.

It didn't take her long to find Morgan as she departed from the queen's throne and walked down the stairs. Mira didn't wait for Morgan to search for her. She walked to her and spun her onto the dance floor without waiting.

"One should be careful; someone, mainly myself, might start to think you're genuinely interested in courting me," Morgan commented as they began a slower dance. This one was strictly for partners. There would be no one interrupting with group patterns, and Adam knew better than to stop this. Though his pacing in the corner might draw attention.

"Oh, I'm past being careful. I've been very intentional about what I want with you." Mira continued to spin them around. Gradually Mira brought Morgan closer to her as her hand sent soft strokes down her back. Finally, Mira brought her hand up and cupped Morgan's face. The enchanter had closed her eyes and smiled as Mira brought them together. She opened them now, her purple eyes locked on Mira's, and Mira saw the desire there, the openness and the need in her expanding pupils and slightly gasping lips.

"I want you," Mira rasped out. She choked down more bile.

"You want me?" Morgan asked.

"Right now." Mira spoke in her ear, continuing to spin them around.

Morgan nodded and led Mira off the floor. Mira smiled when Morgan turned back towards her as they left the ballroom. They got past the guards and any other lingering guests when Mira grabbed Morgan's hand and pulled her into an alcove.

Mira's blood pounded in frustration as Mira further delayed getting to Calla. It was necessary; she told herself. She had to make Morgan want to take her. Mira pushed Morgan against the stone wall and stopped her lips from touching Morgan's with the barest whisper between them, and held it. Morgan's breaths were shallow and rapid against Mira's lips.

"What a tease." Morgan tried to nip at her. Mira pulled back just enough, smiling as she saw Morgan's eyes flash.

"I want to see it," Mira whispered.

"I'll show you just about anything."

"I want to see the dungeon. I want to know with absolute certainty I'm safe here...with you." Mira added as she pressed her lips for a brief moment against the corner of Morgan's lips.

Morgan groaned. "My word isn't enough?" Morgan asked.

"I'm more of a visual person. Besides, maybe seeing her chained will give me some more inspiration," Mira said. She gripped Morgan's wrists and lifted them above her head as she stepped closer, nipping at her ear. "So, will you take me?"

Morgan panted as Mira waited, holding her pinned against the wall.

"I've never met any princess like you."

"You've never met any woman like me," Mira replied, winking.

Morgan took the initiative and pushed Mira back and against the other side of the hall. "Let's go. I'll take you."

Morgan quickly led Mira down twisting hallways dimly lit with fading candles, casting long shadows over them. Their hands were locked together the entire time, as though Morgan feared the moment she released Mira the spell would be broken. Mira didn't mind; she would do whatever it took to ensure Calla's safety.

When they reached the main entrance, Morgan paused as she withdrew an old key and used it on a nondescript door that Mira had passed several times in her search. They walked up a flight of stairs, stopping at the landing. Morgan ignored all the guards, but Mira didn't. She noted how many were posted, where the keys hung, everything.

Morgan pulled her in their fine gowns over wet cobblestones slick with slime and moss.

"Lord Edouard should be done with her by now. He is still expected to make an appearance at —"

A scream ripped through the hall.

Mira just about broke as Calla's scream, coated in unbridled fear, filled the air.

Morgan sprinted down the dungeon in her heels.

"Stop, please," Calla's voice pierced Mira, and she found herself chasing after Morgan.

Mira slipped on the cobblestones in her haste. She scrambled to her feet, scraping her nails over the stones to get back up. She had to get to Calla; she had to stop whatever it was Lord Edouard was doing.

By the time Mira got to Calla's cell, Morgan was standing by the door...observing.

"Stop him. Please." Calla's voice was a whisper that chilled Mira as she approached.

Mira held in her vomit as she saw Calla cowering as far as the chains would allow her, as he removed his belt.

"Stop this, Morgan," Mira said.

"No. I need information from her, and if this is how it needs to be done, then Lord Edouard is the man to do it."

"This is wrong. No matter what she says, you are damaging a young woman. Surely Queen Lyanna wouldn't approve of this."

"Queen Lyanna approves of the results, and I'm tired of waiting."

Lord Edouard removed his boots, and Calla whimpered.

"I want to hear it from the queen herself. Stop him now until I have heard approval from her that she condones this treatment of those under her domain." Mira summoned every ounce of royal snobbery in her voice as she straightened her back and stared down on Morgan.

"She's a traitor. She helped the guard try to form a coup."

Lord Edouard began unbuttoning his trousers.

"So that justifies this?" Mira whispered. She gripped Morgan's arm and stepped close to her. "If you're half the woman I know you to be, you'll stop this."

"You don't know me at all."

"I want to know you better. So, much better," Mira said as she looked Morgan up and down. "I hope you want to know me better, too."

Morgan blinked and nodded. "Lord Edouard, stop. That's enough for tonight. We'll see how pliable she is in the morning."

"But —"

"Now. Don't make me come in there and get you," Morgan ordered.

Lord Edouard put his clothes and shoes back on. He shot Mira a withering glare as he left. Calla remained curled on the floor, her dress providing the barest coverage. Mira's fingers twitched to cover her, to hug her, to hold her close and never let go.

But she couldn't do that. She couldn't go to her friend and reassure her. Adam would have to. Mira tugged on Morgan's sleeve, drawing the torturer's eyes away from Calla.

"Come with me. Lord Edouard got his fun; let's have ours." Mira pouted.

Morgan smiled, all thoughts of Calla gone as she led Mira out of the dungeon and to her bedroom.

CHAPTER FORTY-SIX

Raven

Raven reached for a blade at her back that wasn't there. She pivoted and got into a defensive stance as the woman walked towards her in tight black clothes. Her black hair flowed down her back in loose waves, and her brown eyes glinted in the moonlight.

"And you are?" Raven eyed the woman as she got closer. How had she not noticed her there? She was short and lean, allowing her to hide in small spaces. No wonder Raven hadn't seen her. She was a perfect whisper in the dark. But she still didn't know who she was.

"I'm Tora."

"And how would *you* know who Ian is?" Raven got up and stepped close to her.

Tora smiled, telling Raven that she knew many secrets.

"Because I'm the one the Prince of Ice comes to at night. I'm the one he whispers his secrets to, his desires, his darkest wishes. He tells them all to me." She stopped within inches of Raven.

Raven quirked a smile. Tora was jealous and staking a claim on her territory then. "The Prince of Ice?" Raven smiled down at her. Tora didn't truly know Aleks then, just who he let her see.

"Yes, Prince Aleksander, the man who left you in the throne room."

"Hmmm, I didn't realize I cared enough about him to be left by the…'Prince of Ice', was it?" Raven smirked. This girl would know nothing of value.

Tora's lips tweaked to the side, a hip pushed in the same direction. She twirled a piece of her hair.

"I'll bet you don't actually know who Ian is and you've only come to posture before me instead."

"That's not true. Ian was Prince Aleksander's closest friend when they were children. He may not have been of noble birth or high ranking, but his mother was one of the kitchen cooks. While his father was out selling his carvings, Ian would stay here with his mom, where the prince and his friend would play." Tora spat.

"Why does that matter? I left him alive. He was barely tortured."

"You did leave him alive."

Tora gripped Raven's injured shoulder. Raven held in a scream.

"You know it takes a special kind of enchanter to give another enchanter a poison that's been magically twisted," Tora whispered with glee.

"He wasn't an enchanter. I would have been informed."

"He was. You see, he was so weak, his mark couldn't be distinguished on his skin. There was barely a line." Tora's eyes glittered as she delivered the blow.

Raven had never given an enchanter one of her poisons. If she were ever recruited to torture another like her, she used normal poison, not enchanted ones. The risk was always too high that the enchanter would become addicted and continue chasing potions. Raven winced as Tora squeezed her harder.

"What happened?" It was the only question that mattered.

"After you left, his father found him. Prince Aleksander was with him as well. He had been visiting, you see, wanting to get away from the palace and be 'normal'." Tora rolled her eyes as if the mere idea of normalcy was repulsive. "He was alive in the alley, barely conscious. For a few days, Ian was fine.

Since he was so weak, the poison lasted just a little longer in him, saturated his blood, and made his need for it stronger. As soon as he recovered, the entire family was relieved. Prince Aleksander was summoned home shortly after. It started slowly at first, with Ian. A small potion one day, another a week later. He spaced them out, tried to, at least. It didn't take long before he spent every night in a potion den."

"He should have been given help. They should have known —"

"They thought that because he was such a weak enchanter the effects wouldn't be as severe."

"Bullshit. Every trained enchanter knows the weaker you are, the more susceptible you are to addiction. It gives you a taste of the power you can't have, so they continue to chase it." Raven seethed. Tora still kept her grounded in place in the washroom. Aleks should have known.

"Ian wasn't trained. No one bothered. They said that enchanting even one potion would deplete him for days."

Raven's mouth dropped. That was incredibly weak. Which meant Ian's ingesting of her poison had only made him worse. He would have been...Raven didn't want to think about it.

"Yes, that's right." Tora released her hold on Raven. "No one trained him. With Prince Aleksander away, no one was there to see the signs of what was happening. He chased that power high all the way until his heart stopped by taking Vivifica."

Raven paled. "He didn't...he took Solacium, didn't he? Even though he wasn't dying...he took it."

Tora nodded.

He had taken Solacium, and it had had nothing to fix. When it couldn't find something, it went to the major organs, trying to repair what didn't need repairing. His heart would have exploded. He wouldn't have felt it, not entirely, but the body...it would have...Raven vomited. She didn't want to picture what Ian would have looked like with a heart that had burst out of his body.

"Prince Aleksander was the first one to find him. He had to tell his best friend's parents what had happened. They blamed him, of course. They assumed that because their son was close to the prince, he had been targeted. And Prince Aleksander...well, he's always blamed Snow White. Always wanted to kill her for what she took from him."

"How uh...how did he know it was me?" Raven had been careful. She had barely spoken to the boy.

"Your partner, I think? He said your name just loud enough for Ian to hear it. It was the only thing he could say when they first found him." Tora tilted her head to the side. "It's too bad everyone knows what you look like now. The myth of Snow White is so much scarier without being able to put a face to the name."

Tora left without another word. Raven collapsed onto her straw bed, absorbing the information. Ian wasn't supposed to die. Why hadn't she been told? More questions that she needed answers to, answers she would have to get from the only other person who would know about her assignments...Queen Laila.

CHAPTER FORTY-SEVEN

Raven

Raven didn't even care anymore about who visited her. However, the smell of roses and vanilla that wafted through her open door was new. Raven turned her head to find Queen Laila standing in her room. The queen lifted her head in disapproval of Raven's lack of a response.

"I would love to grovel before you, but I don't really feel like it. So you'll have to excuse my impertinence," Raven said.

"My son's anger can be quite intense." Queen Laila smiled.

Raven huffed. As though that were something to be proud of. No wonder Aleks was the Prince of Ice. If he had displayed anything but cruelty, he probably would have been killed.

"Is there anyone else you would like me to kill? Maybe torture? Or poison?" Raven asked. She was being anything but subtle.

"Oh no, nothing so pedestrian as that. I have more like you at my disposal." Queen Laila stepped closer, her face open and curious. Raven noticed she had only brought two guards with her. "I'm here to offer you an opportunity."

Raven remained still as she focused on the stones in front of her and not the queen. Raven said nothing, refusing to be baited.

"I will allow you time out of your room if you attend etiquette and royal lessons with me as your tutor."

Raven barked a laugh. "Princess lessons? You want to give me princess lessons?" She did look at the queen now. She wanted to see every detail the queen revealed about herself.

Queen Laila stood before her in a gown of black, a gown of mourning. Was she still mourning the loss of her friend? Had they truly been that close? Each time Raven saw the queen, she had to blink to clear out the image of Ella. It was not Ella who stood before her, just her twisted, evil aunt.

"Does it pain you to know that when Lady Tremaine died, the last face she saw looked exactly like yours? It's almost as though you killed her yourself."

"Come closer and say that again," Queen Laila said.

"You can't take me," Raven snarled.

"My offer will stand for one night. Think about it. You'll get some exercise and be allowed to bathe," Queen Laila said before leaving.

Raven turned back to her room and began counting the stones. Why did the queen want to train her? How could it possibly benefit her to drag Raven out of her room each day and teach her how to be a proper princess? Especially when she already knew how to be proper, Lady Tremaine had ensured it.

Raven continued to stare at the wall, the silence ringing in her ears. It roared through her head. How could she even think straight when there was no noise to pull her out of her head?

Raven crossed her legs and breathed in for six seconds, held it, and breathed out for six seconds. Her magic remained cut off. Even with the constant bite of the stone on her arms, she tried. She continued her breathing pattern, sinking farther into herself. If she were only far enough into her core, she would be able to access it. She knew it. The only moment she had felt any type of life had been around Aleks. Maybe she needed the threat of another enchanter posed to her, one close enough in strength to get a rise out of her magic. Aleks certainly fit that. She couldn't remember a time when her magic hadn't woken up in his presence. If she could force a flare out, maybe she could get the shackles off. It had never been done, but there was always a first time for anything. Bearing these shackles couldn't solely be left to the whims of another enchanter. She would find a way.

Though Queen Laila didn't realize it, she had just given Raven the perfect opportunity to test her theories, and if she learned more about the queen and any weaknesses in the process, then it would be even better.

Raven was hauled to her feet by two guards, who chained her wrists together before escorting her out of her room.

"Where are we going?" Raven croaked.

None of them responded to her. They continued to escort her through the palace grounds. Raven kept her eyes wide open as they moved from hallway to hallway, crossing courtyards and back through other courtyards as they attempted to confuse her with their location. Raven rolled her eyes at the misdirection. She knew if she went around the corner and down two more hallways, she would come across the throne room, and that farther down the hallway was the dining hall.

But that's not where they went. Instead, they took her to a washhouse, where they plopped her on the hard stone floor.

"We'll be outside, so don't even think about running." The burly lead guard threatened.

"Does it appear that I'm in any condition to try to run?" Raven huffed. "Are you going to unlock my chains?"

"No."

"How am I meant to bathe myself?"

"You'll think of something."

She waited to move until all of them had left the washroom. She got up slowly and glanced around the room. It was bare except for the large bath in the floor and some towels on top of a chair. She moved the chair first, tossed the towels on the ground, and used the chair to block the door. Raven opened the drawers in the cabinets and had to cover her mouth in delight as she found a tool she could use to pick her manacles. Raven shook out her wrists and freely swung her arms. She walked and stretched, exercising tight muscles.

She wasn't inhibited anymore. Raven blinked, holding back a tear.

Joy swelled, and it felt hollow...fake.

Her magic wasn't dancing with her.

The obsidian shackles still weighed heavily on her arms, pulling the muscles. If only they were easily broken. Raven rubbed her face, smearing the tears into her skin. She didn't know how long they would leave her in here, so she got to work on undressing.

Her clothes stuck to her body and ripped wounds as she tried to take them off. Raven winced, but continued through it. The water in the tub was still steaming as she approached. Part of her tunic remained on her back, but she was hopeful the water would do the rest of the work for her.

Raven sighed as she stepped in and was covered in warmth up to her shoulders. The wounds stung in the heat, but she didn't care. Instead, she leaned forward and rested her arms on the floor of the washroom, rested her head on them, closed her eyes, and dreamed of Aleks.

He walked over to her as she lay in their bed and got under the blankets beside her.

"I've missed you," she whispered.

"I wasn't gone long." Aleks chuckled.

"It was long enough."

Raven jolted awake. She couldn't be sleeping. She was exposed. Someone could come in and —

"You must be exhausted," Tora said. She sat on a chair, one leg propped on a knee, sharpening a dagger.

"Do you even know how to use that?" Raven asked.

"I can't believe I got this close before you woke up." Tora put her foot down and leaned towards Raven. "I've always wondered, do those shackles hurt? I've never seen someone with so many. Are you really that strong?"

Raven remained silent.

"You can't have him. Prince Aleksander was mine long before you, and he'll be mine long after you're dead. Of course, it will take a while for him to forgive me for killing you, but it'll be worth the wait."

Raven still didn't speak. Part of her wanted to see how long Tora would talk for. The other part of her wanted her body to be a little bit more relaxed before having to fight for her life. In her current state, Raven wasn't sure if she would win.

Raven turned her head slowly, testing the muscles in her neck. Then she turned to her feet, flexing her toes under the water before gently moving her legs and flexing muscles that had gone unused for too long. The last thing she examined as Tora continued her odious monologue was her back. It was still healing, and while the bath was relaxing, it would only have a mild effect on her back and its tolerance for movement.

She would just have to move through it.

Raven refused to die at the hands of —

Tora attacked.

She jumped into the bath, sending a wave of water over the edge as she grappled with Raven. She shoved Raven under the water, attempting to hold her below. Raven pounded her fist against Tora's knee before digging her nails into her skin and dragging them down.

Raven was released in time to gasp for air as Tora screamed.

By the time Raven regained her breath, Tora had gripped Raven's hair, her nails deep in the roots of Raven's scalp, and pulled.

Raven gripped Tora's arm and held on, using the weight of her body to flip the fight in her favor. Raven pushed off the side of the bath and slammed Tora against the opposite side, instantly finding release. Raven ripped the dagger out of Tora's hand and tossed it away. If he truly loved Tora...Raven's heart ached at the thought.

"Yield," Raven said as she pressed Tora's arm behind her back.

"I yield." Tora raised her other arm in surrender.

Raven released her pressure and stepped back to let Tora get out of the tub. Raven stepped out behind her, watching her every move. Tora moved slowly, rubbing her spine.

"You know I've had fantasies about this."

Raven turned at the sound of Aleks's voice. He stood in the door, one foot crossed over the other.

"Prince Aleksander," Tora whispered. Her body shook. At first, Raven thought it was from fear, but quickly noticed it was in excitement as she lightly bounced on her toes. Tora gracefully jumped over to him, pressing herself against him. "I'll come to your chambers tonight and we can celebrate the good news."

Tora ran her hands down Aleks's body.

Raven swallowed the bile that threatened her. How could he love that little candied apple? Once again, Raven wanted to curl into the loneliness that confronted her emotions. She rubbed her shackled arms, hoping that maybe, just maybe, some movement would cause an opening for her.

"Good news?" Aleks asked, though his eyes were locked on Raven's. He had yet to glance at Tora.

"Yes, didn't your mother tell you? She approved our engagement." Tora practically squealed as she ran her hands through Aleks's hair down to his neck.

Aleks looked down at her, and Raven wasn't sure which emotion was stronger, the joy at the disdain that crossed his face, or the fear at what Tora's reaction would be.

"I'm not marrying you," Aleks said quietly, as though that would soften the blow.

"This is what we've always wanted. We've planned it for years."

"No, you've planned it for years."

"That's not true. We always talked about how if you were able to marry me, you would, but you were promised to her!" Tora spun around and flung an accusatory finger at Raven.

Raven paused as she tried to get clothes on.

"She's the reason all of us are in this mess. If she had just died like she was supposed to, you wouldn't be questioning anything." Tora cried.

"Tora, even if I wasn't promised to her since birth, I wouldn't marry you. My mother is using you as a pawn in her game." Aleks gripped Tora's biceps as he turned her to face him. "I'm sorry I misled you, but we were never going to be anything serious."

"You're lying. You love me."

Raven almost laughed at the parallels between her and Jason, but kept it together as Aleks tried to calm Tora.

"Tora, what you and I had was a lot of fun, but despite what my mother told you, I won't marry you. I'm sorry."

"It's because of her." Tora went still as she shot a look at Raven.

"No. Raven didn't do anything." Aleks turned Tora so that she wasn't able to see Raven. "All blame is placed solely on me."

Tora stopped fighting him and went slack in his arms. She looked down at the floor, sniffling. Aleks stepped back from her, his head tilted to one side.

Raven took the moment of peace to slip into her pants and slide on a breast band, the whole time keeping her eyes trained on Tora. Aleks had left her side to get a towel for her, and Raven didn't trust her to not try something rash.

He handed Tora a towel.

She threw it back at him, and in the same motion threw a blade at Raven.

Two things happened instantly.

Raven dodged the blade, and a different dagger flew from behind Raven and landed in Tora's chest.

Aleks caught her as she fell, easing her to the floor as her hands clutched the dagger.

Raven spun around and came face to face with Daci.

"Why?" Aleks asked. He glared at Daci.

"Because you shouldn't have to bear the guilt of killing her." Daci walked over with Raven and stood over Tora. Blood pooled beneath her as she stared at them, all life gone from her eyes.

"She didn't have to die," Aleks growled. "Get out of my sight."

Daci's eyes were wide as she bolted. Raven turned to Aleks as he crouched over Tora's body. His hands hovered over her, unable to touch her.

"Here, let me —"

"No, don't touch her," Aleks yelled. He got between her and Tora.

"Aleks, look at me." Raven gently rested her hands on his shoulders.

He shook under her grip as his eyes darted around. Raven cupped his face until she locked eyes with his ice blue ones that were wide and lined with tears.

"Hey, Prince Charming," she held his face, "let me help you. No one should have to care for the body of someone they love."

Aleks scoffed. "I didn't love her." He wiped at his nose, sniffling.

"Even so, you cared for her."

Aleks nodded. Raven let him go as she went to Tora. She closed Tora's eyes and draped another towel over her body. Aleks sat on the floor, head hung from slouched shoulders.

"Come on, we're alerting the guards and then going to your room." Raven pulled Aleks up and gently nudged him out the door. She found some guards, ones who hadn't been bribed to leave her unattended, and told them about Tora.

"What else can I do for you?" Raven asked as she got Aleks to his room. He sat on the floor and stared blankly ahead. She sat next to him, leaning her head on his shoulder.

"Become queen."

Raven pulled away. "The last time I saw you, you were livid with me, and now you're telling me to become queen?"

"It took me a little bit to calm down."

Raven grunted.

"But, I know you were following orders, my *mother's* orders, which means she had you kill Ian. Everything I thought I knew was a lie. You need to claim your throne and fix all of the damage my mother and aunt had caused."

Raven scoffed. "You expect me to just snap my fingers and make it better? I'm sorry your world has been rocked and that you're questioning everything right now, but I don't want to be queen —"

"What about your lessons?"

"What else was I going to do?" Raven asked. She was not about to tell him it was all a ploy to learn more about his mother. "I'm not worthy of leading others, Aleks. What kingdom would want someone who spent their life training and killing people? I've thought long and hard about it, and I can't be the Queen of Evrotia. I just can't Aleks, please don't ask me again."

"Raven, I...I don't know what to do." He stared at the wooden floor between his feet. "I'm always two steps ahead, but ever since my aunt arrested you, I've been behind."

"Well, me becoming queen is not the answer to everyone's problems, despite what everyone thinks."

"If we got married, as intended when we were children, we could change a lot—"

"I knew it." Raven stood and paced around his room avoiding the furniture. "There's always some ulterior motive with you. You want to be king —"

"No, I don't. I have never wanted to rule." Aleks stood and placed himself before her. "I want to change this world. I thought I could from within my mothers spies, but I can't. The only way is with you on the throne. You don't see it, but I do. I see how glorious you would be as queen. You are strong, intelligent, fair, and most of all kind."

"Aleks —"

"I see why Rowan is so devoted to you. I didn't understand, not when I've always seen how my mother and aunt rule, but you're different. You're the one everyone has been dreaming of —"

"Enough," Raven yelled. "Stop. Please. I don't...I don't want it. I hear you, I do."

"Well..." Aleks locked eyes with her, "when you decide to see what everyone else does in you, I'll be there for you, in whatever way you need me."

CHAPTER FORTY-EIGHT

Ella

Ella walked out onto the ship's deck and promptly lost the breakfast she had attempted to eat that morning. They had been on the water for two days, and she had yet to gain her footing on the small ship. David, however, didn't have a problem as he swiftly navigated the currents below them.

"I don't understand how you're not sick." Ella heaved.

"I've always been fine on the water." David shrugged. "What can I do for you? Unfortunately, there is no enchantment that cures seasickness."

"Just your presence is enough," Ella said as she slid down the edge of the ship and sat with her back pressed against the wooden boards. David joined her, his arm pressing against hers. "I must look like a mess." She turned her head to look at David. It was true; she was a mess. She had worn the same loose clothing gifted by the emperor for days, and it was currently covered in sweat, sea salt, and dirt.

"You're right. You look horrendous." David laughed.

Ella gazed into his molten brown eyes and saw everything he wasn't saying. She turned her body to face him.

"What does your magic feel like when you look at me?" Ella whispered.

"What?" David spoke low.

"You told me once that your magic was screaming at you that I wasn't okay. That something was wrong, and it was right. I had just been ordered to kill you. So what does it say now?" Ella asked.

David turned towards her and gently held a hand. "When I touch you like this..." he rubbed his thumb over the back of her hand in small circles, "my magic races around my veins, twisting and turning within me as though I'm in a sparring match with someone who isn't afraid of fighting their prince."

"David, I —"

She didn't get to finish her thought as David pressed his lips against hers. Every single thought was obliterated as her entire focus became the feel of David's soft lips on hers. Swiftly followed by the feel of his hands pulling her closer until she was practically on his lap. Then, his magic spilled over and around her, and for a fraction of a second she felt his magic course through her, and Ella understood. It was though sprinkles of raindrops were kissing her skin all at once, wrapping around her spirit with an energy so pure she could cry from the joy it felt. She had never known that such happiness could exist.

Then, it was gone.

Ripped away as David contained his magic.

Ella bolted up and heaved over the side of the ship.

"That was..."

"I shouldn't have done it." David blushed. "I thought if you felt my magic for a moment, you would understand, and—"

"I understood," she whispered. Gods, she wanted to kiss him again, but the sick all over her shirt stopped her.

David stepped closer and to her, his hand cupping her cheek.

"I'm horrendous, remember?" She mumbled.

"You are the most horrendous woman I have ever laid eyes upon," David whispered as he leaned forward and pressed his lips to her forehead.

Ella held him close, her eyes shut, as she took in the feel of his lips on her skin, his warm hands on the curve of her back, and how the ship seemed to melt away from them.

"Let's run away, David. Just you and me and anywhere else but here." It was out before Ella could even think of stopping it.

David leaned back from her. He raised a hand and held her cheek.

"What's wrong?"

"Nothing. I didn't mean it."

"You know it's okay to not want to always save the kingdom?" David ran a hand through her hair.

Ella nodded slowly, her gaze locked on him.

"I just...I'm tired, David."

"Well, if saving the kingdom were easy, everyone would do it. Luckily, you're not everyone," David whispered.

"At least we get a few more days on this ship to relax," Ella said. She smiled weakly.

"We got what we came for, and now we get to come home and expose Lady Tremaine and the Queen of Trudel to my father. Then we can go back to our lives."

"What does that look like?" Ella closed her eyes, waiting for the blow. He would go back to being a prince, and she would...she would go somewhere.

"Well, that's a much larger conversation, but I'm hoping that whatever comes next will include you by my side...fighting by my side," David said.

"Fighting?" Ella opened her eyes. "Truly?"

"If I've learned anything on this...adventure, it's that you are the smartest, kindest, and best fighter I have had the pleasure of knowing, and I would be a fool to not have you protecting our kingdom."

"Really?" Ella swallowed the tears.

"I promise," David whispered.

“What if it also included me by your side in the throne room?” Ella whispered. She could do it. Had done just that with Emperor Edris. It hadn’t been the worst thing.

“Truly?” David asked.

“I promise,” Ella said. “Now, I need to get a fresh change of clothes.”

“You do look horrendous.”

David laughed, winking as Ella gestured rudely at him.

CHAPTER FORTY-NINE

DREA

The Day of Drea's Accident

Drea jolted awake. Her head pounded behind her eyes. How long had she been out? The last thing she remembered was...meeting Liam at the gardens as he had requested. They had gone for a walk, finding small alcoves to steal kisses before continuing. She had flushed with giddiness each time he had pulled her aside. He wanted to know her answer to going with him to Trudel. She hadn't answered him. Truthfully, she wasn't sure what to say anymore. He had confused her and all of the plans she had for her life.

But then...Liam had...

Drea felt the pulse in the back of her head where the rock had hit her. Liam had knocked her out. He had...confusion warring with heartbreak at his betrayal. Why? Why take her?

Drea kept her body still as she turned her attention to her surroundings. Keeping her eyes closed, she listened. Silence engulfed the room.

An owl hooted in the distance; trees swayed in the wind as they brushed against the building she was in. A soft creak of wooden floorboards told her she wasn't alone. Two sets of feet walked around. So, Liam had a partner. A big one from the difference in the creaks.

Drea wiggled her toes and fingers, seeing how much she could move before one of them noticed she was awake. Ropes prevented her from moving her arms, though they had left her legs unbound. Amateurs.

Her magic...her magic!

Emptiness greeted her where she should have found her core of power dancing. The missing strum in her veins and power in her muscles had dwindled, and each time she tried to summon it...it got farther away.

That jerk had chained her with enchanter's shackles? Whatever his reason was, it couldn't be good for her. With her arms restrained behind her, she had no idea how many shackles had been placed on her. Not that she would need her power for this. Liam might wish he had power by the time she was done. He might be a good fighter, but she knew his weaknesses.

But why take her?

He had to know he couldn't get away with anything. He might be here as part of the diplomatic envoy, but that didn't preclude him from any punishment for kidnapping. Whatever he wanted...it must be good. He didn't know what her mother's mission was, and he couldn't have figured out who she was. She hadn't hinted at anything once. Every conversation they had ever had flitted through her mind as she processed everything around her. Based on the dim lighting, several hours had already passed.

"Glad to see you're awake."

Drea didn't move.

Liam's hands roughly gripped her chin and forced her head up. What had happened? He had never been like this.

"I know you're awake."

"Liam, what's happening? Where am I? Are you okay?" Drea played her damsel card. It was all she had until she determined the full scope of Liam's plan.

"You're going to help me. I've taken us somewhere no one can discover us until I want to be found."

"But why? I would have come with you," Drea whispered. Deep down, she knew she would have gone with him had he asked. Not out of any hubris, but because she had thought...well, that didn't matter anymore.

"You're not this dumb, Drizella. I needed your full attention in a place that was private."

"We've been alone before Liam, I don't understand." And she truly didn't. She didn't know which fact frightened her more, that Liam had somehow duped her, or that she had been so blind with infatuation she hadn't noticed it.

"You're going to help me get to the prince and his champion." Liam smiled as he crouched before her, his brown eyes were twisted in glee.

Drea had never seen him so pleased with himself, so hopeful for what she could do for him. It unnerved her to have missed seeing this side of him. She thought she had known the lengths he would go to prove himself, but the intensity in his eyes indicated he would go much further than she had thought possible.

"Why me? They know you. You've sparred with them. Surely you don't need me."

"I do. They're well protected at the palace. I can't get near them. You know how to sneak around the palace. You know their habits and patterns. You can tell me what I need."

"Why do you think I know this information?" She had been very careful to never mention knowing David or Henry personally.

"That last ball with Henry was weird, and Anastasia confirmed for me that you're friendly with them."

Drea kept her groan inside. Ana probably didn't even realize what she had done, that or she thought it would encourage a different reaction from Liam. "Your kingdom is under a peace treaty. Going after them will start a war, Liam—"

"Precisely! Our queen never wanted to be the queen of Trudel. She wanted to rule Rairene, and if this treaty ends, she can conquer this pathetic kingdom

and become its rightful ruler as she should have eighteen years ago. Then she'll have me to thank for it." Liam puffed his chest.

Drea kept her jaw from dropping. Her mother and the queen had been planning for this exact event for years. "What makes you think I'll tell you anything?"

"You're not the type of lady to handle being tortured." Liam knelt in front of her. "I don't want to do that, though. I still want you to come home with me. We can return heroes, Drizella. Just tell me, and we can be happy. Together."

Drea peered around her prison. She was in a small wooden home with only a table, a few chairs, and a small kitchen. She had no idea where she was as the sun continued to set through the small window. At least he didn't seem to know who she truly was..

Liam was in for a surprise.

She could handle much more than he realized.

"Liam, I don't know anything."

"I don't believe you." Liam made a motion with his hand. "But I think you'll tell me a lot once we're done."

The man with Liam was a large Trudelian warrior and had not been part of the envoy. She would have remembered him. Looking around, she glimpsed her wrists, the enchanter's shackles cool against her forearm. There was only one. Good. Liam didn't know how many he would need and thought this would suffice. Drea quirked a brow. The partner had to be the enchanter and not a strong one. Now that she had adjusted, Drea pulled at her power again, feeling it trickle into her like a poorly damned stream. But it came back to her, one drop at a time. Once she had had enough, she would be able to break free.

Weapons would be necessary for Liam's companion. She might be good, and she might be tall, but even Drea knew she would need leverage to either knock him out or kill him.

Liam dragged the small table over and unrolled a set of knives that varied in length, edge, and sharpness. She tried not to yawn. Drea had used them before and was prepared for what they would do. He paced in front of the table, trying to decide what to use first. She certainly wouldn't help him. Clearly, he needed practice in figuring out how this worked. Decision made, he walked over to her, a knife in his hand. Did he know how to use that particular blade?

That made her nervous.

An unskilled torturer was deadlier than one who knew how to handle themselves. If Liam got too excited by her pain or her fear, he could fatally injure her.

"Question one. Where does Henry go first thing in the morning?"

Drea gazed at him, mouth shut, challenging him. Could he actually do it? Could he hurt the person he wanted to bring home with him?

"Fine." Liam dragged the blade over her leg, slicing through her dress and creating a thin line in her thigh. It stung, but she'd suffered worse.

Hell, she'd done worse to herself.

None of it mattered; she would never betray Henry. Could never betray him. Not Henry. As mad as she was at him. As much as she longed for him to return her feelings, she could never betray the man who knew how to make her laugh and smile. Who made her magic dance the most beautiful routine by the mere presence of him, and when he hugged her...bliss. There was no double life that she had to hide from him in those moments. It was just her and Henry, and he was home.

As the pain grew, and the cuts got deeper and bigger, Drea held onto that feeling of home.

Eventually, Liam began to pace, shaking the knife dangerously close to her face.

"Why won't you answer me? The pain will stop. All you have to do is give me what I want."

"I will never betray him. You think my loyalty is so easily won by a few kisses in the dark?"

"Henry will never choose you. You know this. It's why you were so easily taken by me." Liam crouched in front of her, fiddling with the knife as it dripped her blood onto her dress. "You are so beautiful, Drizella. Probably one of the

prettiest girls in court, but Henry is the prince's champion. You're nothing. You're the daughter of a woman from another kingdom who only holds a title in marriage and has standing due to her friendship with our queen. You bring nothing to the table for him. Why be loyal to someone who doesn't see you?"

"His friendship is more important to me than anything I could possibly gain from him. I will not be the cause of any pain he suffers."

"You've gone weak being away from home for so long. It's pathetic." Liam looked her up and down. "No wonder your mother enlisted my help."

Drea's retort froze on her lips. Her mother had done this to her? "If I'm so pathetic, why haven't you broken me yet?" Drea snarled. Her pulse pounded at his words. Her mother had betrayed her. But she couldn't focus on that. Liam was getting angry, and she needed him riled so that he would make a mistake...even if that meant more pain for her, then so be it.

"We'll see how much longer you can last."

Liam's partner walked over and handed him a vial with a dark, freshly enchanted poison inside. It would be potent. Liam dripped it onto her wounds.

Drea screamed as it burned like fire through her blood.

She kept screaming as her magic continued to trickle back to her, and the shackles weakened. Those shackles became the center of her focus as they moved from dripping the poison into her to pouring the entire contents of the vial over her wounds. She would be free soon, and these two idiots would learn what it meant to threaten her.

To threaten Henry.

The poison continued to rampage through her.

She would get through this.

It would not do long-term damage. She would endure.

Liam continued to ask her questions, trying to get any information at this point about Henry and David. But she wasn't in the room with him anymore. Drea retreated into her mind, escaping the pain and finding her happiness.

She sat in the library, a cup of tea in her hands, as she read. The romance novel comforted her in its normalcy. Just what she required. The sunlight poured in, illuminating her little corner.

Everything was at peace.

"Good morning, Sunshine," Henry spoke softly as he walked in.

Drea stared at him. The sun highlighted his fiery hair and deep green eyes. It was the smile, though, that always made her magic spiral out of control. A smile that illuminated her entire world. She could drown in it and die of pure happiness if that was the last thing she saw.

"Good morning," Drea whispered. She smiled at him as her throat constricted.

Liam was before her as Drea was ripped from her mind palace as one of Liam's daggers was twisted in her thigh.

"Tell me what I want to know, Drea. What's his weakness?" Liam growled.

Drea heaved as she stared him down, remaining silent. She would not give in. Not to him. Drea closed her eyes and pictured Henry again.

Henry got close to her, smiling as he leaned in and brushed his lips against hers.

She fell into the kiss as she rested her hands on the back of his neck and brought him closer to her. She opened her lips to deepen their kiss, pulling him with her as she leaned back into the window.

The library and its books faded away until it was just them.

Drea screamed as she was pulled out once more. Henry's lips were gone, and the enchanter was pouring poison onto her leg. Her mind palace image of Henry overlapped with her reality.

"Drizzie, what's happening?" Henry cupped her face in his hands, rubbing the tears.

"I'm sorry." She stared at him through tear-stained eyes, blinking them away as the pain in her left leg continued to build.

"Don't go. I need you here," Henry pleaded. He pulled her closer, wrapping his arms around her waist and pressing his lips against the curve of her neck.

Liam slapped her.

Drea ignored it. She couldn't leave Henry. She wanted to stay there, where the pain was manageable and Liam didn't exist.

"Don't leave me again," Henry said. His hands ran through her hair before pulling her close.

"I can't. It hurts too much." Drea gulped for air. Her magic danced with longing to stay with him, the man she had loved since the first day she had met him.

"Stay with me," Henry whispered. He ran his hands through her hair, and she shuddered.

Pain exploded in her chest.

What was happening? Drea was ripped from him again as she screamed. A dagger had sliced into her breast.

Drea clutched Henry close. She tilted her head up and kissed him. It was a kiss filled with every ounce of love she possessed for him. Henry's arms wrapped around her as if the act alone could keep her there.

"I'm sorry." Drea held Henry close, pressing her lips against his as the pain crescendoed and she could no longer stay with him.

Drea opened her eyes and came face to face with Liam.

"You're going to regret this," Drea spoke through the blood dripping down her throat.

"I doubt it. Since you refused to help me, you've left me no choice, Drizella. I can't let you warn them, and I will get to Prince David and Henry —"

Drea's hands illuminated as enough of her power gathered, broke through the shackle, and convulsed around her. Liam and his partner backed up, mouths open. Drea used the moment to shove the chair backward, breaking it as she gripped the armrests to rip them free of the chair.

She flipped herself onto her feet and pounced on Liam's partner. She held the fractured pieces of wood in her hands and used it to her advantage as she pummeled him until she knocked him out.

"You crazy —"

"Call me crazy again. Do it," Drea heaved, blinking away the pain that coursed through her body. Her legs felt like liquid that could barely support her. Her arms were leaden with fatigue. She would never let him see her tremble.

"You know, I did like you, Drizella." Liam pulled out a dagger, flipping it in his hands.

Drea was unimpressed.

She'd seen him use that blade many times over the last few weeks, and he had yet to master it. Liam moved first, and Drea dodged to the side.

Her legs collapsed beneath her.

What the fuck?

Drea glanced down to see her dress soaked in blood.

"I told you, you're not getting out of here." Liam jumped, his dagger raised.

She rolled onto her side and onto her knees. The armrests were gripped in her hands. She used them to deflect his thrust, keeping her balance long enough to bring Liam to his knees. Surprise flashed across his face.

"If I'm not getting out of here, then neither are you," Drea said through teeth gritted with pain.

"I'm going to kill Henry and return home a hero." Liam sliced his blade down, cutting deeper into her leg.

Drea screamed as the poison-laced blade connected with her magic. Now that she was uninhibited by the shackles, her power and the poisons rampaged through her blood...and she was helpless.

Darkness crept into her eyes, rapidly eating her vision.

She wouldn't survive this.

She knew it at the core of her power.

Her magic rose to the challenge, facing the poison, clashing in a violent disruption through her body. Drea yelled as Liam gripped her wrists, pinning her to the ground, her injured leg bent beneath her.

"I won't let you get away with this," Drea said. Her voice was filled with tears as the pain ramped up and blinded her.

Liam laughed as he gripped her biceps, holding her.

Drea let her magic unravel, yelling as the pain burned as brightly as her anger.

Raw magic poured out of her as she lost control.

Drea raised her hands as the pain crescendoed, and suddenly her screams became Liam's as her magic ripped across both their faces.

Liam dropped her.

She watched him flee through spotty eyesight as she reined in her magic.

Drea turned her focus in on herself and the magic pouring free.

She grabbed a strand of power and spun it back into a gentle twirl. Then she pulled another strand in. She pulled them all back piece by piece, finding a way to regain control until it spun in a delicate waltz that continued to struggle to hold its form. But it was contained for now.

She was alive.

For now.

Drea lay back on the hard wooden floor, struggling to see the room around her as the poison continued its consumption of her vision, hearing, and touch. She drifted in and out of consciousness, her entire body pulsing. Heat ripped through her leg as blood seeped out.

Until she didn't feel anything anymore.

Not even the steady trickle of blood could be felt.

All she could think of was that she hadn't let Henry down.

He was safe.

He was alive, and Liam couldn't go anywhere near him with a mark like the one she had left on his face. It was the last thing she had clearly seen, angry red lightning streaks across his face from where her fingers had pressed against his skin. It would eventually not be swollen, but it would mark him forever.

Drea attempted to lift her fingers to her face, to feel the scar pulsing on her cheek, but her hands wouldn't move. She frowned, focusing on her fingers, ordering them to move. They didn't. Drea stopped trying. It didn't matter. Not anymore. She was dying. But Henry would live.

She faded out and floated off to her perfect world.

Henry rested his hands on her shoulders before pulling her close.

She breathed him in, relaxing into the smell of sunshine and eucalyptus. Drea closed her eyes and memorized every sensation that passed through her body as Henry held her. His strong arms supported her as safety enveloped her. His hair was softer than usual, and her fingers ran through it seamlessly. His soft lips pressed gently against her forehead. In a world that demanded Henry to be strong, everything that touched her was kind. All she needed was him.

With that thought in mind, Drea let go.

Present Day

Drea walked into Princess Lena's meeting room first thing in the morning. She hadn't even had time to train with Gus. Queen Laila sat perfectly poised in her mirror, and Ana...Ana was in an additional mirror, and she was crying.

She's dead. Ana repeated it several more times, more to herself than to them.

From what Drea could see, a gray stone fortress sat behind her.

Who's dead? Eleanor? Queen Laila asked.

Tressa, the assassin we sent after Ella. I'm staring at her grave. Ana wiped away her tears. *I'm going to find her and —*

You're going to return home and await orders, Queen Laila commanded.

But I could —

No. We believe Prince David is en route to the palace. We need you here for our plan to work. Queen Laila reiterated.

Anastasia nodded as she straightened her shoulders.

"Drea, what did you find out from Henry?" Lena asked, unbothered by Anastasia's whimpering.

"Henry just informed me they're hosting a celebratory ball to honor David's safe return home. It was Princess Celeste's idea to bring happiness back to the people," Drea replied.

It was a horrible idea. David should be brought in discreetly, not by way of a fancy ball. Henry had agreed with her, but hadn't been able to convince the king and princess otherwise. All she could hope was that Ella and David would be successful in their journey to Holodal and that they came back with allies and a way to stop Queen Laila.

Wonderful, we'll plan an ambush after the ball, Queen Laila said as she began to walk in and out of the mirror's view. She continued to wear mourning black, with the only ounce of color coming from the shawl she wore loosely around her shoulders. Queen Laila stopped pacing when a knock came from somewhere within her room. The queen grinned at whatever news was relayed to her. *I have to go. Lenaria, it appears your brothers have both been successful in their missions; see that you are too.*

Lena nodded, her fingers gripping the edge of the table as her mother severed the connection.

What did Cai and Aleks do? Anastasia asked as she wiped away her tears.

"Nothing near as important as our mission. We cannot fail, ladies. I will not have it." Princess Lena stood and locked eyes with Anastasia. "Get home immediately. We have work to do."

For days, Princess Lena whipped all of them into a frenzy. Every novice trained, and every instructor honed their own skills. The plan was simple. A day after the ball, David would be poisoned by one of Snow White's deadliest enchantments; Ella would be found with the poison in her room, and if David survived, Lena would be officially made his queen. So long as everything went according to plan. Several of the novices and one instructor were sent to the palace to infiltrate it as serving staff, while another was sent to one of the merchants that frequently stocked the palace's food supply. Once Lena had been told of her brother's successes, she was determined to see herself atop the Rairenian throne.

Drea and Gus continued their lessons, starting earlier each day as Lena pushed increased everyone's training each day. Gus swung at her, no longer holding back as she sparred with him. Drea ducked his punch as she held out her leg to take his from under him. Gus leapt in time to avoid her attack. She got to her feet quickly and put Gus on the defensive as they continued to fight. She hefted her sword and swung a blow at Gus. He blocked it with his own blade; the metal grinding against each other. Drea released and came in swinging with her fist, catching him off guard and hitting him to the ground.

Gus held his hands to yield.

Drea collapsed to the ground, her breathing ragged.

"Good job," Gus said through his rapid exhales.

"Thanks. You too." Drea stared at the ceiling. "You didn't just let me win because you're exhausted and wanted the fight to end?"

"Of course not, and don't you dare ever level such an accusation against me again," Gus snapped. "As if I would ever just let you win." He continued to grumble incoherently as he crossed his arms.

"My apologies, I just…I had to check." Drea mumbled. She grinned at him when he turned to her. "I just beat you."

A tear gathered in her eye as the sudden realization of what she had accomplished dawned on her.

"I beat you."

"You did." Gus grinned back at her as he helped her to her feet.

Drea rapidly blinked, trying to clear the tears. Tears rushed forward when Gus wrapped her in a hug. Drea embraced him, closing her eyes as she lived in her victory. Her magic unraveled within her, dancing with her as it sang through her veins. She had won a fight, and her leg didn't hurt. She had done it.

"Thank you…for everything," Drea whispered. She gave Gus a squeeze before stepping away from him. "I couldn't have…I couldn't have done this without you." To emphasize her point, she spun in a circle on her left foot without a single concern. A small twitch hit her leg.

"Maybe we don't push it too far just yet," Gus said. He grabbed her cane from where it rested along the wall and brought it over to her. "I'm so proud of you, Drea"

Drea clutched the cane, twisting her hands around it with the sudden urge to break it over her knee.

"How are the novices doing with the extra training?"

"Everyone is exhausted, but they're determined to do their best for the princess," Gus answered, muttering the last few words.

"And how are you?" Drea rested a hand on his arm.

"I'm coping. I'll be ready when she needs me." Gus spoke in hushed tones as they approached the door.

"Understood. Thank you so much for helping me find my confidence again, Gus." Drea hugged him one last time before heading away from him.

"You're not going to get ready?"

"I have a meeting with a croissant and the most delicious tea you've ever tasted," Drea called over her shoulder.

She truly did have a meeting with a croissant and some tea. She just didn't tell Gus that it also involved a guest. Drea had changed in the carriage ride into a simple black gown that brushed the floor with a cloak to match. Lastly, she kept her hair out of her face by pulling it back into a simple half-do.

Henry was already waiting for her, with tea and croissants steaming on their table. His curly red hair fell haphazardly around his face and shoulders. He leaned back in his chair, sipping his own cup of tea. Henry gazed down at the tea and took another sip. She took that as her cue to sit down in front of him and smile.

“Thank you for meeting me so early.” Drea held her cup and breathed in the herbs.

“Of course. Can I ask why we're meeting before the rest of the kingdom has gotten out of bed?” Henry chuckled.

“It's the only time I could spare, unfortunately. Things have begun to move.”

“Oh?” Henry sat up straight and leaned toward her. “Tell me what's happening.

And she did.

Both of them sat in silence at the end of it as Henry processed in minutes what she had been processing for a day.

“Thank you for the warning. I'll make sure David sees his father in private before the ball to tell him everything,” Henry replied. He shifted in his chair, suddenly red in the face.

“Everything okay?”

“I heard you met Gwen.” Henry crossed his arms and rested a foot on one knee.

Ah. “I did. She's lovely. I'm very happy for you.” Drea lied.

“You are?” Henry's foot fell off his knee.

“Yes. Did you think I was going to lie and say she's a horrible person and that you shouldn't marry her?”

“Well...yes, actually,” Henry confessed.

“Oh.” Drea looked everywhere but at him. She could do it; she would remain strong and not give into her heart's desires. “Well, choose someone who isn't as kind as her next time.”

“I'll try,” Henry chuckled. “I'm glad you got to meet her. She may not seem like it, but she's fierce when she needs to be.”

"She'll have to be if she's marrying the future king's champion." Drea took another sip of her tea before biting into her croissant. The flaky crust melted in her mouth as she ate, eliciting a soft sigh.

"Will you be at the ball?"

Drea nodded to nervous to yes with a mouthful of croissant. The last time she had been at a ball...Drea shook the memory away.

Henry reached out and held her hand. "Save me a dance?" he whispered.

"You'll always have a spot on my dance card, Henry." Drea squeezed his hand as she stared into his emerald eyes. What she wouldn't give to stare into those eyes forever. Her magic leapt, begging for release the longer she looked at him. Drea formed it into a soft, melodic dance as she tapped it down.

"Henry, I —"

"Don't say something you can't back up." Henry interrupted.

Drea tilted her head.

"I can't —" Henry paused. "I can't go through that again, Drizzie. Please don't tell me something, no matter how true it is, if you can't follow it with actions."

Drea stared at him, unable to say a single word. Of course, she couldn't back up her words with actions right now. She didn't even know if she would survive this whole ordeal. Drea nodded stiffly.

Henry released her hand, and Drea thought her magic would revolt at the loss of his hand on hers. It rose quickly in her hands, sparkling in the early sunlight before she could contain it. Henry got up and walked away from her as she thought about what she had to do and how much her life, and those around her, would change.

CHAPTER FIFTY

Ella

Ella leaned against the railing and rested her head on her hand as she watched the city of Riset and the palace come into view. From a distance, all five circles appeared no different from each other. They were all citizens living within the beautiful white walls of Riset that had started to yellow with time. The palace rose above them all, made out of the same stone as the wall that shone in the late evening sun rays. Behind them loomed the mountains covered in dense foliage. Before her lay the harbor and its looming wooden barricade and gate that would have to be lowered by several men to allow them passage.

Ella closed her eyes as the salty air blew across her face and through her tangled, braided hair. They were so close to victory. Outside of a freak storm preventing an earlier arrival, everything was going according to plan. Jason was prepared to talk to the king. David had convinced Henry to keep Luca safe. Tonight, they would all be set free. Free from Lady Tremaine's influence. Free from Queen Laila's scheming. And she could...Ella relaxed as she thought about her conversation with David.

He wanted her.

Not just for her appearance or her position, but for her...and for all she could become. And she...she wanted to be beside him, whether it was on a battlefield or in the throne room.

She just hoped they arrived on time.

"Hi."

Ella turned as David walked beside her.

"I'm always in awe of this view. I rarely get to see it, but when I do," David paused as he looked around, "it takes my breath away."

"It's one of the most beautiful things I've seen." Ella confirmed as she stood.

David nodded. He held his hands together as he shifted from side to side on his feet. "Ella, I..." David paused, running his hands through his hair before blowing out a big breath of air.

"Is everything okay?" Ella tilted her head as she watched him.

"Yes, of course, I —"

"Prince David," Jason called as he walked behind them.

"Sir Jason." David tipped his head in a small sign of acknowledgement as he walked over to them.

"I wanted to discuss my meeting with the king, and..." Jason froze as he took in the harbor in the setting sunlight.

Ella turned away when she saw the tears gather. She had only been gone for several weeks and was homesick. What must it have been like for him to have been denied his home for two years? Ella shook herself as she faced them.

"The current plan is for Henry to be in a private room with Prince Lucian, where we will deliver your story and proof to the king. This should give him enough evidence to have a more transparent conversation with Queen Laila and our allies over a shared scry," Ella explained. "David, did you still need to tell me something?"

David blushed. "It can wait."

Ella nodded, turned away from them, and headed to her quarters below. She needed to make sure she had everything and that they could get off the ship the moment it was docked.

Ella flipped her hood over her head as she moved to get off the ship. She faced David and...Ella almost groaned before walking to him. He smiled at her. She frowned.

"David —"

"We're home. We're safe," David chuckled as Ella pulled up his cloak.

"I'm not taking any chances. You're not safe until —"

"We're at the palace, I know."

"No. Not even then. You're not safe until the king knows everything and has the correct conversation."

"I promise to stay by my very protective guard's side until I'm safe."

"Good." Ella looked away to hide a smile as her cheeks flushed.

"But," David lifted her chin, "only if my very protective guard promises to never remove her pendant." David said, tapping the large gem on her chest.

"It hasn't come off since," Ella replied, holding David's hand over the pendant and her heart.

"Good." David leaned down and pressed his lips to her forehead before heading down the plank to the harbor.

Ella watched him go, the touch of his lips on her forehead still pulsing on her skin. She smiled as she followed David and got into the carriage.

CHAPTER FIFTY-ONE

Drea

One Day After Drea's Attack

Drea opened her eyes.

To her disappointment, the first thing she saw was her mother.

Drea turned her head, wincing as the swollen cheek pulled with the movement. She moved her hands to touch it.

"No. Don't move, my dear." Her mother was next to her side in an instant. She began to rest a hand on Drea's shoulder when Drea flinched away. Lady Tremaine slowly removed her hands.

"You sent him after me," Drea accused. If there was anything she was going to remember from Liam kidnapping her, it would be that.

"I did."

"He overstepped. You hired someone for a role they should never have been given."

"You refused to listen to me about Henry," her mother stated.

"I refused —"

"Because of this, you leave me no choice, Drizella."

"Oh?"

"You will end things with Henry, or I will end Henry."

"You would start the war early. Queen Laila —"

"Would find a way to accept the change in plans," her mother stated.

She would do it. She would kill Henry because of the perceived threat he was. She would start a war early all because...Drea loved Henry.

"You would deny me the person I...the man that I..."

"Love?" Lady Tremaine crossed her arms. "Yes. I would deny you love as a sacrifice to your queen. I'll leave the decision to you, my dear."

***

Drea kept her head turned toward the window, watching the rain when someone knocked on her door. Would she ever enjoy being out there again? Would she want to be? She had finally been able to lift her hands to her face to find that half of it was covered in a tightly bound cloth.

Her magic lightly trilled, as best as it could, as it recognized him before she could shift her eye to see Henry walking through her door. Shhhh...Drea whispered to her power. That was all she had to do to control what little amount remained. Drea found that she couldn't bring herself to turn her head and face the pity she would see from him.

"Drizzie." Henry was beside her in a moment.

"Henry." She could barely get his name past her lips.

"How are you?" Henry held her hand, rubbing his thumb over her palm.

Gods, how could she do this? She couldn't. She couldn't lose him.

"I'm okay." Drea had yet to fully look at him. Out of everyone in the kingdom, he was the one person she couldn't bear to see any amount of pity.

"Who did this to you? I'll hunt them down and —"

"I don't know who it was, Henry. They never said anything." Her hands shook in his grasp. She removed them before he began to notice and fiddled with a blanket instead.

"Drizzie, I can help. My father's men can find him, and if they don't, then I'll find him and kill him." Henry vowed.

"No."

"If you're afraid —"

"I'm not afraid." She turned to him allowing him to fully see her. He moved closer to her, his mouth opening as he walked around to be by her side. "Don't you dare say I'm afraid." She took a deep breath, reeling her magic back. She could do this. She would do this one thing. For him.

"Drizzie, I didn't —"

"You should leave."

Henry stepped backward, putting his hands in his pockets. "Okay, I'll see you tomorrow."

"No. You won't." She turned away from him.

"When can I?"

"Never, Henry." Drea's hands shook as she clutched the blanket. "I don't ever wish to see you...again." Her pulse strummed frantically as it twisted her up.

Henry moved so that he saw all of her. "Have I done something?"

"No —" Drea swallowed the tears.

"What happened, Drizzie?"

"I don't want to see you again, Henry." Drea spoke swiftly as though saying it faster might somehow make it easier. But the crack forming deep in her heart said otherwise.

"Look at me."

She locked her eyes on him, challenging him.

"What's wrong? What did I do?"

"Nothing is wrong, Henry...this...event has simply forced me to evaluate what I'm doing with my life —"

"And you wish to erase me from this life? You have to give me a better reason. I deserve that much."

"You *deserve?" Drea raised her voice.*

"Yes. I deserve to know why my closest friend, the person whom I cherish, has decided to no longer have me in their life."

Drea's heart exploded. "I don't want to be with you, Henry."

She could do this.

Despite everything he had just said...she could do this. "I only ever talked to you out of pity for...her...for Ella. You were such a sad puppy after she left, and I couldn't take it anymore."

Drea's singular drop of power raged against her words. It flared at her fingertips as if trying to tell Henry it didn't agree with her. But she couldn't let him see that. Couldn't let Henry know how much this was destroying her.

"I don't believe you."

Drea gathered herself and her magic back into a controllable place before she said more hurtful things. "The first time I talked to you after Ella left was simply because Anastasia dared me. She didn't think I could get you to speak with me." Drea did all she could to keep the pain that welled in the back of her eyes from spilling forth. She was breaking herself...and him. Her magic shrank at her words. Gods, she hoped he would leave soon. Why hadn't he left yet?

"I didn't realize I had become such a joke to you. I'll leave you alone."

Drea ignored the tear that escaped her control as he turned his back on her. She looked out the window once again, unable to bear the sight of his back getting farther away from her. Drea breathed through her mouth, waiting to feel his presence leave her room.

Henry stopped at the foot of her bed, pausing. "I don't know what happened, but if you ever need anything...I'll always be there."

Everything within her screamed to get out of bed and find a way to get to him, to hold him, to tell him that she didn't mean a single thing she had said.

To tell him she loved him.

"Goodbye, Drizella."

Her eyes widened at the use of her name. She kept her gaze locked on the raindrops for what felt like hours. She didn't bother to control the tears as they soaked through the cloth. Saliva flooded her mouth as she curled over and grasped the bucket just in time to vomit. Sweat rolled down her back and forehead.

What was she doing? She couldn't lose him.

Not Henry.

But at least now Henry would live. At least he...

Drea curled on her side and let the sobs shake her body as she wrapped her arms around herself. How could she live without him? Her mother should have just left her to die, it would have been a less painful experience.

***

Present Day

The ball was upon her sooner than she had expected. Granted, everyone invited was surprised by the news and given less than a day to prepare. It was not a lavish ball, so their instructions were to arrive for a feast and a small soiree in the ballroom with the king's closest friends and advisers to celebrate Prince David's safe return home.

Anastasia had arrived home the day before in a flurry of chaos. Tressa's death had wound up her sister, and Drea didn't think anything less than Ella's death could quench it.

"She had everything," Anastasia vented as they sat in Drea's window nook. "She literally had everything, and she shoved it in our faces. Even mother showed favoritism towards her." Anastasia crossed her arms.

"What do you mean?" Drea asked. She couldn't think of a single time their mother had shown Ella preferential treatment.

"All of those hours spent in the attic, that was time Ella got with mother that we will never have."

Drea remained silent in her shock. The time in the attic, of course, was when their mother had been beating Ella with a whip. If that was favoritism to Anastasia...

"I don't think Ella would consider —"

"I don't care about what Ella feels. She got time with mother. Mother always had her train longer and harder than us, all because she thought she was the better fighter."

Drea pressed her hand to her mouth. She couldn't argue with Anastasia. Not when she was searching for any reason to despise Ella more than she already did.

"Has Lena agreed to give you Ella's assassination?"

Anastasia smiled. "I'm not sure yet, but I'm hopeful." Anastasia got up and looked down at Drea. "I have to get ready for the ball, you should too."

Drea nodded slowly as her sister left, leaving her speechless and confused.

***

It took Drea longer than expected to finish getting ready. So long, in fact, that Anastasia was pounding on her door. Drea closed her eyes and breathed deeply before leaving. Her cane weighed heavily in her hand as she walked down the hallway and towards the stairs. Today was a good day. She was going to have a good time at the first ball she had attended in three years. She had ensured she wore flat shoes that wouldn't trip her and had tucked away a blade on her right thigh. By the time she got down the stairs, the carriage was waiting with Ana and Princess Lena inside.

"You're beautiful, Drea." Princess Lena commented as they shut the door and had the carriage take off. "Should we run through the plan once more?"

"Everyone is in position within the palace with multiple safeguards in place should one of them be discovered. Tonight, while everyone is at the ball, one of them will sneak into Ella's room with the bottle missing half of Snow White's poison, and tomorrow morning, David's tea tray will be brought up along with a second one to Ella's door containing the same tea without poison," Ana answered.

"Good. I'll be nearby so that David doesn't have to die if I don't want him to. Truthfully, that will depend on how tonight goes." Lena leaned back into her cushions. "Drea, what will you be doing?"

"I'll be distracting Henry and determining if there's anything we haven't accounted for tonight." Drea shifted in her gown.

"Correct. Let us know if something happens that we need to know about."

Drea nodded.

"We will, of course, do the same if something doesn't feel right." Anastasia added.

Drea tilted her head, but didn't say anything as she processed her sister's words. Drea, of course, didn't tell them that hopefully, right now, Ella and David were getting ready to tell the king everything about them.

She had officially betrayed her sister, queen, and kingdom.

If she were ever to have a moment to redeem herself to any of them, it would have been now.

But she remained silent, letting them ride to their fates.

***

Drea got out of the carriage and let her dark purple gown flutter around her. Though simple, it was beautiful with its depth of color and silver embellishments around the off the shoulder neckline and waist. Her hair was loosely pulled back, with half twisted on top of her head and the rest lying around her shoulders.

Her cane was heavy as she used it to walk up the stairs. Even though she had defeated Gus the one time, she wasn't confident in herself to conquer these stairs alone yet. Other noblemen ascended the stairs beside her, as all of them approached the ball.

They were ushered into dinner, where they sat down at the dais with the king. Drea hid the frown on her face. If King Matthias knew everything, he certainly would not have allowed Princess Lena to sit at his table. Princess Celeste entered first, followed by her father. The king walked around to stand at the head of the room.

"We have gone through some trying times recently. It is my pleasure to inform all of you that Prince David is back home and will be joining us later at the ball to celebrate." King Matthias's voice rose over the crowd as they gasped.

Drea waited for news about Ella, or why David wasn't currently with them, but it never came. She kept her face relaxed as time passed by, and there was no sign or mention of Ella. Odd. She tuned into the surrounding conversations, doing her best to ignore Ana as she flirted with a young nobleman beside her.

Eventually, dinner ended, and King Matthias invited all of them to follow him to the ballroom. Drea began to follow, pausing when Henry walked into the hallway and motioned for her to follow him.

"Henry, what's wrong?" Drea asked as they walked into a small library.

"Ella and David are late. Their ship just docked. The king knows nothing." Henry stepped closer to her.

Gods, he was handsome in his formal attire. The dark green coat and black tunic contrasted beautifully with his perfectly disheveled red hair. Drea paced in front of him, leaving her cane resting against the chair.

"What does that mean? What if everything goes wrong? What happens...to me?" That was the root of it. What would happen to them and the tenuous friendship they'd rebuilt? What if something went wrong, and she lost him all over again?

Henry stepped in front of her and gently held her arms. "Everything will be okay. We know they're safe and on their way. Not everything has gone smoothly, but we've shifted. All we have to do is go down there, bring David into the ballroom, and have him talk to his father."

Drea bit her lip. "What if..." she gazed at Henry through blurry eyes. "I've done a lot of bad things, Henry. I can't...I know we're only friends, but I can't go through losing you again. I thought I could, but I can't." Drea rambled.

Henry gently cupped her face, rubbing a thumb over her cheek, catching a stray tear.

"I don't care about that anymore, Drea. I don't know if I ever truly did," Henry whispered. "My heart has and will always belong to every single version of who you are. No matter what you've done, or what you might have to do in the future, my very essence will always fall in love with you over and over again."

"Henry —"

He rested his forehead on hers. "I will wait for you, no matter how long it takes. I will keep waiting for you, Drizzie."

Drea couldn't form a coherent thought as her heart and magic exploded. She placed her hands around his neck and lifted her head before his lips crashed against hers.

It was a kiss she had waited for for years.

Drea sank into the kiss, memorizing every detail from Henry's soft lips to how his hands had moved to fist the fabric of her gown and pull her closer, wrapping his arms around her. Their kiss went from a tender, light touch of their lips to an all-consuming kiss as their lips fully locked together, and Drea let herself go to fully enjoy kissing the man she loved. Her fingers trailed through his thick hair, holding him closer as they remained locked together.

Henry's arms moved from her waist to under her thighs as he lifted her into the air and walked her backwards until she was pressed against the wall, her ankles wrapped around his waist. Drea sighed in bliss as Henry kissed the gentle curve of her neck.

"Henry," she spoke through breathless gasps, "I love you. I've loved you since the first moment I met you, and I'm so sorry for everything that ever happened. I'm so, so sorry."

How could she have ever willingly given up this man? Her magic rose as her emotions grew, reaching out for Henry, asking to dance with him.

"We'll talk about everything another day," Henry said between kisses that trailed from her neck down her shoulder and arm.

"Another day," Drea agreed between breaths. She bent her head down to kiss Henry's forehead before placing a finger under his chin to tilt his head back. "I promise, but first, I think you owe me a dance."

Henry gently let her slide down to the floor, his body pressed against hers. He let his forehead rest against hers, eyes closed as they caught their breath.

"Let's get you to that dance floor." Henry kissed her hand as he stepped back and led her to the door. "You should probably leave first. I'll wait a moment and find you later."

CHAPTER FIFTY-TWO

Ella

How had everything unraveled so quickly? What was King Matthias doing throwing them a ball and *not* telling them about it? They hadn't gotten to see the king. Hell, she hadn't even gotten to see Luca. David had been taken one day by a group of servants, and her another to get ready. Celeste had chosen her attire for the evening, and Ella could hardly complain about what the young woman had chosen.

Nerves fluttered through her fingers, aching to hold a dagger. Something was off, and she couldn't decide if it was from the surprise ball or something else.

As the final touches were done, Ella sliced into a part of the gown to strap a dagger to her thigh. The maid helping her almost fainted. Ella thought she was going to pass out when she hid two more on her body. But the maid remained conscious and focused on Ella's appearance. It was probably the maid's most important and quickest prep time ever.

Ella gave herself a final once over in the mirror, ready to get to the ball. Her gown was similar to the one she had worn at the last ball. The light blue chiffon fluttered around her with beautiful silver embroidery on the sweetheart neckline and puffy off the shoulder sleeves. The bodice was fitted to her chest perfectly, with not too many layers for the skirts. The enchanted crescent pendant from Jaq rested on her chest, just as she had promised. The maid added some cosmetics to her face, and the final piece to her ensemble was her hair. Ella wanted it twisted with a series of beautiful but effective braids, but the maid wanted it down and pulled back with some ribbons. To compromise it was down, with no ribbons.

She left her room and nearly ran for the ballroom. Ella twisted her hands together as she sped walked through hallways. Servants bustled around her, and a few lords and ladies gave her sideways glances as they headed in every direction away from the ballroom.

She ignored all of them.

She had been in charge of who was invited, though based on the people glaring at her, the right decision had been made. Ella dodged out of one young lady's way as she barreled past Ella in a ballgown. Ella spun to watch her as a young man chased her.

"Excuse me, Lady Eleanor." A palace guard approached her.

Ella paused. "I really have to get to this ball."

"Princess Celeste —"

"Is in the ball," Ella said as she motioned towards it.

"She's not. She's nervous and was wondering if she could see you first."

Ella frowned and searched around the guard one more time before nodding her head and following him.

They walked past the ballroom and around the corner.

"She isn't in her room?"

"When she gets nervous, she goes to the lower balcony," the guard replied.

Ella slipped her hand into the slit of her dress as she walked out onto the balcony. She turned around, looking for Celeste or whoever was there to ambush her. She should have guessed this would be a trap.

"You know, I've always hated you."

Ella turned around to face a second set of doors. Princess Lena, with her perfect hair and immaculate gown, stood before her. The ball gown shimmered in the moonlight as she leaned against the doorway, examining her nails.

"Why?" Ella loosened the dagger in the back of her dress.

"You still haven't figured out who you are yet, have you?"

Ella cocked a hip and crossed her arms.

"She did such a great job of erasing her past. I guess your mom was the coward I was always told about."

"You know nothing about my mom." Ella stepped close to Princess Lena, staring into her ice blue eyes.

"No, you know nothing." Princess Lena stepped closer, cloning the gap between them. You don't even know who she is." Princess Lena laughed as she gripped Ella's arms. "She was my aunt, a member of the royal family, and she left us...for your father."

Ella stumbled back as Princess Lena released her.

"Your mom was meant to be the Queen of Trudel and marry her fiancée. Instead, she left her family, her kingdom, and her duty, all for a lowly duke. My mother had to become queen instead of marrying the King of Rairene. Now, all wrongs will be corrected, starting with you."

Ella stepped back from Princess Lena as though the distance would help it make sense. It couldn't be true. Her mom wasn't part of the royal family.

"You're *lying*," Ella whispered.

"Wish that I were, cousin." Princess Lena said. "Don't you see it in our eyes? Maybe if you saw my brother Aleksander, you'd notice it more. He's the one with the family hair." She examined her nails again.

Ella backed up against the balcony's edge, the cool stones pressing against her for support.

A foot moved behind her.

Ella glanced back and down to see three men in black standing below, swords drawn. She turned back to Lena and found seven more, all with swords pointed towards her.

"So, your goal is to try to kill me?"

"Kill you?" Princess Lena pressed her hands against her chest in mock offense. "I would love to, but I follow my orders. We're taking you home."

"I would rather die." Ella pulled out her dagger, getting into a fighting position. Gods, she wished she had worn a less hindering gown. But she was never going anywhere with her cousin.

"If you don't, she's going to die." Lena smiled.

"Why do I care about her?" Ella glanced at the woman. She had no idea who the blond waif was.

"Ella," Henry's voice cracked.

"Henry." Ella remained in her fighting stance, keeping her eyes and ears open to any movement.

Henry walked cautiously out of the shadows cast by the ballroom. His eyes flicked between her and the blade Anastasia held the woman's throat.

"That's Gwen, my fiancée."

His fiancée? Ella wasn't sure what surprised her more, that Henry was engaged to this woman, Gwen, or that it wasn't Drea. None of that actually mattered. Henry would do everything he could to protect those he loved, or those who were innocent, and while Ella didn't know if he loved Gwen, she was an innocent person.

"I can't go with her, Henry." Ella's eyes darted around, evaluating her options. There were very few. The one she liked the most was killing Lena and running for the mountains.

"Even if you escape, which you can't, the entire kingdom will be hunting you down," Anastasia sneered.

Ella quirked a brow. She had forgotten Anastasia's presence. Anastasia's smirk twisted into something ugly as she removed her blade from Gwen's throat and strutted over to Ella. *What had she done?*

Out of the corner of her eye, she saw Drea step behind Gwen and whisper to her. Hopefully, the girl ran.

Anastasia held out a mirror to Ella as she said, "David's condemning you to the entire kingdom, Ella. I guess he doesn't love you after all," Anastasia taunted.

Lady Eleanor is not whom she claims to be, David said through the mirror. Ella realized it was being sent out over all the mirrors in the kingdom. *In the chaos of the winter ball, she held me hostage with the sole purpose of starting a war between our ally, Trudel. Thankfully, I was able to escape.*

What had they done? How were they getting him to say these lies?

David paused for a moment. *However, during my time as her prisoner, I learned truly frightening information about her,* he paused again.

Ella looked at Anastasia and then at Lena. Both of them radiated smugness.

She divulged to me that she is the assassin that we all know of as Cinderella.

Ella's jaw dropped as Lena circled her. Whoever David spoke to, gasps flew throughout the room.

Eleanor is not only guilty of killing Lady Tremaine, Trudel's ambassador, but...

He wouldn't. Not after everything they had been through. Not after he had seen what his wrongful accusation had done to her. He wouldn't —

She killed our queen.

The people around David erupted.

As a sign of goodwill between our two kingdoms, Eleanor has been arrested and is currently being transported to a ship where she will face judgement for her crimes in Trudel.

Anastasia shut the mirror.

"What did you do to him?" Ella asked. Fire burned inside her at what they had just done. They had just forced David to open a wound that had freshly healed, and gods only knew how long that would take to heal.

"Absolutely nothing. You know how much he despises killers, Ella," Anastasia said.

"You've done something to him." Ella didn't think. All she did was act on what her body wanted to do, and that was to take her dagger and stab it through Lena's heart.

The men who encircled her moved in one fluid motion, tossing ropes around her and pulling tight before Ella got near her cousin.

But they weren't prepared for what came next.

Ella's pendant lit up as the ropes restrained her. Pure power exploded from the pendant, sending a wave of magic from her and catapulting the men away from her.

Ella worked on shimmying out of the ropes.

"Stop," Princess Lena yelled as the men began to move towards Ella again. "Drizella."

Ella hesitated. She couldn't hurt Drea, and if Drea got too close, she wasn't sure what the pendant would do to her and her bad leg.

"Remove that necklace, Drizella. It'll serve as proof to the prince that we have her and that our deal is complete," Princess Lena ordered.

Drea stepped out of the shadows from behind Gwen. She kept her eyes downcast as she fiddled with her cane, letting it lightly tap the stone. She wouldn't actually take the pendant? This was a ruse to help her, just like that night when she had killed Lady Tremaine. Ella couldn't go to Trudel. She didn't know what awaited her there, but she really didn't want to find out.

"Drea, please," Ella whispered.

Drea walked around to where the necklace clasped together and stepped close to Ella. "They have Celeste," Drea mumbled.

Ella's body went slack. *No.*

Drea walked back around to face Ella as she examined the necklace. She reached out her hand towards it, and the pendant instantly began to glow from the threat. Ella watched Drea's brown eyes calculate what this enchantment did.

"Ella, tell the necklace I can touch it, and that once I have it, only David is allowed to possess it."

Ella nodded. The pendant felt intuitive enough. She closed her eyes and pressed her hand to it. Jaq's presence surrounded her with stuffy books and minty magic as it waited to attack any threats. Ella soothed it and gave it an image of what David felt like to her with spiced magic, a stormy shore and pine trees all coated in safety and love.

Drea took the pendant as Ella felt Jaq's presence leave her.

Lena won. Queen Laila had won.

"Tell him you love him, Drea. You never know when your moment will be stolen," Ella said softly. She hadn't gotten to tell David. Not in so many words. She hoped he knew.

The moment Drea backed away, the men moved in and tightened the ropes around her.

Ella turned to Henry. "Whatever deal they've made, they'll break it, Henry. This war will start."

"I know," Henry whispered.

Ella turned to Lena who stood with crossed arms and a smirk. "You'll never break me."

"I'm counting on it." Lena moved quickly as she raised her sword. Before Ella could react, everything went black.

CHAPTER FIFTY-THREE

Drea

Drea moved beside Gwen as the men continued to further restrain Ella now that she was disarmed and unconscious.

"Let. Gwen. Go," Henry snarled. He walked to Lena, and though he towered over her, Henry had never appeared so small.

The corner of Lena's lips curled in delight as she stared at Henry. She appeared to grow bigger as she soaked in the power she wielded. "She may leave."

One of Lena's swordsmen walked over and cut Gwen's bonds. Henry turned and rushed to her side, hugging her close.

"What did you two just do?" Drea questioned, turning her full attention onto Lena and Ana.

Ella remained unconscious as she was lifted into the air between four men who carried her down the stone stairs to a carriage convoy that waited below.

"We did what Mother couldn't and what our queen demanded of us," Anastasia answered. "I wish you could have been a part of it."

"Why wasn't I part of it? Did you want to make sure you kept all the glory?" Drea pressed.

"We knew it would fail if we included you, dear," Princess Lena said, stepping beside Anastasia.

"I find that hard to believe. If anything, I could have helped you capture Gwen, so that she wasn't beaten," Drea replied.

"You can stop acting Drizzie, we know you've betrayed us." Princess Lena asserted.

She was correct, of course. But how she knew...that was a question for another day.

"I would never betray my sister," Drea snapped. "Ana, I love you. It's always been you and me." She gripped the cane in her hands, rolling it back and forth.

Anastasia and Lena stood united before her. Lena even had her arm wrapped around Ana.

"Stop lying to us, Drizella. I've suspected you ever since you were adamant that Ella was dead, and Ana, well, she took a while to come around, but had to admit that it was so odd that you thought Ella was dead. I mean, you could only be so certain if you had either witnessed it, meaning you could have prevented your mother's death, or you had become an insider willing to help spread the lies. So which is it, Drizella?"

"I—"

"You could have prevented our mother's death, and you did nothing," Anastasia accused.

"I was trying to save us...to save you," Drea snapped, setting the truth free.

"I don't need to be saved," Ana screamed.

"Aren't you tired of it, Ana? Aren't you exhausted by the constant scheming? The plotting and political moves being made in the shadows? Don't you wish you could have a life free of the fighting, the hunting, and the pain?" Drea asked. She slowly turned in a circle as Anastasia began to circle her, making sure Ana stayed within her line of sight.

"I would rather have my mother alive than have to live with a deformed, crippled sister," Anastasia confessed as she withdrew a short sword from the skirts of her gown.

"Well...I just wanted you to be happy," Drea said. She blinked against the tears that rose at her sister's words.

"This wasn't part of our deal. You two need to leave." Henry was at Drea's side in a moment.

"No, my traitorous sister is going to accompany us in shackles to be judged for her crimes." Anastasia seethed as she pointed her blade at Drea.

"I won't go with you," Drea said. She gripped her cane, resting her hand on the pommel..

"Then I'll pass judgment now." Anastasia lunged.

Drea had been ready for an attack. Her sister always thought with her heart and used her mind later. Drea blocked her blade with her cane, pushing Anastasia, and their fight away from Henry and Lena. The last thing they needed was one of them getting hurt.

"Ana, it doesn't have to be this way." Drea grunted as Ana pushed back, knocking Drea off balance.

"Surrender, and I won't be forced to kill you. We both know you can't fight me," Anastasia said through angry tears.

"I think you'll find I'm not as helpless anymore." Drea unsheathed a thin rapier from her cane and pressed her advantage. Her leg held against the strain as Drea battled Anastasia.

Drea knew Anastasia would fight with controlled chaos, letting instinct guide her, and Anastasia knew that Drea would be precise and methodical. Anastasia moved first, instantly going for Drea's left leg.

Drea twisted sideways, avoiding the strike and getting in a hit of her own as Anastasia stumbled past her. Anastasia recovered and swiped Drea's legs out. Drea stayed down for a moment, waiting for her sister to follow. Anastasia never could resist someone who was already down. Drea rolled out of the way and sprang to her feet, punching her sister in the face as Anastasia tried to avoid her.

"We could have been heroes together, Drea," Anastasia gasped. She broke through Drea's defenses and got close to Drea, nicking Drea with the tip of her dagger.

"Heroes to whom? The queen? Who really wants this war? You think the people of Trudel, the soldiers of Trudel, care that their queen was snubbed twenty years ago?" Drea questioned. She ignored the pain blossoming in her side as she knocked aside another attack with her cane.

"Our mother cared."

"Our mother had also been snubbed and would have done anything to get back to Lord Elliot," Drea said. "I would rather die on the right side of history for standing up for what's right than living for what's wrong."

"Then you'll die and leave me alone in this world." Anastasia spun with a flourish.

Movement flickered in the corner of Drea's eye.

Lena was behind her.

A smirk pulled at the corner of Anastasia's mouth as Drea scrambled to remember if Lena was a skilled fighter. From what she could remember, Lena wasn't proficient outside of some basic moves. But that didn't change the fact that Drea was pinned between the two. If she faced Lena, her back would be to Ana's, and as much as she loved her sister, a dagger would quickly find a home in her back.

The muscle in her leg took the pause in their fight as the perfect moment to cramp. It was sharp, and it was debilitating as it ground her muscles and squeezed. Drea scrunched her face, letting out a whimper.

"I see your leg has met its limit," Anastasia commented. She pressed her attack, forcing Drea to move.

Her leg buckled at the shift in weight.

Drea fell to her knees as she blocked Anastasia's attack.

"Surrender, Drea. I don't want to see you die."

"You could have fooled me," Drea replied. Her arms shook as she held her blade up to hold off Anastasia's.

Anastasia's eyes flicked to behind Drea, remorse passed across her features.

"Let me protect you, Ana. Please, you're my sister. I just want us to be free." Drea pleaded a final time as she pushed past the pain in her leg and stood, while simultaneously using the head of her cane to pull Anastasia's feet out from under her and force her to the ground. "Yield." Drea pointed the tip of her blade at Ana's heart.

Anastasia flicked her eyes once again away from Drea as a smirk blossomed across her face.

Drea turned her head in time to see Lena throw the dagger.

Henry jumped between Drea and the blade.

"Oops, I missed," Lena said as Henry grunted. "Anastasia, we're leaving. Now." Princess Lena grabbed Ana's hand and whisked her sister to the carriage waiting for them below.

Drea didn't care.

Henry still stood with his back to her, swaying on his feet.

Drea limped around to face him. His face was whiter than Ella's hair as he held onto the dagger's hilt that stuck out of his chest.

"Drizzie." Henry fell to his knees.

"Nononononono." Drea tried to catch him, but the best she could do was support him as she eased him onto his back, blood staining his tunic. "Henry, please..."

"Driz..."

"Shhh, don't waste your energy. You're going to be fine. I promise you'll be fine." Drea found Gwen to the side, arms slack at her sides as she stared. "Get help!"

Gwen shook herself and sprinted away.

"Drizzie." Henry's voice was shallow as he gasped.

"You're going to be fine. You still owe me a dance, Henry, and I swear to the gods if you leave me before fulfilling that promise, I will kill you myself." Drea promised.

Henry blinked in response, a smile tugging at his lips.

"I love you too."

Drea looked at him through blurry eyes as she leaned down and kissed his forehead. "I'm going to save you. I don't care what it takes."

"Drizzie the risk..."

"Henry!" David rounded the corner.

Drea glanced as guards and enchanters accompanied David and Gwen. She turned to Henry as he gripped her hand.

"Drea, let us help him," David commanded as he approached them.

Drea nodded her head. She leaned down quickly and pressed her forehead to Henry's.

"There is no life to live if you're not there beside me. I will fall in love with you in every lifetime. You're mine in this life and the next, but I refuse to have the next life be the one where we get to finally be together. So Henry, you are going to have to fight one last time for us." Drea's hands flickered with power as her magic unspooled and rushed to wrap her in its embrace. It rose quickly, demanding to dance with Henry's power.

Drea opened her eyes as Henry's power unraveled, his life flickering. Drea gripped his hands as her power charged forward to tangle with his, rising to the heartbreak that consumed her as Henry lost control of his magic. Their heartbeats danced together and stopped.

CHAPTER FIFTY-FOUR

Ella

She had let them chain her.

She had let them lead her down to a covered carriage in shackles.

Princess Lena got in with her before the carriage moved and primly folded her hands in her lap, smiling at Ella.

Ella stared her down, watching for any twitch in her expression. But she didn't see any flicker of emotion from her cousin. They rode in silence, the only sound coming from the chains bumping in the carriage. The guards had taken all five chains and locked them to various hooks that had been installed on the carriage walls, which kept her strapped down, unable to move.

When the carriage doors opened, the harbor and a large ship greeted Ella in the moonlight. Several dockworkers moved past them while a few other commoners stumbled out of a pub. More people made their way around the harbor, avoiding the edges of the docks as they staggered. Princess Lena got out of the carriage and stood outside as three guards approached and began unlocking the chains.

Ella watched it all with amusement. At least they took her seriously as a threat. As it was, if given the chance, she would attempt to escape and kill whoever got in her way, and if that happened to her cousin, then it was meant to be. But Ella didn't think that chance would ever come. Not once did the guards let a chain slip or slacken to let her free.

By the time they pulled her out, a small crowd had gathered to watch, and Ella did her best to stand tall.

"That's Lady Eleanor." A woman from the crowd yelled.

"She killed the queen," another shouted.

An eruption of boos swelled throughout the crowd until it was all she heard.

She remained standing on shaky legs.

Ella blinked, surveying the crowd again through blurry vision. She blinked more, trying to clear her vision, making it worse. These were her people. The ones she wanted to protect from the shadows with all her heart. And they hated her.

Ella tried to walk towards the ship, anything to get her away from their disappointment.

But the guards didn't move.

They wouldn't until Princess Lena commanded it, and for some reason she had continued to stand beside the carriage, hands held together in front of her ball gown, waiting.

Ella kept her back straight, her hands fisted at her sides as the chains tightened.

A woman stepped forward, yelling at her as tears streamed down her face. "You killed our queen. You broke our king," The woman said. "How could you do that to them? To us?"

Every word the woman spoke hit Ella in the chest until the woman was directly before her. The guards didn't flinch a muscle when she raised a hand and slapped Ella across the face.

Ella lifted her head. The tears she had been trying to hold back fell forward as the woman slapped her other cheek. Ella stared with wide eyes at the cobblestones beneath her.

Ella looked at the woman with defiant and grief stricken eyes. Her tears betrayed her as they soaked her burning cheeks, but she would not say anything to this woman. She wouldn't have believed her anyway, and Ella knew the moment she spoke, her voice would break, and she couldn't show any more weakness in front of Lena. Instead, Ella straightened her back and stared straight ahead at the crowd that had continued to grow.

It felt as though all of Riset had come to watch her banishment.

Princess Lena continued to stand beside the carriage, smirking. The woman who had bravely approached Ella walked off in a huff. Ella closed her eyes for a moment until footsteps approached her.

It was another upset commoner, except he was brandishing a rusted dagger as he yelled nonsensical words at her. He raised his arm, and Ella prepared herself.

She would die for the city she loved.

David would be alive for now. But at least they could prepare for war. She just wouldn't be there to fight beside him, like he had promised.

The man thrust his arm towards her, and another shot out, catching her attacker's arm.

David? Ella hoped it was him.

The glimmer of hope obliterated her as she stared at Jason.

"You will not harm Lady Eleanor. I think she has suffered enough for one night," Jason growled.

"She should die for what she's done," the man yelled, spitting at Ella.

"You have no idea what she has —"

"Sir Jason, stop." Ella glared at him, hoping he would see the message in her eyes.

Jason sighed and released the men, gently pushing him back towards the crowd.

"Princess Lena, you were supposed to wait for me on the ship, not out here in the open," Jason chided.

"Oops, I must have forgotten." Princess Lena smiled as she strutted past Ella to the ship.

The guards allowed Ella to ascend behind her cousin onto the safety of the largest ship Ella had ever stepped foot on. Though they had been waiting below, the crew hadn't been idle in their preparations. The anchor was lifted, ropes tossed, and the captain strode to the helm and shouted orders to push off.

"Jason, what are you doing here?" Ella asked as the guards continued to hold her.

"I volunteered to be your representative for the crown and ensure you're not—"

"Instantly killed?" Ella laughed.

Jason turned scarlet. "Something like that."

"Well then, Sir Jason, we have a long journey ahead of us."

CHAPTER FIFTY-FIVE

MIRA

Mira snuck out every day to avoid being in the palace. She needed some separation from Morgan, as she and Adam planned their escape route. It was simple, really. She would drug the guards, grab the key, get Calla, sneak through the hidden passageway into Aslar and get on a ship.

All she needed was the ship.

Which is why she was down by the docks, searching for one that would carry Calla somewhere. She couldn't go to Rairene. Ella wouldn't be there to protect her, and she definitely couldn't go to Trudel. Mira bit her lip as she looked at the ships and their destinations.Adam walked beside her, eating a warm, sweet roll, handing her the second one.

"What about the one she came here on?" Adam asked.

"Do you know which one that is?" Mira asked. She certainly didn't.

"No, but I think the head housekeeper knows. We could ask her."

"Let's have that be our last resort. The last thing we need is someone asking questions about us." Mira sighed. All of the ships currently in the harbor were either departing too late, too soon, or going to the wrong destination. Mira had half a mind to send Calla to Grecia; at least she would be protected by Maliah. Mira headed towards a handful of ships that had recently docked.

She walked over to a group of old captains who had congregated together as the crew unloaded their cargo.

"Excuse me, I'm looking to book passage," Mira said, looking at all of them. Each one was old and had what Mira could only describe as an air of gruff snobbery surrounding them. She did her best to not wrinkle her nose as the stretch of unwashed bodies mixed with the salty sea air hit her.

"How many?"

"Three, and we need to leave within the next two nights."

Almost all of them shook their heads.

"Most of us need to give our men some rest before going back out. Where are you headin'?" One captain asked.

"Rairene or Grecia. I'll accept either destination."

"Whatcha runnin' from then?" a short, portly captain asked, winking at her.

"That's none of your concern," Mira snapped. "I mean that it's not anyone's concern but my own. There's no trouble to be had here; I just need to get away with my sister and her husband." She despised haggling, especially sailors who were always trying to pull a fast one on anyone they could.

"I can ya, but it'll cost ya." A tall, intimidating captain walked over to her. His brown eyes were hard in the midday sun.

"What's your price?"

"I leave that to my secondhand. He's practically running the ship now. He's also a hardass."

"Great," Mira muttered as the captain called for his secondhand to come over.

"Christopher, this lovely woman is booking passage with us. Make sure she pays well," the captain said before leaving Mira to deal with a young man.

She did a double take. He was just a few years older than her with short brown hair and piercing blue eyes. While he appeared young, he didn't act like it. His stance was confident, despite his hands being tucked into his coat pockets.

"How much is this going to cost me?" Mira asked.

"You don't want to haggle over the price?" He grinned.

"Let me hear your offer first, and then I'll decide if it's worth it," Mira answered as Adam stood with her.

"You." Christopher's voice dropped an octave in disgust. "I won't book passage for him on my vessel, not after what he did."

"What did he do?" Mira asked. No one had even recognized Adam given how little he went into Aslar.

"He stood by while they took her. He could have stopped them at the ball, but he didn't. I won't betray my friend by taking the likes of him, no matter how much you're willing to pay."

Mira stepped back in shock.

"I'm going to presume this is the ship that carried Calla here and that you're the friend she was dancing with before I interrupted," Adam said.

"You presume correctly." Christopher straightened so that he towered over Adam.

"We're trying to save her," Mira whispered. She didn't know why she trusted Christopher, but inherently, she just knew he could be. "It's why I'm booking passage and need a ship that's departing so soon. She needs to get out of there. Prince Adam and I have a plan. We just need a ship." She stepped closer to him and rested a hand on his arm. "Please help us."

"I'll think about it. Give me the day." Christopher walked away and back onto his ship, taking all of Mira's hope with him.

Mira and Adam spent the afternoon draining their personal coin and stocking up on everything they would need to take Calla into hiding and survive for a few months. Mira paused at a bookseller. She hadn't seen a lot in Aslar and her book loving sister would be desperate for a few good stories. She went into the shop and wrinkled her nose. All of her sisters loved the smell of books. Their eyes went glassy as they talked about the musty scent washing over them or the feel of the paper in their hands as they breathed in the books. But Mira...all she smelled was dust and stale air. However, she was not above venturing into a store that would bring someone she loved happiness.

Mira stepped farther into the shop, passing by an older man with unkempt gray hair at the counter and going straight to the section that held what Calla liked to call her adventurous heroine romance books. Calla claimed it was for research to create enchantments for any situation, lest it be to conquer love or a fire wielding dragon. Mira had a feeling it was for something much deeper than that, but she didn't pry. Her little book worm was happiest when she was off exploring other imaginary worlds and who was she to deny that joy?

Mira surveyed all of the titles and got lost in the options. There was The Maid and The Prince, The Enchanter and The Crown, Thyme for Tea and Baking, The Dragon's Song, and so many more.

"Excuse me," Mira walked over to the bookseller. She was an older woman who had retained all of her beauty. Her gray hair was piled into a perfect bun with stray wisps breaking free. Her green eyes held a sharp intelligence as she turned away from the older man and assessed Mira. "Would you be able to help me? I'm trying to get some stories for a friend, but I'm a bit lost."

"Of course." She smiled at Mira as she stepped out from behind the counter. "I'll be one minute and then I'll come help you," she said to the elderly man, her voice light and wistful.

She walked back with Mira to the books and gazed at the multiple shelves. "Do you know what your friend has read?"

Mira chuckled. "She's read just about everything. But, she's not from here, so if you have anything from writers who live here that would be great."

"What are her favorite stories?" The woman began pulling some stories off the shelves.

"She doesn't realize it, but her favorite books all involve a heroine who is underestimated and defeats the monster, no matter how big. There's always some romance and maybe some spice in there wouldn't hurt her," Mira winked. "But she loves adventures where the lead character overcomes insurmountable odds."

While Mira talked, the bookseller perused the aisles where she either took down or put some back. By the end of it, the woman had a stack of ten books in front of Mira.

"These are all ones that are written by local writers or writers from our neighboring kingdoms."

"Perfect, I'll take all of them," Mira said.

"All of them?" The bookseller sputtered as she took the stack.

"Yes, all of them. My friend has been a bit deprived of books recently and I think she'll devour these in a matter of weeks."

"But the cost, surely you'll want to wait and come back?"

"No, I'll take them now. I promise I can pay for them," Mira said, opening one of many coin pouches she had hidden in her clothing. She paid for all of the books and left with instructions to leave them on the ship that would take Calla to safety.

Mira laid down on her bed and let out a breath of air. She blinked at the hideous pink satin fabric that lay across the four poster bed. Why the queen had chosen pink, she could never guess. She had never seen the woman wear the color, so it wasn't anything she enjoyed. Mira closed her eyes and walked through the plan.

After securing passage at an insanely high price with Christopher for the privilege of allowing Adam on board, they were drunk and back in their rooms to sleep. Tomorrow was the day. Adam was enchanting several potions, one of which she would pour into some ale for the guards, and a much stronger one that she would use on Morgan. Once everyone was passed out, she would signal Adam with her mirror and they would get Calla out of the cell, down through the gates and to two horses that Christopher would have waiting for them. From there it would be an all out race to the boat that already had everything she and Adam had purchased stored away in trunks in their rooms.

They could do it.

Mira had no doubt.

Christopher had wanted to be left out of the plan as much as possible, but would be there with the ship ready to go as soon as they got there.

Mira sat up quickly, holding her head as she waited for the room to stop spinning. She got up on wobbly feet and stumbled over to her vanity. Mira opened a drawer and tossed several items out before she reached the bottom where she withdrew a set of mirrors, each one keyed to a different person.

Mira held the one for Raven and opened it. She pictured her sister as she liked to remember her. Dazzling blue eyes, black curly hair that Mira would kill to have, a beautiful smile, and an air of regality Mira now realized stemmed from her childhood and her innate ability to lead any of them anywhere without a second thought to how realistic the idea was. Though, if Mira was honest, she was always the one with the crazy ideas.

As she thought of Raven and their years together, she waited for the mirror on the other side to open and show her that beautiful face. But it never did. Mira tried three more times. Maybe Raven was busy while out running from her evil stepmother? She closed the mirror after the seventh attempt and put it in her pack. She would try again on the ship. For now, she needed to sleep.

CHAPTER FIFTY-SIX

CALLA

Adam was drunk.

He had stumbled into the dungeon. Calla stared at him as he sat on the floor in front of her, leaning heavily on the metal bars. How his hair was still perfectly tidy, Calla could only guess. She crouched down so she was at eye level with him.

"Adam, are you okay?" Calla asked. Her breath fogged around her as one of the coldest nights yet gripped the air in the dungeon.

"I'm sorry," Adam spoke in slurred Vicurian. His voice was guttural as he tried to put words together.

"Sorry for what?" Calla sat down as close as she could.

"I don't deserve your kindness or your affection. I am truly a beast." Adam continued rambling on.

"Adam, what's wrong?" Calla reached her hand out as far as it could go until the tips of her fingers brushed against his white knuckled hands gripping the bars.

"You're so beautiful. I know you don't think you are, but you are. The way you smile brings more warmth to my heart than anyone ever has before, and your eyes..." Adam reached a hand through to run his hands through Calla's matted hair. "Your eyes have enchanted me from the first day you timidly came into my room and forced me out of my bed."

Tears fell from Adam's face as he burped.

"Why are you telling me this?" Calla didn't even think he realized he was speaking in his native tongue and that she could understand. Her heart had ached to hear these words from him, but she couldn't help but wonder what had changed for him to speak them now.

"I don't deserve you," Adam whispered. His speech was becoming clearer the longer he spoke. "This is all my fault."

"What's all your fault?" Calla could have strangled him.

"All of this. I could have stopped it. If I hadn't been so prideful I could have stopped all of it during the ball. All I had to do was have courage."

"Adam, you couldn't have prevented this. It would have happened either way." Calla reassured him.

"I could have. My people know I am vain and pretentious, but they also know I am brave in a battle and in that moment, I wasn't and now all of this is my fault." Adam motioned towards her. "I'm so sorry for all you've suffered, and now your hands...my fault..." Adam closed his eyes and turned away from her.

"What do you mean 'my hands'?" Calla leaned back.

"They're my fault," Adam confessed.

Calla didn't know what to say. She wasn't even sure she believed him in his current state.

"I trusted that guard...Bastien."

"What?" Calla could barely get the word out.

"I asked him about enchanters and their punishments here and if they might be spared if they could provide beneficial information to the queen."

"What would make you ask him that?" Calla sat backwards, giving herself space.

"You asked me about the strength of enchanters and how you wished you had done more to help Raven."

"So you trusted a royal guard?" Calla almost screamed at him. Her power flickered within her, roaring to life, despite the shackles. How could he have done that? What was he thinking? Those questions and more spiraled through Calla as she watched Adam crumple before her.

"I'm going to make it right, I promise. I'm going to do everything within my power to make this better." Adam reached through the bars and gripped her hand.

Calla yelped, ripping her fingers out of his. Her magic grew and for the first time in days Calla felt as though she could grab it.

"Get away from me!" She backed into her dungeon as far as she could go.

"Calla, please, I'm sorry. I'm so sorry," Adam pleaded. "I'll fix this."

"I don't want to see you again, Adam." Calla got the words out through gritted teeth.

"Calla —"

"Get. Out!" Calla's magic roared in her ears as her heart was shredded.

She waited for Adam to scramble out of her sight before she tried to siphon her magic. She didn't even realize she was able to access it as it overwhelmed her. Calla groaned as she pressed her broken fingers against the stones beneath her and focused her intention on heating the stones. She could do it. She didn't know how to enchant through shackles and broken fingers, but she was about to figure it out.

Calla took a breath and turned her attention away from the pain in her hands toward the cold wet stone beneath them. Her power built inside of her core as she pulled it into a melody that would dance along her veins and out through her fingers —

Calla closed her eyes and clamped her mouth shut as the shocks of power running up her arm turned into sharp spikes that increased in their sharpness as they got to her fingertips.

She couldn't do it. Her power had built, and she had no way of letting it go. Her magic spilled out of her hands, twisting in a pattern she had never seen as her fingers directed it in different directions. Shards of glass seemed to pierce through every broken joint in her hand as her power tried to find release. Calla opened her eyes and blinked, trying to see beyond the black spots obscuring her vision to focus on her hands.

She could do this.

She would let it go.

She could...

She...

Calla screamed as invisible daggers stabbed her hands over and over and over again.

CHAPTER FIFTY-SEVEN

Mira

Mira shook herself as she walked down the hall towards Morgan's room. It had surprised her at first how close to the dungeon Morgan was, but the more she thought about it, the more it made sense. Morgan lived her job. She didn't just love it. She lived for it, and one day, not today, Mira would make her pay for it. But tonight her focus had to be on getting Calla to safety. If she were to do anything tonight, it would be a mercy that frankly Mira didn't think she deserved.

Adam had put together a special enchantment just for Morgan that would put her to sleep and give her some fun nightmares in the process. Mira had poured it into the bottle of wine she now carried with her down the hallway.

After the events with Lord Edouard...Mira shivered at the thought. But, she was here now, wearing one of her best gowns, it flowed around her in thin blue fabric that was sheer enough to leave little to the imagination. Mira always thought she looked like the ocean on a sparkling summer day in this dress. It was one she had worn for special, high-profile assignments at the Tea Room in Rairene. No one said no to her in this dress. Especially not when she let her hair fall freely around her waist and put some cosmetics on around her eyes and lips.

She knocked on the door, shaking herself in anticipation.

Morgan had the desired reaction when she opened her door and immediately dragged her inside. Morgan didn't give Mira time to say a word before she pushed her against a wall and pressed her lips against Mira's.

"You're not..." Mira spoke through heat filled kisses, "going to let...me...apologize?"

Morgan moved away from Mira's lips to shower her neck with gentle bites. "This dress is apology enough."

"I brought wine," Mira said, holding the bottle up. "Want to have some added fun?"

Morgan grabbed the bottle and held it as she continued to lavish Mira with her affections. Mira guided Morgan over to where she held a bottle opener and two glasses beside her fireplace. She broke away from the kisses long enough to open the bottle and pour two glasses, all while Morgan kissed her neck and arms. If Mira hadn't despised all Morgan's existence, she would have liked being able to enjoy this woman. As it was, Mira had to keep back the vomit that tried to rise at the very thought of her.

"You're in an extra good mood tonight," Mira commented. Maybe she had someone new to torture.

"Why shouldn't I be? I got to have fun all day with the traitor's accomplice and now I get to have fun with the most beautiful woman in the entire kingdom." Morgan spoke through shallow breaths.

Mira spun on her toes to face, both glasses filled in her hands. Mira's heart raced to check on Calla. If she was in this good of a mood, it meant that today had been horrible for Calla. Mira held out a glass to her. "To having fun," Mira said as she smiled.

Morgan took the glass and took a sip from it. "To having fun."

Mira took a long drink, encouraging Morgan to do the same, knowing she was protected by Adam's antidote. Morgan drank the entire glass and let it break on the ground as she dropped it in her desire to get Mira on her bed.

Before Morgan could take things farther by removing her gown, Mira spun them and pushed Morgan onto her back on the bed so that Mira was in control.

"I want to take my time with you," Mira whispered.

She had only been with Morgan once, but that was all Mira had needed to know exactly what Morgan wanted, and right now, Mira needed to make this last just long enough that Morgan was passed out thinking something had happened before anything actually did happen.

Adam had warned Mira it might take a few minutes. Since they had to pour it into the wine and not raise suspicions, it would be diluted and take longer to work. So, Mira waited. She teased and played with Morgan, building Morgan's anticipation just until she did finally pass out. Mira tied her up before she grabbed the wine and left to get phase two of their plan going.

Adam waited for her at his room with a small pack and a bottle of ale spiked with a sleeping potion. The moment she knocked on his door, it swung open with Adam on the other side, cloaked with their pack and a cloak for Mira. The one thing she didn't want was to walk through the rest of the palace in her gown. She flung the cloak over her shoulders, grabbed the ale and headed out with Adam behind her.

Mira waved Adam away as they approached the nondescript entrance to the dungeons holding Calla. As she approached, the guards spoke in low voices with the sound of dice being thrown echoing down the hall. Mira straightened her shoulders and walked in.

The guards went silent, all of them standing.

"Oh," Mira stumbled against the wall, feigning intoxication, "this is not where I meant to go." She delicately swung the bottle around as she looked them up and down. "But, maybe I am in the right place," Mira untied her cloak and let it fall to the ground, "do you think I am?"

All of the men walked over to her, smiling.

"You have to join me though," Mira said as she held out the bottle to them.

One of them took it while another started to kiss her neck. Mira giggled as she watched them pass the bottle around. They each took a gulp before setting it down. Mira walked over to it and handed it to them again.

"Come on men, you need to have more to have more fun." Mira winked as she wrapped an arm around one and leaned her body against him. The men all laughed as they drank more. Mira laughed with them as well until they all fell where they stood, passed out.

Mira sprinted down the hallway to let Adam in. As Adam grabbed the keys, Mira grabbed the pack and changed into her black leather suit. As they descended into the dungeon, Mira braided her hair. She secured her daggers and lastly, grabbed her staff as they reached Calla.

They got to the cell and unlocked it. Calla was curled on the floor and before Mira could stop herself, she was hugging her.

"Mira?" Calla's voice was soft and scratchy.

"Calla." Mira's voice caught in her throat as she held her close. Where Calla had previously been voluptuous and comfortable to hug, Mira found more bones and angles pressing into her. But, she still smelled like books and that special spice mix only Calla could smell like.

"How are you hugging me?"

"We're breaking you out," Mira said. She gave a final squeeze to Calla and pulled back to show her Adam.

Calla recoiled. "I'm not going anywhere with him."

CHAPTER FIFTY-EIGHT

Calla

"What do you mean you're not going anywhere with him?" Mira asked.

Calla swallowed her grief at seeing Adam. "I can't go anywhere with him."

"I don't have time for this. We're getting you out of here. Now." Mira pulled Calla to her feet and unlocked the chains around her wrists. "Here, put this on." Mira handed her a loose pair of trousers and a black tunic.

Calla slipped them on over what remained of her gown, sighing as the feel of fresh, clean clothes wrapped around her. Next were the boots Mira helped lace around her calves. Finally, Mira settled a black cloak on her shoulders and raised the hood to cover her face.

"Let's go," Mira said as she shoved Calla out the door.

Calla didn't spare a glance at Adam as she followed Mira down the secret entrance she had used to visit Raven. They got through the dungeon without incident thanks to Mira's guidance. Calla had always been in awe of Mira's skills, but to see them in action, she wished she was in a better mental state to truly appreciate her.

"Hey, it's past curfew, what are you doing out here?" A guard called when Mira stepped out from behind a column.

"Oh, I got lost. I keep getting turned around in here," Mira said as she walked towards the guard.

Calla and Adam stayed hidden as Mira approached. Mira rested a hand on his arm. "You wouldn't mind showing me back to my room would you?"

The guard flushed as he stuttered.

He never saw the dagger Mira pulled out from the strap around her thigh, or before it was firmly planted in his side. The guard fell at Mira's feet as she stepped away, taking her dagger with her. She motioned for them to follow her.

"Give me a dagger," Calla whispered.

Mira looked sideways at her. "You're not going to stab him with it are you?" Mira joked.

"Don't tempt me," calla muttered as Mira handed the blade over.

Calla focused on the dagger, drawing from the small source of power she felt.

"What are you doing?" Adam asked.

"Improving our odds of getting out of here," Calla snapped.

"But how? Your shackles —" Adam started.

"They cracked," Mira said. "When I told you about Morgan, you almost lost control didn't you?"

Calla nodded as she focused on the feel of the blade and channeled her anger into something useful. She had never been good at enchantments for pain or injury, but now, well, she had experienced so much and wanted others to experience it that she knew exactly what to focus on.

"Interficiam per os sicut filum," Calla repeated the enchantment as her power swelled. She curled her intact fingers around the blade and did her best to do the same with the ones that were broken.

Her power fluctuated around her like lightning as it broke through the crack in her shackle. But it was enough. Her power pierced her bones as she held in her scream. Her power flashed, and the enchantment was complete.

Calla handed it back to Mira.

"Belle." Mira cupped her cheek. "What's wrong?"

Calla flicked a glance toward Adam. "Nothing. Give me another dagger."

"We have to go, our time is very limited."

"I know, I'll enchant as we go," Calla said, motioning for another blade.

Mira assessed her, but Calla held firm. She would do this. She knew Mira was thinking about how much Calla hated multitasking while enchanting, and it was true, it made the enchantment less pure to her, but the situation called for it, so she would do it. One way or another. Mira handed her another dagger before leading them on.

Calla allowed herself to focus mostly on Mira as she took the lead by quietly scouting ahead of them. Adam to Calla's dismay stared beside her.

Only three guards got in their way as they continued on in silence. Calla muttered under her breath as she tried to keep her power as contained as possible. It was like shards of glass shredding her apart, but she needed to protect Mira, and that wouldn't be done with shields or potions for strength, it would be done through sharp blades that couldn't be stopped by skin, bone, wood, or metal.

Calla held Mira's staff in her hand as she enchanted her last weapon. It was a beautifully carved staff Mira had whittled away at over the years to create a tapestry of waves and geometric designs in an otherwise useful and discreet weapon.

Mira looked out around a corner before coming back to Calla. "We're almost to the gate. How are you doing?"

"Better," Calla whispered. She held out Mira's unbreakable to her.

"Good," Mira spun her weapon around, testing it. "When we get on that ship, we're going to discuss whatever happened, but for now, I need you focused and together so that we can make it to that conversation.

Calla nodded before she quickly hugged Mira. "I didn't get to hug you back." She squeezed Mira tightly before letting her . Calla had no idea where they were in the palace. She had never come to this side and was wondering why Mira had taken them this way.

A shout rang out above them, followed by several more.

"I guess they found the bodies," Adam said.

"We have to run Calla," Mira said at the same time.

"I'll manage," Calla replied. She would do whatever needed to be done to escape, that or she would die trying.

They got to a long series of stairs that Mira took three at a time as Calla quickly descended behind her, Adam behind. Calla glanced down at the final steps, when she ran into Mira's back.

"Adam, take Calla, and get to the ship. I'll meet you there," Mira said. Her voice was steel and thundered with a command like an ocean during a storm.

Calla looked around Mira to the line of guards standing in their way.

"I can help you," Adam replied as he withdrew his own sword.

"Get her to safety. I'll be fine. It's only five," Mira said. "Now go before there's more."

"Mira we're staying here with you." Calla planted her feet.

"No, my love, you're going to get yourself to safety. If I think you're in danger, I'll be distracted. Now go with Adam, I'll be fine, I promise."

Calla nodded and ran with Adam as they changed course and headed for a different gate. Calla chanced a glance behind her as Mira launched herself into an attack. Mira was a beautiful fighter. She used her staff as an extension of herself to not only take out opponents, but to catapult her body. Mira had always been underestimated due to her role in the house. No one thought twice about a companion being able to defend themselves. But in Calla's opinion, it was the most dangerous job. Mira had to always put herself in positions of vulnerability and weakness to manipulate her targets, while Ella and Raven were always in a position of power. So, Mira had learned to be the best, she couldn't afford not to be.

Calla watched Mira for a moment more, before turning back to follow Adam. She knew Mira would be behind them quickly.

CHAPTER FIFTY-NINE

Mira

Mira dropped the last guard to the ground, breathing quickly. She turned around to make sure all of them were dead.

They were.

"You bitch."

Mira spun around, staff in hand as Morgan launched an attack. Mira blocked her attack, going on the defensive as she avoided the bodies beneath her feet. Morgan advanced on her, a sword in hand.

"How could you?"

"You'll have to be more specific," Mira replied. She pushed Morgan back as she withdrew her last dagger.

"Why target me?"

"You were the easiest target," Mira replied. In truth, Morgan had been a fun challenge for her, and Mira had been intrigued to see what she could get from her. "You were so desperate for someone to pay you any kindness." Mira whispered, watching her words land more pain than any weapon could.

"At least I don't have to use my body to get what I want."

"Sweetie, we both know it wasn't just my body that drew you to me."

Morgan screamed and increased her attack. Mira smiled. She'd handled men bigger than Morgan.

"How does it feel to be the victim? Does it hurt to know you were the one who was taken advantage of? That I didn't actually have any interest in you beyond the knowledge in your head?" Mira taunted.

"You disgust me," Morgan snarled.

"I'll tell you a secret." Mira pushed Morgan against the wall as she summoned every ounce of her anger she had been suppressing. "You disgust me, too. One day I will come back here, and I will make you suffer the most excruciating death not even you could imagine that type of pain for what you did to my sisters."

Mira let all of her anger burst free as Morgan smirked back at her.

Mira glanced around at the sound of footsteps.

"I guess you won't be joining Calla any time soon," Morgan said as she increased her attack, pushing Mira towards the approaching guards.

CHAPTER SIXTY

Calla

Once they got through a different gate, Adam didn't stop. He led her into the heart of Aslar, running over uneven cobblestones and mud. The entire city was silent as night held a firm grasp over them. Calla would have almost found Aslar beautiful if it wasn't for the stench of dirty bodies, sagging homes, and manure that had yet to be cleaned.

Calla didn't see the broken cobblestone until she was falling onto the rough cracked stones, her ankle twisted.

"Can you walk on it?" Adam asked as he helped her.

Calla put weight on it and instantly found her leg buckling. Adam caught her, holding her close to balance them. Distantly, Calla felt her magic trill a song at touching Adam, but she ignored it. Adam lifted her into his arms as though it was the easiest thing in the world. Calla closed her eyes and pressed herself closer to him. Despite what he had done, she still found safety in his arms. Her magic seemed to calm in his presence and her body relaxed.

"I'll have to take a horse," Adam said as he searched for a stable.

Calla didn't have time to tell him she didn't know how to ride before he found one and gently set her on top, bare back. Adam swung up behind her, reins in hand as he wrapped his arms around her and held her in place. Calla remained ramrod straight as they rode through Aslar.

"We're here," Adam said as he dismounted and lifted Calla off.

She slid into his arms, taking her own strength from his. She had always wondered what it would be like to be held by him, he had done it twice tonight, and all she wanted was to be away from him.

"Where are we going?" Calla asked as she looked at the ships. All of them were dark but one.

"Calla."

Calla spun at the voice. "Chip?" She smiled as Chip walked out from the shadows. Calla walked over to him and hugged him before he could stop her. "What are you doing here?"

"Taking you away again," Chip replied as he headed towards his ship.

Adam walked over to her, squeezing her shoulder. "You need to get on the boat and get out of here."

Calla nodded. "We should get on while we wait for Mira."

Adam didn't follow.

"Adam, let's go, I'm sure Mira will be here any minute."

"Christopher, will you come help Calla?" Adam called. He stepped closer to Calla, holding her hands gently in his. He spoke softly as Chip walked over. "Calla, you have always been an inspiration to me and reminded me of what it truly means to be a prince to my people and to be brave not only when it's easy, but when it's hard."

"Adam, you can tell me all of this on the ship."

Adam spoke in Vicurian. "I love you, Calla. I know you're mad at me and that I don't deserve you, but I wanted you to know how much you mean to me." He bent forward and pressed his lips to her forehead, his hand running through her hair.

Adam stepped back. "Christopher, make sure Calla gets on the ship. I'm going back for Mira."

"She'll be here in a minute, have some faith in her." Calla's voice rose as Adam started to walk away from her.

"I need to make sure Mira makes it," Adam said. "I'll be back soon."

"Then I'll wait here for both of you," Calla said as she hobbled over to him. Calla wrapped her arms around his neck, pulling her head closer to his. "Please come back to me. Bring Mira back."

"I'll come straight back. Now get on the ship," Adam whispered. He hugged her tightly before getting on the horse. "Get her on the boat, Christopher. Just as we discussed."

Chip walked over and gave Calla the support she needed. They got on the deck of a ship Calla knew all too well. She turned just in time to watch Adam riding back towards the palace, the horse galloping over cobblestones.

The plank was lifted, and the door to the deck was locked shut.

"What are you doing?" Calla limped over to the crew who hoisted the plank onboard. "Chip, what are they doing?" She spun around and fell to the ground. "Put that back."

"They're following orders."

"Their orders are to wait for Prince Adam and Princess Miraya," Calla said. She set her hands down and yelped as her broken fingers protested the weight. Chip was at her side in a moment, lifting her by her underarms to her feet.

"They're following Prince Adam and Princess Miraya's orders," Chip whispered as he wrapped his arms around her, restraining her.

"No. No. They're supposed to be here." Calla whimpered as the ship began to push off from the harbor deck. "Stop this ship Chip. Stop it right now. I can't leave them."

"You are my priority, both of them know what they're doing," Chip replied, continuing to hold her.

"Adam!" She couldn't see him anymore.

He was gone. Mira was gone. Chip was leaving them behind when he could wait.

"Can't we just wait for him? He didn't even get time to try to retrieve Mira," Calla begged. She sank to the ship's deck with Chip still holding her close, his arms no longer comforting as she leaned against him.

"Those are not my orders. They were very clear that all that mattered was that you got on this ship."

"Do you know what could happen to them?" Calla asked. She bent forward to curl in on herself.

"I'm so sorry Calla. I can't let you go. Not until we're out at sea and I know you're safe."

"Please Chip, if our friendship means anything to you, you will stop this ship and wait for them. Please, I am begging you. Don't make me leave behind the two people I love most."

"They knew what they were doing, Calla. Don't let their sacrifice for their most important person be for nothing." Chip replied.

"Please." Calla's vision blurred as tears poured over.

"I'm so sorry," Chip repeated. He adjusted his hold on her, keeping her close as he rocked them back and forth.

CHAPTER SIXTY-ONE

Mira

The guards shoved Mira to her knees. She stifled a groan as the stones dug into her. She would not cower before Queen Lyanna. Mira shook her hair out of her face, watching the queen pace around her throne room.

Morgan leaned against a column in the back, a scowl on her face. Mira smirked.

Her victory over seducing Morgana washed away as a servant ran in and handed the queen a message.

Queen Lyanna smiled as she made a motion for someone to come in.

Mira kept her head facing forward.

They had gotten away. She had ensured it. Calla and Adam were free. They were on a ship, sailing away from her.

Adam crashed to his knees beside her.

Mira kept herself from looking at him. Though she still heard the shackles around his wrists and his haggard breathing.

"She's safe," Adam whispered.

Mira straightened her shoulders.

Queen Lyanna continued to pace. "Well, it's time to decide what to do with the two of you," she said. Her voice had yet to rise an octave.

Mira wasn't sure if that was good or not.

"Your majesty —" Adam started.

"You." Queen Lyanna interrupted Adam. "I took you into my home. I agreed to have my daughter, my only daughter, marry you. And you've thrown that generosity in my face."

"Your majesty —" Mira said.

"And you, a disgraced princess from a worthless kingdom, how dare you come here under false pretenses extending a hand of friendship and support. You can imagine my surprise when I heard from King Arthur he had disowned you, and that while his alliance with me continues, he had not in fact sent his youngest daughter to me."

Queen Lyanna circled around them, her voice rising with each moment that passed.

"I will not insult your intelligence by asking what you were doing when you orchestrated a dungeon break and released a spy."

Mira and Adam remained silent.

"So the question is, what am I going to do with you?" Queen Lyanna's pacing slowed until she stopped in front of them.

"I am a princess of Grecia —"

"I don't care who you are," Queen Lyanna's voice echoed around the room.

Mira didn't flinch.

She was a princess of Grecia.

The sister to Ella and Raven, and Calla.

She was not afraid of this fake queen.

"I am a Princess of Grecia, I am not afraid."

Queen Lyanna yelled as she continued to storm around the throne room. Mira closed her eyes for a moment, keeping herself centered. She opened them in time to find Queen Lyanna charging toward her.

"I am a princess of Grecia, your majesty." Mira stood and glared down on the queen. "The simple act of chaining me would cause an incident with my father. No matter what you say about his opinion of me, I am still a princess of Grecia and he will take this treatment as an insult."

"I no longer care about maintaining that alliance."

"Should anything happen to me, it's not my father you'll have to worry about." Mira leaned in close to her.

She was a princess of Grecia, and she did not grovel before others.

More importantly, she was a sister to Ella, Raven, Calla, and Maliah.

"As I said," Queen Lyanna's voice was quiet as she stepped closer to Mira until the two of them were inches apart. "I don't care about who you are."

Mira gasped.

How had she missed it?

The pain was so sharp she couldn't gasp for air. Her vision darkened on the edges. Mira didn't even notice the weapon was a black gauntlet with seven daggers piercing her chest until it was removed from her body.

Mira thought about Ella's smile and how when she hugged you, the world seemed right. How Raven laughed so hard she would snort and that anything she baked was filled with sugar and her love. Calla's steadfast love of books and pure view of the world. Maliah would be so mad at her. Each one of them had made a difference in her life, and now she would never get to tell them how much she loved them, how much she missed them, and how badly she wished could see the reckoning they were going to rain down upon Queen Lyanna.

She locked eyes with the queen who stared at her, and Mira smiled.

"You. Lose," Mira whispered as she fell to the ground.

CHAPTER SIXTY-TWO

Raven

Raven observed herself in the mirror. Who had she become over these last few weeks? No one she recognized. Queen Laila had had her hair trimmed and detangled so that it now perfectly curled down past her shoulders. The gown that had been *chosen* for her was a deep red with gold embroidery along the hem. She had wisely not been allowed a weapon of any kind. In fact, anything she could have used had been removed. Even her hair brush was taken each day by the maid that brushed and styled it. If this was what it meant to be a ruler, she didn't want it.

Her princess lessons had been enlightening. They were tedious and Raven found that if she hadn't lost all of her memories, she would have wanted to block out all of these. Raven learned that Queen Lyanna was meticulous, organized, demanding, and had a love for tea with honey and sandwiches. Raven took in all of the lessons from the correct fork to use to strategic thinking while analyzing the queen. She gave away nothing to Raven. They never spoke about her sons, her husband, or daughters, and whenever someone had a message for her, it was delivered on parchment.

Two guards waited for her outside of her room, guiding her to wherever it was Queen Laila would be meeting her that day. Raven rubbed her hands over the enchanter's shackles that coated her skin. Despite the length of time they had been on her, she was in a perpetual state of cold. She couldn't even enchant her thick fur cloak to emit heat.

The palace was quieter this morning, subdued, as though everyone had been told to hunker down and face an oncoming storm.

As they continued to walk she realized they were heading towards the throne room. The guards led her in through the back entrance to stand behind Queen Laila and her throne. Aleks was already there, standing to the right with Prince Cai and their half brother, Liam. The rest of the room was mostly empty, save for a select few noblemen and guards.

Queen Laila sat on her throne, overlooking the large series of stone steps. She wore a gown of green that was so dark it appeared almost black.

"Announcing Lady Eleanor of House Aumont," the court crier said.

Raven's heart stopped. Ella was here? She turned forward as the large wooden doors swung open to reveal an entourage of guards escorting her best friend.

Anastasia led the charge beside a woman who Raven could only assume was Princess Lena with her blond hair and blue eyes. As befitting Anastasia her face was smug as Ella followed in behind her wearing a plain black tunic and loose training pants. Shackles embraced her wrists, as she was pulled forward on a chain leash by Anastasia. Defiance flashed in Ella's eyes as she took in everything. Raven could only imagine what the journey here had been like for her, yet she held her composure the entire time. She had yet to notice Raven as she took in the grand throne room. Why was Ella in chains? What had happened?

"I have to admit that I expected a bit more of a welcome home," Ella remarked as she reached the base of the throne.

"You are getting the welcome a criminal deserves," Queen Laila spoke softly.

Raven shifted at the queen's voice. Criminal? What had Ella done? Raven turned her attention off Ella for a moment and found Jason.

If her heart hadn't stopped beating before, it certainly did now. He was just as she remembered, if not a little bit older. Out of all the people who could have come with Ella, he was the last person she was prepared for. The spark of her power flared for a moment before the shackles ripped it from her. Her heart pounded in her ears. Queen Laila said something and gestured towards her, but Raven could barely hear it as she locked eyes with Jason.

"Princess Astrid has been a guest of mine for a few weeks now," Queen Laila said.

Raven tore her eyes from Jason and stepped forward to look at Ella. Her arms ached to hold her sister within them and never let her go. Whatever had happened, they would be okay because they were together. Out of the corner of her, Raven noticed Liam move to stand behind her as the ever faithful watch dog. His magical burn seemed especially prominent today, Drea's gift for what he did to her. If his kill didn't belong to Drea, she would have found a way the moment she saw him to take vengeance for her. As it was, Raven wasn't sure if Ella was about to launch herself at him. Her stance hand shifted, and she straightened her back as she realized who Liam was.

Queen Laila stood and descended in a graceful cascade to Ella.

"I'm honored that I finally get to see the kingdom my mother called home. She seemed to love it."

"Did she?" Queen Laila circled her, "She had a funny way of showing it." She turned her attention to Jason. "Dear niece, who is your escort?"

Jason stepped forward. "Sir Jason, I'm here as an ambassador and to be the voice of the king in all matters pertaining to Lady Eleanor."

"Interesting. Why would King Matthias send a nobody knight to speak for one of his subjects?"

"I volunteered." Jason stood taller, not giving an inch of ground to her as she examined both of them.

"Really? Why?"

"Lady Eleanor recently reminded me of what's important in life and ensuring her safety is important to me."

"Goodness, my dear niece, you have left quite the impression on him. What did you say to him?"

Ella shrugged. "I'm just good with people."

Raven couldn't hold back the smirk as Ella appeared to grate on her aunt.

Queen Laila turned her back on Ella, a dangerous move in Raven's opinion. "Prince Cai, do you think your cousin has a way with people?"

Prince Cai gave Ella a look Raven was familiar with, and her spine crawled with the urge to get between them.

"I think she has a way with certain men."

"Prince Aleksander, your thoughts?" Queen Laila asked.

Though she could feel Aleks' eyes on her. He knew who Jason was, and what had happened. She wasn't sure what she would see if she made eye contact with him. Ella had turned to her cousin, tilting her head in such a similar fashion to both of her aunts that Raven had to shake her head.

"I don't have enough information or personal experience to speak on how influential my cousin is, no matter the gender of the person."

"Astute observation." Queen Laila walked back to her throne and sat down to gaze down on them once more. "What am I going to do with the lost, forgotten princess of Trudel who murdered my closest friend and ambassador?"

Before the queen could say anything more, the doors opened again, and a messenger ran into the room. "I have a message from the Queen of Evrotia."

"I'm in the middle of something important," Queen Laila snapped. She tapped her nails on the hard stone throne. A characteristic she shared with her sister, Raven noted.

"She was most insistent," he stuttered. Raven blinked as the messenger looked at her for a split second and she could have sworn it was Daniel's face she was seeing from under the cloak.

Queen Laila motioned for him to bring her the message.

Daniel withdrew a mirror and opened it.

"Not here—"

Sister, I require your aide in the weeks to come. I will forgive you your trespasses in harboring Astrid's impostor if you assist me with your army. The heir apparent, Princess Maliah of Grecia has declared war on me after the death of her 'beloved' sister, Princess Miraya. Your naval armada should suffice.

Raven stumbled backward before locking eyes with Ella.

Mira wasn't dead. She couldn't be dead.

Yet, Queen Lyanna had stated as much. She wouldn't lie about the reason for needing an army. Raven's fisted hand rested against her chest as though that would hold back the wave of grief swelling inside.

It couldn't be true.

"You idiot, mirror messages are for me, alone." Queen Laila stood as two guards stood on either side of the Daniel.

Raven looked down at him. He knew. He had known they were private, yet he had played it so that Raven could hear it.

"Who is Princess Miraya?" Ella demanded. She stepped forward from her entourage of guards, the chains jangling.

Raven's heart stuttered. Of course, Ella wouldn't know. Raven closed her eyes at what the truth meant.

"She's a nobody princess banished by her father," Queen Laila dismissed.

"Then why declare war?" Ella tilted her head, examining her aunt.

Raven stepped out of the shadows before Queen Laila could respond. "She's more than a banished princess," Raven answered as she locked eyes with the queen.

She knew what she had to do.

But first, she had to break her best friend's heart.

Raven didn't give herself a moment of hesitation, knowing this was her only chance. Heart pounding, Raven said, "that nobody princess prefers to be known as," Raven's voice cracked as she swallowed her heartbreak, and locked eyes with Ella and said, "Mira." Raven's heart seemed to split open and swallow her whole as the pain of saying her friend's name shuddered through her body.

"What?" Ella's face paled as she stepped backward, shaking her head.

"And I, Astrid—"

"We have a deal, *princess*," Queen Laila hissed.

"I," Raven moved to stand abreast of the queen, "Queen Astrid, declare war on my father's usurper, the impostor, Lyanna, and anyone who stands with her."

To be continued.

GLOSSARY

Enchanters Potions

Force - red potion – gives you enhanced strength

Velocity – yellow potion - makes you incredibly fast

Insomnia – purple potion - keeps you awake for prolonged periods

Spotlight - green potion - gives you intense focus on a particular goal

Vivifica - blue potion - reduces physical or mental pain

Fray - black potion - enhances skill during combat

Solacium - white potion - heals wounds and illness

Callidus - gray potion – stealth, ability to slip past enchanted mirrors or not be seen

Snow White's Poisons

Mire — induces hallucinations

Fenith — the sensation of bones breaking

Frost — induces hypothermia

Blaze — induces high fever

Malice — cold sweats with hallucinations

Wraith — mindless paralysis

Golden Apple — instant death that turns you pale and makes your lips dark red

<u>Enchanters Mark Power Ranking from most powerful to least</u>

Midnight

Obsidian

Onyx

Black

Dark Brown

Chestnut

Medium

Light

Tan

Pale

Did you enjoy The Traitor's Blade?
Want a free way to support an Indie Author?
Leave a Review.
Reviews help with social proof and gets the book promoted more on Amazon.

Go to Amazon and look up The Traitor's Blade to leave your review!

THANK YOU!

This book taught me a lot about self-care, burn out, and how having a support system around you is what makes the difference. This book really did take a village to come into its final form. To my husband TJ, you're one of the top reasons this book even made it across the finish line. Not only are you my rock to lean on, but you're the one who puts wind in my sails when I begin to lose faith in myself, and help me weather the storms when I get lost in them.

Tammy, you helped me when I was stressing out about publishing this book while also two months out from my wedding and gave me the best ever sister chat. It was that chat that helped me realize it was okay to give myself the space I needed to focus on one thing at a time. Thank you for being the best adoptive sister a girl could have, no matter how far away you are.

For my sisters Lauren and Ashley and bonus mom Elsa. Who would have guessed that working for a credit union and bonding over The Bachelor would have led to three relationships that I hold close to my heart. It's my biggest honor to be called your sister and daughter. The three of you have supported me so much throughout this process whether it's bringing my first book on cruises to be left for others to read, reading my early draft, or completing the book when you don't like to read. Each of these make my day and bring me so much joy.

This book is dedicated to my League of Ladies. Arpi, Brittney, and Puneet, the three of you were my sounding board for more social media, cover input, advice, and more than I could ever begin to fully list. Our friendship means more than the three of you could know. It's not often that I find a group of ladies that I have cliqued with so easily and who have accepted me into their group so quickly. I am so thankful for all of the late-night conversations we've had where I'm waffling back and forth over font, colors, etc., and have each of you talk me through it and make the best decision. I love you all so much!

To my Alpha Readers Christina, Brittney, and Gary. Both of you gave me such amazing insight after reading The Traitor's Blade before anyone else. Thank you for all of your work on this. I know it's a lot of work to be an alpha reader and your comments and hard work helped me out so much.

I have to thank Jessica McLennan for all of her support and love. She's always there for me and her never ending ability to help me and answer questions about the chaos that is social media will never go unnoticed or unappreciated.

I have to thank two people who have been incredibly instrumental and helpful in getting this book created. Beth Gilbert designed this beautiful cover, she can be found on Instagram @bethgilbert_art. Her work is beautiful and amazing and she's one of the sweetest artists to work with. And my beta reader/editor August Head. Your edits, remarks, and comments always impress me and push me to think about my characters and make sure the story is on track to match what I want.

Kelsey grew up in a beautiful seaside town where adventures were just a few minutes from her doorstep. Her hot chocolate addiction fuels her when she writes, along with the sound of rain and cold weather. She loves to create worlds about dragons, assassins, and magic. When she's not writing she can be found hiking and traveling or just bingeing the next good show. She currently lives in Northern California with her husband and their two adorable cats Milo and Kida.

CONNECT WITH ME!

www.ingramcontent.com/pod-product-compliance
Lightning Source LLC
LaVergne TN
LVHW010553100826
845148LV00014B/2699

9798988185277